Caitlin Moran is the eldest of eight children, home-educated on a council estate in Wolverhampton, believing that if she were very good and worked very hard, she might one day evolve into Bill Murray.

She published a children's novel, The Chronicles of Narmo, at the age of 16, and became a columnist at The Times at 18. She has gone on to be named Columnist of the Year six times. At one point, she was also Interviewer and Critic of the Year - which is good going for someone who still regularly mistypes 'the' as 'hte'. Her multi-award-winning bestseller How to Be a Woman has been published in 28 countries, and won the British Book Awards' Book of the Year 2011. Her two volumes of collected journalism, Moranthology and Moranifesto, were Sunday Times bestsellers, and her novel, How to Build a Girl, debuted at Number One, and is currently being adapted as a movie. She co-wrote two series of the Rose d'Or-winning Channel 4 sitcom Raised by Wolves with her sister, Caroline.

Caitlin lives on Twitter with her husband and two children, where she spends her time tweeting either about civil rights issues, or that picture of Bruce Springsteen when he was 23, and has his top off. She would like to be remembered as 'a very sexual humanitarian'.

Also by Caitlin Moran

The Chronicles of Narmo
How To Be a Woman
Moranthology
Moranifesto
How to Be Famous

How to
Build
a *Girl*

Caitlin
Moran

EBURY
PRESS

This edition published in 2020 by Ebury Press
First published in the UK in 2015 by Ebury Press
First published in the US in 2015 by Harper Perennial,
a division of Harper Collins

1 3 5 7 9 10 8 6 4 2

Ebury Press, an imprint of Ebury Publishing
20 Vauxhall Bridge Road,
London SW1V 2SA

Penguin
Random House
UK

Ebury Press is part of the Penguin Random House group of companies whose
addresses can be found at global.penguinrandomhouse.com

www.penguin.co.uk

A CIP catalogue record for this book is available from the British Library

ISBN 9781529103199

Printed and bound in Great Britain by Clays Ltd, Elcograf S.p.A.

Penguin Random House is committed to a sustainable future
for our business, our readers and our planet. This book is made
from Forest Stewardship Council® certified paper.

To my mother and father, who thankfully are nothing like the parents in this book, and let me build my girl how I wanted.

AUTHOR NOTE

This is a work of fiction. Real musicians and real places appear from time to time, but everything else, the characters, what they do and what they say, are the products of my imagination. Like Johanna I come from a large family, grew up in a council house in Wolverhampton and started my career as a music journalist as a teenager. But Johanna is not me. Her family, colleagues, the people she meets and her experiences are not my family, my colleagues, the people I met or my experiences. This is a novel and it is all fictitious.

PART ONE

A BLANK PAGE

ONE

I am lying in bed, next to my brother, Lupin.

He is six years old. He is asleep.

I am fourteen. I am not asleep. I am masturbating.

I look at my brother and think, nobly, 'This is what he would want. He would want me to be happy.'

After all, he loves me. He wouldn't want me to be stressed. And I love him – although I must stop thinking about him while I'm masturbating. It feels wrong. I am trying to get my freak on. I can't have siblings wandering into my sexual hinterland. We may share a bed tonight – he left his bunk at midnight, crying, and got in next to me – but we cannot share a sexual hinterland. He needs to leave my consciousness.

'I have to do this on my own,' I say to him, firmly, in my head – placing a pillow between us, for privacy. This is our little, friendly Berlin Wall. Sexually aware adolescents on one side (West Germany), six-year-old boys on the other (Communist Europe). The line must be held. It is only proper.

It's little wonder I need to masturbate – today has been very stressful. The Old Man didn't get famous, again.

Missing for two days, he returned this afternoon, just after lunch, with his arm around a dishevelled young man, carbuncular, in a thin, grey, shiny suit and a pink tie.

'This, *cock*,' my father said, fondly, 'is our future. Say hello to the future, kidders.'

We all politely said hello to the cock, our future.

In the hallway, our father informed us, in a cloud of Guinness, that he believed the young man was a record company talent scout, from London, called Rock Perry – 'although he might also be called Ian'.

We looked back at the man, sitting on our collapsing, pink sofa in the front room. Rock was very drunk. He had his head in his hands, and his tie looked like it had been put on by an enemy, and was strangling him. He didn't look like the future. He looked like 1984. In 1990, that was an ancient thing to be – even in Wolverhampton.

'Play this right, and we'll be fucking *millionaires*,' our father said, in a loud whisper.

We ran into the garden, to celebrate – me and Lupin. We swung on the swing together, planning our future.

My mother and my big brother Krissi, however, stayed silent. In our front room, they have seen the future come – and go – before. The future always has different names, and different clothes, but the same thing happens, time after time: the future only comes to our house when it is drunk. The future must then be kept drunk – because the future must, somehow, be tricked into taking us with it, when it leaves. We must hide ourselves in the fur of the future, like burrs – all seven of us – and ride its ass, all the way out of this tiny house and back down to London, and fame, and riches, and parties, where we belong.

So far, this has never worked. The future has always, eventually, walked out of the door without us. We have been stuck now, on a council estate in Wolverhampton, for thirteen years – waiting. Five children now – the unexpected twins are three weeks old – and two adults. We have to get out of here soon. God, we have to get out of here soon. We cannot hold on being poor, and not-famous, much longer. The 1990s are a bad time to be poor, and not-famous.

Back in the house, things are already going wrong. My mother's hissed instruction to me, 'Get in that kitchen, and bulk that bolognese out with peas! We've got guests!' – means I have now served Rock a plate of pasta – I curtsey a little, when I hand it over – which he is shovelling into his mouth with all the passion of a man who desperately wants to sober up, aided only by petit pois.

With Rock trapped by the hot plate on his knees, my father is now standing, unsteadily, in front of him, doing his pitch. We know the pitch by heart.

'You never *say* the pitch,' the Old Man has explained, many times. 'You *are* the pitch. You *live* the pitch. The pitch is when you let them know you're one of *them*.'

Looming over the guest, my father is holding a cassette in his hand.

'Son,' he says. 'Mate. Allow me to introduce myself. I'm a man of … taste. Not wealth. Not yet – heh heh heh. And I have gathered you here today, to lay some truth on you. Because there are three men without whom none of us would be here today,' he continues, trying to open the cassette box with booze-swollen fingers. 'The Holy Trinity. The alpha, epsilon and omega of all right-thinking people. The Father, the Son and the Holy Ghost. The only three men I've ever loved. The Three Bobbies: Bobby Dylan. Bobby Marley. And Bobby Lennon.'

Rock Perry stares up at him – as confused as we all were the first time Dadda said this to us.

'And all every muso on Earth is trying to do,' Dadda continues, 'is get to the point where they could go up to these cunts, in the pub, and go, I hear you, mate. I hear you, mate. But can you hear *me*? You go to them, "You are a buffalo soldier, Bobby. You are Mr Tambourine Man, Bobby. You are the fucking walrus, Bobby. I know that. But I – I am Pat Morrigan. And I am *this*."'

My father finally gets the cassette out of the box, and waves it at Rock Perry.

'Do you know what this is, mate?' he asks Rock Perry.

'A C90?' Rock asks.

'Son, this is the last fifteen years of my life,' Dadda replies. He puts the cassette into Rock's hands. 'It doesn't feel like it, does it? You wouldn't think you could put a man's whole life in your hands. But that's what you've got there. I guess that makes you like a fucking giant, son. Do you like feeling like a giant?'

Rock Perry stares down, blankly, at the cassette in his hand. He looks like a man who feels quite confused.

'And you know what will make you like a *king*? Putting this out, and selling ten million copies of it, on compact disc,' Dadda says. 'It's like alchemy. You and me, we can turn our lives into three fucking yachts each, and a Lamborghini, and more fanny than you can beat off with a stick. Music is like magic, cocker. Music can change your life. But before it does – Johanna, go and get this gentleman a drink.'

Dadda is now talking to me.

'A drink?' I ask.

'In the kitchen, in the kitchen,' he says, irritably. 'The drinks are in the kitchen, Johanna.'

I go into the kitchen. Mum's standing in there, wearily holding a baby.

'I'm going to bed,' she says.

'But Daddy's just about to get a record deal!' I say.

Mum makes a noise that, in later years, Marge Simpson will become famous for.

'He's asked me to get a drink for Rock Perry,' I say, carrying the message with all the urgency that I feel it deserves. 'But we don't have any drink, do we?'

My mother gestures, with infinite fatigue, to the sideboard, on which stand two half-full pint-glasses of Guinness.

'He brought them back. In his pockets,' she says. 'Along with that pool cue.'

She gestures to the pool cue, stolen from the Red Lion, that is now propped up against the cooker. In our house, it looks as incongruous as a penguin.

'It was in his trousers. I don't know how he does it,' she sighs. 'We've still got one from the last time.'

It's true. We do already have a stolen pool cue. As we don't have a pool table – even Dadda can't steal that – Lupin has been using the first stolen pool cue as Gandalf's staff, whenever we play *Lord of the Rings*.

This conversation about pool cues is interrupted when, from the front room, there is a sudden blast of volume. I recognise the song instantly – it's Dadda's latest demo, a song called 'Dropping Bombs'. The audition has obviously begun.

Until very recently, 'Dropping Bombs' had been a mid-tempo ballad – but then Dadda found the 'reggae' setting on his Yamaha keyboard – 'The fucking Bobby Marley button! Yes! Get in!' – and has re-worked it accordingly.

It's one of Dadda's 'political' songs, and it's dead moving: the first three verses are written from the point of view of a nuclear bomb, being dropped on women and children in Vietnam, Korea and Scotland. For three verses, the bomb impassively imagines the destruction it will cause – destruction narrated by Dadda, using a 'robot' microphone effect.

'*Your skin will boil/And the people will toil/To make sense of it all/And crops from burnt soil,*' the robot-bomb says, sadly.

In the last verse, the bomb suddenly realises the error of its ways, rebels against the American forces that made it, and decides to explode in mid-air – showering the astonished, cowering people below with rainbows.

'*I was blowing people up – but now I'm blowing minds,*' the last chorus runs, accompanied by a haunting riff played on Yamaha keyboard-voice number 44: 'Oriental flute.'

Dadda thinks it's his best song – he used to play it to us every night, before bed, until Lupin started having nightmares about burning kids, and started wetting the bed again.

I go into the front room, carrying the two half-full glasses, curtseying, and expecting to find Rock Perry enthusing wildly about 'Dropping Bombs'. Instead, I find Dadda shouting at Rock Perry.

'That's not on, mate,' he's roaring, over the music. 'That's not *on*.'

'I'm sorry,' Rock says. 'I didn't mean–'

'Nah,' Dadda says, shaking his head, slowly. 'Nah. You can't say that. You just don't *say* that.'

Krissi, who has been sitting on the sofa all this time – holding the ketchup bottle, in case Rock Perry wants tomato sauce – fills me in, in a whisper. Apparently, Rock Perry compared 'Dropping Bombs' to 'Another Day in Paradise' by Phil Collins, and Dadda has become furious. This is curious, because Dadda actually quite likes Phil Collins.

'But he's *not a Bobby*,' Dadda is saying – lips tight, and slightly foamy. 'I'm talking about the *revolution* here. Not fucking – *no jackets required*. I don't care about fucking jackets. I don't *have* a jacket. I don't *require* you to not require a jacket.'

'I'm sorry – I just meant – I actually quite *like* Phil Collins …' Rock is saying, miserably. But Dadda has already taken the plate of pasta off Rock, and is pushing him towards the door.

'Go on then, you cunt,' he says. 'Go on. You cunt. Can fuck off.'

Rock stands in the doorway, unsteadily – unsure if this is a joke or not.

'No – you can *fuck off*,' my father repeats. 'You – fuck-y off-y.'

He is saying this in a Chinese accent. I'm not quite sure why.

In the hallway, my mother approaches Rock.

'I'm so sorry,' my mother says, with a practised air.

She looks around, for some way to make it better – then picks up a bunch of bananas, from a crate in the hallway. We always buy fruit in bulk, from the wholesale market. My dad has a fake ID card, which asserts the holder that he runs a corner shop in the village of Trysull. My dad does not run a corner shop in the village of Trysull.

'Please. Have these.'

For a moment, Rock Perry stares at my mother holding out a bunch of bananas. She is in the foreground of his vision. Behind her is my father, carefully turning up every setting on the stereo to its maximum.

'Just … one?' Rock Perry says, trying to be reasonable.

'Please,' my mother says, pushing the whole bunch into his hand.

Rock Perry takes them – clearly still utterly bewildered – and starts walking down our path. He's only halfway down when my father appears in the doorway.

'Because – THIS IS WHAT I DO!' he shouts to Rock.

Rock starts a gentle trot down the path, and crosses the road in haste, still carrying his bananas.

'THIS IS WHAT I DO! THIS IS ME!' Dadda continues

to shout, across the road. The neighbours' net curtains are twitching. Mrs Forsyth is out on her front doorstep, with her customary disapproval. 'THIS IS MY FUCKING MUSIC! THIS IS MY SOUL!'

Rock Perry gets to the bus stop, over the road, and very slowly crouches down, until he's hidden by a bush. He stays that way until the 512 arrives. I know, because I go upstairs, with Krissi, and we watch him from our bedroom window.

'What a waste of six bananas,' Krissi says. 'I could have had those on my cereal all week. Great. Another irredeemably bland breakfast.'

'MY FUCKING HEART!' my father bellows, after the departing bus – banging his chest with his fist. 'You know what you're leaving here? MY FUCKING HEART!'

Half an hour after the shouting – when 'Dropping Bombs' ends, after its triumphal, twelve-minute-long finale – my dad goes out again.

He is going out to top up his heart, back in the same pub he found Rock Perry in.

'Perhaps he's going to see if Rock left behind a twin that he can also abuse?' Krissi, says, caustically.

The Old Man doesn't come home until 1am. We know when he comes home, because we hear him crash the van into the lilac tree, on the drive. The clutch falls out, with a distinctive crunching sound. We know the sound of a clutch falling out of a Volkswagen caravanette. We have heard it many times before.

In the morning, we come downstairs and find, in the middle of the front room, a large, concrete statue, in the shape of a fox. The statue does not have a head.

'It's your mum's anniversary present,' Dad explains, sitting on the back doorstep, smoking, and wearing my pink dressing gown, which is too small for him, and which reveals his testicles. 'I bloody love your mother.'

He smokes, and looks up at the sky. 'One day, we'll all be kings,' he says. 'I am the bastard son of Brendan Behan. And all these cunts will bow down to me.'

'What about Rock Perry?' I ask, after a minute or two of us considering this inevitable future. 'Are you going to hear from him again?'

'I don't deal with bullshitters, kidder,' my father said, authoritatively, pulling the dressing gown over his balls, and taking another drag on his cigarette.

We find out later – through Uncle Aled, who knows a man who knows a man – that Rock Perry is, indeed, a man called Ian, who is not a record company talent scout at all, but in fact a cutlery salesman, from Sheffield, and the only 'deal' he would ever be able to sort out for us is an eighty-eight-piece canteen of electroplated cutlery, £59, with an APR of 14.5 per cent.

And so that's why I'm lying in bed, next to Lupin, having this tiny, quiet wank. Half from stress, half from pleasure. For I am, as I have recorded in my diary, 'a hopeless romantic'. If I can't go on a date with a boy – I am fourteen, I have never gone on a date with a boy – then at least I can go on a date with me. A bed-date, ie: a wank.

I come – thinking of the character Herbert Viola in *Moonlighting*, who I think has a kind face – pull my nightie back down, kiss the sleeping Lupin, and go to sleep.

TWO

Thursday. I wake up to find Lupin's huge, blue eyes staring at me. Lupin's eyes are massive. They take up half the room. When I love him, I tell him that his eyes are like two blue planets spinning in the galaxy of his skull, and that I can see satellites, and rockets, sailing past his pupils.

'There's one! And another one! I can see Neil Armstrong! He's carrying a flag! God bless America!'

When I hate him, I tell him he has a thyroid condition, and looks like a mad frog.

Because Lupin is quite nervy, we spend a lot of time together. He has bad dreams, and he often leaves the bunk bed he shares with Krissi to come into my bed, because I have a double bed now. The circumstances of me getting a big divan were mixed, emotionally.

'Your nan's dead – and you're getting her bed,' Dad had said, last April.

'Nan's dead!' I wailed. 'Nan's DEAD!'

'Yeah – but you're getting her bed,' Dad said again, patiently.

There is a huge dent in the middle of the mattress, where Nan lay and, latterly, died.

'We lie in the shallow depression her ghost left behind,' I sometimes think, in my more maudlin moments. 'I am born into a nest of death.'

I read a lot of nineteenth-century literature. I once asked my mother what my trousseau would be, upon someone taking my hand in marriage. She laughed hysterically.

'There's a pair of curtains in a bin bag in the loft you're welcome to,' she said, wiping the tears from her eyes.

But that was when I was younger. I wouldn't do that now. I'm more aware of our financial 'situation'.

Me and Lupin go downstairs, in our pyjamas. It's 11am and a day off from school. Krissi is already up. He's watching *The Sound of Music*. Liesl is in the thunderstorm, getting it on with Rolf, the Nazi post-boy.

I feel a bit restless, so I stand in front of the television for a minute, blocking his view.

'Get out of the way, Johanna. MOVE IT!'

This is Krissi. I want to describe Krissi, because he is my big brother, and my favourite person in the world.

Unfortunately, I think I am his least-favourite person – our relationship often reminds me of a birthday card I once saw that showed a big St Bernard with its paw on the face of a small, yappy puppy, with the caption, 'Out of my way, small fry.'

Krissi is a big dog. At fifteen, he's already six foot: a massive, soft tank of a boy, with big, soft hands, and an incongruous blond afro that always gets commented on at family gatherings.

'Oh here he comes – "little" Michael Jackson!' Aunty Lauren will say, as Krissi comes into the room – hunched over, trying to make himself look smaller.

Neither Krissi's personality nor features suit being a six-foot boy. He's pale, with pale blue eyes and pale hair – taking after my mother, he barely has any pigment at all. His mouth and nose are very delicate – like that of silent movie siren Clara Bow. I once tried to open this topic up for debate with Krissi, but it garnered very bad results.

'It's funny, because you've got a big old face – but then a really bitchy-looking nose and mouth,' I told him. I thought these were the kind of conversations we could have.

But it turned out that this was the kind of conversation we could *not* have. He said, 'Get bent, Grotbags,' and left the room.

Not knowing what kind of conversation we can have is one of the reasons I am Krissi's least-favourite person. I am always saying the wrong thing to him. Mind you, to be fair, Krissi just doesn't like people, full stop. At school, he has no friends – his soft hands, freaky hair and sheer size, plus a visceral hatred of sport, mean that David Phelps and Robbie Knowsley often snare him around the back of the big bins, like two terriers hassling a moose, and call him 'gaylord'.

'But you're not a gaylord!' I would say, indignantly, when Krissi told me this. Krissi would look at me, oddly. Krissi looks at me oddly a lot.

Right now, he's looking at me oddly whilst throwing a baby doll at me, which strikes me in the face, with quite some force. For a boy who hates all sports – preferring, instead, to read George Orwell – he has quite the bowling arm. I clutch my face – then lie on the floor, and pretend to be dead.

I used to pretend to be dead a lot, when I was younger – ten, or eleven. I don't do it so much now. This is because 1) I am becoming more mature. And 2) fewer and fewer people are believing I am dead any more.

The last time it actually worked. I lay at the bottom of the stairs pretending I'd fallen down and broken my neck, and my mum found me and absolutely freaked out.

'PAT!' she wailed – the note high and full of fear. The fear made me happy, and calm. Even when my dad looked at me and went, 'She's smirking, Angie. Corpses don't smirk. Fuck knows I've seen enough to know. Corpses are terrifying. I've seen dead men that would freeze your innards so badly, you'd shit *snow*.'

I *liked* them both looking at me, and talking about me. It made me feel safe. I was just checking they loved me.

Today, Mum does not sound concerned when she finds me on the floor, pretending to be dead.

'Johanna, you're raising my blood pressure. GET UP.'

I open one eye.

'Stop being such a *prat* and make Lupin's breakfast,' she says, leaving the room. The twins are crying.

I reluctantly stand up. Lupin still gets a bit scared when I pretend to die. He is on the sofa, wide-eyed.

'Jojo got better,' I say to him, bravely, going over and getting hugs. I put Lupin on my knee and he clings to me, slightly traumatised. It's a good, tight hug. The more scared children are, the tighter they hug you.

After my restorative hug, I go to the kitchen, get the massive box of Rice Pops, the four-litre carton of milk, the sugar bag, three bowls and three spoons, and bring them back into the front room – milk awkwardly under my arm.

I lay all the bowls out on the floor, in a row, and slop out cereal and milk. Behind me, on the TV, Maria is towelling down sexy wet Liesl.

'Feeding TIME!' I shout, cheerfully.

'Move yer HEAD,' Krissi says, gesturing wildly for me to move out of the way of the television.

Lupin is methodically putting spoon after spoon of sugar on his cereal. When the bowl is full of sugar, he keels over sideways, and pretends to be dead.

'I'm dead!' he says.

'Don't be a such a prat,' I say, briskly. 'Eat yer breakfast.'

*

Twenty minutes later, I was bored of *The Sound of Music*. The bit after Maria and the Captain get married goes on a bit, although I could relate to it on some levels: for instance, coming from a similarly large family, I totally appreciated that it took the driving force of an impending Nazi *anschluss* for Maria to get all those kids' shoes on, then go for a walk up a mountain.

I went into the kitchen and started preparing dinner instead. Today it was shepherd's pie. This would require a huge pan of potatoes. We ate a lot of potatoes. We were basically potatarian.

The old man was sitting on the back doorstep, with his hangover, in my pink dressing gown that showed his knackers. Of course he had a hangover. Last night, he'd drunk enough to steal a concrete fox.

When he'd finished his cigarette on the back step, he came into the house – cock and balls still hanging out of the dressing gown.

'Pat *mit* coffee,' he said, making a gummy Nescafé. Sometimes he spoke in German. His old band had toured there in the 1960s – the stories he told always petered out with '… and then we met some, er, *nice ladies*, who were very friendly,' and my mother would look at him with an odd expression that was half-disapproving, and half, I realised much later, turned on.

'Angie!' he yelled. 'Where are my trousers?'

My mother shouted from the bedroom: 'You haven't got any!'

'I must have!' my father shouted back.

My mother stayed silent. He was going to have to work this one out for himself.

I carried on peeling potatoes. I love this peeling knife. It fits so snugly in my hand. Together, we must have peeled tonnes of potatoes. We are a good team. It is my Excalibur.

'It's a big day today. I've got to have trousers,' the old man said, sipping his coffee. 'I'm re-auditioning for the role of "Pat Morrigan, Abject Cripple". My greatest part.'

He put his coffee down, and started practising his limp across the kitchen.

'What do you think of that one?' he asked.

'It's great limping, Dad!' I said, loyally.

He tried another limp – dragging his foot a bit behind him.

'That's my Richard III,' he said.

He carried on doing his Practise Limp.

'I think your trousers are in the wash,' I said.

'Should I do some sound effects?' he asked. 'Some of my best groaning?'

My dad loved the theatre of a medical assessment. The yearly appointment was a real treat for him.

'I was thinking of working in some back pain, too,' he said, conversationally. 'My back would be gone by now if I'd been limping like that for twenty years. Just the start of a hunch. Nothing too dramatic.'

The front doorbell rang.

'That'll be my nurse!' Mum called, from upstairs.

Three weeks ago, Mum had the Unexpected Twins. All autumn, she'd complained about getting fat, and stepped up her already demented running regime – going from five miles a day, to seven, then up to ten. Through slanting sleet she pounded the streets around our estate – a tall, white ghost, as pale as Krissi, with an oddly bloated belly that would not diminish, however fast she ran.

Then, at Christmas, she'd found she was pregnant with twins – 'Santa's got a fucking rich sense of humour,' she said, coming back from the family planning clinic on Christmas Eve. She spent the rest of the evening lying on the sofa, staring at the ceiling. Her sighs were so hard, and despairing, that they made the tinsel on the Christmas tree shimmer.

Currently, she has post-natal depression – but we don't know this yet. Dadda keeps blaming her 'moodiness' on her distant Hebridean ancestors – 'It's your puffin-strangling DNA, love. They all veer towards suicide – no offence' – which makes her, obviously, even more moody.

All we know is that, two days ago, when she found out we'd run out of cheese, she cried for an hour, onto one of the twins.

'That's not how you wet the baby's head!' Dad had tried to jolly her along.

When she carried on crying, he went to the corner-shop and bought her a whole box of Milk Tray, and wrote 'I LOVE YOU' on the bit where it's a pretend gift tag that says 'From' and 'To', and she ate all of them whilst sniffing, and watching *Dynasty*.

Before Mum had the Unexpected Twins, she was a very jolly mother – she used to make big pans of soup, and play Monopoly, and have three drinks and put her hair up in two buns and pretend to be Princess Leia in *Star Wars* ('Get me another drink, Pat. You're my only hope.')

But since she had the twins her mouth is always in a thin line, and her hair is unbrushed, and the only things she says are either very sarcastic, or the sentence, 'I'm so tired.' That's why the Unexpected Twins don't have names yet. That's why Lupin cries a lot, and why I spend a lot of the time I *should* be spending reading nineteenth-century novels, or masturbating, peeling potatoes, instead. Just now we don't have a mother. Just a space where one once was.

'I'm too tired to think of people's names,' she says, every time we ask her what she's going to name the twins. 'I *made* them. Isn't that enough?'

In the interim, me and Krissi and Lupin have started calling the twins 'David' and 'Mavid'.

'Let's put these knackers away,' Dad said, now, pulling his dressing gown around him, and avoiding the front door. 'I don't want a free ball inspection.'

One of the twins – Mavid – was crying in the double-buggy in the hall. I picked him up on the way to the front door.

The health visitor was standing on the front doorstep. She was a new one. Mavid continued wailing. I jiggled him a bit.

'It's all go around here!' I said, cheerfully.

'Good morning,' the health visitor said.

'Would you like to come into the front room?' I asked, mindful of my manners. I am going to show her these babies are looked after, by the whole family – even though their mother is just currently a ghost.

We entered the front room – Lupin and Krissi's blue eyes looked up, resentfully, at the intruder. Krissi held up the remote, and made a great play of effortlessly pressing 'Pause'. The Von Trapps' *Edelweiss* stopped mid '*Bloom and grow*'.

After a small, resentful pause, Krissi and Lupin sighingly shuffled up on the sofa, and the midwife sat in the space, smoothing her skirt over her knees.

'And so – how is Mummy?' she asked.

'Okay … physically,' I replied. Mum did seem to be okay. Apart from her blood pressure. But that had been my fault, for pretending to be dead. So I wasn't going to mention that.

'Babies sleeping okay?'

'Yeah. They wake up a couple of times in the night, but, you know. That is the ineffable nature of the young!' I said. This woman was bound to be impressed by what an engaged big sister I was. Also, my vocabulary.

'And is Mummy sleeping well?'

'Yeah. I guess. Not bad. Up when the babies are up, then back off.'

'And how are … Mummy's stitches?'

This, I was slightly thrown by. I knew my mother had had forty-two stitches after the birth, and that she was washing the stitches every day with warm salty water – because she made me go and get the warm salty water – but my mother hadn't passed on much more information about her vagina than that. I knew from *Spiritual Midwifery* (Ina May Gaskin, Book Pub. Co., 1977) that post-partum women were often loath to share the details of their births with the virgins of the tribe, so I wasn't unduly concerned about it. Still, I did have some info, and I was going to share it.

'Washing every day with salty water!' I said, with the same cheerfulness.

'And are the stitches hurting at all?' the nurse persisted. 'Bleeding, or weeping?'

I stared at her.

'Would Mummy prefer not to talk about it in front of the children?'

We both looked at my siblings, racked along the sofa. Their eyes were round.

'Children, could you give Mummy and the nurse a bit of "private time", please?' the midwife said.

The horror dawned on me like … nuclear.

'Ohmygod this is amazing,' Krissi said. 'This is actually a new era.'

'*I* haven't had a baby!' I said, in a panic. Did she think I'd had *five children*? Oh, this was fucking rich.

'These aren't *my* babies!' I looked down at tiny red-faced Mavid. His fingers were caught up in the incongruous pink cellular blanket wrapped round him.

'Aren't you Angie Morrigan?' the nurse asked, looking at her paperwork, panicked.

'No – I am Johanna Morrigan – her *fourteen-year-old* daughter,' I said, with as much dignity as I could muster.

My mother finally appeared in the doorway, walking slightly gingerly from those stitches that she has, in *her* vagina – and not me, in mine.

'Mrs Morrigan, I'm so sorry – there was a slight misunderstanding,' the nurse said, standing up, panicked.

All my siblings were sliding out of the doors, like butter across a hot pan. I handed Mum Mavid – 'I have taken good care *of my infant brother*,' I said, pointedly – and bolted after them.

We went into the garden, climbed over the broken fence at the bottom, and ran into the field.

Krissi had been saying '*Aaaaaaaaaaaaaah*' all the way there. When we sat down, in a circle, hidden in the long grass, he finally ended this with '… *aaaaaaaaaaah* you're our MUM.'

They were all howling laughing. Lupin started crying from the noise. I lay face down and shouted, 'GAH!'

This is all because I am fat. If you're going to be a fat teenage girl, it becomes hard for people to guess how old you are. By the time you're in a 38DD bra, people are just going to presume you're sexually active, and have been having rough, regular procreative sex with alpha males on some wasteland. Chance would be a fine thing. I haven't even been kissed yet. I want to be kissed so much. I am angry I haven't been kissed. I think I would be really good at it. When I start kissing, the world is going to know about it. My kissing is going to change everything. I'm going to be the Beatles of kissing.

In the meantime, kiss-less, I am now presumed to be the holy virgin mother of five children. I'm actually four better than Mary. Look at me, with all my squabbling Jesuses, laughing at me.

'Mum, can I have NUMMY MILK?' Lupin is saying, pretending he wants to breastfeed from me. Oh, this would never have happened if I was thin, like my cousin Meg. Meg has been fingered five times. She told me this on the Badger Bus to Brewood. I'm not quite sure what 'fingered' is. I'm worried it might happen to your arse. Meg wears dungarees. How would he ever even have got access up there?

'Mummy, can I go BACK INSIDE?' Lupin shouts, pushing his head against my groin, as everyone becomes breathlessly hysterical. The whole thing is so embarrassing that I have forgotten how to swear:

'GET TO … BUGGER,' I shout. They laugh more.

A call comes from across the field, from the house. It's Mum. Our real Mum. The one who actually did have five kids.

'*Can somebody find your dad's trousers?*' she's yelling from the open bathroom window.

An hour later, and I'm driving through Wolverhampton town centre, with my dad, who's now wearing his trousers. We found them under the stairs. The dog was lying on them.

Wolverhampton, in 1990, looks like something bad happened to it.

'Something bad *did* happen to it,' Dad explains, as we go down Cleveland Street. '*Thatcher.*'

My father has a very personal and visceral loathing of Margaret Thatcher. Growing up, my understanding is that, at some point in the past, she bested my father in a fight which he only just escaped from – and that, next time they meet, it will be a fight to the death. A bit like Gandalf and the Balrog.

'I would fucking kill her – Thatcher,' he would say, watching the miners' strike on the news. 'She has cut the balls off everything I love about this country, and left it bleeding on the ground. It would be self-defence. Maggie Thatcher would walk into this house and take the fucking bread out of your mouths in order to prove her point, kids. The bread out of all of your mouths.'

And, if we were eating bread at the time, he would take it out of our mouths, to illustrate the point.

'Thatcher,' he would say, eyes burning, as we cried. 'Fucking Thatcher. If any of you ever turn up on my doorstep and tell me you've voted Tory, you'll be sailing through the air with my boot-print on your arses before you know what's hit you. We vote *Labour*.'

The town centre is always quiet – as if half the people who should be here had left some time ago. Buddleia grows through the top windows of Victorian blocks. The canal basin is solid with old washing machines. Whole roads of factories have closed down: the ironworks, the steelworks, all the locksmiths, save Chubb. The bicycle factories: Percy Stallard, Marston Sunbeam, Star, Wulfruna and Rudge. The steel jewellery and japanned-ware workshops. The coal merchants. The trolleybus system – once the largest in the world – is just a series of dream-like veins left on old maps.

Growing up during the Cold War, and the persistent threat of nuclear apocalypse, I have always vaguely presumed that the nuclear apocalypse had, in fact, already happened – here. Wolverhampton feels like the ruined citadel of Charn in *The Magician's Nephew* (C. S. Lewis, Bodley Head, 1958). A city that suffered obvious, massive trauma when I was very small, but to which no one refers now. The city died on their watch, and there is a communal sense of misplaced culpability about it. This is what dying industrial cities smell of: guilt, and fear. The older people silently apologising to their children.

As Dadda drives into the centre of town, he starts the same rattled monologue he always does.

'When I was a kid, at this time of the day, all you'd hear was the "tramp tramp tramp" of men's boots as they walked to the factories,' he says. 'Every bus would be full, the streets would be seething. People used to come here for work, and get it, the same day. Look at it now.'

I look around. There really isn't the 'tramp tramp tramp' of men's boots now. You don't see any young men until you go past the job centre, by the Molineux, where they suddenly appear in a long, patient line – all in tight, mid-blue market jeans, thin-legged, hair at various lengths, smoking roll-ups.

As Dad waits at the lights, he rolls down the window, and shouts out to one of the men in the line – he's about forty, in a faded Simply Red t-shirt.

'Macks! Alright cocker?'

'Cracking on, Pat,' Macks says, calmly. He's about twenty away from the head of the queue.

'See you in the Red Lion,' Dadda says, as the lights change.

'Arr. Save a brasser for me.'

Into the centre – Queen's Square. This is the heart of Wolverhampton's youth scene – our Left Bank, our Haight-Ashbury, our Soho. To the right – five skaters. To the left – three goths, sitting around the Man On 'is 'Oss – a statue of a man, on his horse. This is our sole landmark – Wolverhampton's equivalent of Lady Liberty.

My dad winds down the window.

'Cheer up! It might never happen!' he shouts at the goths, doing 40mph in a 20mph zone.

'Alright, Pat!' the smallest goth shouts back. 'Your clutch is sounding fucking well bandy.'

Dadda drives on, chuckling. I am astonished.

'You *know* her?' I ask. I didn't think goths knew anyone on this existential plane. You don't think of goths having, say, neighbours.

'It's your cousin, Ali,' Dad says, winding his window up, and driving on.

'Really?' I ask, craning round to look at the little goth receding in the rear-view mirror. I didn't recognise her.

'Yeah. She gone goth last year. Tell you what – you aye gonna run out of freaky cousins in this town any time soon, kidder.'

We drive on. Even though my father has nine siblings, and twenty-seven nephews and nieces of sundry persuasion, vibe and intellect (cousin Adam, famously, once ate a very small light bulb during a party), I had no idea we had a cousin who'd gone *counter-cultural*. We never really see Uncle Aled, as he lives in Gosnell, and once screwed my father over on a deal with a second-hand tropical fish tank.

This is unexpectedly exotic – to have a goth cousin. All the cousins I've met so far wear pink dungarees, and love Rick Astley.

Today Dadda is, as he said before, re-auditioning for his greatest role yet: that of Pat Morrigan, abject cripple. He *is* actually disabled – some weeks, he can't get out of bed – but, as he says, you can never be *too* disabled. People have different *perceptions* of what disability is. His job is to present his disability in such a way that there will never be a particularly picky invigilator who orders further tests, while suspending our benefits for six months – leaving five children and two parents destined for the poorhouse.

'I'm here to eradicate *doubt*,' he says, parking the van up on the kerb outside the Civic Centre.

Today he's being assessed to see if he's due another twelve months on his Disabled Badge. The badge – bright orange, with a picture of a stick man in a wheelchair on it – allows him to park nearly anywhere. Yellow lines, pavements, personalised parking bays with people's names on them. It's like being royal, or famous, or a superhero. We see our father's disability as a distinct bonus. We are proud of it.

He limps, carefully, across the plaza – 'You never know if they're watching you,' he says, nodding to the windows above. 'Picking you off in their sights, like *The Day of the Jackal*. Gotta keep The Limp turned all the way up to eleven' – and into the Civic Centre.

The Civic Centre is, essentially, the centre of all begging in Wolvo. Rent, benefits, general council hassle – this is where it gets resolved. Everyone who approaches this building is trying to get something out of someone who works in this building.

As a consequence, the building gives off the vibe of a medieval castle in the middle of a particularly listless, passive-aggressive siege. Instead of pouring boiling oil on the approaching locals, there will be the presenting of impenetrable paperwork, instead. Or 'referrals'. The promise of an outcome in the post within fourteen days. Infinite soft delays. I'm often reminded of Graham Greene's advice, in *Travels With My Aunt* (Bodley Head, 1969), where Aunt Agatha instructs him to always greet any bill with a letter beginning, 'In reference to my letter dated 17th July …' There is, of course, no letter dated '17th July'. But such a letter causes crucial, almost-infinite, confusion in the enemy.

Dad greets everyone he comes into contact with here with a cheerful, showbizzy familiarity – 'Alright Barb. Alright, Roy. Nice one, Pamela!' – which, looking back now, he clearly copied off Joey Boswell in *Bread*.

Wherever he got it from, his attitude is in marked contrast to nearly every other claimant in the building. Their poses range from 'servile' and 'broken', to 'furious' and 'at end of my tether, threatening to leave my children here and go on the game if the housing benefit doesn't come through' – punctuated by the odd, confused pensioner, or Care in the Community client, silently crying in a chair.

My father, meanwhile, has a calm, Zen, lordly air about him. He smiles at everyone. He enters like a king.

'Those people behind their desks wouldn't *have* a job if it weren't for people like me,' he says. 'In a way, I am *their* employer.'

As I am currently reading about causality – I've got to the 'Philosophy' section in the library – I have a brief debate with him about the timeline of this logic.

'The poor will always be with us, Johanna,' he explains, breezily. 'Before Nye Bevan, my mother raised nine kids on parish hand outs, and all the villagers got so depressed seeing her begging for bread they voted for the Welfare State the minute the Second World War ended. It demeans a society to rely on random acts of mercy, Johanna. Imagine if we had to go and knock on Mrs Forsyth's door every week, asking her for … ham.'

Mrs Forsyth is our formidable over-the-road neighbour – a martinet of a woman with a perm, and house-slippers for housework. She was the first in our street to buy her council house under the Right to Buy scheme, and immediately tarmacked the entire front garden – a great pity, as it had the best, most scrump-able raspberry bush on the estate.

My father is absolutely right. Mrs Forsyth would be very angry if we kept turning up on her doorstep, requesting baked goods, and loo roll.

'The bottom line is, Johanna, no one wants to have their trip to the corner shop spreckled with crying orphans with only one fucking eye left. It's a societal pisser. The suffering poor have always been here. The Welfare State paid for that problem to go away. No more frozen kids in shop doorways any more. Much more cheerful. You've read your Charles Dickens, haven't you?'

'I've seen Disney's *Mickey's Christmas Carol,*' I reply, dubiously.

'Aye. Well then. There you go,' he replies. 'It's been established that the correct thing to do is to give the poor the biggest turkey in the butcher's window. That's what decent people do. And I'm gonna go get my turkey.'

Whilst he's in the medical assessment room, being assessed, I sit in the waiting area, looking at each person in turn, and working out a) which celebrity they most look like and b) whether I would, on that basis, have sex with them.

To me, the matter of losing my virginity is far more pressing than Wolverhampton's industrial decline. It has gone beyond urgent: it is essentially dragging the whole family down. I've got it into my head I should have sex for the first time whilst I'm still under-age – it feels like … *cheating* to wait until it's legal. *Anyone* could have sex when they're sixteen. Try doing it when you're fourteen, hang out only with your brothers and wear your mum's bra. Not even *Challenge Anneka* would have a go on that.

I run my 'Sex Test' on the other men in the room. There's a man in a body-warmer who looks like Mark Curry off *Treasure Houses* – no. Man in tasselled shoes who looks like Radio One DJ Mike Read – no. Man with hair coming out of his nose who looks like a Spike Milligan cartoon – no.

I count five men who look like Freddie Mercury. In 1990, in Wolverhampton, a moustache and leather jacket is still an avowedly heterosexual look. I wouldn't have sex with any of them. Well, I probably would, to be honest, if they asked me. But it's unlikely.

Today, like every other day, I'm going to go to bed still a fat virgin who writes their diary in a series of imaginary letters to sexy Gilbert Blythe from *Anne of Green Gables*.

I'm still thinking of Gilbert when, much later in the day, I take the dog for a walk. Bianca is a nervous Alsatian who, unlike our previous dog, will not tolerate being dressed up in children's clothing or having toys tied to her back in the manner of small, stuffed jockeys – but whom I love, nonetheless.

'We have a bond, don't we?' I ask Bianca, as we go down Marten Road.

In many of the nineteenth-century novels I read, young women adopt wild animals – such as a wolf, fox or kestrel – with whom they enjoy a psychic bond.

So as we cross the road, I communicate with Bianca in the usual way – using only my mind.

'I can't wait until we live in London,' I tell Bianca, who is quivering in the gutter, doing her business. I turn away, to give her some privacy. She is quite a private dog, I think. 'When I get to London, that is when I will start being me.'

Quite what that is, I have no idea. There isn't a word for what I want to be yet. There isn't a thing I can gun for. The thing I want to be hasn't been invented.

Obviously, I know *some* of what I want to be: primarily, I want to move to London, and be hot. I imagine London being like a very large room, into which I will walk, whereupon the entire city will go 'COR! BLIMEY! YOU DON'T GET MANY OF THEM TO THE PAHND!' like Sid James in the *Carry On* films. I want that. I want everyone – men, women, Minotaurs – I read a lot of Greek mythology, and I'm out for whatever I can get – to want to have absolute, total sex with me, right in my sex-places, in the most sexual way possible. Sexually.

This is my most urgent mission. My hormones are rioting like a zoo on fire. There's a mandrill with its head ablaze unlocking other animals' cages and screaming, 'OH MY GOD – FREAK OUT!' I'm in the middle of a sexmergency. I'm wanking my hands down to the bone.

But, on the other hand, away from my genitals, I also wish to be … Noble. Profoundly noble. I wish to devote myself to a cause. I want to be *part* of something. I want to swing into action, like a one-woman army. An arm-me. As soon as I actually find something to believe in, I'm going to believe in it more than anyone else ever has ever believed in anything, ever. I am going to be *devout*.

But I don't want to be noble and committed like most women in history were – which invariably seems to involve being burned at the stake, dying of sadness or being bricked up in a tower by an earl. I don't want to *sacrifice* myself for something. I don't want to *die* for something. I don't even want to walk in the rain up a hill in a skirt that's sticking to my thighs for something. I want to *live* for something, instead – as men do. I want to have fun. The most fun ever. I want to start partying like it's 1999 – nine years early. I want a rapturous quest. I want to sacrifice myself to glee. I want to make the world better, in some way.

After I've walked into the room of London and everyone's gone 'COR! BLIMEY!', I then want them to burst into applause, as they do to Oscar Wilde when he walks into a restaurant on the opening night of another daring play. I have visions of all the people I admire – Douglas Adams, Dorothy Parker, French & Saunders and Tony Benn – coming up to me, and murmuring, ' I don't know how you do it, darling.'

Right now I don't know how *I* do it, either. I have no idea what I should pour all of this itchy, fidgety feeling into. But if it's something that requires telling anecdotes that make a circle of cigarette-smoking *bon viveurs* helpless with laughter (Stephen Fry and Hugh Laurie, wiping tears from their eyes: 'You really are precious. Are there more in Wolverhampton like you? Is it some cauldron of delight?' Me: 'No, Stephen Fry and Hugh Laurie. It was just me. The boys at school used to call me "A fat gyppo".' Stephen Fry: 'Mere duffel-headed lollygaggers, dear heart. Eschew them. More champagne?'), then I'm ready for it.

So far, the only plan I've come up with is writing. I can write, because writing – unlike choreography, architecture or conquering kingdoms – is a thing you can do when you're lonely and poor, and have no infrastructure, ie: a ballet troupe, or some cannons. Poor people can write. It's one of the few things poverty, and lack of connections, cannot stop you doing.

I am currently writing a book, in the endless, empty hours of the day. It's about a very fat girl who rides a dragon around the world and through time, doing good deeds. The first chapter is about her going back to 1939, and making Hitler see the error of his ways, via a very impassioned speech, and making him cry.

There's also a huge bit about the Black Death, which I prevent by introducing stringent quarantine conditions on merchant ships sailing into major British ports. I'm very into the idea of sorting things out through superior paperwork. This is my favourite transformatory power.

Three days ago, I wrote a love scene with the girl and a young, hot wizard that I was very proud of – until I found that Krissi had obviously discovered the manuscript, and written 'Lordy do, wench,' in the margin. Krissi is both a harsh and unwanted editor.

'Anyway, I reckon we're going to leave Wolverhampton by the time I'm sixteen, tops,' I continue, confidently, to Bianca. 'By then, I will have absorbed all the life-lessons that poverty and ignominy are kindly teaching me, and will have a refreshing perspective other people at the Oscars won't have. They will be charmed by my cheerful nobleness – and that will, undoubtedly, lead to sex.'

My sexy, noble reverie is broken by a call of 'OI!'

I ignore it, and keep walking. No good comes of 'OI!' One thing Dadda has taught us is to always walk away from 'OI!'

'OI!' it comes again. 'You BITCH!'

I look around. A very angry man in a Wolves top is standing in his front garden.

'YOUR DOG!'

I look around for Bianca. I can't see her.

'YOUR DOG'S IN MY FUCKING GARDEN!'

Shit. I've broken the psychic connection with Bianca by thinking about fucking. Where is she? I whistle, and she comes bolting out of the shouting man's back garden.

'I'm so sorry!' I say. My voice is high. I know it will antagonise him, as I have my mother's voice – middle-class, with the words more cut-glass than usual; sharpened by nerves.

'I unreservedly apologise – that was completely unforgivable. If it's any consolation, her disposition is mild–'

'I'll come after you, and stick a fucking axe through its head!' he shouts.

I walk on, shaking, to Violet's house. I am quite rattled by the man's sudden invocation of an axe, and need to talk to someone, and Violet is my newest and best friend. She is also my only friend – apart from Emily Pagett, who reminds me of Baba in *The Country Girls* (Edna O'Brien, Hutchinson, 1960), in that she often spreads lies about me – but which I tolerate, because she also tells me gossip about other people, which is fascinating. Even if it's also not true. I recognise that, ultimately, you have to make your own amusement.

So, in the meantime, I go to see Violet – a seventy-two-year-old woman who lives at the end of our street, with her two Siamese cats, Tink and Tonk.

For the last few months, I've been visiting Violet a few times a week. I think it's a delightful thing – for a young, teenage girl to befriend someone of another generation.

'She is like a window into the past,' I think to myself. 'Also, a *widow* into the past – because her husband is dead.'

Violet has a biscuit barrel in the shape of a pig that brims with top-quality branded biscuits. It would be fair to say that I visit the biscuits as much as I visit Violet. Once, she had run out of biscuits. That afternoon had been difficult for both of us.

But today, everything is well: 'Shall we have tea, and biscuits?' she asks, putting things on the table. I put my hand in the barrel. It makes a snorting pig sound. It snorts at you every time you take a biscuit – which even my balmy exuberance can't help but interpret as slightly judgemental. Still.

'Lovely weather,' Violet says.

'Yes,' I reply. 'Incredibly temperate!'

Tink and Tonk come into the room, and coil around my chair legs, like brown smoke.

'Did Dennis like it when it was temperate?' I continue.

I'd read in David Niven's *The Moon's A Balloon* (Hamish Hamilton, 1972) that the worst thing about losing a spouse was that people seemed too scared to ever mention them around the grieving partner.

Learning from the mistakes of David Niven's Hollywood friends – although not Clark Gable, who apparently always mentioned Niven's dead wife, because he'd lost his own wife, sexy comedienne Carole Lombard, several months earlier, in a plane crash – I always mentioned Dennis to Violet whenever I could, in order to keep his memory alive for her.

Sometimes, this is difficult. I once tried to bring Dennis into a conversation about people I fancied.

'Would I have fancied Dennis?' I asked.

However, when Violet showed me a picture of him, I wasn't quick enough to stop my face from betraying the fact that, no – I would not have fancied Dennis *in the least*.

I was hoping for some b&w shot of a hot Resistance fighter from the Second World War, lolling on a Spitfire. Instead, Violet was showing me a recent shot of Dennis, on holiday at the Butlins in Pwllheli, where he looked like the BFG from *The BFG* (Roald Dahl, Puffin Books, 1984). Even with my free-wheeling open-mindedness, I couldn't fancy Dennis – a man whose ears looked like two long pieces of bacon.

Violet had ended up crying that day. I had taken no pleasure in eating her biscuits, and had limited myself to just one – a bourbon.

Today, Violet says, 'Dennis *loved* it when it was temperate. I really think he preferred temperate to all the other temperatures.'

I happily bite down into my coconut biscuit. Dennis loved it when it was temperate. I am totally helping this mourning old woman with a pig-barrel biscuit jar. Today is ending up alright, after all.

Twenty minutes later, I am walking down the road, back to our house, very rapidly.

The last ten minutes have been so odd that I feel light-headed – like my head is actually a balloon that is simply going to snap off my neck and float away, leaving me to collapse, headless, in slow motion, on the pavement.

God I really *do* feel odd. I stop, and sit on the grass verge, and put my head between my knees.

'I have just made the biggest mistake of my life,' I think.

Sitting in the calm of Violet's house, with her quietly nodding, everything had been going fine until I had suddenly felt a terrible, fatal need to *share*. The midwife thinking I had a stitched-up vagina, the Civic Centre, my ongoing lack of being kissed. And then, on top of it all, a man with an axe threatening to kill Bianca.

'I am always asking Violet about bloody dead Dennis,' I thought – 'but she never asks *me* about *my* life. She probably thinks I am *happy*. Ha! Ha! She has no idea of how much bravery and nobleness it takes to present my constantly cheerful persona to the world.'

'Everyone else has friends they share their problems with,' I thought. 'Teenage girls are *always* telling each other their problems. Well, Violet is *my* friend – so I'm going to tell her *my* problems. A problem shared is a problem halved!'

In the next three minutes, I was to find out what a massive, pernicious cauldron of bullshit that was – one of the biggest lies ever told. For, as I told Violet about how much I hated this estate, and how I couldn't wait for Dadda to get off disability benefit and become famous, the old lady stiffened on her chair. Tink and Tonk came upon her lap and sat, equally cold-eyed, staring at me.

I began to falter. Around the bit where I was going, '… and we'll never fit in here – not while Lupin still wears a poncho,' Violet spoke, in a voice I hadn't heard before.

'I had no idea you were on benefits,' she said.

I stopped speaking.

'I had no idea you were on benefits,' she said again. 'Dennis was shot in the leg during the war, he was terribly injured, and he never claimed a penny of Disability Benefit in all the years he lived.'

I can't believe that Dennis has screwed me over twice now. This fucking bacon-eared ghost is my nemesis.

'I have seen your father mending your car, on the drive!' she continues. 'He was doing it this morning! He seemed quite healthy. I had no idea,' she says again, for the final time, 'that you were claiming disability benefits.'

Still sitting on the grass, I am biting my knees. I know exactly what will happen next. Our father has told us a million times what happens if you tell the wrong person the wrong thing. Violet will ring social services, and report that she's seen my dad mending the car – on one of his good days! On one of his few good days! – and that he's fit for work. And there will be a two-week delay – paperwork – and then someone will knock on our door, or send a letter, and then what will happen … I don't know. What happens to families when their benefits are taken away? It is the great unknown.

I run through all the available options I have ever used, or known, that can make something better. I can only think of one.

'Dear Lord Jesus,' I think, rapidly, in my head, as I approach the house. 'I know I haven't believed in you lately and I hope you don't take that personally, but as you are probably already aware, given your monitoring system, which I imagine to be comprehensive, things are quite bad here, and I want to offer you a deal. If you make it so that they don't take our benefits away, I will–' and I pause here, trying to think of the greatest thing I can offer.

It's a pretty pathetic list. I can make no monetary donation to the church. I have no children to baptise. What else is

Jesus into? I'd offer to commit the rest of my life to a nunnery, but I'm pretty sure Wolverhampton doesn't have a nunnery – unless it's that weird building round the back of Argos with the high walls, that's always having meat delivered, out of a truck.

Desperate, and improvising, I finally offer Jesus the nearest I have to life spent as a Bride of Christ: 'Jesus. If you get us out of this – like, really totally clear this up – I promise I will not wank for *six months*.'

I think about this. Six months is – maths maths maths maths – one twenty-eighth of my life.

'*A month*,' I compromise, hastily. 'Definitely a month. I will not touch myself for a month. Not even idly whilst in the bath. Not even after looking at the picture of two hippies doing oral sex in *The Whole Earth Catalog*, where you can see him put his fingers inside. This will be my holy sacrifice to you, oh Lord.'

We have been brought up resolutely atheist, but I'm pretty sure this is the kind of thing Jesus is into: kids not wanking. He'd have to be down on that. This has got to be a good deal for him. Definite score.

'I'm going to say "Amen" now. This is a deal now. We are square on this. You will sort this out. Violet will not rat on us. Amen.'

THREE

Do not think any less of my terror of utter destitution when I tell you that I managed nine days without abusing myself.

Let me be clear – these were nine *terrible* days. Days where I was wracked with a sexual frustration that often bordered on actual pain.

At fourteen, I was in the first, devout flush of my relationship with my sexuality. It was the first limitless pleasure I had ever experienced. Food ran out, books ended, albums fell into the run-out groove, clothes fell apart and the TV reverted to pages from Oracle, or Ceefax, by 1am – but with wanking, I could lock myself in my room and come over and over, thinking of a million different people, and never stop: save for snacks and small, refreshing naps, when necessary.

For a few seconds, you could be utterly gone – outside time and space and thought. Behind the clocks and above the sun and before words began. Nothing but white light and joy. Even the thing I loved most in the world – Rik Mayall as Lord Flashheart in *Blackadder* – was not as good as that single, non-hungry second.

At first, my trusty ally in this was the family hairbrush. By day, I used it to brush my hair, before cutting my fringe with the big kitchen scissors. And by night, I rode the handle of that grooming item like a limitless fuck-pony – doubling its functionalities at a stroke. It was a bit like Bruce Wayne and Batman, in that regard. Bruce Wank. Multitasking. Two very separate lives. Always with the disguise. That brave old brush. And Gotham *never knew*.

The hairbrush, however – although loved, greatly; in the wrong way – was not perfect. It was obvious after only a couple of weeks that it was too narrow, and a bit pointy, and that even the other big benefit of using it – being able to lovingly brush my bush, so that it looked posh, like we were going to a wedding – was not enough.

Thankfully, around that time, I decided to combat my burgeoning underarm odour issues by shoplifting a bottle of Mum roll-on deodorant, and realised on the bus on the way home that it was shaped – astonishingly, usefully, blatantly – like a cheerful, chunky cock. With its pink-domed lid and carefully contoured bottle, the thinking behind British teenage girls' most popular deodorant of the late 1980s was a truth hidden in plain view: Procter and Gamble were selling adolescent girls Starter Dildos for 79p.

Did they know? Of *course* they knew. They knew – *and* they were playing mind-games with us. For what reason – other than a knowing sadistic streak – would they have named something millions of teenage girls were fapping themselves senseless with 'Mum'? It was their way of fucking with our minds. The real test of how horny we were. Are you so desperate that you'd have sex *with your Mum*? To which my simple answer was – locking the bedroom door, and lying on the floor – 'Yes.'

However, I did have limits. I would never buy (shoplift) the blue or green bottles of Mum – because that would be like having sex with a Smurf, or an alien. For a compulsive masturbator, I was pretty vanilla, really. And I was totally sexually faithful to my Mum for nearly three years. How many people can say that?

*

So, yeah. Nine days. It was a hot day – I put on a sundress and accidentally seduced myself. I promised me it wouldn't go any further than heavy petting, but then I got carried away, and ended up doing myself, guiltily and hard, thinking about some monkeys I'd seen having sex in an Attenborough documentary.

I knew there was no point in even trying to explain this to Jesus – our whole deal was crocked – and so I addressed him directly, in a business-like manner.

'Jesus, I'm sorry. I have wasted your time with a fake deal. I acknowledge that this means you are off the case, and that I am now totally on my own in saving the family from destitution. I shall go back to not believing in you again. We will revert to our former positions. Sorry about all that. Take care. Lots of love to God. Amen.'

And I regretfully killed Jesus, in my head, just as I had resurrected him nine days ago, at the top of Eastcroft Road.

From this moment on, to protect us all, I had a new plan: to stand guard.

'What are you doing?' my mother asks, coming into the hall. It is the beginning of the summer holidays, and everyone is running around, shrieking. But I am sitting here, again, at the bottom of the stairs, eating my cereal.

'Just … hanging,' I say. 'There are good ley-lines here.'

My mother stares at me. Clearly, something *is* going on, *has been* going on for some time – but then, on the other hand, I am just sitting on the bottom stair. Technically, there's nothing wrong here, and a mother of five has to pick her battles, lest she die of exhaustion.

'Well, don't …' she starts. There's a pause. In the front room, a baby starts crying. Her attention disappears entirely. 'Just …'

She goes to the baby.

My plan is this: all bad news comes in brown envelopes. I know this, from experience. So, every day, I am going to intercept the post, looking for any franked 'Wolverhampton City Council'. That, will clearly be the letter of doom – the one announcing that they have 'received information' about our family, and are withdrawing our benefits.

And, when that letter comes, my plan is: to burn it. Then when the follow-up letter comes – I will burn that, too. And I will keep burning the letters – one after another – until I come up with a better plan, which surely I will if I can buy time until, like, September. I will, surely, be loads cleverer by then. By September, I will have come up with a better plan to save my family from certain ruination.

However my vigil by the front door has not gone unnoticed by my siblings, as a) I am absent from all their games now, and b) they've had to step over me to get upstairs to the toilet.

'Come and *play* with us, Johanna,' Lupin begs, on the third day of the holidays, hanging off the outside of the bannister, where he climbs up, like Spiderman.

'Get off the stairs, you lumpen blockade,' Krissi says, pushing into me as much as he can on his way up.

But I do not move. I am like Greyfriars Bobby, waiting on the grave. I am a constant guard. I am going to save this family.

It turns out to be the most miserable summer holiday of my life. Last year, on the day we broke up from school, we flooded the back garden with a hose: the low-hanging branches of the hazel-tree reflected in the brown soup. It looked tropical – a bayou.

We had jumped out of the kitchen window into it – the water up to Lupin's knees, all of us soaked. And then we had climbed up the tree and sucked cubes of frozen Ribena, singing the Beach Boys' 'I Get Around' in shrill, high voices until the neighbours leaned out of upstairs windows, and told us to shut the fuck up. We had a *plan*.

This summer, well, this summer is already ruined. I cannot lose myself in a game with the kids, lest I miss the clatter and flap of the letterbox. I sit on the edge of their games, half-heartedly joining in, constantly jerking and bolting to the door – then coming back, temporarily relieved, but fearful of the next post. In the daytime, I am distracted.

And at night, I lie awake next to the sanctuary-seeking Lupin, playing, in my head, over and over, the moment the letter can't be stopped any more, and my parents learn the truth, and turn to me, broken, terrified, and go, 'Johanna – *what have you done to us? What have you done, Johanna?*'

What have I done? What will be done?

In truth, I am basically going mad. I feel I have betrayed my family. The fear that I have put our poor, rickety family – with its ghost as a mother, and an undiscovered popstar as a father – in peril makes me feel constantly unwell; like a terrible brain-fever. I am over-adrenalised. I am flooding with it – I am sick with it, I am drowning in it. I feel like I am perpetually thirty seconds away from the Apocalypse knocking at our door.

All this adrenalin works by way of a second, freak, hormonal high-tide – a bad, shadow puberty. Just as testosterone and oestrogen fused new neural pathways, when I was twelve, so, now, at fourteen, the adrenalin burns out a whole new map of them – fly-overs over and subways below what was already built; places where terrifying thoughts can hide, or travel faster. Faster faster faster. Terror makes me think faster, with a hectic, tumbling gallop that sometimes flattens me – it feels like it will never stop.

I sit in the front room with my family as they discuss various plans for the future – buying a new back door, or visiting uncles in Wales – and think, 'But when that brown letter arrives, we won't be able to do *any* of this. We'll be in the poorhouse, barbecuing rats over a lit candle, and it *will all be my fault.*'

The adrenalin makes me constantly restless. My fists are clenched. I grind my teeth in my sleep.

In later years, I can always recognise someone else who received this shot of fear at an early age – other kids from frangible houses; kids who felt the sand collapsing under their feet; kids who sat awake in the dark, imagining their whole families burning down, and planning planning planning who to save first from the future, and the flames, like *The Amazing Mr Blunden* (Antonia Barber, Puffin Books, 1972). Children raised on cortisol. Children who think too fast.

'This is probably what it's like to be bitten by a radioactive spider,' I think, gloomily, in the second month of my breakdown. I do feel insect-like. My eyes feel shiny, and black. The adrenalin keeps the pupils dilated – blasted.

I confide a little of this to Krissi – my new, unhandle-able worry – and he recommends I read *The Metamorphosis* by Kafka (Bantam Classics, 1972). I read two chapters and get so freaked out I have to leave the book on the landing, away from my bed. Turning into something else seems terrifying.

Surely I cannot suffer this much and it count for *nothing*. Someone must be keeping score of every time my heart falls out of my chest, like a spasming clock; noting the hogsheads of adrenalin I am soused in – without ever saying a word to anyone. I will learn the lesson of this fear: I will never tell anyone when I feel bad again. I will never confide a weakness. It does not work. It makes things worse.

It's really best not to tell people when you feel bad. Growing up is about keeping secrets, and pretending everything is fine.

In the end, I go where I always go when I need information on something baffling, poisonous or terrifying: the library. The answer will be here, surely – among the 20,000 books, calm and waiting, on the shelves. I go and sit on the floor in the medical section. By the time four books are stacked around me, I learn what this feeling is called: 'anxiety'.

I am surprised. 'Anxiety' is when you wring your hands because the milkman is late. I have used the word 'anxiety' in sentences about missing the first minute of *Watchdog*, or wondering what I will get for Christmas.

However, there are many kinds of anxiety, apparently. My cross-referencing has, over the course of two hours, taken me to a volume called *The Courage to Be* by theologian Paul Tillich (Yale, 1963).

Tillich characterises anxiety into three categories: 'ontic anxiety' is the fear of fate and death. The second is 'moral anxiety', from guilt or condemnation. The third is 'spiritual anxiety', prompted by an empty life, without direction or meaning.

Identifying my anxiety as mainly 'moral', with a side-order of 'ontic', I rifle, eagerly, through the pages, to discover the cure for these awful feelings. Right at the end, I find Tillich's ultimate conclusion about anxiety: to simply accept it. 'It is part of the human condition,' he says, calmly.

I lean against the bookshelves, and consider Tillich's suggestion for a few minutes. I consider accepting feeling like this for the rest of my life. Boiling in this quicksilver, electrocised soup for ever – nerves jangling like the tiny bell over an empty shop door, just after a nuclear explosion has left the shop full of the dead, and me the only one standing.

'The thing is,' I say, to Paul Tillich, in my head, 'the thing is, Paul, that ultimately, I don't think my anxiety is ontic, moral *or* spiritual.'

I look at him.

'At the end of it all, I just need some *money*, Paul,' I say.

Paul Tillich nods.

If I were rich, none of this would matter.

I just need some money.

FOUR

Here are the ways you can earn enough money to support a family of seven if you are fourteen years old:

So, yes.

I was a cleaner for one day – I answered an advert in the *AdNews* for someone to work in a big house on the Penn Road on Saturdays, put on my best hat, tied the dog up outside the house and knocked on their door.

I spent three hours cleaning their kitchen, their bathroom, their black-and-white tiled hallway. She got me to scrub off the limescale on her taps, with a toothbrush, and to bleach the big bins out the front – split teabags covered my arms with tea-leaves, and in their patterns I read my immediate future: to smell quite bad.

At the end of it, she asked me how old I was, and I said, 'Fourteen,' and she explained it would be illegal to have me back again, and gave me a tenner, and I left. I think she'd suspected I was underage from the start, but didn't want to clue me in to the full extent of employment law until her bins were soused.

In American films, kids on the hustle for cash make lemonade – then sell it out the front of their houses, to thirsty passers-by.

I discussed this possibility with Krissi. He just looked at me, and then out of the window, at our street.

'We haven't got any lemons,' Krissi said, finally.

'When God gives you no lemons – make nonmonade!' I said, brightly.

I did not sell lemonade outside our house for cash, in the anxious summer of 1990.

In the front room with my parents, as we waited for *Catchphrase* to come on, I casually raised the subject of what a teenage girl could do to raise money.

'Get a paper round,' my mother says. 'I used to have a paper round. I saved up for a record player. That's how I bought all my Stones records.'

My mother has the first seven Rolling Stones records, kept separately from all my father's records. They're the only band she's ever liked. Sometimes she puts on 'You Can't Always Get What You Want' when she's mopping the kitchen floor, and shouts along to it, angrily.

'You always did love a dirty rock 'n' roller,' my dad says, now, squeezing her thigh, right at the top, where it definitely starts to be rude. Mum squeezes him back, at the top of his thigh. They stare at each other in a soppy, slightly charged way, and look a bit stupid. I clear my throat, loudly.

My parents stop being sexual at each other on the sofa, and turn back to me.

'The trick to getting a paper round is to hit the newsagents in the last quarter,' my dad says, with a professional air. 'Autumn. Then you do three months, cash in all the tips at Christmas, and then sack it all off in the New Year, when it gets really cold and miserable. You're just in there for the jackpot round.'

Unfortunately, when I go down to the newsagents the next day – to activate this brilliant plan – I discover lots of other people know this cunning trick, too: there's a waiting-list for a paper round until next spring. 'Unless you want to do The Wordsley,' the newsagent says, doubtfully.

The Wordsley is the rough estate – three grey tower-blocks in a scrubby wasteland, like a three-pin plug that's waiting to be plugged back again, and turn back on the dead, surrounding area.

There's a rumour that someone was crucified on the Wordsley – they nailed his hands to a plank and left him round the back of the clinic. It's one of the things we 'know' about Wolverhampton – like how we 'know' the man called The Cowboy, who walks around the town centre dressed like a cowboy, used to live in America; and the beardy tramp who lives in a tent on Penn Roundabout has refused so often to be moved on that the council have run a power-supply to his tent, so he can watch TV and have a fridge.

Wolverhampton is an unexpectedly interesting place to live, if you know where to look.

The summer goes on, and I'm still trying to get rich. My 'lucky four-leaf clover' pendants scheme runs into trouble when one of the kids I sell them to takes his apart – it's a piece of card-board on a string with a four-leaf clover Sellotaped to it – and realises I've just taken a three-leaf clover, and stuck a fourth leaf onto it. I have to refund all (six) of my previous customers.

Then, on one impossibly exciting day, there is a casting call in the *Express & Star*: 'Wanted: children for the Grand Theatre's autumn production of *Annie*.'

Not only is this an advert specifically offering employment to children – the first time I have seen such a thing outside reproductions of Victorian papers, calling for nimble-fingered lasses to work as bobbin-doffers – but knowing the entire score to *Annie* is one of the few genuine qualifications I actually have.

I take the *Express & Star* into the garden.

The kids are busy on our latest project – a snail farm. In an old roasting tray full of grass, earth and daisies, we have over thirty snails, of varying sizes. We can tell the difference between every one. Each one has a unique personality. Each one is named after one of our heroes.

'This is Archimedes,' Lupin is saying, of a snail he is bathing in an old tobacco tin full of water. 'He gives wise council.'

Archimedes looks rather limp. He has been 'soaking' in the 'tub' for some time.

Krissi, meanwhile, is busy with a pair of scissors.

'You'll never guess what I found in the *Express & Star*!' I start, waving the page.

Krissi scowls: 'I'm in the middle of an operation.'

'Lesbian Dennis and the Duchess of York are poorly,' Lupin says, pointing at two snails on a plank.

'They've got tangled cancers,' Krissi says.

I go over to look. Lesbian Dennis and the Duchess of York do, indeed, appear to have 'tangled cancers' – they are joined together by two mysterious white tubes. Krissi is angling the scissors between them.

'They were like this when we found them,' Lupin says. 'They've been stuck together for three hours. We *monitored* them.'

Krissi rolls up his sleeves.

'They can't get away from each other!' Lupin says. 'They're *trapped*!'

'Shhh Lupin,' Krissi says. 'I'm going in.'

He snips the white tubes. The snails writhe, quite violently for snails, and retreat into their shells – emitting huge, outraged bubbles. We all sigh, in relief.

'They're free! The snails must be so glad,' Lupin says, taking each one, and putting them on a lilac leaf.

Lupin surrounds them with lilac blossoms, 'To get better.'

'So – what you on about?' Krissi asks – wiping the scissors on his dungarees with a business-like air.

The snails continue to emit billows of agonised foam.

'They're putting on *Annie* at the Grand!' I say, waving the *Express & Star*. 'We already know all the words! There's no one in Wolverhampton who knows *Annie* better than we do! We should all go to the auditions! You could play the chorus orphans, in the orphanage!'

Krissi regards me keenly.

'"*You*" could all play the chorus of orphans?' he asks. '"*You*"? So who are *you* going to play, then?'

'Well.'

I pause.

'Annie,' I say.

Krissi becomes instantly hysterical. As he laughs, I feel what the sonic waves of his laughter are breaking against – my huge, round face. The American football-player solidness of my body. Mum's bra, under my shirt – far too large, which I've tried to tighten using blanket-stitch (*Young Girl's Guide To Sewing*, 1979). Krissi does not think I could play a semi-starved yet cheerful eight-year-old American orphan, in the Great Depression.

'Annie,' I say again, trying to sound firm, and hopeful.

'*Mannie*, more like,' Krissi says. '*Ham-mie*.'

But I know it's because Krissi secretly wants to play Annie himself. I know that this is why he is laughing.

We spend all morning rehearsing *Annie* in the garden. I am surprised Krissi joins in, now he's so old – but he does. Not only is he a great Pepper, but he also does all of Miss Hannigan's lines on the side. He's a very convincing Miss Hannigan. Yet again, I feel proud of my older brother. This is a solid morning's

graft. I am determined we will be the best-rehearsed gang of
orphans the Grand has ever seen.

We break for lunch – crackers and cheese, eaten sitting up
the tree; passing the packet between branches, like a flock of
fat, ragged birds.

Then we continue rehearsing right up until 4pm, when I
make the phone call to The Grand.

Everyone gathers around the phone.

'I'm calling about the audition for *Annie*?' I say, using my
poshest voice – the same one I used when talking to the man
who wanted to put an axe in Bianca's head. This is my 'talking
to people' voice. I wear it, like a hat to church, whenever I am
talking to someone from outside the house.

'There are five of us. We're quite a gang! The Morrigan
Gang! Between new-born and fifteen! And you wouldn't need
to rehearse us much – because we already know *all* the words!'

It would be too boring to go into the bit where the lady told
us we'd need to have at least a Grade 3 tap-dancing certificate,
and extensive experience in amateur productions, and to basically not be a big gang of fat mental kids, and to fuck off.

'I can assure you – we have a *lot* of experience in being
amateur!' I say, when she mentions the 'amateur experience'.
She doesn't laugh. No one ever laughs when I make these
kind of jokes. When Bill Murray says shit like this, people
completely lose it. I wish I was Bill Murray. I hope everything
I've read about evolution is wrong, and I eventually evolve into
him. It's one of only three plans I have.

I put the phone down, and look at my siblings. They look back.

'You know what Annie says about tomorrow. Hang on for
it!' I tell them.

'I *told* you this was stupid,' Krissi says, taking off his Miss
Hannigan wig.

*

The next day, Krissi has to admit that Lesbian Dennis and the Duchess of York have died. They are dried up in their shells, and don't respond – however much we poke them right in the centre, with sticks, and, then, latterly, pins.

When it's clear that the Duchess of York is dead, Krissi sticks a needle right through her. He does it with a calm, cold air – as our chief snail surgeon, I guess this is medical research he needs to do.

We sing 'Tomorrow' again, as we buried them, and Lupin cries.

But as Mother Superior tells Maria in *The Sound of Music*, where God closes a door, he opens a window. Two weeks later, in the *Express & Star* – our sole portal to everything in the world – there is an announcement.

Under the headline 'Calling Young Wordsworths!', a competition is launched, inviting 'budding young Midlands' poets' to submit poems, on the theme of 'Friendship'.

The prize is a cheque for £250, your poem being printed in the *Express & Star*, and the opportunity to read your poem out on *Midlands Weekend* – the Midlands' Friday night magazine TV show, which is watched by everyone in the West Midlands.

'You should enter that poem competition, Johanna,' my mother says, as I eat my corned beef hash.

With my newfound, anxious belligerence, I don't tell Mum I've already got two-thirds of the poem written. I like to keep as many secrets as possible, these days – by way of trying to undo the big, fatal one I let get away. It's how I know I'm growing up. By keeping secrets.

But for the last two days, I have, quietly, been doubling-up in my efforts to save the family: as I sit guarding over the letterbox, 7am–12pm, for any attempted delivery of our doom, I am also writing pages and pages of poetry, in my notebook. I have carefully counted them, and I have already written over 2,200 words towards this poem. I have even managed to rhyme 'friendships' with 'lends chips', which I think is pretty epic.

If anyone in the West Midlands is going to earn money by writing this year, it's going to be me. It's really, totally going to be me. I'm having that £250.

And I do! It is me. I win. A letter arrives, and everyone screams, and Mum immediately frets about what I'm going to wear to be on television – 'You'll have to wear your dad's jeans – you're too fat for your old ones' – and Dad rings up Uncle Jim to borrow £40 for petrol, 'To get our kidder to Birmingham,' and puts £10 in the tank, then spends the rest on new shoes for Lupin, and getting fish 'n' chips, to celebrate, which is fair enough.

And I spend a week in nerves, and then Friday wearing Dad's jeans – sitting on a chair, staring at the clock; literally doing nothing other than staring at the clock – until it's finally 5pm, and time to drive to Birmingham, with my poem in a folder marked: 'Johanna's Folder: POEM'.

Halfway up Brierley Hill, he turns off *Brothers In Arms*, and points to the quiet, street-lit valley below. All empty industrial estates, and small, coiled ribbons of housing.

'When I was a kid, you'd come up this hill, and all of that –' and he gestures to the valley in front of us '– was on *fire*. The foundries and the forges and the ironworks. The potteries. The whole place glowed – sheets of sparks, fifty foot high. The fires never went out. It looked like *hell*. Mordor. That's what your *Lord of the Rings* is about. Tolkien was from round here. He was writing about how the Industrial Revolution turned the Midlands from Hobbiton into Mordor.'

A man who'd spent all day in a forge, or a mine, he said, would go into a pub and drink fourteen pints – 'And he wouldn't get drunk. It would just be replacing the sweat. You'd sweat that hard.'

You'd see men sitting in corners with one foot gone – one hand crushed. Or an empty chair. It was brutal work – humans as tiny columns of meat amongst hammering, burning and explosions.

As he told these stories of his father's work, and his father's friends, he spoke as if he wasn't sure if it was a bad thing or a good thing that men no longer stood in the centre of fires, and sweated.

Like so many of the men I knew, he was in two minds about Britain's industrial decline. I guess it was like the death of an unstable, punitive mother. She was an unstable, punitive mother. But at least you *had* a mother. Everybody needs a mother. Perhaps.

'If you're working class, and you want to get out of here, you either become a boxer, or a footballer, or a popstar,' he says, finally. 'That's your only way out. Obviously, I chose being a popstar.'

There is a small pause here, as we both consider his career, so far, as a popstar.

'But you,' he continues. 'You've got your writing.'

'It's only one poem, Da.'

'If you can write one good thing, you can write *anything*,' Dad says, firmly. 'You practise every day, and you'll get so good you'll be able to write 1,000 words about … a light bulb. Or … my arse.'

'Your arse.'

'Or *your* arse. You've found another way out, kidder!' Dad says, banging the steering-wheel with the palm of his hand.

'Another way out of the shit. £250 for a fucking *poem*. Good blag. Well *done*.'

I writhe with happiness – the way cats do, when a stranger bends and touches their face, in the street.

At the *Midlands Weekend* studio, everything is white lights, and hustle. Going from our dimly lit, purposeless house to this … hive … is disconcerting. Everyone is smartly dressed, with new shoes, and has a general air that they have pay-cheques, and go to restaurants, and then have sex.

I have never been in a building with people who go to restaurants, and have sex. I have never been to a place, or done a thing. It is intoxicating. Things get done here.

A woman called Amanda puts me and Dadda in 'the Green Room', which isn't green, and I drink four cups of squash, and feel an anxiety that feels like all the other anxieties I have ever had, but played at double-speed. Everything feels utterly unreal. I feel like I'm about to swoon.

'Everything feels utterly unreal. I feel I might be about to swoon,' I tell Amanda, as she finally ushers me on to the studio floor – leaving Dadda behind, in the Green Room, doing 'thumbs up' as I leave.

'Oh, don't swoon!' Amanda says. 'The feature after you is a cockatiel who's learned how to skateboard, and we'll have to pad him out for six minutes if you swoon. He attacked a researcher earlier.'

The show is going out live. I am put into position, for the presenter to walk over to, when it's time for my bit. As the cameras circle around me, I look down, and see myself – through the cameras – on the monitors, grouped around on the floor.

And I really wish I hadn't.

At home, we have no mirrors in the house – not one. Mum won't have them: 'They'll just break, and bring bad luck.'

So for the last fourteen years, I've always had to just … guess what I look like. In order to see myself, I draw myself, over and over, in my drawing pads – with huge eyes, and long hair, and beautiful dresses trimmed with fur, and pearls. There's a chance I *could* look like this, after all – and surely it's more useful to draw yourself like this than not?

Of course, I've often seen my reflection, dimly, in dark shop windows, up town – but these windows did not know me; they had only seen me for a second, walking – so how *could* they know what I looked like? How could glass reflect so quickly? The glass, in its haste, was wrong.

But here, in the monitors, in the studios, I can see myself, full-length, in colour, for the first time in my life.

And although it should have happened somewhere else – and over something far more dramatic, and noble – as I look at myself on the monitor, I feel my heart break.

Because my biggest secret of all – the one I would rather die than tell, the one I wouldn't even put in my diary – is that I really, truly, in my heart, want to be beautiful. I want to be beautiful so much – because it will keep me safe, and keep me lucky, and it's too exhausting not to be.

And standing here, looking at myself, in cold horror, in the monitor, I can see what a million people are going to immediately notice: that I am not. I am not beautiful at all.

I am a very pale, round-faced girl with a monobrow, and eyes that are too small, and lank hair the colour of dead mice, and I am not beautiful at all. And I am fat – a solid, pale fatness that makes me look like a cheap, white fridge-freezer that someone's wheeled onto the stage, and then painted a worried-looking child's face on it, due to a terrible unkindness.

I look at me in the monitor, and I can see me very quickly looking down at the poem in my hands, and reading it very intently – because I don't care what I look like. I am a poet, and a writer, and I deal with hearts and souls and words, and not meat and vanity and a dress that would have made me look better. It doesn't matter that I am ugly.

I will just have to work out how, exactly, that is true. I will prove that it doesn't matter that I am ugly, later on.

And as *Midlands Weekend*'s presenter, Alan 'Wilko' Wilson, walks towards me – cameras foreshadowing his move across the studio floor, like courtiers bowing, as they reverse – and I start to vaporise with nerves, I suddenly remember a very, very important thing about *Midlands Weekend*. The key thing about *Midlands Weekend*, in fact: Everyone in the Midlands hates this show. They only watch it to slag everything on it off.

Appearing on *Midlands Weekend* is like offering yourself up as a sacrifice to every bored, casually-spiteful channel-flicker in the Midlands. They're going to kill me.

And at that point, my brain kind of explodes.

'FRIENDSHIP', BY JOHANNA MORRIGAN.
Who is my best friend? My bosom-buddy, my pal?
My best friend is my beast *friend*
My dog – who looks like Limahl.
Not for me a human
Who might give away secrets and hopes
Who betrays your loneliest whisper
Or crushes your heart, and then gloats.
But, oh! The wolf of Wolverhampton
We run in a pack of two
You've seen me through the RUFF! And smooth
And I know I'm gonna stick with you.

*You cannot hug me with your paws – I know, I know, I've
tried,*
*But Bianca, I know that you can always hug me – hug me
with your eyes.*

'Johanna Morrigan there – from the Vinery estate in Wolverhampton!' Alan says, walking into my shot. 'Now, Johanna, I
have to ask you a question.'

'It would be inappropriate for us to go on a date, Alan,'
I reply.

I didn't know I was going to say this to Alan until I did – my
brain is white with fear; it's a completely automatic response.
The joke *made* me say it, as Krissi and I used to say.

To my surprise, Alan becomes immensely flustered. Years
later, he got investigated by Yewtree, and was found to have a
collection of teenage girls' knickers, so, retrospectively, I can
see why he was alarmed.

'Hahaha! Johanna! I see you have a *zany* sense of humour,'
Alan says, recovering, and looking at the camera. 'So you love
your dog, yes?'

'Yes, Alan.'

'You've always loved your dog?'

'Yes, Alan.'

'Johanna, we had an old friend of the show on last week –
Judith Trevalyn, from Redditch council. And she was suggesting
that the so-called "Devil Dogs" – Rottweilers, Dobermanns,
pit bulls and German shepherds – should all be *put down*. How
would you react to your "wolf" being *put down*?'

'Like I put in the poem, Bianca's my best friend,' I say
earnestly. 'Having Bianca put down would be like killing *my
best friend*.'

'And how would it make you *feel*?'

I consider this. 'I'd go mad!'

I don't want the idea of me 'going mad' to sound *too* heavy, so I pull a comedy 'mad' face. Eyes crossed, grimacing. Whirly-whirly finger to the forehead.

This doesn't seem enough – Alan pauses, as if waiting for me to say something more. I obliged.

'We're like Shaggy, and Scooby Doo,' I continue. 'Best friends forever.'

To clarify this point, I do what, as I know now, you should *never* do if you're a freaky fat teenage girl on a live TV show, in the grips of your first ever wave of utter, existential self-loathing, and being watched, ultra-critically, by everyone in your home town.

Without explaining why, I break into a very impassioned impression of Scooby Doo.

'Ri ruv my rog!' I say again. 'Revveryrody ruvs my rog!'

I take a breath. I can feel what I'm going to do next.

'Scooby Dooby Doooooooooooo!' I conclude, howling. I am giving this impression *everything*.

'Scoooby Doooby Dooooooooooo!'

On the car-ride home with Dad, he stays almost completely silent. It takes an hour from Pebble Mill to the Vinery, and he says nothing until we're nearly home – turning off the Penn Road, and onto the estate.

'Johanna,' he says.

He looks across at me. I have cried and cried and cried and cried until my sinuses are solid. I am burning up. I *want* to burn up.

To this end, I have zipped my anorak right up, to generate heat. I want to leave nothing in this passenger seat but a pile of ash and what looks like a charred leg of pork, such as I have seen in the photos of spontaneous human combustion in *Beyond Explanation?* by Jenny Randle (Robert Hale, 1985).

I have had to put the poem on the dashboard, to dry out – I've cried so much onto it.

'Johanna,' he says, as if preparing to give me a piece of information he should have given me long ago – perhaps at birth – but fatally forgot, until now. He sounds like he's kind of blaming himself for everything tonight, and is going to prevent it ever, ever happening again.

'Johanna – our name's "Morrigan". Not "Prat".'

I must remember. I am a Morrigan. Not a prat.

For the next few weeks, things are quite difficult. As we are in the phonebook, a small yet dedicated band of people from school take it upon themselves to ring the house and scream 'Scoooby Doooby Doooooo!', then slam the phone down again.

I deal with this with all the coping mechanisms I know: lying under the bed with the dog reading *Little Women*, and eating jam sandwiches dipped in instant hot chocolate.

I thought it had all blown over when, two Tuesdays later, Dad came into the house, looking furious. Someone had drawn a Scooby on our back gate, in black gloss paint, and written 'Mystery Machine' on the side of the van.

'People drawing fucking … American retard dogs on the house, Johanna,' he said, warningly, as if I were on my last chance. 'Fucking *branding* my vehicle.'

The only person we know who can re-spray the van is Johnny Jones, who fortuitously nicked a spraying kit from Wickes when he was working there – but he's up in Leicester at the moment, visiting his ex-wife.

So for the next two weeks, we drive around in the 'Mystery

Machine', and my dad has to park it up close to walls, and hedges, to hide the writing, and this makes him very irritable.

Not least when – pale with hangover – he gets out of the van outside the butcher's, and the butcher greets him with, 'Rikes – a ghost!'

And of course, I can't go out onto the estate at all now. After wearily sitting and guarding the front door, the delivery of the last post is no longer a relief to me. Before I set fire to myself, uselessly, on *Midlands Weekend*, I would whistle for the dog and go straight down the library, and spend the afternoon there, with all my authors, hanging.

But now, neither I, nor the rest of the kids, can leave the house in daylight. There's a bunch of youths who keep shouting 'Oi – Shaggy! It's Shaggy!' at Lupin. With my NHS glasses, meanwhile, I am 'Fat Velma'. I couldn't have chosen a worse cartoon to reference. I'm a borderline fucking genius at handing ammunition to the enemy.

And so, as summer heats up, we are all trapped inside, on top of each other. Everyone is treating me like I'm a massive dick. This is totally fair enough.

The only good thing that happens in this entire, awful stretch is the prize cheque for the £250 arriving.

We cheer the envelope. I open it – still shamed but, at least, wealthy. I am full of astonishing plans for this money. This, at least, has made the pain worth it.

Then, the week after, the clutch goes on the van, and my father appears in the door of my room.

'Gonna need that dosh, kidder,' he says.

He spends £190 on getting the car done, and the rest goes on the overdraft (£30) and the Red Lion (£30).

*

So now, broke again, still lying under the bed, I stare up at the underside springs, three inches above me.

Downstairs, the phone rings. My mother answers it.

'Yes, yes – very funny. Is that Barbara Lemon's kid? Sod off.'

Another Scooby call.

I feel like Scout Finch, when Atticus is being victimised by the whole town – except, instead of trying to save a wrongly prosecuted black man from the electric chair, I wrote a poem that sounded like I'm a lonely leper virgin that wants to have sex with my dog, and then did an impression of a major Hanna-Barbera cartoon character on live TV instead.

Not only have I not earned a fortune which will keep my family safe, but I have now also made us even more of a freakish laughing-stock on the estate than we ever were before. Which – given that the huge Buddha in our window means that our house is regularly referred to as 'Big Daddy's House' – is saying something.

'*I am a drop of poison in the well/That can't be taken out again*,' I think to myself, sadly. I love quoting my own poetry. '*I am the spore that flew over the citadel wall. And* I was the fattest person they've ever had on *Midlands Weekend*.'

I lie there for a minute, until the truth dawns upon me – like a torch shone down a badger-hole, accompanied by the sound of spades, clanging.

There are no two ways about it: I am going to have to die.

PART TWO

HOW TO BUILD A GIRL

FIVE

I am thrilled by the idea of killing myself. It seems like such a gratifyingly noble thing to do. A monster has come to town – me – and there is only one hero who can kill it: me.

I'm not *actually* going to kill myself, of course. For starters, I suspect I might put up a struggle, and fight dirty – perhaps biting – and, secondly, I don't actually want to *die*. I don't want there to be a dead body on the bed, and it to be the end of everything. I don't want to *not live*.

I just … want not to be *me* any more. Everything I am now is not working.

I basically want to live in the 'easy like Sunday morning' bank advert – a huge, warehouse flat in London, in which I am wearing a fluffy towelling robe, and reading the paper.

And then, later, I will be going out in a beautiful green dress, and saying something so funny, someone *has* to have sex with me. That's what I want. That's my future life.

Lying under the bed, I consider the chances of this scenario happening to the current Johanna Morrigan. They are blindingly small. I just don't have the *resources*.

'I'm gonna need a bigger boat,' I think.

And so, I just … start all over again. I have read, many times, the phrase 'A self-made man', but misunderstood what it meant. I presumed it was describing, not a working-class boy made good in industry – smoking a cigar, in slightly over-shined shoes – but something more elemental, and fabulous, instead. Someone mage-like, who had stitched themselves together out of silver gauze, and ambition, and magic.

'A self-made man' – not of woman born, but alchemised, through sheer force of will, by the man himself. This is what I want to be. I want to be a self-made woman. I want to conjure myself, out of every sparkling, fast-moving thing I can see. I want to be the creator of me. I'm gonna begat myself.

The first thing I'm burning is my name. 'Johanna Morrigan' does not have good associations any more. 'Johanna Morrigan' is the answer to the local question, 'Who do you think has fucked up recently?'

I compile a list of possible new names, and take it in to Krissi.

He is on his bed knitting himself a bobble hat whilst listening to an Agatha Christie audiotape, from the library. A big, pale boy hunched over a tiny pair of needles. Krissi becomes very angry when you tell him that knitting is for girls.

'Knitting was primarily a male hobby at its inception,' he says – big pale hands clacking the needles. 'You'd anger a lot of Scottish fishermen if you told them it was a girl's habit. They'd beat you with a giant salted cod, Johanna. And I'd pay to watch.'

I turn the audiotape off, just as Poirot has a *tisane*.

'Poirot isn't going to find it difficult to work out who killed you,' Krissi says – pretending to stab me through the heart with the knitting needle, and turning the tape back on again.

I turn it back off again.

'Krissi, I'm getting a new name. What do you think would be good?'

'"Hamburglar". Now fuck off.'

'Seriously, K.'

Krissi knows how low I am. Two days ago, he found me

lying face-down, and crying onto a sanitary towel, which I had positioned under my eyes, by way of acknowledging the sheer volumes of sorrow. He did laugh at this, but also looked sympathetic.

'I still think "Hamburglar",' he says – but knits quieter, like he's listening.

I've tried to choose a name that's thin, and light and powerful, like an aluminium glider: I am going to climb onto this name, wait for a thermal, and then fly it all the way down to London, to my future.

It's got to work in print – it must suit black ink – but it also needs to sound cheerful when shouted across a bar. It must sound like a joyful yell.

The list of names I make are evidence alone of why, on the whole, it is best for girls not to become mothers in their teens. For whilst teenage girls are more than capable of raising a child perfectly well, the kind of name a teenage girl is apt to choose is poor.

'How about "Juno Jones"?' I ask.

Briskly: 'They'll call you "Jumbo Bones".'

'"Eleanor Vulpine"?'

A look.

'"Kitten Lithium"?'

'Is this actually for a human being? You're not getting Iggy Pop to name the new *Blue Peter* cat, or something?'

'Yes – it's for me. How about "Laurel Canyon"? It's where, like, Crosby, Stills, Nash & Young lived in the Sixties. The hippy Valhalla. I could be Laurel Canyon.'

'I hate Crosby, Stills, Nash & Young. I think they're cunts.'

I blink. Blimey. Krissi smiles.

'Not really!'

But his eyes are cold.

'My favourite two are "Belle Jar" and "Dolly Wilde". Belle Jar like in *The Bell Jar*, you know – Sylvia Plath – and Dolly Wilde, who was Oscar Wilde's niece. She was, like, this amazing alcoholic lesbian who was dead scandalous, and died really young.'

Krissi looks at me.

'And these are the names you've chosen to lead to a happier, better life?'

'Krissi seriously – which one do you like best?'

'You can't be just "Johanna Morrigan"?' he asks.

'I can't be just Johanna Morrigan,' I say. 'I can't.'

Krissi sighs.

'Ip dip do/The dog's got the flu/The cat's got the chicken pox/So out goes you.'

An hour and a half later, I'm in the big chemist's in Queen's Square, shop-lifting black Rimmel eyeliner into my coat pocket, with an immense sense of destiny. I feel happy, for the first time since I left Violet's house.

It's morally okay to steal this eyeliner, because I need it. I need it, to draw Dolly Wilde's face onto my own.

SIX

I love Dolly Wilde. She's my new pet. She's an early nineties prototype Tamagotchi. I am my own imaginary friend. In many ways, it's the best and healthiest hobby I could have discovered right now: me. I am going to take my run-down shell, and upgrade myself.

On the wall above my bed, I start Blu-tacking up things I think will be useful in this task – a collection of attributes I would wish to gift myself, now I'm starting again. It will be like those scenes in detective shows, where they pin up all the clues on the wall, and then stare at it, whilst music swells, until – suddenly! They know who the murderer is, and grab their coat, and run out of the room.

I am going to put every clue I have about how to be a better me on this wall, and I will stare at it whilst listening to *The Best Of The Hollies*, until – suddenly! I will know who I am, grab my coat, and run out of the room, to have sex.

I cut the pictures out of the *Radio Times*, and from books, and magazines at jumble sales. The women: Barbra Streisand in *Hello, Dolly!*, Anne of Green Gables and Miranda Richardson as Queen Elizabeth I in *Blackadder* – a triumvirate of irrepressible gingers. Then the brunettes: Dorothy Parker, in her furs; Kate Bush, in her nightie; Elizabeth Taylor, in her excelsis. I appear to have no time for blondes – except for Bugs Bunny, dressed up as a woman, as he seduces the fool, Fudd. That is a woman I could be, definitely: a cartoon man-rabbit dressed up as a girl, trying to have sex with a stuttering bald man. I could definitely do that.

I assemble the men, on my wall: my imaginary coterie of brother-lovers. Dylan Thomas smoking a fag. The young Orson Welles, pranking the world with *The War of the Worlds* and not giving a shit. George Orwell – so noble! So clever! So dead so young! Tony Benn, inventing stamps and the Post Office Tower. Rik Mayall as Lord Flashheart in *Blackadder*, kicking the door in and shouting, 'WOOF!' A picture of Lenin when he was very young – I don't know exactly what he went on to do, but I do know that he looks hot here – all brown eyes, natty scarf and floppy hair. No one this handsome could be *that* bad, surely.

And the words: the rest of the wall is words. The page from *On The Road* about the burning Roman candles. Scarlett O'Hara's 'With God as my witness, I will never go hungry again' speech, which I stare at, thoughtfully, whilst eating cheese sandwiches. The lyrics to 'Rebel Rebel' and 'Queen Bitch'. When Bowie yelps that he could do better than that, I hear another young person stuck somewhere, looking out of the window and imagining how much better they would invent the world, if they were just given the chance to lay their hands on the machinery. If they could just bust into the engine room for twenty-four hours, with a tool box.

Some of it, I write directly onto the paintwork, so it will never be lost, or blown away. I am collaging myself, here, on my wall.

And as I assemble the inside of my head, like a new hang-out, so I alter my appearance, too. At jumble sales I eschew my typical purchases: stuff that my parents would have described as 'vibey'. As with most hippies, they love bright colours – a chunky, hand-knitted jumper with rainbows would be greeted with, 'You'll look fucking natty in that, son!'

But I am going to be wearing this stuff no more. No more colour.

I'm in black, now. Black, for business – like an evil highwayman. Boots, tights, shorts, blouse: all in black, with a black, tailed waiter's jacket that's slightly too tight over my tits, but no matter. I am Chick Turpin. I am Madame Ant. I'm planning to hold up some passing stagecoaches, heading towards London, and steal a new life from whoever's inside.

I dye my hair black, too, with shoplifted Movida – security in the chemist's appears to consist of the sign 'Shoplifters: Will Be Prosecuted' on the door. Winningly, someone has amended it by scribbling out letters with a black felt-tip, to read, 'Hope: Be Cute' – which I am now adapting as my new motto.

You can nick anything from the chemist's. Like bright red lipstick, too – which I am splashing on like there's no tomorrow.

When school starts again, in September, the reveal of my new, black hair gets several comments.

The best one, from Emma Pagett: 'Aww, wicked – you look dead like Winona Ryder!'

The worst, from Craig Miller, who's standing behind her: 'You look like a *dead* Winona Ryder, more like. HA! HA!'

I am unperturbed by his comments. Craig Miller is a boy who makes girls he *fancies* smell farts that he does on his hand. He is not Giacomo Casanova (*History of my Life*, Longmans, 1967–72), who I know would fancy me, as he loves clever women; and, also, big arses.

A month after *Midlands Weekend*, I am coming downstairs to do my post-monitoring shift by the front door dressed like Edward Scissorhands, moonlighting as a waiter. I spend the hours embroidering *(Traditional and Folk Designs*, Alan & Gill Bridgewater, Search Press, 1990) my name, 'Dolly Wilde', onto all my clothes: across the breast of my jacket, on the turn-up of my shorts, across my thigh. I am branding me. I do not want to forget my name.

Making Dolly Wilde is my business, now. I enjoy the feeling that deciding who I am is *work*. I now have a career – the only person in our house to do so. I find my anxiety levels have dropped enormously

On this particular Tuesday, today's project, I have decided, is 'Networking'. I'm being very serious about the business of me. In business-bible *The Practice of Management* (Peter F. Drucker, Harper & Row, 1954), the advice is that you should 'find other people in the same line of work, and make contact'.

Cousin Ali has recently reinvented herself – *viz* 'going goth' last year – so I'm going up town, to network her.

And I'm taking my business associate with me.

'What do you want?'

I blink.

I'm standing at the Man On 'is 'Oss statue, with my cousin Ali and her gang of four goth boys – one of which I recognise from school. Oliver. I'm pretty sure he's the only kid in Wolverhampton called Oliver. I remember him before he was a goth – every day, in the dinner hall, kids would stand around him in the queue saying 'Please sir – I want some more!' in quavering voices, and then pushing him into a wall. Really, with those kind of stats, it was just a matter of time before he went goth.

I say 'Hola!' in my most cheerful way, but it doesn't seem to be working.

'You want something?' Ali says again.

I shift, awkwardly. I'm pretty sure I've read this correctly – that this is the outpost for loners. That, culturally, this is what I should be filed under: 'Goths, sitting by statue/war memorial'.

People with no upper-body strength, who read poetry. These are my people. I am wearing my black waiter's jacket, black boots, black tights and so much eyeliner that I look like a puffin.

Given this effort, I thought the counter-culture would just … let you in. I didn't know there was an *interview process*.

I blink again. 'I'm your cousin. Johanna. Pat's kid.'

Ali looks up for a minute – a hard, evaluating look.

'You look like Fat Nanna,' she says, eventually.

'I got her bed!'

Ali's lips thin: 'I got the budgie cage. Gonna put a hamster in it.'

Silence.

Ten feet away, my business associate – Lupin – is chasing a pigeon. I've dressed him up brilliantly: he's currently obsessed with tigers, and I've made him some tiger ears and a tiger tail, which is pinned to the back of his trousers. He's chasing the pigeon whilst shouting 'RARGH!' at it.

A boy looks up: 'Ali – is she with you?' Ali shrugs. I shrug, too. The boy shrugs back. I shrug again.

Fucking hell – is this what being a teenager consists of? No offence, but I've had livelier days potty-training Lupin – during the phase he used to poo behind the sofa, then throw it into the potty and ask for a reward. Actually, that really was quite fun.

'You a goth, then?'

The boy is talking. He's looking at my outfit, which is all black.

'Well – is being a goth really a straightforward, binary, "black or white" issue?' I ask, in the manner of an elderly professor on *The World at One*, gesturing to their white faces, and black clothes.

Nothing.

Man, I have seen clips of Gilda Radner tearing up *Saturday Night Live* with this kind of shit. I don't think anyone in this town is ever going to laugh at my jokes. They just don't get semiotic deconstruction here. Maybe I will have to move to New York.

'I'd say I'm … "goth-curious"?'

Still nothing.

'What bands you into?'

The boy is talking again. Ali is utterly limp, letting him quiz me.

I think for a minute.

'Well, Beatles, obviously. Zeppelin. *The Best of Simon & Garfunkel*. All that …'

I think.

'… shit.'

The boy is staring at me. Clearly, this isn't impressing him.

'Don't you like anything *recent*?' he asks, eventually.

'Of course!' I say, confidently. 'Roachford. Dire Straits. And Michael Jackson – even though he seems like a bit of a prat.'

I also like Tina Turner – I've worked out a whole dance routine to 'Steamy Windows', using a broom in lieu of a cane – but I'm not telling him that. He's staring at me like this conversation is a game I'm losing badly.

'… but mainly John Coltrane, and Charlie Mingus,' I put in, quickly. 'All the hot, bad jazzers.'

I'm lying. I hate jazz. I think it sounds like people being completely mad. But my dad plays it a lot, and I recall his sage advice: 'Whenever you need to win a situation – talk about jazz, Johanna. It confuses people.'

The boy continues to stare. Ali moves slightly away from me. I wait for a minute, but it seems like this conversation is over.

'Well,' I say. I can't believe jazz has failed me. I wonder what else my dad is wrong about.

'Well, just gonna …' I stand up. Lupin is twenty feet away, in pursuit of a hobbling pigeon that has only one foot. 'Just … off now.'

Ali barely nods. The boy completely ignores me. This initial meeting with Wolverhampton's counter-culture has gone badly. A proper 0/10. I have failed on preparation.

I'm going to need a much bigger boat. This is my recurrent problem.

I look across the square, to Record Locker – Wolverhampton's independent record shop. I make a decision.

'Come, Lupin,' I say, standing up, and holding out my hand to him. 'We must away – to pastures new.'

This was the traditional parting line of *New Yorker* critic Alexander Woollcott – traditionally uttered after some disaster, such as drunken collapse, or massive social *faux-pas*. Lupin takes my hand – still trying to kick the pigeon – and I walk across to the store.

I wish these cunts knew about Alexander Woollcott. They would respect me, even as I walked away. Instead, I can just hear them laughing:

Ali: 'Oh, my *God*.'

I am about to do what is, undoubtedly, the bravest thing I have ever done. Record shops are not for womenfolk. This is a known fact. They are the gang treehouse with 'No girls allowed' written on the side – the young, music-loving person's equivalent of the gentleman's smoking room. In my most paranoid fantasy, when I open the door, all the music will stop, and everyone will look up – like in a Wild West saloon bar, when a stranger walks in.

When I open the door, the music does actually stop, and everyone looks up. The music stopping is just a coincidence – it's the end of the record – but everyone looking up isn't. The people here, hunched over the racks, are boys in army surplus jackets and Doc Martens, with long hair; a couple have tatty black leather jackets on. There's a pair of Madchester flares by the seven-inches. They are all well-qualified members of the counter-culture. They are allowed to be here.

By way of contrast, I'm a fat girl in a black waiter's jacket and a blouse, holding hands with a ginger six-year-old wearing tiger ears and a tiger tail, who is looking at a perambulating pigeon and shouting 'THE EAGLE IS COMING!' very loudly.

Side two of *Bummed* starts, and they all look away again. A couple are smirking. I don't care. I have regular, fulfilling sex with a hair brush, and am the bastard son of a bastard son of Brendan Behan. They will all rue the day. Eventually.

'Alright,' the man behind the counter says. He has greasy black hair and is wearing a Sepultura t-shirt – which I can tell, merely from the logo, is an internationally recognised sign that he kills and eats women.

'Just browsing!' I say, cheerfully, and walk over to the first rack of records, looking purposeful. It's the 'M's. I look at the record sleeves, in what I hope is a knowledgeable way, and try and work out what bands I would like, judging by the cover-art. Morrissey. *Viva Hate*. Bit gloomy. Mega City Four. Piercings. In the nose. That would *hurt*. I wonder if, when you blow your nose, bits emerge. From the hole.

Lupin picks up a Van Morrison record, then fumbles it, and drops it.

'You looking for something in particular?' the man behind the counter asks, shirtily. A couple of boys look up again. Shall I try jazz again?

'*Escalator over the Hill* by Carla Bley,' I say.

This is my dad's worst record by a long chalk – an experimental double-album of free-form jazz opera that clears the front room every time he puts it on, pissed. Even he can't listen to it for more than half an hour without making moaning noises, like he's in pain. He moos.

'It's pretty obscure though, so you probably haven't got it,' I say, pityingly. *Confuse them with jazz.*

'It's *jazz*,' I clarify, helpfully.

'Johnny Hates Jazz?' the man says, loudly. 'No, we haven't got any Johnny Hates Jazz.'

'No,' I say, slightly panicked. 'Not Johnny Hates Jazz.'

Even I know Johnny Hates Jazz are shit. Girls with perms like them. Walking in this shop and asking for Johnny Hates Jazz is basically a death sentence.

But it's too late – the boys are giggling now.

'No – not Johnny Hates Jazz. Carla Bley,' I try again, desperately. 'It's a jazz-opera, oh fuck it, look, I'll try somewhere else.'

I prepare to sweep out of the shop, but Lupin's holding a magazine.

Hurriedly, I try to wrestle it out of his hands.

The paper tears. I look up, stricken. If he's going to charge me for the magazine, I have no money. I'll have to … be killed and eaten by him in his backroom, repeatedly, until I've paid it off.

'It's free,' the man says, gesturing us out of the shop with his hand. 'It's free. It's a free magazine. Take it. Take it.'

'Come, Lupin,' I say, opening the door with as much dignity as I can muster. 'Let's go and see Alexander Woollcott. He's waiting.'

The boy by the rack nearest the door bends over, and hands me something.

'Your son's tail,' he says, handing me Lupin's tiger tail.

Again with the 'son' thing. Jesus. He is NOT MY SON. I AM ACTUALLY A VIRGIN, ACTUALLY. Although I obviously don't say this.

On the bus on the way home, Lupin lolls against the window, in some kind of daze, and I take the sticky, torn magazine from his hands, and flick through it. It's a free musician's monthly magazine called *Making Music*. The cover promises to take the eager reader through the entire back-line rig of Del Amitri's current tour, reveal the 'Mic Secrets' of Midge Ure, and show us around the LA studio of legendary session bassist Pino Palladino. I've essentially found the contents of my dad's head, printed out. Even though I'll read *anything* – you can quiz me on the ingredients in Birds Strawberry Trifle all you like; I've read that packet – even I can't read this.

But on page four, there's a column called 'J Arthur Rank', which prints the 'utter nonsense them magazine people write'. Angry musician readers send in lines from the music press, which they find vexingly pretentious.

Craig Ammett, reviewing The Touch in *Melody Maker*, claims, 'This is the sound of God exploding – slowly. And the debris hitting Dali in the face.'

Ian Wilkinson in *Disc & Music Echo*, meanwhile, is denigrated for lauding Sore Throat's LP as '… an overnight evolution from in-joking musical amoebas, to mighty sonic dolphins'.

And David Stubbs, again in *Melody Maker*, describes prog-rock band Henry Cow's sound as '… dragging a moose around on stage, and sucking on it'.

'Nobble these nerds!' the J Arthur Rank column urges. 'Go to work on the Bozos behind the Typewriters!'

This is, apparently, terrible writing. The music press is, obviously, some manner of Versailles, filled with decadent, lace-cuffed dandies typing grandiloquent nonsense about hard-working musicians in bands. These are puffed-up fop parasites, riding on the mighty back of the noble rock beast. Lollygaggers, poseurs – petit-maîtres riffing toss late into the night, making no sense, making the world an infinitely worse place. These people are, really, no better than scum.

And I think: I love this stuff. I could do this. Fuck writing a book about a fat girl and a dragon. I could be a music journalist, instead. I could easily write this stuff. It would be a doddle. This is better than poems about my dog, or my dad's arse. This is what I've been waiting for.

This is my way out.

SEVEN

A week later, in Central Library. A beautiful Victorian building, filled with tatty eighties plastic shelving – and, now, me.

In the upstairs Audio-Visual Library, there's a huge, wooden table, on which newspapers and magazines are laid out for everyone to read.

Previously, I'd always pitied the old blokes sitting at the table, reading *The Sun*. Looking at the tits on Page 3, in the library.

'Oh, Nye Bevan,' I would think. 'That you would live to see social provision used for this!'

Now, however, I'm all over this facility – as the table also provides the week's music press: *Melody Maker*, *NME*, *Disc & Music Echo* and *Sounds*.

Once I've stood watch over the door for the morning post, I walk into town and spend my weekend at this desk, reading the music press. No – *studying* the music press. This is my work, now. I am studying my future.

I still have my business associate with me – Lupin, sitting at the table, dressed as a tiger, reading books from the Children's Library. Sometimes, if Mum's having a bad day with the babies, I have to bring them with me, too – for 'fresh air'.

So I sit, reading. There's so much to learn. Turns out, *loads* has happened since the Beatles split up. It's not just Dire Straits and Tina Turner, after all. In a notebook, I write down what sound like the most amazing bands – The Smiths, My

Bloody Valentine, Teenage Fanclub, Primal Scream, Pixies, Stone Roses, The Fall, Pavement.

All their names sound new, and bright: like places, rather than bands. Full of people who are alive, and still making music. There's a record label called Creation, and everyone on it appears to be a garrulous, hell-raising Celt. There's a pub called The Good Mixer in Camden, where everyone goes to drink. At the Astoria, there's a place called The Keith Moon Bar, where aftershow parties go on until 1am. 1am!

I could just walk through the door in these places and *talk* to someone. I could be *in* this. I feel like Marco Polo, hearing about China. I know I need to go there. I know this will be my thing. I have found my destination. My people will be waiting for me there. These magazines are describing *my* future life.

I try to interest Krissi in my new-found obsession with music – these dispatches from my newfoundland. I come into his bedroom, and throw myself on his bed.

'Oh my God, the new Sonic Youth single sounds amazing. Kim Gordon is pretending to be Karen Carpenter – but with fucked up scuzzy buzz-saw guitar all over it, like she's fore-telling her own doom.'

'Who's Karen Carpenter?' Krissi asks.

'No idea,' I reply, happily.

'And what's "fucked up scuzzy buzz-saw guitar"?' Krissi continues.

'Nope. No idea,' I admit. 'But it sounds like it must be *awesome*.'

I will do soon, though. I will soon know what fucked up scuzzy buzz-saw guitars sound like – because I've ordered the album. Central Library allows you to order any album you like for 20p. Having rinsed Dadda's pockets for loose change when I found him passed out, face-down, in the hallway, a couple of days ago, I've ordered ten – the bands that *Disc & Music Echo* recommend most highly.

'It can take six to eight weeks for them to arrive,' the librarian tells me, warningly, looking down at the cards that say un-libraryish things like 'Jane's Addiction: Nothing's Shocking', 'Babes In Toyland: Spanking Machine' and 'Bongwater' on them, in my round, childish hand.

'Oh, that's okay,' I say. 'Gives me time to imagine them.'

She stares at me.

This is my new thing – to imagine music from words. I lie on top of my duvet, imagining what these albums might sound like. It's a process a little like magic, or second-hand thought-throwing. I make whole albums in my head, whilst I wait for the real ones to arrive. I look at the album covers, and infer melody from the colours – the sunset ice-cream swirl of the Cocteau Twins' *Heaven or Las Vegas* or the red satanic appliqué of Jane's Addiction's *Ritual de lo Habitual*. Excited – inspired – I start to incorporate them, synaesthetically, into my sexual fantasies – coming in coppers, in paisleys, in the crimson bursts of Lush's *Scar*.

As the autumn turns colder, and harder, in November, I am coming to a library of imaginary music – head full of colour, staring at the cold moon outside.

Trying not to wake Lupin up, beside me.

Of course, there's only so long you can wank to a wholly imagined record collection before you become desperate to hear it, and take some form of action.

John Peel is mentioned in these magazines, over and over – John Peel's legendary sessions on Radio 1, where all these bands play, at some point: a nightclub in the radio waves you can get into whatever your age, and whatever you're wearing.

Even a fourteen-year-old girl can enter wearing her long, Victorian-style nightie, long after everyone else in the house is asleep.

At midnight, plugging my dad's huge headphones into the radio, I lie next to Lupin – sleeping – and try to find Radio 1, from the tuning information given in the *Radio Times*. Scrolling through the bandwidths, I hear familiar bursts of Kylie and Simply Red and Gladys Knight, but I keep going – these are not the droids I am looking for.

Finally, at 97.2FM, I find a Liverpudlian drawl, talking about his 'not inconsiderable efforts to locate the tour dates for hotly tipped Ipswich trio Jacob's Mouse', and failing.

This is it! I'm in the door! This is Uncle Peel, of whom they all speak! I am, finally, going to hear the counter-culture of 1990 for the first time! This is where it hangs out!

Peel finishes his morose, Eeyore-like rant about the tour dates, and introduces the next record.

'There's no nicety of something as bourgeois as an introduction here, I warn you,' he says, laconically, before cueing the song in.

The sudden noise, through the headphones, is disconcerting – a massive, evil-sounding slab of guitar, seemingly played with the sole intention of terrifying anyone who hasn't yet lived through a roughly equivalent sonic experience, such as riding their tricycle under a malfunctioning cement-mixer full of dying children.

Then the vocal starts – a man who sounds utterly possessed, screaming out an urgent warning: '*He's outside your house! He's outside your house!*'

I have never been more terrified in my life. This is most assuredly not 'Steamy Windows' by Tina Turner. This 'John Peel show' is, clearly, some manner of CB radio, by which demons communicate with each other, as they scheme to consume the Earth. And still the warning goes on: '*He's outside your house! He's outside your house!*'

I turn the radio off, and take the headphones off, trembling. Jesus Christ. I need water. I get out of bed, and go to get some, from the desk. As I pass the window, I look out, and there is – a man; and he's outside my house.

A man, just standing under the streetlight opposite. With all the impossible menace that a man, alone, has. Why would he be here? Why? WHY? There's never *anyone* around on our estate. Oh, this is pure diabolism.

Seeing a movement at my window, he looks up. His face is pale. He looks right at me. In my horror, his face appears to melt a little – turning into Edvard Munch's 'The Scream', which I have seen in *The Key to Modern Art of the Early Twentieth Century* (Lourdes Cirlot, Bateman, 1990).

Stifling a scream, I get back into bed, and put the radio under a pile of clothes, on the floor – burying it, lest it now be radioactive with fiendishness.

I hug the sleeping Lupin to me – a cross between a comfort and something I am absolutely prepared to offer up to the man, as a sacrifice, should he suddenly, with his evil logic, appear in my doorway.

I am too young for the counter-culture, I think. I just can't handle it. If I get through this night without dying of pure terror – which I currently greatly doubt – I am going straight back to the Beatles tomorrow. Lovely Beatles, with your harmonies about love being old and love being new! I should have stuck with you! I am never, ever trying to listen to John Peel again. There's no way I can be a music journalist if you have to listen to stuff like *this*.

*

Years later, of course, I realised that there were no demons – that this was merely some fairly anodyne speed-metal, and that the man outside was just a man, standing at the bus stop, waiting for the 512.

But I've started to make my stand, now, as a nascent teenager, and it will be difficult to back down. My recent make-over – as a goth rejected by other goths – has not gone unnoticed within the family.

'You've changed. Wearing black all the time. It's like having a big fat crow trapped in the house,' Mum says, one day, as I come down the stairs. 'A big fat crow, flapping at the windows. It's depressing. Can't you wear a nice dress?'

'Black is how I am inside. Because there's no lighting inside the human body,' I tell her.

She just looks at me blankly, and shrugs.

She never gets these kinds of jokes – where I try to subvert classic teenage cliché. I've tried explaining them to her before, and she just emits a little, blank, dismissive 'Oh' – rather like the Queen would if someone said, bullishly, 'Check my fucking wedge – I've got *twenty quid*.'

'Oh.'

She doesn't like the make-up, either.

'I once nearly blinded myself with a mascara brush,' she says, looking querulously at my eyeliner.

I don't want to point out that that says far more about her than it does about me. She might as well be telling me a story of how she once confused 'Push' for 'Pull' on a door, then banning me from using doors again – 'Lest you *also* be betrayed by doors.'

And there's a whole series of 'You've changed' conversations – like we're trying to collect some kind of set.

'You've changed,' she says, as I come downstairs wearing a small black lace wedding veil.

'Well, that's good, isn't it, Mother. Otherwise I'd still be excreting via your umbilical cord.'

'You've changed' – as I watch the Happy Mondays on *Top of The Pops*, and practise my Madchester dancing.

'Well, that is the nature of the passing of time.'

'You've changed' – as I bleach my moustache in the bathroom.

'Yes. I've decided the "Indie Hitler" look wasn't going to work for me, after all.'

The kids like my new look, anyway.

'You look like an evil princess,' Lupin says, admiringly, playing with my black veil.

Evil princess. I'll take that. It's better than what I had before, anyway – 'Pudding-like outcast.'

I could probably work with 'Evil princess'.

The next night I listen to John Peel again, like an evil princess would. It doesn't seem so terrifying, the second time around. Like stormy weather, all you have to do is wait, and it will clear. Yes, there's lots of dance music – Peel loves Acid House, which I have decided, definitively, is not for me: I don't have the right clothes for it; nor do I know anyone with a car who can take me to a rave, and so, for this reason, I am out. I am like those uptight teenagers in 1963, hearing the Beatles, and saying, sniffily, 'What a racket! I prefer the honest joys of skiffle!'

But sometimes, and suddenly, these barrages of me-excluding noise part to reveal things I find astonishingly beautiful, and useful to me and my heart, in their current position. I lean over and press 'record', in order to keep them forever – minus their first seven seconds.

I keep these tapes for years. Mazzy Star. The Sugarcubes. Loads of African hi-life guitars – which I patronisingly think are almost as good as the stuff on Paul Simon's *Graceland*, and record in the pious interest of 'having broad tastes', even though, if I'm being honest, I subsequently always fast-forward through them.

But it's all there, on a cassette, if I want and need it – and I want and need it: I want and need all these new colours and ideas and voices, on little grey cassettes I can keep in my pocket, like charms. Like books before them, I know each of these songs could, in the end, prove to be the thing I need: a way out. A place to go.

John Peel is *my* World Service – my club-house in the sky, where I meet with all the other kids like me, also clutching empty cassettes, who want to hear the latest headlines: someone has written a brilliant song in Boston! In Tokyo! In Perth!

For this is the thrill of Peel – finding out there's a world six inches under the pavements. The counter-culture. The underground. It's always been there – like the buried rivers that run under London. And when the time comes that you cannot stand your surface-level any more, and you feel there is nowhere left to walk laterally, you can stop right where you stand, take a hammer from your pocket, and smash between your feet, and go down. Go deeper.

Drop, like Alice, into a bright new world of Mad Hatters, imperious Queens and riddling Dormice, and wars that have raged endlessly, since time immemorial. Punks hate hippies and mods hate rockers and ravers hate indie-kids. Patti Smith coldly rages against Jesus, Primal Scream are higher than the sun, and Ivor Cutler stands on a stony beach with an accordion, singing surreal Hebridean stories about girls who squeeze bees for honey.

And sometimes – as if it's a festal occasion – Peel plays the hits. The first time I hear The Stone Roses' 'I Am The Resurrection', I dance in my bed, lying down, with the headphones on – arms cast out wide, feeling excited, for the first time, to come from a battered industrial town. Things happen in these kinds of towns that could never happen anywhere else – proud, poor kids make things happen with more heat, and intensity, and attack, than could ever be managed somewhere with pleasant villages, or well-tended gardens.

I finally understand what my father says when he says, 'I am the bastard son of Brendan Behan – and you *will* bow down to me.' The working classes do things differently. I can hear it. I can see we are not *wrong*. We are not just poor people who have not yet evolved into something else – ie: people with money. We *are* something else – just as we are. The working classes do it differently. We are the *next* thing. We power popular culture – just as, before, we powered the Industrial Revolution. The past is theirs, but the future's mine. They're all out of time.

'JOHANNA!' Krissi hisses. I take my headphones off. He has apparently been calling my name for some time, from his bunk bed.

'If you're having a fit, I'm very happy to push a wooden spoon into your mouth,' he says. 'Stop *wriggling*.'

'This is not *wriggling*,' I say, putting the headphones back on. 'This is *dancing*. I am *dancing*, Krissi.'

EIGHT

I'm over at Uncle Jim's house. The place is rammed. It's 28th November 1990, and Margaret Thatcher has just resigned as prime minister, after an internal party coup that has made the *Nine O'Clock News* impossibly exciting for the last week.

With each development, my father has been on the edge of the sofa, like he usually only is for a cup final featuring Liverpool, shouting 'Go on! Stuff it up the cow! Fucking *have her*!'

When Mrs Thatcher suddenly, dramatically, appears behind BBC reporter John Sergeant after the first vote, and Sergeant looks visibly startled, Dad shouts, 'She's behind you! Fucking hell – she just pops up like the fucking skeleton army in *Jason and the Argonauts*, don't she? Tebbit's been sowing his fucking teeth. Medusa, innit? With snakes in her hair. Look at the fucking snakes in her hair, kids.'

We look, and feel that we can see the snakes.

And now, she's gone.

'Resigned? Booted out, more like. Got the sack. See how you like it up you! She doesn't like it up her!' my dad is crowing, opening a can of Guinness. Everyone raises their can in the air, and toasts: 'She doesn't like it up her!'

The kitchen is full of uncles and aunts, smoking and drinking. All the uncles and aunts are here – it's a proper tribal meeting. Even the Welsh ones, and the ones from Liverpool – they were born across the country, by Fat Nanna and Evil

Granddad, as they were repeatedly bombed, then moved, then bombed again, during the war, and then looking for work, in the years that followed.

The mining uncles from Wales have always scared me – pictures of them in the photo albums showed them black, teeth gleaming. As a child, I always confused them with the Black and White Minstrels, and worried they might be racist. I have imagined their house, in the mines – a hollowed-out cave off a main shaft, with the aunties desperately trying to keep the doilies and the tablecloths clean, in the dark, lit by a lamp.

When I finally visited Uncle Jareth's house, in Swansea, I was amazed to see it was a normal council house, with walls, and roof, and a garden, and felt uneasy – until they showed me the coal-hole. I presumed Uncle Jareth slept there, on the coal, like a dragon on its hoard, and felt satisfied. I resumed playing 'It' with the Welsh cousins, who were unexpectedly blond and golden, like they stole all the sunlight Uncle Jareth should have had, during the day. Miners' children are always very clean. I have noticed this.

'This lot'll be out on their arses by New Year,' my dad continues, reviewing the remaining Tory cabinet. 'Poxy bunch of suits compared to her. They're nothing now their mummy's gone. They've gassed the hive! The Queen is dead! The Tories will be hanging from the lamp-posts by Valentine's Day!'

All the uncles cheer. All the aunts look disapproving, and continue removing clingfilm from plates of sandwiches.

The uncles move outside, into the back passage, and continue talking about politics. They can only talk about politics because no one can ever ask, 'How's work going?'

With the exception of Uncle Jim – whom we refer to as 'The Rich Uncle', because he's the union rep at a car plant – none of the other uncles have work, now. Dockyard workers, car-plant workers, miners – big men sitting restlessly on tiny sofas in tiny houses, on the dole.

Some of them have 'sidelines' – Uncle Stu once turned up at our house selling household cleaning products, from a tray. Dad bought some bleach off him, and then they sat in the front room, getting drunk. Later, I heard Mum saying that she'd seen Uncle Stu crying.

Uncle Chris's three sons have all joined the Army: 'Fighting for the country that fucked them,' Dad says, bitterly – but he doesn't say it to their faces. They've all been trained how to use deadly weaponry. My dad, although ostensibly reckless, picks his fights very carefully.

With the men gone, the women can discuss other topics. Women always have other topics – because they can talk about their families, and their wombs, and how giving birth to various members of their family damaged their wombs. Aunty Viv has a story about once being in the kitchen, and coughing out her uterus into her knickers. Whenever she tells it, all the other women light fags and go, 'Tell me about it!' It's completely terrifying.

'So – I see your Johanna's become a Child of the Night,' Aunty Viv says, to my mum, nodding her head at me. I am, as always now, completely in black, and semi-blind with eyeliner.

'I'm actually protesting the Biafran War. Also, against "Cold Turkey" slipping down the charts,' I say, arranging sausage rolls on a plate.

No one here has read the famous letter John Lennon sent to the Queen when sending back his MBE – so, yet again, this great joke is completely wasted. I'm going to have to start writing these down.

'I bet that hair dye's sodded your grouting, Angie,' Aunty Soo says, flicking ash into the sink.

'It's like having a big black crow, moping around the house,' my mother confirms.

'You've already used that line,' I tell her.

'I'm your mother,' she replies. 'I can call you a big fat crow ten times a day, if I like.'

'Ah, she's not a crow – she's a black swan, aye you, Johanna?' Aunty Lauren says. 'The black swan of the family.'

Aunty Lauren is ace. Aunty Lauren has 'a bit of a past' on her – in the sixties, she was one of the hippies who poured Fairy Liquid into the fountain in Queen's Square, and filled it with foam. It was on the front page of the *Express & Star*. In the corner of the picture, you can just see the corner of Aunty Lauren's handbag. She's shown us the picture frequently.

Last Christmas, she invented 'The Snowman' – the usual Snowball of Advocaat and lemonade, but topped up with vodka.

'Drink a couple of those and, in the morning, your kids wake up and find you've melted,' she cackled. 'They're left in their pyjamas, just holding your wet scarf and crying. That's why it's called "The Snowman"!'

An hour later, she tripped over the sofa, dancing to Fleetwood Mac.

'So what you doing at the moment, Johanna?' Aunty Lauren continues. 'Fifteen now, aye ya? You worked out what you wanna be yet?'

'I'm going to be a writer. A music journalist,' I say.

I've seen dozens of films about what happens to someone in the working classes announcing that they want to do something 'arty' – like be a writer, or singer, or poet. All the assembled relatives will look furious, and start saying things like, 'Your dreams are no good – you've got to put bread on the table, pet!' and 'You've always thought you're too good for us, with your *fancy London ways*.' I am absolutely braced to become an outcast. I am ready to be a young Tony Hopkins, storming out of the room, to find my muse alone.

That is not what happens.

'Ah, good on ya, Jo!' Aunty Lauren says, immediately. 'Good for you, turning all of that bullshit into cash.'

'Cracking!' Aunty Viv says – which is frankly astonishing, given that she once told me off for getting her Little Stephen to mime the Barbara Dickson/Elaine Paige duet 'I Know Him So Well' with me, because it 'made him look bent'.

'You know what,' Aunty Soo says, 'I knew a kid at school who ended up writing the pop reviews in the *Express & Star* and it was a bostin' job – he ended up going to Edinburgh, with the Moody Blues.'

Suddenly everyone in the kitchen is going on about people they know who were writers, or went into the music industry, and what a great career it is for a young working-class person to aspire to. I feel obscurely aggrieved. Can't my family do *anything* normal? I'm supposed to be feeling rejected and outsiderish right now. Instead, my Aunty Soo's tipping me off that, if you become a music writer, 'You get all your drugs free, so I hear.'

'Johanna doesn't need drugs – she's got sausage rolls,' my mother says, pointedly. She's been sitting, palely, on a chair in the corner, and watching gimlet-eyed as I put a whole one in my mouth.

With as much dignity as I can muster, I take the plate of sausage rolls and go into the front room, to offer it to the cousins.

'SOZZER ROZZERS!' I shout, spitting crumbs, as they fall upon the plate. I've never counted how many cousins I've got. There's a good dozen in here – playing a game where they have to get around the room whilst not touching the floor, by climbing over the sofa, chairs, mantelpiece, etc.

My goth cousin Ali is sitting in the corner of the room with her Walkman on, viewing them disdainfully. I do a quick circuit of the room – climbing on sofa, chair, window-sill, mantelpiece, back to the starting point, still eating the sausage roll, shouting '*That's* how you do it' to the awestruck toddlers – then sit next to her.

'Alright,' Ali says.

As I suspected, Ali is being a lot more friendly today – now she's not showing off to some boy, and is also surrounded by small children she wants to distance herself from, as their elder.

Still, I'm not going to utterly prostitute myself to her affections for a second time. As a power move, I turn the plate, so she has to take one of the more battered sausage rolls. She takes a shit one. I accept this oblique apology with a nod. She ignores it. We sit in silence for a minute, watching the kids hit each other with cushions.

'You wanna go for a fag?' she says, suddenly.

I feel as startled as if she'd said, 'Shall we go and milk a bison?'

'Yeah,' I say.

We pick our way over the wrestling children, and go and sit on the front doorstep. She takes a packet of Silk Cut out of her pocket.

'The cigarette brand of the working-class woman,' she says.

She puts one in her mouth, and proffers the packet to me. I take one.

'Does your mum know?' I ask.

'These are hers,' she says, lighting it, shrugging. I put mine in my mouth, but she doesn't offer me the lighter, so it just … stays there.

She exhales a contented line of smoke, which we watch blow straight back into the house.

'So,' she says, finally. 'How's Tina Turner?'

'Oh, I'm over Tina Turner,' I say. I'm not. I did an amazing 'Nutbush City Limits' last night that made Lupin cry laughing.

'I've been reading *Disc & Music Echo*,' I add. 'I've been getting into the Stone Roses, and the Happy Mondays, and Bongwater. I mean, I haven't heard Bongwater yet. But they're my favourites.'

She stares at me.

'I'm waiting for them to come, from the library,' I add. 'And I've been listening to John Peel.'

'Are you into John Kite?' she asks, like it's a test.

'Who's he?'

She exhales again – clearly working out if she can be bothered to tell me. A quick look up and down the street confirms to her that there's literally nothing better to do right now.

'He's this brilliant Welsh council-estate pisshead,' she says, eventually. 'Like a cross between American Music Club and Harry Nilsson? And gobby. He's just done this live album where between songs it's like stand-up comedy – and then he sings about his mum being mental.'

'I can relate,' I say, giving my unlit cigarette a cowboyish twizzle.

'I've drawn a picture of him,' Ali says, getting out her sketchbook. 'I draw pictures of all my favourite singers.'

She shows me her sketchbook. Ali's quite a bad drawer. I look at one bony blonde.

'Is that Zuul, from *Ghosbusters*?' I ask.

'It's Debbie Harry,' Ali says. 'Her chin's really difficult. That's John Kite.'

She points. We look at a scruffy man, done in pencil, smoking a fag. He looks like a fat young man made from broken bedsprings.

'I love John Kite,' Ali says. 'That's another one of him – but I did his hair wrong, and turned it into Slash from Guns N' Roses.'

We flick through her pad – Ali still smoking.

'There's a lot of Slashes,' I observe.

'Whenever anyone goes wrong, I turn them into Slash from Guns N' Roses,' Ali says. 'You just scribble in lots of hair, and put a top hat on it. That one,' she points, to a Slash in a Puffa jacket, behind a keyboard, '*was* Chris Lowe from the Pet Shop Boys.'

Ali finishes her fag, and grinds it out on the step.

'So you haven't got any records yet – but you want to be a music journalist?' she asks – almost as if she's interested.

'No. And yes.'

Ali pauses, and thinks.

'Well, yow've got to fake it 'til yow make it, kidder,' she says, finally. This superlative gay drag-queen motto, rendered in a flat, Wolverhampton monotone, by a depressed goth.

'Fake it 'til yow make it.'

I'm still thinking about how brilliant this idea is – a third big truth I have learned in a year, along with 'Never tell anyone your secrets' and 'Don't do impressions of Scooby Doo on live television' – when the uncles suddenly spill out of the front door and into the front garden.

Uncle Jareth has been down the off licence, and has bought a bottle of Asti Spumante, and the other uncles are now busily digging a hole in Uncle Jim's front lawn.

'Gonna lay down this vintage!' Uncle Jareth is saying. 'We bury this bottle here, right – then on the day Thatcher dies, we dig it back up again, and toast her coffin.'

The other uncles roar their approval. Jareth back-fills the hole, manically – enjoying the sweat.

Uncle Jim looks at the hole, as Jareth lays the turf back on top, and bangs in a stick, by way of a marker.

'All we can do is outlive the bitch,' he says, quietly. 'We've seen her come in, and we'll see her go back out again. We will out-run this. We will out-run *all* of them.'

Everyone is quiet for a second – staring at the ground, smoking, in the way only men can. Then Dadda shouts 'Because we are the BASTARD SONS OF BRENDAN BEHAN, AND THEY WILL RUE THE DAY!', and everyone cheers, and Uncle Jim goes in to get more beers, and the chairs from the kitchen.

It's getting dark. In the house over the road, another celebration has started to spill out into the street. Someone is playing 'Tramp The Dirt Down' by Elvis Costello. They're going to make a night of it.

If you want to know why we're poor, and why Dadda doesn't have a job, here's why: back in our house. By Dadda's bed. A big, white pot of pills. Daddy's pills.

Daddy was in a band, and when they didn't make any money, he got work as a fireman, and one day – it was a very bad day – he got trapped on top of a burning factory.

And when he woke up in hospital, they told him he'd broken nearly a quarter of all the bones in his body when he jumped. They did sixteen operations on him, and now he is the Tin Man – all screws and plates and tiny metal joints that we pretend to oil, with an oil-can, whilst he lies on the sofa.

He showed us a list of all the bones that snapped, and the x-rays, and it was interesting to look inside a foot, or a shoulder. There was a portion of his right foot that looked like powder – all the bones exploded into sand. And the screws looked just like the screws you would find inside a toolbox – except they were inside a man, a real man, who was our daddy.

Daddy was very poorly and we had to be careful of his legs: you could not climb on Daddy, or bounce on Daddy. Daddy could not do piggybacks, or races. If it was rainy, you had to cover Daddy with a blanket, because the pain got worse then, and it made rainy days particularly gloomy, because he filled the whole sofa, and his knuckles were white, and you could feel the shouting coming; waiting on the front door step, in the hallway.

'I've got a bone in my leg,' he would say, as we trailed away from him, with the unread story, or the unplayed-with puppet. 'I am Arthur Ritus.'

And his mouth would be thin, and the leg stiff with metal under the blanket, and the rain and the rain, and the ants under the sofa, and the rain.

And he would say, on these most awful days, 'I'm gonna get the band back together, and get us out of here, kids. I promise you that. I promise you. We're not staying here. This time next year, there'll be no more beans on toast. I'm going to be limping out of here, into a limo, and into the Ritz – and *you're all coming with me*!'

And that was 1982, when there was just me and Krissi. And now it was 1990, and there was Lupin, too, and the twins. We would need a very big limo, now. One of those long ones, from America, that you see on *Whicker's World*. Which we will not get whilst we are on Invalidity Benefit, Income Support and Child Benefit.

But some bits of Daddy ached more than others. We didn't know at the time, but years later (during a night in The Bell – this is why we drink; all the truths are kept behind the bar! In the optics! Ask away!) one of Daddy's colleagues told us about what really happened that night.

That, before he jumped from the roof – as the gas canisters were exploding around him, one after another – Dadda had started screaming the same thing, over and over again: 'It found me! It found me! It found me! It found me!'

And that he was shouting it right up until he hit the car park.

And what happens, when 'it' finds you, is that something happens to your eyes. When you get angry, they go very pale blue, like bone china made of real bones, and your anger becomes so big that it fills the house, and everyone lives in it. You caught it, off the explosion. *You* are exploding, now. You are trying to be bigger than the explosion. Because you never stopped being scared of the explosion.

Anger is just fear, brought to the boil.

And the thing about scared people is, whenever you ask them for advice, on whatever subject, they only ever have one thing to say to you: 'Run.'

A bad day.

I am sitting on the wall, in the garden. I am crying. Thatcher resigned two weeks ago, now – but I'm not crying about that, of course.

Dad is sitting on the steps up to the lawn, smoking angrily. I came to him with a question, and his reply has been long, and furious. I have chosen the wrong day to talk to Dadda – a white-knuckle day. A day he's in pain. This is why his reply has gone on for half an hour, and has become louder, and more furious. I started crying about ten minutes ago. I am now kind of hysterical, but I can feel the speech is coming to an end:

'… and so if you do want to be a writer, Johanna,' he says, lips thin, and white, with fury, '… if you want to be a fucking writer – then *be* a fucking writer. Just fucking *write*. Write something! WRITE SOMETHING. Stop fucking going *on* about it.

I can't *stand* you going *on* and *on* about it. Get *on* with it. What are you *waiting* for? *Get out of here.*'

And he gets up and limps, heavily – quietly moaning, in pain, 'Fucking legs,' back into the house.

I'm hiccupping too much to say what I want to say: it's not as easy as that! It's not as easy as that, Dad. I'm only just fifteen, and it's not as *easy* as that. I can't just be a writer. I still haven't heard any new music! I get scared on the bus alone! I sit at my desk and I do not know where the words are hidden! It's not as easy as that!

It is as easy as that.

NINE

Dolly Wilde is sitting on a low wall outside IPC Tower in London, on the South Bank, wearing eyeliner, and her hair piled up into an ornate eighteenth-century do, fastened into place with Biros. Behind her, the Thames is wide, flat and brown, with St Paul's doming in the middle of the horizon, seeming to emit a low humming sound, like a gong. This is London where John Lennon and Paul McCartney sat, eyeball to eyeball, guitar to guitar, playing the greatest game ever played on Earth – being the Beatles, in 1967, and where Blur are currently getting pissed in The Mixer. This is the best place in the world.

In the best place in the world, Dolly sits, with a notebook in her lap, which she is pretending to write in, as she is almost an hour early for her appointment, and is trying to keep herself 'looking busy'. She is sitting on a wall because she has never gone into a café or a pub before, and is obscurely worried she might do the wrong thing in there. She is, however, secure in the knowledge that she is well-practised at sitting on walls, and so that is what she is doing. Here's what she is writing in her notebook:

Everyone in London looks weird, they all wear camel-coloured coats – not like Wolverhampton where you have ONE COAT and it's either navy or black and waterproof.

They all walk very fast. Their faces are different – their features all flow backwards off their noses – their noses look like the nose-cones of jet planes. They have velocity. *Everyone here has a purpose. You can feel the money, in this place. You can hear it being made. I never understood why people voted for Margaret Thatcher before – it never made sense in Wolverhampton – but it does here. I understand why people here think miners and factory workers belong in a different century, and country. I can't imagine anyone I know being here. The people walking by talk like they're in a movie. I* do not *feel like I'm in a movie – unless that movie is* The Elephant Man. *Maybe I should have a bag over my head. That might work. I am so nervous! I can't help but think everything would be much easier if I'd EVER KISSED SOMEONE. The kissed generally have more authority.*

Dolly Wilde pretends to suck on her Biro, like it's a fag, then realises she's still holding it like a pen, and turns back into Johanna Morrigan. She has managed to be Dolly Wilde for approximately nine minutes.

This is worrying – because she is about to go in for a job interview as Dolly Wilde, as there is no way that Johanna Morrigan will get a job at *Disc & Music Echo* as a music journalist. Johanna Morrigan has signed all the letters to *D&ME* as 'Dolly Wilde' – she has picked up the phone and spoken to them as 'Dolly Wilde', and the twenty-seven album reviews that she sent them – all carefully written out on Uncle Jim's computer, and printed out on his Daisy Wheel printer ('Daisy Wheel'! I could have called myself 'Daisy Wheel!') – one sent, each day, for twenty-seven days, all have the byline 'Dolly Wilde'.

Except, of course, it's not really a byline yet. A name doesn't turn into a byline until it's in a magazine, or newspaper. Until then, it's still just your name, but typed.

And today is the day Dolly Wilde goes into *D&ME* and finds out if she is going to turn into a byline, or just remain a name that is typed.

I have spent the last two years building 'Dolly Wilde – music journalist' as assiduously as I can. I have now borrowed 148 albums from Central Library, listened to pretty much every John Peel show, and am now an expert on the indie/alternative music of 1988–92. I have done a lot of thinking, in my room; I can now tell you what the music of the nineties sounds like, to a sixteen-year-old girl. There are three kinds.

There is noise. White noise. Ride and My Bloody Valentine and The House of Love and Spaceman 3 and Spiritualized and Slowdive and Levitation. Noise like a non-stop InterCity train going through a station, at night – but instead of you watching it from the platform, skirts whipping, you climb onto the tracks, face-on, like Bobbie in *The Railway Children* – and you open your mouth wide, it drives right into your head and starts doing mad, fast, cold circuits round your veins.

You can't argue with noise or reason with noise – noise cannot be right or wrong, it cannot fail and it cannot fall, and there has never been this noise before, so you cannot fault it or belittle it. I love this noise. If someone asked me 'What are you thinking?' I would point at the noise.

I am eating this noise like mouthfuls of freezing, glittering fog. I am filling with it. I am using it as energy. Because what you are, as a teenager, is a small, silver, empty rocket. And you use loud music as fuel, and then the information in books as maps and co-ordinates, to tell you where you're going.

*

The second music, in 1992, is the music of working-class boys. Manchester. Madchester. The Mondays, and the Roses. I love the records. I love the swagger, the euphoria – the way Northern, working-class pride on E sounds like half the country finally standing on its feet again, after the eighties, and glorying in its power and inventiveness. But I fear the men. These are the same scally boys on my estate that I walk past with my head down, hoping they won't shout at me: I could never be their friend.

Their eyes would immediately give away their brutal analysis of me: that, ultimately, they would not fuck me. I would, therefore, become instantly invisible again, in their presence. Girls like me are invisible to boys in bands like this. I am not in their songs. I am not Sally Cinnamon.

I am not Ian Brown's spun sugar sister.

So my love – all my actual, fierce *love* – is for the third kind of music of 1992 – the stuff that's noisy *and* itchy. The music where I *do* find myself in the songs, all written by sexy, clever, angry freaks.

1992 is full of them – it's a rare high-tide for the vengeful, literate and odd. The Manic Street Preachers in wedding dresses with grenades in their mouths, singing about the First World destroying the Third. Suede in their jumble-sale blouses, singing about council houses, and insisting that everyone is bisexual after 11pm. Girly-men. Men in eyeliner, and glitter, like Marc Bolan and David Bowie laid a clutch of dragon eggs in 1973, and they've just begun to hatch.

And, most dazzlingly of all, the girly-girls themselves. Women.

For there's a storm in America, and the rain has now blown in over here, just in time for me: Riot Grrrl. A bunch of women like some League of Extraordinary Gentlewomen – writing fanzines, putting on female-only gigs, hanging out with each other, trying to make a space – in the crowded, swampy jungle of rock – that is for women alone.

They are all warriors, dressed in petticoats and sturdy boots – Kathleen Hanna from Bikini Kill paid for her guitar by stripping; Courtney Love punches out people who abuse her.

Courtney Love punched Kathleen Hanna, too, but this is the way of the rock star – let us not forget Charlie Watts punching Mick Jagger after Jagger called him 'My drummer'. 'You're *my singer*,' Watts snarled, before adjusting his cuffs, and walking away. Sometimes, in the jungle, you fight each other. The jungle is hot, and you get angry.

The songs they write are like drunken conversations with friends, in pubs, at the point just before you start dancing on the tables. 'Rebel Girl' by Bikini Kill has Kathleen Hanna starting to describe a proud, odd woman as if she hates her, but then explains that this girl is her hero, and she wants to fuck her.

And when Courtney Love sings 'Teenage Whore' – part self-loathing, part-pride – I feel oddly calm, yet excited. Hearing women singing about themselves – rather than men singing about women – makes everything seem suddenly wonderfully clear, and possible.

All my life, I've thought that if I couldn't say anything boys found interesting, I might as well shut up. But now I realise there was that whole other, invisible half of the world – girls – that I could speak to, instead. A whole other half equally silent and frustrated, and just waiting to be given the smallest starting-signal – the tiniest starter-culture – and they would *explode* into words, and song, and action, and relieved, euphoric cries of 'Me too! I feel this too!'

The news has hit Britain: they're making new kinds of girls in America. Girls who don't give a fuck. Girls who dare. Girls who do it because other girls do it. Girls that would like a girl like you.

Hibernating – incubating – pupating in my bedroom – I feel I know these freaky bands – the boys and the girls – totally: they, too, have lain under their beds, knowing that they can't be who they are any more, and that they need to build a bigger boat. They are all in the furious, messy, white-light act of self-creation, trying to invent a future they can be in.

I can imagine their bedrooms – lyrics scrawled on the walls in marker-pen, coats on the floor smelling mustily of jumble sales and thrift stores, carrier-bags full of battered, copied cassettes of Bowie, Stooges, Patti Smith and Guns N' Roses, and all of us meeting, without knowing, in the middle of the night, at John Peel's late-night lock-in – headphones on, trying not to wake the other people in our crowded houses. We're all doing the same thing. We're all just trying to get through these years to a better place, which we are going to have to make ourselves.

I know what I have to do: I have been put on Earth to get everyone in Wolverhampton into liking these bands. That is the purpose of my life.

From a practical point of view, I am ideally placed to do this, among all humanity – for the bus stop for the 512, over the road, is essentially a trap in which shoals of future fans are forced to wait for twenty minutes between buses – easily enough time for me to win them over to the cause, given enough volume.

I drag the stereo over to the window – a trailing life support of wires, black and red and yellow, across the room – and put it on the windowsill. I then climb up next to it, swing my legs out of the window and put the stereo on my lap.

'I'm going to educate this town,' I say to the dog. 'I am going to make Wolverhampton as good as ... Manchester. We're upgrading.'

I put on 'Double Dare Ya' by Bikini Kill, as loud as I can.

'Yes, peasants,' my demeanour says. 'I *am* blowing your mind. The day has come. No longer need you listen to Zucchero and Check 1-2 Featuring Craig McLachlan. I have brought you The Good Shit.'

Of course, the bus queue does what all British bus queues would do, in similar circumstances – they turn back, and ignore me ... All save for one woman – in her fifties, maybe – who just stares at me.

At the time, I thought the expression on her face was one of disgust. Thinking about it now, however, I can see it's one of terrible pity, instead. I'm a child in a nightie, sitting on a windowsill, holding a stereo on my lap, blasting music onto the street, trying to change a town with one record, in case I die.

An hour later, I'm still sitting in the window, writing 'MANIC STREET PREACHERS' on the stereo with Tippex and blasting out Hole when the Volkswagen pulls around the corner – clipping the kerb quite notably, and thudding back down on the tarmac so heavily you can hear all the pots and pans rattling inside, even from here.

The van comes to a halt outside the house, and then nothing happens for a good minute or so. I know, from experience, that this is because Dadda is drunk, and trying to focus enough to work out how to open the door.

When he does, he emerges, shitfaced, and initially confused by what is happening. He hears the music – Courtney Love screaming her head off – and then looks up and sees me, in the window, speaker on my lap.

'Dadda!' I say.

'Kitten Cat!' he replies.

It's just like those 'Papa!' 'Nicole!' Renault adverts, but on a council estate.

I suddenly feel sorry for Dadda – coming home, and finding out that everything his generation had ever achieved has just been blown out of the water by mine. His wound will be sore. His heart will be heavy. His records will all die.

Dadda cocks his head, like a dog, and his expression changes. Something's happening.

'You know what you need to do?' he says.

I can't hear him properly, and cup my hand around my ear.

'You need to PUSH THE MID-RANGE UP, AND KNOCK THE DOLBY OFF,' he shouts up to me – giving a business-like nod.

He then tamps his fag out, and walks into the house. I hear him fall over, as usual, before he reaches the stairs.

So these are the reviews I have been sending – one a day – to *D&ME*. Ride, Manic Street Preachers, Jane's Addiction, Belly, Suede, the Stone Roses, Aztec Camera, the Lilac Time and My Bloody Valentine.

And now the deputy editor has summoned me down to their offices. I get Mum to write a sick-note to school – 'Please allow Johanna the day off, she has a terrible earache,' she writes, adding, to me, 'From listening to all that bloody *wailing*' – and I am here, outside, waiting.

I remember Krissi's last bit of advice, as I left the house – so early – to catch the bus, to catch the train, to come down to London. I was applying eyeliner in the mirror, and singing.

'Whatever you do,' Krissi said, looking up from his George Orwell, 'just … don't be yourself. That never works.'

I look at my watch. It's 1pm. Time to go in for the meeting. I stand up.

'Good luck, kidder,' Dad says.

Oh yeah. Because I've had to bring my dad with me. He's going to sit on this wall outside *D&ME* and wait for me. He's got new shoes on.

'I'm not letting you go down to London on your own,' he said, flatly, when I said I'd been asked to go for a meeting. 'I know what a cunt I was when I was a teenage boy – and I'm not having you mix with cunts like me in the big city. This cunt is keeping those cunts *away*.'

Obviously, I'd pleaded for several hours to be allowed to go on my own – but he'd been absolutely adamant.

'Besides,' he said, in the third hour, 'I quite fancy checking out the Old Smoke. See my old stomping grounds.'

'Well, why don't we just bring *Lupin* down, too, and *the twins*,' I say sarcastically, crying. 'Why don't we make my new job a *huge family outing*?'

'London? YES PLEASE YES YES!' Lupin shouts, jumping up and down on the sofa.

'Don't be a prat, Lupin,' I say, pushing him onto the cushions, quite softly. He starts crying – then leaps onto me, and we wrestle on the floor. I like wrestling Lupin. I find it very relaxing. When I finally pin him to the floor, I do this thing where I pretend to give him heart-compressions, which I have learned off *Casualty*.

'BREATHE Lupin, BREATHE! Stay with us! One-one thousand, two-two thousand!'

If you do this to someone, they can't breathe, and they also laugh hysterically.

I keep doing it until Mum tells me to get off, and make the tea.

D&ME is on the twenty-ninth floor, the receptionist tells me. She has to check my name is on a list – 'We get … *bands* …

turning up,' she says, with a look of disgust – before letting me through the security gate.

I've never gone up twenty-nine floors before – this is the highest I've ever been. In the lift, I entertain the notion that this might be the day that I discover I'm scared of heights, and that I might step out of the lift, look out of a window, scream and faint – but as I get out of the lift, I am pleased to report back to me that I'm fine.

D&ME is to the left of the lifts – its doors are covered in stickers, broken records Blu-tacked on, and a letter from a PR company that begins, 'Dear TOTAL cunts. FUCK YOU.'

Inside is a room that, in its man-ness, makes the Record Locker look like the communal ladies' changing rooms at Dorothy Perkins.

This office is essentially built out of trousers, confidence and testicles. There are piles of back issues everywhere – yellowing, fraying. Desks piled high with records and CDs.

Around one desk are some men – I'm too panicked to count how many – gathered around another man who is sitting on a chair, with a dirty bandage around his head, smoking a fag, and coming to the end of a very long anecdote.

'…so I wake up under the table, yeah, and he's *gone* – the whole band are *gone* – and there's a bill for £300, and an *actual human shit in the ashtray*. Well, I *think* it's a shit. I'm standing up and freaking out – totally freaking out – and shouting "THIS IS A SHIT! THIS IS AN ACTUAL HUMAN SHIT!" when the club-owner comes over and points out that it's a cigar. And that I'd already tried to light it.'

'Yes – but the *bandage*, Rob,' the editor says, as everyone laughs. 'You still haven't explained how you came back from Amsterdam looking like you'd got confused at Dover and went to Vietnam, instead. I'm presuming the drummer punched you. That's why you have drummers. To punch journalists.'

'I think he tried to pull Marianne, and she dropped a chair on his head,' another man offers.

'Nah. I fell over in Duty Free on the ferry on the way back, buying 200 Marlboro,' Rob says, shrugging – gesturing with the fag in his hand. 'The on-board nurse was *laaaaahvely*. I gave her the advance tape of the band's album, and she showed me the cupboard where they keep all the pills.' He pats his pockets, contentedly.

A thought suddenly occurs to him. 'Here,' he says, a look of worry spreading over his face, 'I hope she doesn't have any snide brothers. Otherwise, there's going to be copies of it all over Camden Market by Monday, and Ed Edwards is going to go completely brain donor.'

During this anecdote, I have been putting myself in the most obvious place I can, so I can be noticed. It is, clearly, time I announced myself. As the anecdote finally finishes, and the men laugh again, I take a step forward.

For one awful moment, I know, utterly and absolutely, that I – a fat teenage girl from a council house, in a top hat – will not be able to cope with this situation. I do not know what to say to these rangy rock 'n' roll men.

And then I have what I still, even now, consider to be my single greatest moment of genius: I will just *pretend* to be someone who does. That's all I have to do. Ever. Pretend to be the *right* person for this weird situation. Fake it 'til you make it.

'Hello!' I say, brightly. 'I'm Dolly Wilde! I've come to London, to be a music journalist!'

All the men turn and look at me. Their expression is a bit like one I saw in a documentary, where someone once put a single flamingo in a zoo-enclosure full of camels, for reasons

I can't recall. All the camels stared. The flamingo stared back. Everyone seemed fatally confused.

In this confused silence, one man silently reaches into his jeans, and hands another man a fiver. The man nearest me nods to them.

'There was a bet in the office. A couple of people were convinced you were a forty-five-year-old bloke from The Wirral, on a wind-up.'

'Not yet!' I say, cheerfully. 'But who knows where the coming years will take me! Life is like a river!'

'I'm Kenny,' a man says, standing up. He's a very big, very bald, very gay man in a pair of astonishingly bold cut-off shorts. He has the air of a queeny galleon about him. He has six laminated passes hanging around his neck, like a Hawaiian *lei* garland, and clearly, at no point, has ever given a fuck about what people think about him. In later years, I asked him how a gay man mainly into prog-rock ended up working for a magazine dedicated to incredibly straight, borderline unlistenable indie – all of which he hated. 'I *never* mix work with pleasure,' he replied, wryly.

But, now: 'You've been speaking to me, on the phone,' Kenny says.

'You're the Deputy Editor!' I say. I am getting this question *right*.

'Yes,' he says. There's a pause. 'So –' he spreads his hands '– want a job?'

'Yes please!' is what I should say. I've been offered a job less than a minute after walking through the doors. I'm winning.

But, at the time, all the films I have watched, and books that I have read, have led me to believe that, whenever you can, you shouldn't say the politest thing, or the rightest thing – but the most *legendary* thing, instead.

On the way down, on the train, I have planned what the most *legendary* response to a job offer would be, and it's what I say now:

'Work for you?' I say. 'I would love to! I would really, really love to!'

I pick up a paper napkin on the desk, dip it into a glass of water, and then make as if to go and wash the walls.

'First I'll do the walls,' I say, to Kenny, 'and then the floors – that way, if I drip …'

This is dialogue from *Annie* – the scene where Daddy Warbucks asks Annie to live with him for a month, and she initially misunderstands, and thinks he wants her to be his maid, instead.

When I imagined delivering this line, I imagined everyone at *D&ME* laughing.

'We offered her a job on the most left-field music news-paper in the country – but she parodied both her working-class background *and* obsession with musicals by pretending that we'd offered her a job as an office-cleaner, instead! Legendary!'

There is no way everyone in this office won't have seen *Annie*. This line is going to be a killer.

Everyone in this room has not seen *Annie*. There is an awkward silence.

'It's from *Annie*,' I offer. 'The musical?'

More silence.

'No big musicals fans at *D&ME*?'

'Musicals are strictly for homosexuals and womenfolk,' Kenny says, drily, in a way that's so post-post-post ironic it actually stops being communication, and simply becomes confusing, and unhelpful.

'I quite like *The King & I*,' says the man with the bandage.

'You've had a recent blow to the head,' Kenny replies.

These are all jokes! This is a jokey office! Obviously I feel bad about *my* joke not working, but not *too* bad – only about six Dyings, out of ten. It's no 'Scooby Doo on live TV'.

'Well, now you're part of the team, Annie, do you want to sit in on the editorial meeting?' Kenny asks. 'I can't think why a teenage girl on the threshold of an amazing life wouldn't want to sit in on the process that results in us putting Skinny Puppy on the cover, and losing 20,000 readers in a single week.'

'Hey!' Rob says, angrily.

'Have you ever heard Skinny Puppy?' Kenny asks me.

'No, sir,' I say. I've decided to start calling people 'Sir' and 'Ma'am'. I saw Elvis do it once, on telly, and it looked really cool.

'Well, don't,' Kenny cautions. 'It's just horrible. Like someone burning a load of simple children alive.'

The Editorial Meeting happens in an adjacent room. Smoking appears to be pretty much mandatory, as does talking all over each other. Most people wear black, and everyone seems amazingly confident – they all seem to know what their character-types are, and stick to them consistently: there's an angry man, a cynical man, a clever man, the man with the bandage on his head. This meeting is a scene they've played out many times before, and they all know their roles and tropes. As I am new, I have no idea what mine is, other than to sit here feeling very, very anxious. I stay very quiet.

There is a twenty-minute discussion about next week's cover: it's Lush, a boozy bunch of raconteurs that sound a bit like a baby My Bloody Valentine, and are fronted by Miki Berenyi – a half-Japanese, half-Hungarian Cockney with a cherry-red bob.

'She is damn fine-looking woman,' Rob says, to general agreement, as everyone looks at her picture. 'A damn fine-looking woman.'

That is what is being decided in this meeting. That Miki Berenyi is a damn fine-looking woman. I am still absorbing the exact ramifications of this – there are many – when Kenny suddenly turns to me and goes, 'So, the Upfront section. New bands. You got anything? Who are the benighted Midlands youth going wild over these days?'

I think. I have no idea. How would one know what new bands there are? I've learned everything I know from *D&ME*. Where does one even *find* new bands?

'There's a quite interesting three-piece from Derby,' a boy on the other side of the table cuts in, during this awkward silence. Along with me, he's the only person during the meeting who's been quiet. He's what my dad would call 'a dark lad' – Pakistani, maybe? – and I've presumed that he's staying quiet for the same reason I have: we feel odd in this room.

'A dancey kind of thing – they do big orchestral samples over mournful break-beats. Kind of like Shut Up and Dance, if someone had given them *Now That's What I Call Classical Music* for Christmas. The lead singer looks like Catweazle,' he continues, in a very dolorous Birmingham accent. 'They played the 69 Club in Wolverhampton last week,' he adds, directly to me, 'didn't they?'

'Oh yeah!' I say, pretending I know this. 'Yeah – I have heard of them. Yeah. I think Peel played them last week. Sir.'

I have absolutely no idea if Peel *did* play them last week – but given that Peel plays around a hundred songs a week, I'm on pretty safe ground *re* anyone ever actually finding out if this happened or not. This is a solid, utilitarian lie.

Kenny nods, decisively, to the dark lad.

'You want to follow it up?' he asks. 'Find out if there's a single, do it then?'

The boy nods. I've just worked out who he must be – he writes under the name 'ZZ Top', and covers a lot of rap, dance and hip-hop. I never really read his reviews because I find rap, dance and hip-hop vaguely terrifying. I don't have the right clothes to be into them, and it all seems a bit intense. I file these genres along with heavy metal and speed metal, under: 'People who would kill, then eat me.' I like bands with lead singers who look like I could, with the wind in the right direction, beat in a fight. I reckon I could probably deck Morrissey, if I had to. I've had practice – on Lupin. But I do not think I could fight my way out of a misunderstanding with Ice T.

'Right!' Kenny says, drawing the meeting to a close. 'Off you all jolly well fuck to the pub. Same time next week?'

As everyone files out – shoving each other, talking – I hold back, because I have no one to shove. I note ZZ Top is doing the same – presumably for the same reason. We slowly put our notepads in our bags, and walk out at roughly the same time. ZZ opens the door for me, and I curtsey, and start walking though.

'Thank you, sir,' I say, like Elvis would. I'm going to stick with this Elvis thing.

'Didn't I see you on *Midlands Weekend*?' ZZ asks. My heart very usefully empties all four chambers of blood into my face, and my guts turn to ice.

'HAHAHA!' I say. 'HAHAHA!'

'You were, weren't you?' he persists. 'Something about a Scooby Doo? I was at my parents. You *really* freaked Wilko out. They should have had that clip on *It'll Be Alright on the Night*.'

He looks like he wants to say more, but I cannot bear this conversation. It is making me profoundly anxious.

'Well, I obviously owe you all a *massive* apology. BYEEEE!' I say, and run into the Ladies' toilets – leaving him standing, in the corridor, holding his rucksack.

I am the only person in the Ladies. There is a stack of *BMX Weekly*, whose office is on the same floor as *D&ME*, by the bin.

This room is, clearly, used mainly for storage – because there are no ladies for the Ladies.

I go to the toilet and have some *Midlands Weekend* flashback-induced diarrhoea, and then notice that my period has started, in its usual, completely random, stupid way.

'Oh, fucking *great*,' I say to my knickers – rubbing the blood off as best I can, and then stuffing a wodge of loo-roll in my pants. *Annie*, *Midlands Weekend*, not saying anything during the meeting, and now *Carrie* in my pants – this is my most glamorous and successful day ever. I flush the toilet, and execute a slightly awkward waddle over to the basins – stride impeded by the makeshift pillow in my knickers. I wash my hands, looking at myself in the mirror.

'Well, this is where you say something wise to yourself,' I say, aloud.

I can see where I have drawn Dolly Wilde on top of my own face – the two uneasily co-existing – but perhaps others can't. If I walk and talk fast enough, maybe no one will notice. All I need is a moment to compose myself, in here. Just a moment to compose myself. Perhaps the next eighteen years.

'Something wise,' I repeat.

But I've got nothing. I look like Dolly Wilde, but I'm still acting like Johanna Morrigan. That's going to have to change. Because this is the place I need to be. I need to be able to keep coming back here, and make this *my* place, because this is how you get to meet bands, and make money, and be in the music. This is the only door I have ever seen that opens onto my future.

When I finally get out into the corridor, everyone has gone. I drop twenty-nine storeys on my own.

TEN

So now I am a writer. A writer! I have three albums to review this week – 200 words each – for which I will gain the princely sum of £85.23. And that *is* a princely sum.

However, the day-to-day business of my new job proves unexpectedly difficult. We have a computer – a Commodore 64, given to us by Uncle Jim – in the front room, wired into the television, and on my first day at 'work', a Saturday, I march into the room with my notebook, and my CDs, and prepare to clock on.

Lupin is on the computer, playing *Dungeon Master*.

'Hop it, small fry,' I say, in a not unkind manner. 'I need to commune with my muse. Clear off.'

'But it's my turn,' Lupin says, implacably. Not looking away from the screen, he points to the 'Computer Rota' – the painstakingly assembled schedule, written on a piece of A4 paper stuck to the side of the television, that we devised a year ago, after months of bloody warfare. And it is true. 'Lupin – 9am–11am' is right before 'Johanna – 11am–1pm'.

But now, surely, everything has changed.

'Yes – but this is *for work*, Lupin,' I explain, sitting on the edge of the chair, so that I'm crushing him a little bit. 'Jo-Jo needs to write 200 words on the Milltown Brothers album. Lupin go play with Sticklebricks for a while.'

'It's *my turn*,' Lupin says, doggedly.

'Not any more,' I say, sliding into the chair beside him, and forcing him to pop out, like an oily pea from a pod. 'You've been out-ranked. Leg it.'

'MUM!' Lupin shouts, falling out of the chair.

'Yes – MUM!' I shout, not moving from the chair.

When my mother arrives in the room, holding a twin, I find she is unexpectedly sympathetic to Lupin's cause.

'It is his go, Johanna,' she says, firmly.

'But he's just … mucking around. He's just –' I look at the screen '– killing a ghost. And not even a real one. An imaginary one. But I'M AT WORK,' I explain.

'We can't change everything just because you've got a job,' Mum says. 'Everyone is equal in this house.'

'Except Dad,' I say, sulkily. 'He always gets the biggest pork chop. *And* he has dibs on the telly when the American Football's on. We never get to watch *That's Life*.'

'Johanna, you will just have to wait your turn,' Mum says. 'I cannot give you special treatment. There are a lot of people in this house, and we have to be fair to all of them.'

'I don't want *special* treatment – just *logical* treatment. My need is *greater*. As a professional writer, I am now simply *more entitled* to access of the computer than Lupin is. It's like … if we were trying to hammer out foreign policy right now. If I were Boutros Boutros-Ghali, you'd listen to me more than … Karate Kid here.'

'I'm not going to argue with you, Johanna. You are not Boutros Boutros-Ghali,' my mother says, leaving the room.

'Please let me go on the computer,' I whisper to Lupin.

But Lupin now has the self-righteousness of being backed up by my mother.

'It's my go,' he says, stubbornly, sitting back down. I sit on him a bit more – to make my point – hiss, 'Frankly, *mean*!' at him, and then go into the kitchen to make myself a very strong Horlicks – my drink of choice, in times of crisis. I intend to drink it angrily, whilst nursing a sense of increasingly sleepy injustice.

Dadda is in the kitchen, frying himself some bacon, and wearing my pink dressing gown.

'Ah – it's Hunter S. Thompson!' he says, as I open the jar. 'How is life in the cruel and shallow money-trench they call rock?'

'Lupin's being a dick,' I say, sulkily. 'I'm not allowed on the computer for another hour.'

'Aye, don't worry about him,' he says, blithely – pouring bacon fat over the bread. 'I need to talk to you, about our plan.'

'Our plan?' I ask.

'Yeah. How we storm the citadel, now you've got your foot in the door.'

I look at him, lost.

'Johanna, I've spent twenty years waiting for someone to come along and get me a record deal,' he says, getting HP Sauce out of the bottle with a knife. 'I've been waiting in pubs, and sending off demos, and hanging around studios talking to engineers who say they know someone who knows someone who's Peter Gabriel's guitar-tech. I've been waiting for the one person who can get us out of here. And all this time, the person who was going to get me a deal was right here.' He looks at me. 'It was you.'

'Er …' I say.

'Johanna – this is it, kidder!' He takes a bite of his sandwich. He looks happier than he has in years. 'We've just got to have one hit single, and we're out of here. One poxy song. Even better if it's seasonal. Look at Noddy Holder. All he's got to do is put a Santa hat on once a year, shout 'IT'S CHRISTMAS!' and then put his feet back up again, the jammy git.'

'Just get my name out there, in the paper,' he says. 'That's all I need. Just get me one big nob.'

Thinking, 'Just one big nob? But that is very much my plan for *me*,' I go back into the front room, laughing to myself at how sexually liberated I am. For an unkissed virgin, drinking a double-shot of Horlicks, I am *totally* Riot Grrrl. I give thanks to my big sisters, across the Atlantic, for my lessons in red-hot drive-by sassing. I have no thoughts at all as to how to help my father.

2.30pm, and I'm finally in my rightful place – at the computer – typing away, when my attempt at a new power-dynamic in the family hits another hitch. I'm halfway through a difficult para-graph trying to describe the Milltown Brothers' indisputable jangly guitars as anything other than 'jangly' – so far, I've got 'quite jingly' – when a wailing sound issues from the kitchen. I hear my mother going to investigate, and then her feet in the hallway. She appears in the front room, furious.

'You got Lupin to make you a sandwich?' she asks, looking extremely riled.

'To be fair, I've made him *millions*, over the years,' I say. 'I thought he'd enjoy learning a new skill. And I'm on deadline! I'm starving!'

'He's just taken half his thumb off on the cheese-grater,' she says.

Now I cock my head: that wailing sound from the kitchen does – yes – sound *exactly* like an eight-year-old boy who's grated his thumb off. That's *exactly* the pitch.

'Johanna. We're a *family* – not "Johanna Morrigan and her Supplicants",' my mother says. 'You can't go lording it over the kids.'

Obviously I can't *tell* her that I'm trying to single-handedly save our family from potential ruin, because then I'd have to tell her about the potential ruin – which was all my fault in the first place.

'If I don't keep this job, then my only future career-options are working in Argos, or being a prostitute,' I say, wildly.

'Maybe you could work in Argos *as* a prostitute,' my mother says, merrily. She appears to be enjoying this conversation. 'They could list you in the catalogue, and people could queue up, and wait for you to come down the conveyor-belt.'

Because I am well-read, I know what a terrible cliché it is for a teenager to shout 'I HATE you. I never ASKED to be born', so I refrain.

Besides, I have used this line before, and my mother replied, very calmly, 'Well, as Buddhists, we believe children *do* actually ask to be born. You would actually have *requested* me as a mother, Johanna. So if it's not working out, I'm afraid that's down to your poor karmic judgement in picking me. Sorry.'

On this occasion, I just put my headphones on, and listen to John Lennon's 'Mother' in the most sarcastic way I know how.

And so the weeks play out.

A phone-call. Kenny, at *D&ME*.

'We haven't heard from you in a while,' he said, laconically. 'Been busy?'

I can't tell him that no one's currently allowed to use the phone at the moment, while a red bill for £78 sits on the dresser, and that I've been praying hard that he'll call me, and offer me more work.

'Yes!' I say, brightly. I have learned all the lessons from the Editorial Meeting, and I know how to talk, now. I know what kind of person I need to be when I'm talking to Kenny. 'I've been partying hard, Kenny! It's hard to schedule in all of the fucking, and *then* all of the drinking.'

I'm sitting on the stairs in my nightie, watching one of the twins in his buggy, quietly and peacefully being sick all down his chin.

'Well, if you could put the boys down for just one minute, Wilde,' Kenny says, amused, 'we've got some more of that writing business you seemed so keen on. Smashing Pumpkins at the abstrusely named Edwards Number 8, in Birmingham. Fancy 600 words on that? Next Thursday. We thought it was time to give you a bigger piece. Take you up a notch. It's a promotion! Plenty of time to stock up on the emergency drinking and fucking, before temporarily getting down to work. Yes?'

'Yes, sir!' I say. I will work out exactly how – with my no money, no money at all, until I actually receive my first, dawdling pay-cheque – I will get to Birmingham later. Perhaps Birmingham will, in the next week, move closer to Wolverhampton, and I can simply walk there!

'Record company's press officer is Ed Edwards – he's utterly fucking useless, but then, they all are,' Kenny sighs, before giving me Ed's number. 'Get on the guest list. You can even have a few drinks while you're there! Keep the receipts, there's a good chap. Sadly, I don't think IPC's expenses run to claiming "some fucking", as well – although you could give it your very best shot.'

'Expenses?'

I feel like I've just been shot in the head by a bag of gold.

'Expenses?'

This is a magical word. 'Expenses.' Oh, most beautiful word! Expenses means ... *more money*.

'So can we claim travel expenses, as well?' I ask. I've crossed all my fingers and toes, and legs, willing him to say 'Yes'.

'Well, eyebrows might rocket if you go First Class, or pedalo there on a ... swan, but generally, yes. IPC mercifully acknowledges that you're not going to "Birmingham Edwards Number 8" for anything as pleasurable as … pleasure,' Kenny says, before ringing off – leaving me lying on the floor, staring up at the ceiling, mouthing, 'Yesssssssssssssss.' I have a big new job. I have been *promoted*.

Whilst Lupin might be unwilling to be helpful towards my new-found role – that of 'important employee of a national publication' – my father, with his eye on my position as 'someone helpful to *his* career' – is much more helpful. This is having mixed results.

At this moment in time – Thursday night – he is trying to reverse the caravanette into a parking space outside Edwards Number 8 that's marginally too small for it, by insistently nudging at a pile of bins that are in his way. Presumably this is making a loud banging and scraping sound outside – but he's playing 'Buffalo Soldier' so loudly inside the van, I can't tell. The bass is making the gear-stick vibrate.

The last week has been exciting. By which I mean, awful. Having asked my dad for a cash advance to cover my train fare to Birmingham, he outright refused, on the basis that, 'I know what I was like on late-night trains when I was a younger man, and I don't want you meeting any cunts like that.'

'You've already used this line on me,' I say.

'And you've already used that line on your mother,' he replies.

He has insisted that he will drive me to Birmingham.

'You can get me on that guestie, like, can't you?' he says. 'Pat Morrigan, plus one. Just like the old days. Good to check out the competition. See what the young salty lads are doing. It'll keep me on my toes.'

His enthusiasm for modern alternative rock music, and his chivalric impulses towards me, would be even more admirable if he hadn't made the offer after hearing that music journalists can claim 'refreshments' on expenses.

'Well,' he says, now, locking up the van, and rubbing his hands. 'Time for those "refreshments".'

His disabled badge has allowed him to park right outside the venue, in what I think might actually be a bus stop. This, and the bin-banging, has made us the subject of much curiosity to the queue of people outside Edwards Number 8. It's an arrival that very much begs the question, 'Who the *fuck* are you?'

Dadda limps confidently towards the doorman. This is, in essence, a blag, and he is always high, and in his element, during a blag. He once referred to his proposal to mum as 'a blag'. 'I blagged her on Brighton beach,' he said, knocking back a Guinness. 'Blagged your mum.'

'We're on the guest list,' he says, in his 'explaining things to a peasant' voice. 'Johanna Morrigan, plus one.'

The doorman looks at the guest list, doubtfully.

'Er, no,' I say, to my dad – and then to the bouncer. 'It's, erm, Dolly Wilde. Dolly Wilde plus one.'

'Dolly Wilde?' my dad says – looking at me properly for the first time in months. I am all in black, obviously – and also wearing my top hat, from a jumble sale, in honour of Slash from Guns N' Roses. I look pretty amazing. Or, at least, I don't look like I did last year.

'Dolly Wilde?'

'It's my writing name,' I say. 'Dolly Wilde.'

'Arrrrr,' the old man says, appreciatively. 'Arrrrrr. Writing name. Nice one.'

'She was an infamous alcoholic lesbian,' I add, cheerfully.

'Bostin'!' Dad says, as the doorman unclips the red rope, and lets us in.

I've never been to a gig before. My first ever gig – and I am being paid to be here. Everything is novel to me. It's very early – no one's really here yet – and the house-lights are still up. I can see we're in what was once an Edwardian music hall, with a long, shabby bar right across the back. The walls have been painted a murky, 'rock' black, and everything – floor, walls, ceiling – is scuffed and chipped and reeks of cigarettes and toilet block.

This is where rock happens! This is where young people come! Rock music smells of toilet and cigarettes! I am learning! I am *very* excited. I feel like I am on a threshold of some kind.

'I'm just going to get some of those aforementioned *refreshments*,' Dadda says, heading towards the bar, and giving a 'man-nod' to the barman.

I go down the front, right by the stage. I want to make sure I have bagged a good view of both bands – Chapterhouse are supporting; they're a pretty hot band right now – in order to make my review the best review *D&ME* has ever had.

I stand right in front of the central microphone – where lead singer Billy Corgan will be – and consolidate my position by getting out my notepad and pen, opening the notepad on the first page, and writing 'SMASHING PUMPKINS – BIRMINGHAM EDWARDS NO. 8, BIRMINGHAM, 19th November 1992.'

I turn around, and see my dad is leaning back on the bar, drinking a Guinness, and talking to the man next to him. He sees me, and raises his Guinness, in salute.

'*Just refreshing*,' he mouths.

I nod.

The first band aren't on for another hour and thirty-seven minutes, yet. I sigh. Maybe I am a little bit too early.

'BIRMINGHAM EDWARDS NO. 8, BIRMINGHAM, WEST MIDLANDS, GREAT BRITAIN, EUROPE, THE EARTH, MILKY WAY, INFINITY,' I amend, in my notepad, in my swirliest writing.

I am sixteen, and I am getting paid by the word.

10.11pm. Well. This is all turning out to be a bit confusing. I've managed to hold my position – in front of Billy Corgan's mic-stand – but under duress. For, as I'm rapidly learning, there's this really weird thing that Smashing Pumpkins fans do: a kind of intense, pushing, leaping dance, to the band's songs.

At first, I thought it was just a tradition they had for the opening song – you know, like when 'Oops Upside Your Head' comes on, at a wedding, and everyone rows across the floor. I presumed everyone would stop mucking around after the first song, and settle down, and basically stop jumping on my head.

But Smashing Pumpkins are now three songs in, and it's clear this leaping around is no mere one-song tradition. Instead, there is a constant thrashing up against each other, as if everyone's trying to start a fire by rubbing themselves together – using Tad t-shirts as kindling.

Writing my important on-the-spot impressions of the gig – 'Corgan looks v serious! D'Arcy has drink of water' – is becoming increasingly difficult, as most of the time I'm having to hold my notepad in my mouth whilst using my hands to keep my top hat on my head. This audience is no respecter of someone wearing a bold chapeau.

As the opening chords of the fourth song start, there is a particularly energised shove from the back, and I lose both my hat and my notepad.

'Jesus CHRIST!' I shout. 'This is DERANGED!'

I kneel to retrieve my hat, and then fight my way out of the crowd – to observe, from the side. These people are mental. To think! I've always been scared of raves, because I thought they'd be too loud and sweaty. This is, surely, loads worse.

I stand at the side. I've decided I will be an onlooker of youth culture tonight. Besides, can I really analyse what's going on if I'm taking part in it? I'm a rock critic, not an *animal*. My place is to stand at the side, watching.

The gig goes on for what seems like forever. I'm very tired – it's past 11pm and I'm usually in bed listening to the Beacon Radio phone-in by now. Every Friday they do one on the supernatural. It's always very interesting. There's a woman in Whitmore Reans who's got a ghost in her hallway, and she always rings in to tell us what he's doing.

'Harry' – that's the ghost's name: Harry – 'had a right cob-on this week. Knocking all my telephone directories off the table.'

I don't know any of the songs the Smashing Pumpkins have played – I'd stolen 20p to order *Gish* from the library, but it hadn't arrived in time. A lad in Brewood has borrowed it before me, apparently. Bastard – but you can tell which ones the most famous ones are, because everyone goes particularly mad when they start. Some people crowd-surf, which I'd always presumed was just something that happened in America, and seems a bit weird to see in Birmingham – as if everyone here had started referring to petrol as 'gasoline', and were fretting over going to Junior Prom.

'This is not your culture!' I feel like telling them. 'You should be dancing like how people dance to "Tiger Feet" by Mudd on *Top of the Pops*! Or doing The Lambeth Walk! That is the British way!'

During a boring – slow – bit in the set, I go to the back, and see how my dad's doing. He's found a drinking buddy, and is pretty wankered.

'This is Pat,' he says, introducing me to a man who is also drunk. 'Because I'm Pat too! We're two Pats! He's a Protestant,' he adds, in a stagey whisper, 'but we've sorted it *all out*.'

He makes it sound like they've actually resolved the entire Northern Ireland conflict – and that, once they've made a phone call from a phone box, after the gig, there will be peace between our two nations once more.

'Are you okay to drive?' I ask him.

'Never better,' he says, trying to put his glass on the bar and missing slightly.

'I've got to go backstage afterwards – say hello to the band,' I say.

I don't know why I presume this. I think maybe this is like a party that the Smashing Pumpkins have thrown, and that it would be rude not to introduce myself, and thank them, before leaving.

I give Dadda my hat and my notepad, and go back down the front for the last two songs. Even though I don't really like Smashing Pumpkins – I find them a bit *dirge-y* – I cannot pass up this opportunity to fully experience my first gig. Awkwardly, and grudgingly at first, I do as the others do. I stiffly bounce on the spot, carefully – as if warming up for PE.

'Rock music needs very supportive bras,' I note – holding onto my bosoms as I leap up and down, doggedly. This is something the music press had never mentioned. They have so little guidance for girls.

On a chorus, people behind me push against me, and so I push back – I am rubbing up against boys, which, I note with glee, is my most sexual experience so far.

'I am roughly 7 per cent less virgin now!' I think, as I feel a skinny boy's ribs xylophone on my back.

In less than ten minutes, I get soaked to the skin in a heady cocktail of my sweat, and the sweat of others. Clouds of steam rise off the mosh-pit, and mingle with the dry-ice.

When I finally stagger away – the band's last chord ringing out in infinite feedback – my hair is as wet as Hairwash Day, and I am partially, thrillingly deaf. This is like that one time I did a cross-country run, and got some adrenalin – but without someone shouting 'FASTER, Morrigan!' at me. I can see the appeal.

It's surprisingly easy to blag my way backstage. Indeed, in future years, I never find it quite this easy again, no matter how many passes and laminates I have. I think it might be that the security at Birmingham Edwards Number 8 are utterly unused to small, fat, wet, over-adrenalised girls going up to them and saying, 'I'm a journalist! I'm here to see the band!' very loudly, because their hearing's shot.

As a rule of thumb, you know a band's security has failed quite spectacularly when a sixteen-year-old girl in a top hat – holding a shredded notepad that she finally found kicked-out by the speaker-stack, and her drunken father, and her drunken father's friend, Pat – manage to get into the band's dressing room.

The band are sitting around – slumped, sweaty, exhausted. The atmosphere in the room is tense – in later years, reading about their career, I find that around this time, guitarist James Iha and bassist D'Arcy Wretzky are in the middle of a messy break-up, drummer Jimmy Chamberlin is starting to dabble in what turns into a considerable heroin addiction, and Billy Corgan is entering into a depressive phase – partly triggered by the fact that he's currently so broke, he's living in a garage.

'Hiya!' I say to this room.

I don't really know how to talk to bands – I don't really know how to talk to people – and for some reason, I presume that the key thing to do is be 'a bit sorry' for them. The Pumpkins are obviously exuding a fairly 'down' vibe, and I surmise that this is because they have come from America – land of big cars, *Dynasty* and Elvis – to Birmingham, and are sad about this. Obviously, I don't know about Billy Corgan's garage at the time. I presume all Americans have huge houses. I mean, even in *Roseanne* they have a massive house, with a porch – and Roseanne just works in a hairdressers, sweeping up hair.

I sit down next to D'Arcy, because she's a girl, and do my sympathetic face.

'Long day, huh?' I say. 'You probably really want a brew. Like, a cup of tea. That's what we call tea here. "A brew." Not, like, a brewski. Beer. Not that.'

D'Arcy looks up, confused.

'You look knackered,' I continue.

She looks even more disconsolate and confused.

'But you rocked!' I add, quickly. 'You were AMAZING! OH MY GOD! I've never seen a gig like that before!'

This is quite true. I have never seen a gig like that before. I have never seen a gig before.

'How's the tour going?' I ask. 'Is it exciting?'

'Oh, you know …' she says. She has an American accent. It's the first one I've ever interacted with. Previously, American accents have only ever come out of the television. 'It's kinda mind-blowing to come to Europe, and there be people who've heard of us.'

She says 'Europe', 'Yuuuuurp'. It's *very* exciting. Genuinely foreign. But she's still staring down at the floor. There's an awkward pause. The whole band are glassy-eyed – seemingly borderline traumatised by the gig they've just played. I don't have a clue what to say next. A voice suddenly comes from the doorway.

'Tell ya what – yorra a tight little unit!'

It's my dad. He is speaking with great authority. Everyone turns to look at him. He's leaning in the doorway, still holding his pint of Guinness.

'A tight. Little. Unit,' he reiterates. 'Your drummer's good, mate,' he says, to Billy Corgan, hero of grunge. 'Got a bit of a *jazzer*'s air to him. And your bird –' he gestures to D'Arcy Wretsky, hero of grunge '– your bird, is fucking *fit*.'

Everyone stares at my dad.

'Lads, lads!' Pat – Dad's friend – chirps up. 'You were fine – *fine* – but do you not know any party songs? Or "Protestant Boys"? That's a hell of a song. It always gets a room lively. "*The Protestant Boys/Are Loyal and True/Stout-hearted in battle/And stout-handed too …*".'

I decide it's time to away, to pastures new. We have probably met enough Smashing Pumpkins now.

When the review runs, it contains every single superlative word I can think of – partly as my way of making up to the band for having had to meet my father and Pat, and partly because, as soon as I get back into my dad's van, and have him drive back to Wolvo, pissed, I just want to go back into that room and have that massive sound come up inside me again.

Now I know what happens at a gig, I will be ready for it, next time – I will come in just a t-shirt and shorts and boots, and fight my way to the front, like a quietly determined soldier, and then let the band take my head off. I want to walk into rooms like that every night, with a sense of something *happening*.

A gig, I realise now, is a place where people come together and give permission for anything to happen. Things can be said and shouted and sung; people get pissed; people get kissed – there is a communal agenda of joyous wilding. These are the boardroom meetings of young people, where we establish our vibe.

By way of contrast, everything else I am doing is just sitting, and waiting.

God, I want to go out again.

When the review runs – headline: 'MOSHING PUMPKINS!' – it is accompanied by a big picture of the band, and takes up half a page. 'This is the night where it all begins for the Smashing Pumpkins in the UK,' I have written.

> *Every cool kid in the Midlands has come to pay obeisance to the new Emperors of Mournful Grunge. Little matter that Billy Corgan's singing-style is somewhat 'yowling' – that of a cat out in the rain, who has just realised the cat-flap is locked against him. From the first, crashing chords of 'Siva', every kid in the venue has the same look on their face: 'I, too, have felt like a cat locked out in the rain, Billy Corgan! I live in Bilston! You have to wait 45 minutes for the 79 bus! Thank you for writing a song that finally expresses how that feels!*

I look at the review with utter glee. I can take up half a page, now. I am worth exactly half a page. It is exciting to chart my growing abilities, as a writer – like the bit of wall in the kitchen where our growing heights are marked off, every six months, in a scratchy rainbow of different-coloured pens. 'Lupin – Halloween 1991.' 'Kriss – Xmas 90.' 'DOLLY, first lead review, *D&ME*, 1992.'

Kenny tells me that when I hit fifty reviews, I will be 'seasoned' enough to do my first interview.

By January 1993, I have interviewed nineteen local bands. I file my copy promptly, with all spellings combed through, using a dictionary, and all my best words and phrases deployed like bonnets, tippets and jewels, to fascinate the eye, and inspire wonder.

In February, when my income often reaches a heady £100 a week, I go into the school at 11am, and sit outside the school secretary's office, listening to Jane's Addiction on my Walkman, subtly air-drumming, until she emerges.

'I'm resigning,' I say, cheerfully, to the secretary – pulling the headphones down to my neck so that we can both hear Perry Farrell screaming *'SEX IS VIOLENT!'* tinnily, from my chest. 'I won't be able to continue my education any more, as I'm running away to join the circus. I've sold my soul to rock 'n' roll.'

'And have you informed your parents of this?' the secretary asks me, calmly, as if she's heard this all before.

'Not yet,' I say, breezily. 'But they'll be cool with it.'

I hand her my school tie.

'Give this to Tim Watts in 10J,' I say. 'He needs it. He keeps chewing his. I think he's still teething. His voice hasn't broken yet. I think he might have a chromosomal abnormality. Also, just so you know, it was Andy Webster who set the fire-alarm off last year, Annette Kennedy lets people finger her for 20p on the playing fields, and Mrs Cooke has no control over RE lessons – Tim Hawley, the Evangelist with a hare-lip, stands on the desks and does a "snake dance" while she's writing on the blackboard. He often drops his trousers and shows people his privates. I think he's quite troubled. Also, quite lopsided. One ball is twice the size of the other. I have no idea if that's normal – but I will soon, because I'm going to go and get my kicks now, while I'm still young.'

The school secretary seems unimpressed with this classic quote from Rizzo in *Grease*, and merely puts the tie in her pocket and says, 'I'll inform the head, and send a letter to your parents.'

I go out to break, and tell my friends I'm leaving school.

'No *way* man, you're so lucky,' Emma Pagett says, eating Chipstix, eyes bulging. 'You're a *legend*.'

Across the playground, I can see Krissi looking at me, disapprovingly.

I take the long way home – I stopped off at the playground, where a gang of thirty kids wrote farewell messages on my school-shirt in felt-tip. I have a cartoon mouse saying 'WICKED!' on my arm, 'MADCHESTER RAVE ON' on my back, and 'UP YOUR BUM' on my collar. I look like the wall on the Girls' toilets.

When I get in, it's gone 6pm, and Mum and Dad are in the front room with Krissi. They look like a furious intergalactic senate, on the brink of declaring war on a rogue Jedi, ie: me.

'What you playing at, Johanna?' Dadda says. 'You've left *school*?'

'You're going straight back there tomorrow, and saying you've made a mistake,' Mum says.

'I can't. I've given them my tie. And this is my only shirt,' I say, pointing to 'UP YOUR BUM' on my collar.

'You can stay up all night scrubbing it off while you explain to us what the *hell* you think you're doing,' Mum says. 'You can't just *leave school*.'

'But everyone's at school to get a job – and I've already *got* one,' I say. 'I mean, if I stay at school, I won't be able to *do* my job. Gigs don't finish until 11pm – I actually fell asleep during a swimming lesson last week. I was just floating face down, like the dead body in *Sunset Boulevard*, while people threw floats at my head. I'm already having to turn down things because of a stupid maths lesson. I'm never going to need maths! I'm going to be so good at English that I'll earn tons of money, and hire an accountant! I've planned it all. I'm not *stupid*.'

I have never seen Mum look more angry. It's even worse than when, when we were much younger, me and Krissi dressed a life-sized baby-doll in Lupin's clothes and threw it out of the bedroom window, screaming 'NO LUPIN NO!' just as she was pulling up in the car. That bollocking lasted a full day.

This one goes on a week. That night, we argue until midnight – me crying hysterically from 9pm onwards.

At 7am the next morning, she wakes me up by pulling the duvet off me.

'SCHOOL,' she says. But I refuse to go. It gets shouty quite quickly.

'As I work with the English language, I'm very loath to use a cliché like "I'm SIXTEEN now, I'm IN CHARGE OF MY LIFE",' I say, resolutely not moving. 'It would be a trite piece of dialogue. So I'm going to "show, and not tell" instead.'

And I pull the duvet back over me.

'This is me not going to school,' I clarify, in case she hasn't got it. 'I'm in charge of my life. Ask Lupin to make me a thumb-sandwich.'

Mum does not find this call-back to an earlier transgression amusing. After twenty minutes, she leaves, to be replaced by Dadda.

'You've got to get an education, Jo,' he says, sitting on the bed. His attitude is much more conciliatory. Gentle. Almost … doubting. 'You know? Pass those exams. Get those pieces of paper.'

'*You* didn't,' I say. Dadda left school at fifteen to join his band. We know all the stories – gigging working-men's clubs; playing strip-bars and US Army bases; eating steaks and learning how to play poker with prostitutes; and being only six months away from making it – really making it.

'Yes,' he says. 'I didn't.'

There's a pause, as we both telescopically zoom around the house in our minds' eyes – the stair-carpet, tattered and flapping on every tread. The bookcases made of bricks and planks: a piece of furniture widely known, on *The Antiques Roadshow*, as 'The council estate escritoire'. The leaking shower, and the baby buggy with the broken handle, and the mouse-shit in the back of the cupboards. One of the twins is crying downstairs.

He sighs. His face looks suddenly very sad. I get up, and hug him. He pulls me onto his knee, for the first time in years.

'You will *really* fuck your knees up,' I say, aware of how much bigger I am since the last time he did this.

I put my head on his shoulder. He smells of fags, and coal tar soap, and sweat.

'Oh, my daughter,' he says.

I want to say, 'I won't fuck it up. I won't fuck up … like you, Dad. I've learned your lessons. I know this is going to work'. But then that would acknowledge that Dadda did fuck it up, and didn't make it work, and make his face even more difficult to look at.

So I just say, 'Go ooooooooooon. Let me,' instead.

I hear him go downstairs to talk to Mum. I hear the low murmur getting louder and hotter, until it's turned into an argument.

'You *know* it's more complicated than that!' Mum shouts, at one point.

I put my headphones on, and listen to Courtney Love singing 'Teenage Whore'. Courtney left home at fourteen, and became a stripper – and she's *absolutely fine*. I don't know why they're worrying.

The argument between Mum and Dad lasts a week. She is obdurate that I should stay in school and finish my exams – he keeps saying 'Let her go for it, Angie', while she rattles red bills around on the dresser and frets about me 'fucking herself up with a load of druggie freaks'.

I stay in my room, writing my reviews – only adventing downstairs to make cups of tea in a very respectable manner, projecting the most innocent and aggrieved air I can.

In the end, after a week of rowing, she capitulates: 'On both your heads be it,' she says, 'But don't say I didn't warn you.' Then she says, looking at Dadda, 'I don't think you've thought this through. It's going to be more difficult than you think. It's a lot for Johanna to take on.'

I hug her, screaming, and then him – him for much longer.

'I *promise* I'll make this work!' I say. 'It will be good for *all* of us! I will be able to contribute to the house! It will be like when Jo March writes short stories to help Marmee out, in *Little Women*! Or when Pauline Fossil gets the role of Alice in *Alice in Wonderland*, in *Ballet Shoes*. I'll give you fifteen shillings a week, towards board and keep! If Daddy goes to war, we can send him blankets, and brandy!'

'The only war I'm going to sign up for is the Class War,' Dadda says. He quotes his favourite line from a film: 'Your dad wants to shoot the Royal Family, and put everyone who's been to public school in a chain gang. He's an idealist.'

He then adds: 'But we could definitely use the brandy.'

And it seems he will get the brandy sooner than we all thought: the next day, Kenny rings up and says, 'Congratulations, Wilde: you're going to Dublin next week, to interview John Kite.'

ELEVEN

I am on a plane. I'M ON A PLANE. I'm on a plane. I have never been on a plane before. Of course, I'm not going to tell Ed Edwards that – Ed Edwards, press officer for the record label the legendary Welsh pisshead John Kite is signed to. I don't want him to pity me. I don't want him to see what I look like when I do something for the first time. I don't want anyone watching me *change*. I will do all my changing in private. In public, I am, always, the finished thing. The right thing, for the right place. A chrysalis is hung in the dark.

I was surprised how little resistance my parents offered to me going to Ireland on my own. My mother said, 'You're going, alone, to hang out with a band, in another country? I'm not sure I like that. What are these people *like*?' – clearly imagining Led Zeppelin in their pomp, throwing fourteen-year-old girls out of the hotel window, and putting live fish inside televisions.

But I'd shown her interviews with John Kite – him talking about welfare, and the Beatles, and his favourite kind of biscuits – and she sniffed, and said, 'Oh, he's not a *proper* rock star then. He's just a *musician*,' in such a way as suggested that musicians didn't have penises, and therefore would not be a threat to me.

Dadda, on the other hand, was mainly interested in 'the blag': 'They putting you in a nice hotel? Are you flying first class? And taxi from the airport? Ah, record companies. Benevolent mother to us all.'

Once he'd worked out it was costing John Kite's record company just under £500 to send me to Ireland, he seemed content to let me go: 'Big companies show how much they love you by how much they spend on you,' he said, wisely, smoking a fag. 'They're not going to spend half a grand on throwing you to the wolves.'

So here I am – just me, with my tiny rucksack, on a runway, about to go to another country. I note to myself, cheerfully, that last week, my former class at school made *their* first venture abroad: a French exchange-trip. Emma Pagett got billeted with a family who put her in a bunk bed with a twelve-year-old who kept saying 'Kenny Everett' in a 'posh' English voice, and had salami and cheese for breakfast. Her subsequent letter on this seethed with outrage:

'We all went into town to see if we could find cornflakes. Tim Hawley was crying,' she noted, with satisfaction.

By way of contrast, I'm staying in a hotel that has a *swimming pool*. With a *star*.

'Bono's been asked to be put on the guest-list tonight. Bono!' Ed says, sitting in his plane seat like it's a chair in a pub. He's got the paper in his lap. He's preparing to *read* while we fly. He is going to do a crossword. A diversion – for the bored!

I will *not* be reading while we fly. My face is pressed against the window. When we fly, I am going to be absolutely present for every metre, and every cloud. No one will *ever* have flown more than me.

'Bono! Brilliant,' I say. 'I can make him personally apologise to me for … everything.'

I am currently pretending I hate U2 – mainly because I have noticed everyone on *D&ME* hates U2, and I guess they've just … seen through the whole thing.

Secretly, however, U2 are one of my favourite bands. If I hear 'Who's Gonna Ride Your Wild Horses?', I sob, and can't stop until I imagine Bono hugging me. I would love Bono to hug me. I would love Bono to give me 'the Bono Talk' – the infamous speech where he takes hot, young, bewildered things to one side, and counsels them, and vows to defend them, in the rock equivalent of Glinda's kiss upon the brow.

When you get the Bono Talk, that means you're saved. I would love to be saved. I would love someone to empirically tell me what I should do. Having to guess – improvise – all the time is so wearying.

'He's on at 10pm – it's a late start over there – so we'll eat first,' Ed continues, filling in nine down. 'Then after the gig, you get John all to yourself.'

The plane starts to taxi along the runway. I had no idea they went so fast. This is the fastest I have ever gone. We are already going too fast – and then we accelerate. Planes cruise at 600mph. Is this 600mph? This speed is inhuman, and unholy. It's angry. Planes have to become furious before they can fly. They kick the ground away, and punch into the clouds, screaming. We are fighting our way into the sky. The earth drops away, like we weighed it. You count to three, and the trees and roads and houses become tiny. You count to six, and the towns have shrunk down to a grey patch, stuck to a motorway.

'… he's not pleased with the piece in the *NME*,' Ed is saying, confidingly. 'They put in all that stuff about his ex-girlfriend that was supposed to be off the record, and his mum rang him up, crying …'

Shut up, Ed – the world below us has turned into a map. A real map! The woods look like the 'Woodland: deciduous' markings of Ordnance Survey. It is just as they drew it! Who knew! Who knew you could put the whole world on paper, after all! The artists were right! This is so reassuring!

'… and when we got to MTV, the only luggage he had was a carrier-bag with a pair of headphones in, his passport, and a bottle of duty-free mead. Mead! I mean – who drinks mead?' Ed gives an amused chuckle. 'John is *mad*.'

The windows go pale grey – we've flown into the clouds. Rainclouds are dirty, and wet – looking out of the window at them makes you feel you have temporarily gone blind. The inside of a raincloud is like a bubble of night. And then the plane pulls up higher – the clouds ripping across its nose – and we suddenly burst out into bright, bright brilliant sunshine.

And in the same way my first dose of adrenalin anxiety blasted through me like black flood-water, two years ago, this is now the opposite.

Sitting in seat 14A, in the sun, I float on a full-moon tidal joy unlike anything I have ever experienced. I am getting incredibly high on a single, astounding fact: that it's always sunny above the clouds. Always. That every day on Earth – every day I have ever had – was, secretly, sunny, after all. However shitty and rainy it is in Wolverhampton – on the days where the clouds feel low, like a lid, and the swarf bubbles and the gutters churn to digest – it's *always* been sunny up here.

I feel like I've just flown 600mph head-on into the most beautiful metaphor of my life: if you fly high enough, if you get above the clouds, it's never-ending summer.

I resolve that, for the rest of my life, at least once a day, I will remember this. I think it the most cheering thought I have ever had. When we finally land in Dublin, and I go off to meet John Kite, I am essentially drunk on the sky.

John. He was not a beautiful boy, nor a tall one. He was round, like a barrel, in a shabby brown suit he'd mended himself –

and his hair was neither one colour nor the other. His face was slightly crushed, and his hands shook a lot for a man of twenty-four – although, as he put it, later, 'In dog-years, my liver is sixty-eight.' But when the wind blew in on the street corner, you could see his heart beat under his shirt, and when the conversation accelerated, you could hear his mind chime, like a clock. He was bright bright bright, like the lantern above a pub door in November – he made you want to come in and never leave. He was company – good company – the only company for me, I soon found.

When I first saw him, he was in the saloon bar of a pub off Temple Bar, arguing with a man who was boasting about smoking eighty cigarettes a day.

'But what cunt counts them?' Kite asked, popping his cuffs.

He smoked every cigarette with ceremony – as if each one were hand-crafted, and contained a little gold – rather than being easily available from corner shops, in packets of twenty.

He'd walked into the pub – over an hour late – like a judge walking into court. This was, clearly, where business would be conducted – but this was also the theatre of the human heart, where all things happened and all things would be revealed, given the fullness of time.

He was still arguing with the man – 'You smell like you smoke less than fifty a day to me, my friend. You are borderline odourless, for an obsessive' – when Ed went over, and touched his elbow.

'John,' he said. '*D&ME* is here!'

'Alright,' John said, nodding, to me.

'This is Dolly,' Ed said.

'Alright – Duchess,' John said again. He turned, looked at me, and was suddenly fully engaged. All the lights went on – like someone had plugged in the Wurlitzer. The dance-floor flooded with jivers.

'Dolly,' he said, 'it is a pleasure to meet you. Shall we brutalise ourselves, with gin?'

John was a beamer – a proper beamer. When he smiled, he looked like all his life, he'd never wanted to do anything more than sit at this table with me, and smoke, and talk, while we watched people pass by the window.

He smiled when I said that I would only drink Coke – 'But thank you' – and he laughed when I said I didn't smoke: 'I applaud you, Dolly,' he said, lighting a fag. 'I applaud your fucking brightness. The thing is, when you start smoking, you think you've bought a fun baby dragon. You think you've charmed a fabulous beast, as your toy, that will impress all that see it. And then, twenty years later, you wake up with your lungs full of cinder and shite, and the bed on fire, and you realise the dragon grew up – and *burned your fucking house down*.'

And he coughed – a big, hairy man-cough – to prove it.

And he clinked my Coke glass with his gin glass, and beamed until his eyes were just lines of joy, and we just started talking and never really stopped: families, and madness, and *Ghostbusters*, and our favourite trees – 'Broadly speaking, I never met a tree I didn't like – save the lime, which is an irredeemable cunt' – and Larkin, and Tolstoy, and dogs. And whether 'Septuagesima' was a better word or phrase than 'gibbous moon', and council estates, and what it was like to go to London for the first time, and feel ashamed of your shoes: 'Although not any more,' he said, putting his feet up on the table. 'Handmade brogues. £20 in Oxfam. They only hurt when I walk. But look how beautiful the *burnish* is. The vamp is of calf-skin; the closure-style – Derby.'

And within twenty minutes – and then, for the next twenty years of my life – I knew a very important thing: that all I wanted to do was be near John Kite. That things would now divide, very simply, into two categories: things to do with John Kite, and things not to do with John Kite. And that I would abandon anything in the latter in a heartbeat if the chance of the former was on offer.

I had met a good boy who could talk, and every so often I would look up, and see us reflected in the mirror, under the low golden pub lamps, as the fog curled wetly outside the window, and it was the happiest picture of me never taken. We looked so happy together.

John Kite was the first person I'd ever met who made me feel normal. That when I talked 'too much', it was not the point where you walked away, going, 'You're *weird*, Johanna' or 'Shut *up*, Johanna' – but that that was when the conversation actually got good. The more ridiculous things I said – the more astonishing things I confessed – the more he roared with laughter, or slapped the table and said: 'That is *exactly* how it is, you outrageous item.'

I told him about wanting to save the world, and wanting to be noble, and how being at the *D&ME* made me feel like an odd toddler. I told him about my hat coming off at the Smashing Pumpkins, and my dad and Pat turning up backstage, pissed, and he slapped the table, weeping laughing.

Emboldened, I told him I fancied Gonzo from *The Muppets*, and he took it totally seriously, and said, 'You, my friend, would *adore* Serge Gainsbourg. Have you ever heard any? He looks *exactly* like Gonzo. *Exactly*. It's my contention that they modelled him wholly on the dude. Oh – you and Serge are in the stars! I will send you a tape the *minute* I return home! For myself, I have always suspected Mary Poppins would be *filthy*.'

'This is the happiest you've ever been,' I told myself in the mirror, in the ornate Victorian bathroom, two hours later.

I was having a little girl-to-girl chat with me – getting a second opinion. Goosing my own Maverick.

'You've made a friend! You're making a friend *right now*! Look at your face, in the middle of friending! You are hatching an attachment! Because the thing about John Kite is – the *important* thing about John Kite is–'

The door opened, and John Kite's head suddenly appeared – hair slightly ginnish over his forehead, fag in hand.

'Duchess, I've put Guns N' Roses on the jukebox, and they've emptied our ashtray with aplomb, and you really can't waste any more time pissing, you know. It's already 4pm.'

By 5.30pm, we had decided to move on – a man in a battered hat, who gave every impression of having only recently misplaced the pig under his arm, informed us that a pub called 'Doran's' had the best whisky selection in Dublin.

We never found that pub – we wandered the streets excited by the fog that had descended; excited by how things would loom out of it, solid for a second, and then melt away again, a second later. Everything had the dreamy air of *Through The Looking Glass* to it – I would not have been surprised if a lumbering giant Rook, or knitting sheep, had materialised and then dematerialised on the invisible conveyor-belt we seemed to walk parallel to.

At one point, we walked down a street and nearly ended up in the Liffey – it came upon us so rapidly – and we sat on the cold stone, on the water's edge, and looked across at the faint, bright lines of buildings on the opposite bank.

At 8pm, in the new, gentle dark, John turned to me, dirty blond forelock in his eye, and said, 'Duchess, this is one of those great afternoons where you make a friend for life, isn't it? We just seem to be … a lot the same.'

*

We got to the gig an hour late – Kite coming through the doors in his fake fur coat like some fabulous, Welsh, pissed pimp-hustler. I was holding his hand. I banked every jealous look, and became limitlessly wealthy on them.

In the dressing room, as Ed tried to give John black coffee – and John continued to calmly drink whisky, whilst batting Ed away like a moth – I looked around, and thought, 'I am back-stage! I mean, I *am* backstage. *I am the backstage.* I'm not just audience any more. I'm with the band.'

I looked across at 'The Band'. He was trying to take off his tie, with some difficulty. It was a knitted, woollen thing – 'But I'm going to put a bow-tie on, to perform,' John said, firmly, 'because I believe in a more formal attire when singing songs of heart-break. A sense of authority conveys comfort, to the weeping.'

Because the theatre was packed – loud, hot; everyone slightly angry with everyone else for being into this singer they thought was their special secret – there was nowhere for me to stand and watch the show.

'You'll sit there,' Kite said, with a flourish – pointing to the edge of the stage. We were standing in the wings, waiting.

'No *way*,' I said – but he'd already taken my hand and walked onto the stage with me, into the applause, which was solid, and filled the room, and felt like something you could actually see. Along with the white lights in your face, being on stage felt like opening the front door and finding the White Cliffs of Dover on your doorstep, waiting – ranked up from the stalls to the Gods. The White Cliffs of Dover stood, patient and huge, above us.

'This is the Duchess. She's with the band,' he said, pointing to me. I waved at the audience, sat on the very edge of the stage, and then concentrated on looking appreciative of Kite, in a business-like manner.

'And I'm The Band,' Kite continued. 'I am reliably informed by *Melody Maker* that I'm going to break the more fragile hearts in two, so – safety goggles on.'

I sat on the stage, and cried all the way through the gig. I must have looked like an art installation – 'Crying Girl Is Affected By Sad Songs'. I tried not to – but by the time the second song started, I was gone: John's songs had a breakable, scared quality to them that I recognised from sitting up alone, at night, and finding the future terrifying.

The song about his mother's breakdown – 'Subject to Melody' – had him singing *'A poor boy all alone/In a burning home/Choosing which one will walk out last,'* started me off; and by the time his stubby, pale fingers were picking through 'We are the Cavalry' – *'You remind me of a field of crucified saints/Kindness is a wound/And at closing time/We wash the blood with/Our hair dipped in wine'* – I was snotting all into my mouth and having to eat it, silently shuddering.

At one point he looked across and saw me weeping, and it seemed to throw him for a minute – he looked like he might stop the song. And then I bravely smiled, and he smiled back – as gleeful as he had been in the pub – before going back to his sad, sad chorus.

And that was the point I knew I just loved this filthy, ugly, loquacious man in a fur coat, who would spend the day roaming all over town, looking for bright lights, and laughter – and then at night come on stage, and unbutton two buttons on his waist-coat, with his clumsy, fat fingers, and show you his heart beneath.

After the gig, he stayed backstage for three drinks – which, being John Kite, he inhaled like vapour in less than ten minutes – and then he shrugged everyone off, with a cheerful 'Gotta be grilled by the Duchess now', and took me back to the hotel, for the interview.

I only had one cassette for my recorder – a single C90. It had never occurred to me that, in the end, I would spend from midnight until 5am talking to him. He'd drunk just enough to never stop talking, and I had never learned to stop talking in the first place.

He told me about his mother being committed when he was nine years old – how his dad was a drunk, and he was left with three younger siblings to look after. And that he would put on his mother's coat, and sit his small, motherless brothers on his knee, and hug them, so they could smell the coat, and pretend it was her.

'I read that was what you do with puppies,' he explained. 'And they all looked like little puppies, Duchess. Puppies left in a cardboard box, under a bridge.'

And how they were so poor that they'd steal firewood from the council bonfire, on Bonfire Night, and take it home in the pram – the baby sitting on top. And how, when he went to visit his mother in the hospital, feeling so broken and small and old, she would never hug him, or touch him. She could not bring herself to make any physical contact. Instead, at the end of the visit, she would kiss the tips of her fingers, and press them to his mouth – saying 'And that is John's goodbye.'

In turn, I told him about my family – my drunken dad, the dreary estate. How I'd brought about our impending ruin, and how I was running as fast as I could to outstrip it. How Mum had become an angry ghost, who didn't like who I was now. That Mum thought that Dolly Wilde wasn't who I *really* was at all.

'Oh, God – people always want to tell you what you're *really* like,' he said, with contemptuous dismissal – as if this were a wholly repulsive hobby; like Morris dancing, or wanking cats. He lit a fag. 'What a fucking bore people are.'

We talked until dawn, when John put pillows in the bath in his en suite, to make me a bed.

'You gonna *Norwegian Wood* it, love?' he said, as I crawled off to sleep in the bath.

Once I was in – it was unexpectedly cosy; like lying in an egg – Kite came and laid his fur over me. A white bath, full of fur.

'Is it still early?' he asked, hopefully, sitting on the side of the bath.

'John, it's 5am,' I said.

'Well,' he said, thinking. 'We might as well keep talking, then.'

It would be boring to say how much we laughed. He lay in his bed, and told stories, and would go quiet – asleep? – and then he would giggle, and then I would giggle, and he would say, 'You put the phone down,' and I would say, 'No, *you* put the phone down.'

At one point, he staggered in for a piss, three feet from where I lay – a thunderous unloading of whisky, Guinness and gin.

'You put the phone down,' he said.

'No – *you* put the phone down.'

'Love you, babe.'

He flushed, and went back to bed.

We were like two kids on a camping holiday.

First a taxi, then the airport. A plane. I think the shadow of the plane is a whale, in the Irish Sea. I love how it is following us, all the way back to Britain. Heathrow. Piccadilly line. Victoria line. Train. Wolverhampton.

512 bus. I have fallen out of the sky onto the 512 bus. My clothes still smell of Ireland, but I am back here. The Penn Road! With your monstrous knotted trees! I salute you!

My rucksack is on the seat beside me – heavy from the three ashtrays Kite insisted I steal. Two from pubs, one from the hotel.

The hotel one was the one he was most firm about. I had woken at 9am, and found him sitting at the table, by the window – the ruins of breakfast around him.

'There were no flowers on my breakfast tray,' he explained, vexed. 'No carnation. No rose! This will necessitate the separate, time-consuming purchase of a buttonier.'

He gestured to his empty lapel, where there was usually a flower.

'I must register my *dissatisfaction*,' he said, stuffing the ashtray into my rucksack, with a flourish – following it with all the miniature shampoos, lotions and soaps, before attempting a hand towel, and failing.

'This is negative customer feedback, to the hotel manager,' he said, emptying the minibar into my side-pockets.

The bus jolts a lot, down the Penn Road, which is making holding the pint glass of Guinness I have in my hands tricky. The Guinness is my big souvenir from Dublin.

At 10am this morning, in the taxi on the way to Dublin airport, I'd made Ed Edwards stop the cab outside a pub while I ran in, bought a pint of Guinness, and then asked the barman, with as much legendariness as I could muster, 'Could you gift wrap this? I need to take it to England.'

Between us, we'd devised a method whereby I'd put a coaster on top, like a lid, and he'd then swaddled it in almost a whole roll of clingfilm, from the pub kitchen. I have spent the subsequent seven and a half hours tenderly carrying this sticky brown mummy all the way from Dublin airport to Wolverhampton.

I have done this because, for as long as I can remember, my father has had a recurring rant about the ultimate unsatisfyingness of the Guinness in Britain.

'The only good pint of Guinness,' he will say – stubble flecked with creamy foam – 'is made in Dublin. The water's different. I'd give my *balls* for a proper pint of Guinness.'

And so I have brought this pint for him – a proper Irish pint, from Ireland. This pint – brought through the sky, and over the sea. I am finally buying my old man a good pint of Guinness.

As I walk through the door, holding the glass – kids throwing themselves at me, one already crying – I hold it out to Dadda, and tell him to sip it.

He tears the clingfilm off – looking at me, confused – and then takes a sip.

'Christ. That's flat,' he says.

An hour later, I go up to my room. I put on John's album, *Forestry*, as loud as I can.

As it played, I remembered how he looked when I told him about how it was the first time I'd been on a plane – 'Aww, love! I wish I'd seen your fucking face! I bet you loved it, you fucking ingenious whore! I bet you *exploded*!'

I liked telling John Kite that it was the first time I'd done something. He seemed to find my innocence joyous. I can't imagine telling anyone else. Other people seem to find my inexperience a liability. John Kite is the first person I've ever met who doesn't make me feel I am weird.

I start writing a list of things I want to talk to John about that I can't with anyone else, headed, firmly: 'The Next Fifty Conversations with John Kite.'

I tear pictures of John out of *Melody Maker*, *D&ME*, *NME*, *Select* and *Sounds* in the library – surreptitiously – and Blu-tack them to the wall, next to the Manic Street Preachers, Brett Anderson and Bernard Butler, and Kurt Cobain, wearing a dress. I start writing my diary to him, instead of to Gilbert Blythe. I put the three ashtrays on the desk, and stare at them.

If I smoked, I could smoke using John's ashtrays, and it would be like we were smoking *together*. Maybe I should start smoking. Maybe that would be the right thing to do.

Four days later, I get a letter. A long, cream-coloured envelope, with my address scrawled on the front in a looping hand, in grey Biro, and a cassette inside, with 'Gonzo Gainsbourg' written on it, in the same pen. I've never seen grey Biro before. Who the fuck knows where to get a grey Biro? I put the cassette in my stereo, and press 'Play', as I read the note.

'Hiya Duchess,' it begins – the best two words I have ever read in my life. My first and only christening. 'Hiya Duchess.'

Thought you'd want to know our alcoholiday ended with me in the swimming pool of the hotel at 11am, asleep on a sun-lounger, still in the big fur. I thought I'd go for a dip to sober up, lie down to have one of your copyright 'profound thoughts' TM, and, when I woke, an entire family in cossies and trunks were standing around me, with their mum at the back going, 'Leave the man alone! Keep away from him!'

No one's ever called me a 'man' before – I felt proud, and stern. This could be my gateway into adulthood.

Good to meet ya, princess – I will see you soon, yes? Let's make it soon – I don't want to have to wait twenty-four years to meet you again. I'm going for a walk. I ain't left the house in three days.

Love, The Band.

The cassette John has copied for me is Gainsbourg's *Melody Nelson*: it sounds incredibly, unbearably sexual. Dark and astonishing. Like a future I'm both scared of, and will run towards. Coupled with the letter, it pops a part of my child-brain, and I suddenly burst into tears.

I think I cry for at least half an hour – the kind of crying that is like rain where it starts without warning, and violently, but eases off into sudden rainbows, and blackbirds calling out in gratitude as they swoop across wet lawns. The weeping of relief.

Without even knowing what I'm doing, I lift the letter to my face, to see if I can smell any faint trace of John's hands – hands that make the music. The hands that play his guitar. I don't know why, but his hands break my heart.

Oh thank God thank God thank God, I think – I am not going to die having not received a letter. I get letters now. People write me letters. I am friends with the music. I can go out into the world, can make friends. It's working. I'm with The Band.

TWELVE

The next few weeks are some of the worst of my life, because I have discovered something amazing: that some people aren't just people, but a place – a whole world. Sometimes you find someone you could live in for the rest of your life.

John Kite is like Narnia to me – I've pushed through his fur coat and into a land where I am Princess Duchess, High Chatter of Cair Paravel. In John Kite, people walk down the street holding pigs, and we walk on stage holding hands into the bright light, and I fly over tiny maps to great theories, and I sleep in the bath-tub, still talking. I wish to be a citizen of John Kite forever – I want to move there immediately. I know he is the most amazing person in the world. Things happen with John Kite.

'I can't live here any more,' I tell the dog, sadly. I have climbed out onto the shed roof, and encouraged the dog to come with me.

'I can't stay here,' I continue. 'It doesn't work. The house is too small, and nothing happens, and I will never be older than twelve here.'

Since I've been up in a plane, and seen the houses turn into matchboxes, all the houses in Wolverhampton seem to have shrunk. I'm like Alice when she gets bigger, then smaller, then bigger again, in *Wonderland*. My scale has changed. I am still at 30,000 feet. I can't fit through tiny doors. I have dreams that I stand up and stamp on the houses, and flatten them, and run away. I need to run away to London, where John Kite lives, and where I will be the Duchess, and live in a variety of bars.

But I can't. For the awful thing is that now I know what I want – to be roughly no more than fifteen feet away from John Kite for the rest of my life – I can't have it. Now I've filed my John Kite feature to Kenny, I can't help but notice that work has dried up completely. Kenny is a bit odd with me on the phone: 'Do you like the feature?' I ask him.

'Well, you left us in no doubt where you stand on the man,' Kenny says, and changes the subject.

The piece runs on the eighteenth – I walk to the newsagent and there it is, billed on the front:

The stand-first, written by Kenny, describes my night out with Kite: 'Dolly Wilde flies to Dublin, racks up a £217 bar-bill, ends up in John Kite's bath, and explains why Kite is now "More important than the Beatles" [Really? Ed].'

In the feature, I've tried to describe what it's like being so close to the music – to hold its hand, and stand on stage with it, and talk to it, and then listen to it going to the toilet. I have one objective in the piece: to make every single person who reads it want to buy John Kite's records. I call him a 'dirty, crusading angel', and a 'filthy choirboy', and 'a beating, bleeding heart in a tattered suit'. After each of these descriptions, Kenny has written '[Oo-er, Madam – Ed]', or '[Blimey! Ed]', which makes me feel uneasy.

But Kenny hasn't written anything after the paragraph where I describe how John's face looks when he sings – how his fringe is wet in his eyes, and his whole demeanour is that he will sing this song to you, and then jump over the side of a ship, and swim to Paris, to start a new life, because he is embarrassed he has been so truthful. So maybe it's okay.

It is my first ever love-letter, although I don't realise at the time – perhaps the mood of over-wrought semi-hysteria should have alerted me. Or – more prosaically – the bit where I went, 'I am in love with John Kite. His music, that is.'

At the time, I think that is so subtle. I might just as well have written a 2,500-word repetition of the phrase, 'I HAVE A MASSIVE CRUSH ON JOHN KITE.'

But after the feature runs, Kenny stops calling me and offering me work. There is an ominous silence. There are no more trips down to London, no matter how often I ring him. Perhaps I should have stayed at school, and got those A levels, and resigned myself to being finger-banged by Craig Miller, who isn't in a band at all. Maybe I have made a mistake.

For the first two weeks, it isn't so bad, as John is on tour in the US. I lie on my bed with the music press, and read the reviews that come through with the eagerness of a mother reading letters from the battlefield, from her son.

'What's he up to now?' I ask, fondly, as I open the page on his gig in New York, where he had apparently 'charmed the crowd' with his 'shambolic between-song banter', which is 'less the announcing of the [non] hits, and more a stand-up routine delivered by a torch-singing Withnail'.

'I know how funny he is, because he is *my friend*!' I think. 'I have seen him be funny for *just me*. I have heard the jokes no one else has. I saw him do a piss. No one there would have seen him do a piss.'

A week later, the accompanying feature comes out, written by Rob Grant, who is on Kite's US tour. That was when things go bad for me, as I enter the third week of *Anno domini Nostri Kite*. Oh God, the agony of reading this piece.

Lying on top of my bed, eating raisins, I read how Grant has basically gone in and stolen my perfect night – the night I would have asked for before facing the electric chair in the morning.

He's been there for the gig, for a 3am trawl around whisky bars and, eventually, Kite sitting out on the balcony of his bedroom, at 6am, as the sun comes up, singing Grant his new songs as New York honks into life below them.

There has been breakfast in a diner – 'Excuse me, ma'am, but this jukebox doesn't work.' 'That's because it's a cigarette machine, sir' – and then they took the ferry out to the Statue of Liberty, drinking whisky miniatures and chaining Marlboros on the top deck, with the sky blue and new above them.

Each paragraph makes me progressively more furious. I chew the raisins to pulp, black pulp. Grant doesn't need this day – he didn't even fucking want it! His favourite band are Can, and he probably spent the whole fucking weekend moaning that he wanted to get back to his wife and kids!

I, on the other hand – I would have eaten that amazing day whole. I would have squeezed every fucking dot of glitter out of the night sky, and then been riding the balcony railings at dawn. You could have shot me dead at midday and I would have died with a smile on my face. *Why* had I not been there? In an exquisite torture, there were people who were writing about *the life I should have been in* – but instead, I am here, doing nothing, just waiting, and dying. Someone else is writing my diary, now – and not putting me in it.

It is because while I am in this room, I don't exist.

'You actually don't exist while you're in your bedroom,' I say to the dog, so that she knows this important fact. 'Teenage girls in bedrooms aren't real.'

I pull my knees up into my chest, in order to become more like a bullet or a cannon-ball, and look up at my wall, where all the pictures of Elizabeth Taylor and George Orwell and Orson Welles have been obscured by new pictures of John Kite. It perfectly represents the inside of my head.

'I have got to get out of this room,' I tell him. 'Please wait for me. Don't have all the fun now. Don't fill up on other people who aren't me. Don't ruin your appetite.'

I bite my hands. I am doing more biting, these days – on my knuckles; on the thumb knuckles. This is like a grown-up version of sucking your thumb – biting. This is what grown-ups do when they needed comfort – they bite their hands, quietly, in their rooms. It quells the anxiety – focused it down into two, small crescents of tooth-marks on my skin.

'I am getting out of this room.'

And I know how. Next week, John Kite plays his homecoming gig in London, at the Falcon. I am getting out of this room. I am going to get on a train to London, and get back in this game.

I bounce downstairs, joyfully, to tell Mum I am going to London to see John Kite. I am already planning my outfit – maybe a flowery dress, from the charity shop. John would like a girl in a flowery dress. I could *kill* John Kite in a flowery dress. In a good way.

Halfway down the stairs, I can see something bad has happened. Mum and Dadda are leaving the house – Mum crying, and Dadda slamming the door in his haste – and Krissi is standing, with a brown envelope in his hand. Because I've imagined this minute so often, you'd think that I would know how to cope with it. But I don't. I'd never, ever been able to imagine past this point.

'What's happened?' I ask.

'They're doing us, Johanna,' Krissi says. 'They're cutting our benefits.'

'Why?' I ask.

I feel like I will wet myself, like when the children are terrified or have hurt themselves – but will simultaneously cry myself to death, too, in one, fast-forwarded, pyroclastic self-immolation.

'They've "got some information",' Krissi says, grimly.

THIRTEEN

For the next six weeks, whilst pursuing their 'information' about a 'possible irregularity' further, the Social Services are cutting our benefits. Mum and Dad do maths on a series of backs of envelopes, and work out we've lost 11 per cent of our income.

Initially, I am relieved – I have been expecting 50 per cent, 90 per cent – every penny taken from us, and then what? Not even the poorhouse, in 1993 – maybe we would have to move into an aunt's house, like families fallen on hard times in nineteenth-century novels. A spare family in the spare room, existent on charity. Seven Jane Eyres, of various sizes – throwing themselves on the pity of Aunt Reed. I'd have to sleep in a cupboard, and Lupin would be haunted by ghosts.

11 per cent, by way of contrast to this utter ruin, seems … manageable? After all, if I cut off 11 per cent of my hair, I'd barely notice. For a moment I think 11 per cent isn't so bad.

What I'm failing, momentarily, to consider is that we are already on the very edge. There are no investments to cash in, to tide us over this 11 per cent dip – no bonds, savings or shares. There are no 'little luxuries' to cut back on, like going to the hairdressers, or a subscription to a magazine. We cut our own hair, and read magazines in the library. There are no grand plans we can temporarily shelve, during this cash lull – like replacing our car, or decorating the front room. We were never going to replace our car, or decorate our front room.

And there's no one we can borrow from – for one of the truths about the poor is that they tend only to know other poor people, who also couldn't afford an 11 per cent dip, and can't subsidise ours.

The truth is, when you are very poor, that 11 per cent bites into the very bones of your existence. 11 per cent less means choosing between electricity, or food – electricity and food that is already rationed, and fretted over. 11 per cent is not very much – but, when you are very poor, it may form the bedrock of your survival.

And now you are standing on so much less than you were before. You are unstable. You are liable to fall.

The new maths of our existence has now been carefully worked out, on a piece of paper, stuck to the wall. Our new budget now, with no wriggle room for anything extra – not a pot of jam, nor a new pair of shoes. We cannot do anything other than stay very still. We are on 11 per cent less of was-never-enough-in-the-first-place.

The morning after my parents have made their new budget, I go into their bedroom, when they're in bed, and sit on the end.

'Look,' I say. 'This isn't as bad as it seems. I'm earning now! When that cheque finally arrives, I can give you money!'

Making this offer, I have a combined feeling of relief and fear. I'm relieved that I can give the family money, and stop all this worry.

Besides, surely, the more money I give my parents now, the less angry they will be when they finally find out it was me that fucked up. If I can earn, and then give them, say, £1,000 before the big discovery, perhaps they won't be angry with me at all! Perhaps I can buy their forgiveness! I will make them *indebted* to me! This is a good plan!

However, my mother immediately holes this plan.

'When that cheque comes – *if* it comes – you're going to put half of it into a savings account,' she says, firmly. 'And half of everything that comes after, as well. Me and your dad have discussed it.'

'*What?*'

'You don't know what's going to happen in the future, Johanna,' Dadda says. 'Leaving school is a risk …'

'It's not!' I say. 'Everyone else on *D&ME* is like *thirty*, and they have, like, *houses* – it's just a normal job!'

'You're so early in your career, Johanna,' Mum says. 'You need savings.'

Dadda gets up to go to the toilet – 'Just going to water the allotment, love' – and Mum leans forward, whispering. For a moment, she looks like she used to, before the twins came.

'If your dad had had savings, he wouldn't have had to give up music when the band broke up,' she says, urgently. 'When things go wrong, you need money, so you don't get … stuck.'

She looks at the twins – asleep on a mattress by the side of the bed.

'What happened with our benefits?' I ask.

'I'm sure we'll find out soon enough,' my mother says. She speaks with the kind of flat sadness that comes from being tired, and trapped. The kind of sadness that makes you wild with fear, when you see it in a parent.

And then Dadda comes back into the room, and she slumps back on the pillows, pretending to look like her normal self again.

The next day, two men appear on the front door step, and take away the television. We've always rented – everyone on our estate rents. Whoever has £300 to buy? – and now it's the first of the desperate cuts to be made.

The children line the route from the front room to the front door like it's a funeral – weeping as it leaves the house.

We then go back into the front room, and stand around the empty spot – like sad woodland animals around Snow White's dead body.

'This is like our mother is dead. Our *real* mother,' Krissi says. Even Krissi is crying, a bit – and Krissi never cries. The last time he cried was when he fell backwards off the bunk bed onto some Lego, and a chunk of skin came off his ear.

Lupin is properly hysterical – it's halfway through the first season of *Twin Peaks*, which we have been obsessed by.

'We'll never find out who killed Laura Palmer now!' Lupin wails, dribble coming out of his mouth.

Even my suggestion that we 'play' *Twin Peaks* – wrapping Lupin up in bin bags, and leaving him up the garden – doesn't lighten the mood. After twenty minutes Lupin complains that he can't breathe properly – even though we've made ample holes in the plastic – and the game is abandoned. We sit up the tree, sombrely, contemplating a future without television.

'No *Blue Peter* or *Saturday Superstore*,' Lupin mourns.

'Or *Crimewatch*,' Krissi says. We love *Crimewatch*. We regularly take down the number plates of every car that comes down our street – lest it contain a murderer, and become a vital clue. *Crimewatch* presenter Nick Owen's oddly menacing catchphrase – 'Please, don't have nightmares. Please, sleep well' – is our traditional way of saying goodnight to Lupin, after we've told him a long and gruesome horror story.

Now, this farewell rings hollow in our ears. For the nightmare has, finally, come, and it is worse than a murderer.

It's not just the television. Everything must be cut. There are no more boxes of fruit and vegetables from the wholesale market now. Dadda buys a 50kg sack of wholemeal flour, and at least one meal a day now consists of chapattis – flour, water and salt mixed into a dough, flattened into plate-sized rounds, by hand, grilled, and then covered in margarine.

We find that by pricking them all over with a fork, before cooking, you can double the amount of melted fat they can absorb – which makes them marginally tastier. There are competitions to see who can get the most margarine onto a chapatti – a competition I am winning, with over a tablespoonful – until Mum finds out, and rations the margarine, too: 'That price-sticker – 79p – *means* "79p". Not "free to little piggies".'

We become experts at finding sell-by-date bargains. For a while, the local supermarket discounts huge tins of saveloy sausages, in brine, and we eat them three times a week, with boiled white cabbage, and lots of own-brand ketchup, or salad cream. We live on ketchup and salad cream. Without them, there would truly be a riot. The sum contents of our morale comes in 1kg own-brand condiment bottles.

A gas bill lands, then an electric bill. Mum arranges a second overdraft, to pay them: so now we're going backwards, twice as fast. Lupin's shoes wear out – but there's no money to buy any more: he wears Krissi's old wellingtons. His feet are perpetually soft, and wet, and white with sweat.

My shoplifting rockets – 'Hope: Be Cute', the sign in the chemists reminds me, as I stuff my pockets with tampons and deodorant. Like Robin of Locksley before me, I am stealing sanitary towels from the rich, to line the knickers of the poor.

Shoplifting's harder, now, as there's no more money for bus fares up town: I have to walk in and out: six miles there, six miles back, along the dual-carriageway, lorries whipping the hat off my head, over and over.

Often I take the twins with me, in the buggy – just so I'm not lonely during the walk. Or Lupin, and the dog – I sing to them, as we walk. I sing 'I Am The Resurrection', and 'Cemetry Gates' by The Smiths.

These songs mean even more to me now the money's run out. Even the handfuls of 20ps to hire new CDs are gone – and so my record collection is stuck on the 148 records I had before: these 148 records, pirated from library CDs, are my whole world. A lighthouse in the distance that only I am steering to. A place I will get to, eventually.

In Central Library – pockets still full of stolen tampons, dog tied up outside – the twins sleep in the buggy while I read the *D&ME*, *Melody Maker* and *NME* I've walked six miles to. To get all the value, I read every word – even the gig-listings, at the front, which are nothing more than a register of the small-to-mid-sized venues across Britain in 1993: Rayleigh Pink Toothbrush, Derbyshire Wherehouse, King Tut's Wah-Wah Hut, Buckley Tivoli, Windsor Old Trout. I can recite all of these, like a rosary of places where people still go, and things still happen – and to which, one day, *I*, too, will go, and *I*, too, will happen. I will not stay stuck here. I refuse.

One week, there is an interview with John Kite in the *D&ME*, billed on the cover. I reflect on how useful it is when your friends are a bit famous, and interviewed in magazines. It's a lovely way of being able to catch up with them in your spare time. So handy. Look how we are keeping in touch!

In the first paragraph alone, I learn that John has been given a new necklace by a fan in Germany – a crucifix, 'For if I have a sudden death-bed situation and need to hastily kick-start my sclerotic Catholicism', has written a song on mushrooms called 'Increase The Lexicon', and has had a small tattoo, of a Welsh dragon, inked onto his pale, soft upper-arm: 'Although, I will be frank with you – the place we went was not reputable, and it looks more like a long cat, with eczema.'

The main part of the interview, however, is about class – currently a big issue. All acts are being asked about the recession, and the Major government, and benefits, and politics, and poverty. Everyone is asked where they stand.

And, so, this question now falls to John Kite – a Welsh working-class boozer and infamous bar-room monologist – in an interview with Tony Rich in *D&ME*. Sitting in Central Library with the rain pouring down outside, I read it.

> *'There's one big difference between the poor and the rich,'* *Kite says, taking a drag from his cigarette. We are in a pub,* *at lunch-time. John Kite is always, unless stated otherwise,* *smoking a fag, in a pub, at lunch-time.*
>
> *'The rich aren't evil, as so many of my brothers would tell* *you. I've known rich people – I have played on their yachts* *– and they are not unkind, or malign, and they do not hate* *the poor, as many would tell you. And they are not stupid –* *or at least, not any more than the poor are. Much as I find* *amusing the idea of a ruling class of honking toffs, unable to* *put their socks on without Nanny helping them, it is not true.* *They build banks, and broker deals, and formulate policy, all* *with perfect competency.*
>
> *'No – the big difference between the rich and the poor is* *that the rich are blithe. They believe nothing can ever really be* *so bad. They are born with the lovely, velvety coating of blithe-* *ness – like lanugo, on a baby – and it is never rubbed off by a* *bill that can't be paid; a child that can't be educated; a home* *that must be left for a hostel, when the rent becomes too much.*
>
> *'Their lives are the same for generations. There is no* *social upheaval that will really affect them. If you're* *comfortably middle-class, what's the worst a government* *policy could do? Ever? Tax you at 90 per cent and leave your*

bins, unemptied, on the pavement. But you and everyone you know will continue to drink wine – but maybe cheaper – go on holiday – but somewhere nearer – and pay off your mortgage – although maybe later.

'Consider, now, then, the poor. What's the worst a government policy can do to them? It can cancel their operation, with no recourse to private care. It can run down their school – with no escape route to a prep. It can have you out of your house and in a B&B by the end of the year. When the middle-classes get passionate about politics, they're arguing about their treats – their tax-breaks and their investments. When the poor get passionate about politics, they're fighting for their lives.

'Politics will always mean more to the poor. Always. That's why we strike and march, and despair when our young say they won't vote. That's why the poor are seen as more vital, and animalistic. No classical music for us – no walking around National Trust properties, or buying reclaimed flooring. We don't have nostalgia. We don't do yesterday. We can't bear it. We don't want to be reminded of our past, because it was awful: dying in mines, and slums, without literacy, or the vote. Without dignity. It was all so desperate, then. That's why the present and the future is for the poor – that's the place in time for us: surviving now, hoping for better, later. We live now – for our instant, hot, fast treats, to pep us up: sugar, a cigarette, a new fast song on the radio.

'You must never, never forget, when you talk to someone poor, that it takes ten times the effort to get anywhere from a bad postcode. It's a miracle when someone from a bad postcode gets anywhere, son. A miracle they do anything at all.'

The feature goes on – Kite proceeds to get, as he always does in interviews, quite drunk, and the mood lightens as he talks about his forthcoming European tour, and his recent adoption of a sloth at Regent's Park Zoo ('The physical similarities between us are striking. I would hope, in reversed circumstances, the sloth master race would be as considerate towards me.')

But in Central Library, I'm trying not to make it obvious I'm crying. This is what it's like! I am in a bad postcode! I am these words! I love John Kite. *He* knows about the 11 per cent. I want to leave the twins' buggy by this table and just run – run to wherever he is and shake his hand, and roll up my sleeve and show him a new tattoo which *I* would have got, and which would read 'WV4 – Bad Postcode'.

I want to take this interview with me everywhere, like an introductory document – to the supermarket, to the council offices, to *D&ME* – and show it to people, saying, 'This is what it's like. This is what is happening to me. This is why I am so tired.'

I am so tired. Tired – but so so so wired to the moon.

Because the one thing I haven't confessed to anyone is how I know all of this is my fault. That our sudden, terrifying, grinding poverty is my fault.

The atmosphere in the house is already terrible – three times I've had to herd Lupin and the twins into the bedroom and play Simon & Garfunkel's 'Bridge Over Troubled Water' really loudly, while Mum and Dad screamed at each other downstairs. These arguments always end with Dad leaving the house to go to the Red Lion, where Johnny Jones gets him pissed – leaving Mum to shuffle and re-shuffle the bills on the dresser; as if each contact with her hand might rub away at the total.

Krissi is, obviously, very deeply depressed. He'd planned to go to university – but now seems like a bad time to discuss something that will involve spending money, and involve upheaval, and so he has become almost totally silent. It's like he's temporarily pretending to be dead.

And it's my fault – all my fault – and the anxiety is killing me. The adrenalin-surges I had whilst sitting at the letter-box, waiting – are nothing compared to these new ones: my hands sometimes go numb. I get the shits. My thoughts are so fast and terrifying that I often think of the bit in Bob Geldof's auto-biography (*Is That It?*) where, after his mother dies, he finds himself leaning on a nail that protrudes from the wall – pushing the point into his forehead, like an amateur trepanning.

That's what I'd like to do, I think. Have a long, cool, clean nail, right in the middle of my head. That would calm me. And no one would blame me – a girl with a nail in the centre of her skull. They would put me in a hospital – and, because I would be broken, and ill, I would be safe. If I broke all my bones, no one would hate me. If I was in trouble. If I was at the bottom of the stairs. If I was smashed up. If I died.

If you can't save yourself from attack by being powerful – and I, palpably, have no power. My hands are empty – then perhaps you can save yourself from attack by being ruined, instead. Blow yourself up before the enemy gets to you.

The reason I'm so scared is that this has all happened before. We have been this poor before – in a house this angry, where Dadda's eyes went completely cold, and everything seemed to end – when he first stopped working, in 1986.

There is a story about this which I will tell you now – it used to make me sad, but it doesn't make me sad any more. You can have it.

When it was my eleventh birthday, I wanted a birthday party. I'd never had a party before. This is when I had just made my one friend – Emma Pagett – and I wanted to invite her over.

My mother said that this was possible – my birthday present would be £10, and I was absolutely free to use that money to buy party food, and host my friend.

I made my own cake – I was a cheerful cook. You cream the marge with the sugar, beat in eggs, fold in flour, bake, sandwich together with buttercream, and jam, and then you have cake.

Krissi took a picture of me, when the table was fully laid: cake on a plate covered in tin foil, for festivity, and me in my baker's boy cap, like John Lennon. I am standing by the table, and showing off the goods with an elegant hand gesture – like Anthea Redfern, drawing attention to the canteen of cutlery on *The Generation Game*.

But, all the while, Dad stayed in bed. It was one of the days where he just … didn't get up. Just lay in bed, next to his big, white bottle of medicine, with his eyes almost white.

At 3pm, my mother came into the dining room, where I was sitting, on a chair, reading *The Railway Children,* waiting until Emma arrived, at 4pm.

'Your dad's not feeling well,' my mother said. 'He's gone to bed. He … doesn't want you to have Emma over, in case he needs to …' – she thought for a minute – '… have a bath.'

I don't remember how I told Emma, on the phone, that she wasn't to come over. I wouldn't have told her about how, sometimes, when your daddy has fallen off a building, he doesn't like people to come to the house. That he won't let anyone in, or out.

I suspect I would have said I didn't feel well – that I had a stomach-ache, and so she shouldn't come over.

And that was true, in the end – about the stomach-ache. Because I ate everything on the table. I ate my whole birthday.

And then I went to bed.

FOURTEEN

Still, life in Wolverhampton now is not without its excitements. On Thursday, we take Lupin to the dentist, where he has five teeth removed.

Here, perhaps, is the reason he has been crying so much. It's not that his nature veers instinctively toward the melancholic, and pensive, after all – it's just that his teeth are riddled with rot. The dentist has to gas him and take out five of them, in an hour-long, brutal, surgical punch in the face.

'They're only your milk teeth, son!' Dadda says, cheerfully, as we drive him home in the van – lying flat out in the back, head on Krissi's lap. 'Your *starter* teeth! Now you're getting your Man Teeth through! Soon you'll be biting through bricks – like Jaws!'

Lupin is holding the bag of sweets he's been given, as a treat. We have no other reward system available to us. He's been paid for his teeth in Black Jacks, Refreshers and Fruit Salads. And he's paid for his Black Jacks, Fruit Salads and Refreshers in teeth. In a way, it's a perfect circular dental system for children.

'When I was a kid, we *all* had rotten teeth!' Dadda says over his shoulder, gleefully. 'All of us! Every uncle! Your Uncle Jim had one that came through black. *Came through. Black.* We called it "The Demon Tooth". Your Fat Nanna had false teeth by the time she was twenty-eight! She used to say she lost a tooth for each child.'

'It looks like Lupin has, too,' Krissi says, coldly – looking around the van full of siblings.

None of us can stop staring at Lupin. He's still groggy – drunk – and when he opens his mouth, it looks like a fifth of his face is missing. Red, wet gaps in his head. He doesn't have a mouth any more – just a hole.

Krissi silently puts his finger on Lupin's cheek, pointing something out to me: they've split his lip, too, while he was under. His teeth *and* his lips. All they've left is a pulpy mess – with a single incisor left, on the right, like a Martello tower, sitting on an empty shoreline of blood. Poor Lupin.

When we get home, Mum has made the house ultra-tidy – in the way that it usually only is if visitors are coming. Today's honoured guest is Lupin's pulped mouth. He's given the best bit of the sofa – with the most functioning springs in it – and the best blanket over his knees, and, when he comes round fully from the anaesthetic, in order to cheer himself, he gets us all to do increasingly humiliating things in exchange for sweets from his bag.

Krissi has to pretend to be an orang-utan that's trapped under the armchair. I have to say that I fancy a series of esca-latingly mortifying people – starting with Mr Bennett, the caretaker from *Take Hart*, and ending with The Glove from *Yellow Submarine* – until I start crying, and Mum has to come in, and chide everyone for letting it get out of hand.

We all pretend we're doing the humiliating things to cheer Lupin up. In reality, it is pretty much for the sweets. Tea is macaroni and boiled white cabbage. We are looking for John Kite's 'tiny, hot, cheap treats'. Lupin gets a whole can of rice pudding to himself, with a spoon full of jam in it, because, with no teeth, he can't eat macaroni and boiled white cabbage.

'I've got the best tea!' he says. We let him have this victory.

*

'These are amazing,' Krissi says, later. We're in the bedroom – all the kids, in a circle, on the floor. We're all playing with Lupin's teeth. Krissi has got a pin, and is carefully scraping out the soft rottenness in a molar.

'Does it have a smell? A rotten smell?' Lupin asks.

Krissi sniffs it, carefully.

'Nah.'

There is a bad smell in the room anyway. Ten minutes earlier, Krissi had taken a match and held it to a tooth – to burn off a shred of gum that was still stuck to it.

'Like human bacon,' he'd said, striking the match.

It gave off an odour like burning hair – but then, maybe that was the tooth itself. There are now black scorch-marks on the side of it. Who knew you could have so much fun with teeth!

I am using three of the teeth to cast my I Ching. My hexagram is forty-four – 'Coming To Meet.'

I look through the book of the I Ching, to see what it means.

'"We see a female who is bold and strong",' I read. 'That must be me! I will marry John Kite!'

I do double thumbs-up to the whole room. I whoop myself. I punch the air.

I read on.

'"It will not be good to marry such a female."'

Everyone does an 'I told you so' look.

I look down at Lupin's teeth.

'I'm going to cast again,' I said.

I once recast my I Ching nine times in a row – until it came out good. I keep redoing it until it says that I will move to London, and live in a flat on Rosebery Avenue, and get married to John Kite, with Stephen Fry as our minister. Sometimes, getting that future right takes all night. But I have time enough on my hands now.

The Book of The I Ching is being used a lot, at the moment. As the investigation into our benefits grinds on, we all become obsessed with fortune-telling. We're trying to regain some sense of control, however trifling, over what will happen next.

For some reason, Mum decides that Krissi has 'The Sight', and gets him to do everyone's fortunes, every couple of days – infinitely pressing 'refresh' on our future, until we get one we like.

'It's going to be exactly the same as yesterday,' Krissi snaps, shaking the divining coins onto the floor.

With time pressing, however, the main focus of our fortune-telling sessions is, still, Dadda.

Knowing he's now on a deadline – world fame or the poorhouse! Double or quits! – Dadda has been redoubling his efforts to return to this Elysian land of rock and honey. By familial consent, he's taken £10 out of the weekly food budget to send twelve, newly finished demos down to record companies in London. Finally finding a use for the sur-really impractical calligraphy pen I was given for Christmas, I write the addresses on the Jiffy bags – Virgin Records, Island Records, WEA – and send them the latest version of 'Dropping Bombs', which has now been re-worked as a 'baggy' classic, in the style of the Happy Mondays.

Dadda's recent adoption of modern music has come as some surprise to me. When he came into the front room as I was watching *Top of The Pops*, I absolutely expected him to launch into a classic ex-hippy's rant about how rubbish all modern music is. Not only was I braced for this – I was looking *forward* to it. I would be able to argue with him, indignantly, on behalf of my generation, and feel deathlessly, furiously teenage.

Instead, he stood there for a minute, in the doorway, watching the Mondays doing 'Step On', clearly off their faces, and said, appreciatively, 'They've got some balls on them. Look at them! Twatted!'

He added the last almost ... *lovingly*.

So now, when these baggy-filled Jiffy bags are posted, Krissi – instructed by Mum – casts Dadda's fortune. Again.

'So – when am I getting my first million, then?' he asks, coming into the front room, rubbing his hands together.

We all gather round, to hear the news – Dadda lying on his side, on the floor, after the first few minutes, as his knees can't bear his weight.

The coins say we may have to wait a little longer than we ideally hoped for our wealth – 'Fucking hell – I hope not past March. The MOT's due, and it's your Chris's wedding, in fucking *Hull*' – but our fortune is, most assuredly, coming. It is in the I Ching.

At the end of the reading, we all give Krissi a round of applause. Everyone is cheerful.

'That's *that* sorted, then,' Dadda says, slowly getting off the floor. 'Argh! Knee! Johanna – it's time for us to strike, now. While the auspices are good.'

'Yes!' I say, because there isn't anything else to say. There's a pause. 'How?'

'We can take London *together*,' Dadda says. 'You should talk to some of these people at the record companies. Get a bit of a buzz going about me. Hype me up.'

'Yes!' I say again. And then: 'How?'

'I dunno,' Dadda says. 'What do bands do these days to get publicity? Maybe we should ask the I Ching again,' he says.

'The I Ching is tired now,' Krissi says, firmly. 'You have to let it ... *regenerate* for a while.'

'Me and you should put our heads together,' Dadda says, to

me. 'Come up with some plan. Get all P. T. Barnum on this. Me and Johanna will think of something.'

I am pretty sure I can think of nothing.

Later that night, Krissi lies in bed, in his bunk, staring up at the ceiling. Lupin is asleep in the bottom bunk. I can tell he wants to say something. Finally:

'It's all bollocks, you know,' he says. 'Every single one I've done is bollocks. I haven't even read the book.'

He keeps staring up at the ceiling.

'What?'

'I can't read the future. I can't do the I Ching. It's all bollocks. Of course it's bollocks, Johanna.'

'But – but you said I'd have a boyfriend by Christmas!' I wail.

I'm sitting on the edge of my double bed, dressed in Dadda's old thermal long johns, and am wearing a face-pack made of oats, which I read about in *The Brownie Guide Handbook*. Apparently it's good for spots – which I am gaining rapidly since we started living on a diet that is 90 per cent boiled white cabbage and chapattis with margarine.

Krissi looks at me for a minute. Sometimes, he looks at me with something that is almost – almost – pity. That is what he is doing now.

'Oh, yeah. That'll definitely happen,' he says, eventually, turning over, and pulling the duvet up over his head.

I wait until everyone's asleep, and then put my hand to my fur. My sexual fantasies have become quite medieval recently – as an extension of all the fortune-telling books we've been getting out of the library, I've branched out into the rest of the 'Supernatural' section, and have been reading a lot about witchcraft.

The books on witchcraft are full of pornography, I've discovered, to my surprise. Obviously they don't *say* its pornography – they are simply historical reports from women, often nuns, who have had sex with the Devil.

History, it seems, is full of nuns who've had it off with Satan. If the Devil fucks you in the missionary position, he is an incubus. If you straddle him, he is a succubus. There is a lot of technical detail to learn about fucking the Devil.

'The young neophyte, seemingly drugged, is pushed into the midst of the assemblage, and made to stand naked in front of the coven,' one account reads. '"Young neophyte!" the High Priest calls. "You have served me well! Stand up and join these assembled here so that they may look upon you, and do as they desire!" She is submitted to the carnal desire of any member of the coven who request her, and will assist in mass perversions.'

Anyway. Yadda yadda yadda. The bottom line is, I wank a lot thinking about medieval demons.

Stressed after the day we've had, I start thinking about being laid out on an altar, and being forced into 'conjurations of lust' with a succession of demons and horny priests. The wheat fields are parched, and failing, and unless they fuck a virgin in a Black Mass, everyone in the village will starve.

Imagine having sex with someone being *useful*. Everyone needing you. Or else the crops would fail. It's so hot. Mass perversions. Mmmmmm. It's either thinking about this, or John Kite, and every time I think about him, I cry. So I think about the Black Mass, instead.

'Johanna.'

Silence.

'Johanna, what are you doing?'

It's Krissi. He's awake.

'Er … I'm just a bit … itchy. Having a scratch.'

Silence.

'You've been itchy quite a lot, recently. Late at night.'

Another silence.

'You're very itchy, Johanna.'

A very long pause. Eventually:

'I think I have … nits.'

The next day, Krissi asks Mum if he can move out of the room he shares with me and Lupin, and have his own bedroom.

'Of course!' Mum says, brightly. 'I'd be delighted! I'll just pull a fabulous big bedroom for you – out of my arse! Do you want a pony, too? And a stable? I've got one of those up here too, I think!'

'I could have the dining room,' Krissi says, coldly.

This throws Mum.

'The dining room?'

'Yes. I've thought about it. We all eat in the front room anyway.'

This is true. All meals are plates on laps, on the sofa, or floor. Or standing in the kitchen, eating lumps of cheese and bread, on the hoof.

'You can't have the dining room,' Mum says, flatly.

'I need my own bedroom,' Krissi says.

There is a new, impressive immovability to him, since all plans for him to go to university seemed to go quiet. A sense of 'And that was the *last* time you ever got to screw me over. From now on, I am unyielding. I will fight'.

Obviously I know he's asking to move into the dining room because I have wanked him awake over weeks of Satanic fantasies – so I am guiltily provoked into immediately backing him to the hilt on this plan.

'I think Krissi *should* have his own room,' I say. 'He's seventeen, and needs his privacy.'

'I really do need my privacy,' Krissi says, resolutely not looking at me. 'And I need more room, for my seedlings.'

Krissi has recently taken up gardening, with the intention of growing vegetables, so that we don't die of scurvy. Our bedroom is full of random pots labelled 'Marrow', 'Peas', 'Tomatoes' and 'Chilli'.

As is the way of our family, there then follows a gigantic, heated debate on the subject of Krissi having the dining room, in which everyone piles on, and uses the opening of one sibling request in order to put in *their* requests for things, too. At one point, Lupin is angling for a bicycle, a bedside lamp and a Transformer.

But by 4pm, Mum has capitulated. Krissi's bed is in the dining room – where the table once was. And the table is now in my bedroom, where I will use it as a desk 'for my writing'.

By nightfall, the dining room has a sign on the door that says 'Alan Titchmarsh's Sex Pad' – written by me – and Krissi is arranging his seedlings on the makeshift shelving system constructed of planks and bricks.

And I – I have a desk! At last! No matter that half the table is covered with boxes of toys and clothes – the other half, marked off with a strip of Sellotape, is all mine: a place where I can finally write.

I move all my pictures and quotes from over my bed, and put them on the wall behind the desk, instead. I have new things to add, that I have found in the last few weeks. Larkin's 'Lines On A Young Lady's Photograph Album', with the lines *'A real girl, in a real place'*, and *'invariably lovely'* picked out in red. *Invariably lovely. Invariably lovely. A real girl, in a real place.* I put a big picture of John Kite next to it. That was when I was a real girl, in a real place.

There's also a list titled 'My Best Words', which I have been collecting as assiduously as others might collect butterflies, or brooches: *Shagreen. Uxorious. Mimosa. Cathedral. Colloidal Mercury. Iodine. Waxwing. Lilac. Jaggery. Atholl Brose. Zoo.*

In these weeks where I am getting so little work, I feel I have to gather a better grade of weaponry: I must make sure I have all the best, sharpest, most potent words on my wall – so that, when I am called into battle again, I will be able to fight instantly, unbeatably – and never be relegated again.

I also have the central pages of the *London A-Z* pinned to the wall, which I have been studying and learning like my times-table. I want people to think that London is where I come from – that I was born in London, and was just accidentally misplaced. When I go back among the adults there, I want to seem as if I know this place better than they do: I want to be able to immediately and casually be able to say, 'Yes – Rosebery Avenue, EC1. You would get there via the Clerkenwell Road. You pronounce Marylebone Road "Marra-lee-bun Road", and the pubs around Billingsgate Market stay open all night, and into dawn, and breakfast. You see, I know all the roads in London. I know all of London. This place is not mysterious to me. I always knew I would come here. This is my real home. We had another life quite by mistake – but it is all better now. It's all quite better now.'

I am going to get back down to London as soon as I can, where I will be a real girl, in a real place, again.

One good thing happens, in this otherwise broken-gollum month: on the 29th, I finally receive a cheque for all the work I had done for the *D&ME* so far: £352.67. I go up town, and buy a telly from the junk shop, and install it in the front room to whoops and cheers. The kids run over and kiss the television, leaving kiss-marks all over the screen.

'We are back in *business*,' Krissi says, plugging it in, turning it on, and lighting the front room back up with its beautiful, flickering glow. We watch the news for the first time in months, and the weather, and cookery programmes. *Spitting Image* have made a John Major puppet that's all grey, and can't understand why the economy is going down the pan. There aren't as many jokes.

'Telly was funnier when Margaret Thatcher was Prime Minister,' Lupin says, wisely.

That night, we sit up until 3am watching *Hammer House of Horror*, and eating piles of grated cheese. I love money. A broken thing can become unbroken. I *knew* I could prove Paul Tillich wrong. All I *did* need was some money. Money makes everything better.

FIFTEEN

Finally, the call comes – Kenny asks me down to another editorial meeting: 'It feels like we haven't seen you in a while, Wilde.'

For a moment, I blink at the name – it's been so long since I invented Dolly Wilde, and no one else has used that name in weeks.

'Thursday, midday, Wilde,' Kenny says. 'Come with ideas. God knows we could use them.'

It looks like I have been forgiven, for whatever I did wrong in my John Kite feature. Or, at least, I am being given another chance.

Excited by hearing Dolly's name again, I remember how much I loved her, and I resurrect her in earnest.

I prepare Dolly for London like I am her lady's maid: in the sink, I first bleach her hair, and then dye it cherry red – the colour of Dorothy's shoes, the colour of Miki Berenyi, from Lush. I build Dolly's eyes up, with swooshes of black eyeliner; I dress her in hold-up stockings, a black dress and her top hat.

I have made my notes, now, you see, on how to build a girl, and put her out in the world. Everyone drinks. Everyone smokes. Boozy Miki Berenyi is a damn fine woman. You come into a room, and say things, like you're in a play. You fake it 'til you make it. You discuss sex like it's a game. You have adventures. You don't quote musicals. Whatever everyone else is doing, you do that. You say things to be heard, rather than to be right.

You keen at street-lights, thinking they are the sun.

Wolverhampton train station, and I get onto the train like I am a bullet, being shot out of a dirty gun. The view from the window is like flicking through a book: rooftops, back gardens, canals – wastelands like plates of over-boiled cabbage. I can't wait wait wait to get out of this town, and be in London again. I'm going to make every moment like a hot mad dream that I can sick back up into my mouth, at will, and taste again and again when I'm back here, eating chapattis and staring at dirty walls.

When you come out of the tunnel, outside Euston Station, the walls are high, and white, and draped with ivy. It looks like you are entering ancient, wealthy Rome.

D&ME. Lift. Corridor. Going straight into the always-deserted Ladies, I head to the mirror.

'Hello again,' I say to myself. I'm prepared, this time. I have a packet of fags in one hand – Silk Cut, the cigarettes of the working-class woman – and, in the other, a bottle of booze. I've made an executive decision to start drinking, here, in front of my peers at the magazine. This is what I do now.

It had taken me a long time to decide which bottle of booze I was going to buy, and bring down here. It seems to be a key thing in being adult – your drink of choice. In books, people make snap judgements as to your character, wholly based on what drink you choose.

'Ah, a whisky man!' they say. Or, 'But of *course* – champagne!'

In the end – in the off-licence by the station, next to a shaking tramp – I went for the bottle of Mad Dog 20/20, the bright green 'fortified wine' so popular in the nineties.

Not only is it cheap, and a cheerful colour, but I have also observed that this is the empty bottle most regularly found next to makeshift campfires of burnt bed-springs and car batteries, on The Green. This has worked by way of a very successful low-rent viral marketing campaign on me – marking MD 20/20 out as the premiere alcohol of choice for young people such as myself.

I think about having a nip of Mad Dog *before* I go into the meeting – right now, in the Ladies – but decide not to.

There's no point in drinking if no one's watching.

The Meeting Room is nearly full when I walk in. They're sitting on chairs, and on the table, talking and smoking.

'Ladies and Gentlemen – MR ELTON JOHN!!!!!' I announce myself. Most people laugh – so I'm *already* winning compared to last time.

'Wilde,' Kenny says, looking up at me, and my hair, and my MD 20/20. 'You've gone Joplin.'

I open the bottle of Mad Dog, and offer it to the room.

'Aperitif?' I ask. Everyone demurs. I take a small swig from the bottle.

This is the first alcohol I have ever drunk. It's fucking appalling – a brutal assault on primarily, it feels, my eyes, which bulge, and fill with tears.

'Ah, thank God. That's better,' I say, putting the bottle down on the table, and wiping my mouth with the back of my hand. Fake it 'til you make it. 'Last night was *vicious*.'

There is more amused laughter. This 'boozy rock child' thing is going down far better than all the stuff about *Annie*. I have, clearly, found my niche.

'Well, before Wilde locates and then throws a television out of the window, we'd better start this meeting,' Kenny says, kicking the door closed from where he sits.

If I had to review me at this Editorial Meeting, compared to my first one, I would give me a solid seven stars out of ten. Not only do I make three jokes that make the room laugh – on the subject of Prince being a sex symbol, I say, 'I'm sorry, but, speaking as a woman – which I almost always am – Prince is just too small to be sexy. Unless you put jump-leads up his arse, and used him as a vibrator.' BIG laugh for that one – but, by the end, I'm quite pissed, too.

If I'd had to guess, before, what 'being pissed' felt like, I would never have guessed this unusual result: your knees feel warm, and your anxiety alchemises down into something syrupy, and pleasant, and malleable. Like all medicines, it tastes revolting – but it makes you better. *It makes you better.* If I had just four spoonfuls of this a day, I would never need to bite my knuckles again. Alcohol is the cure for biting, and worry. Mary Poppins drinks her spoonful of rum punch. John Kite watches her, lasciviously. My thoughts spiral up, on a pleasant alcohol vortex.

At the end of the meeting, Kenny gives the customary indication that the business is over – 'Off we jolly well fuck to the pub!' – and this time, off I jolly well fuck to the pub, too.

This is the second pub I've ever been in – and Dublin didn't count, really, because I only drank Coke in there.

This time, however – expansively medicined on the MD 20/20 – I suddenly realise that, of all the buildings in the world – art galleries and hospitals and libraries and good homes – pubs are the *best* kind of building. As my dad has always insisted, they are the palaces of the proletariat. The castles of cunts.

In 1993, pubs are at the height of their splendidness, and nobility. Every street corner in every city is studded with one of these glorious Victorian citadels: opulent with gold-gilt mirrors, huge mullioned windows, and tables varnished and re-varnished brown so many times, that they look like they've been lacquered with beef gravy.

Each table has an ashtray in the centre – and, when you all sit down, you realise that this is the hub of your group.

Through the afternoon and evening, the table will whirl round and round, faster and faster, like a wheel – but as long as you can keep flicking your fag-ash into the hub, at the centre, you will not fall off the table, or go flying out of the door. It is good of pubs to put their ashtrays in the places least prone to centrifugal gravity. Landlords are men of safety, and science. These buildings have been proven to work.

'Dolly – what do you want?'

The staff of *D&ME* have taken a large table, and Kenny is getting the drinks in. I have £4 in my purse, which I reach for, but Kenny gestures for me to put it away.

'What you drinking?' he asks, again.

'Another MD 20/20 would go down nicely, sir,' I say. Kenny looks at me.

'Yes – I don't think they sell Mad Dog here,' Kenny says, carefully. 'Although we could go and ask one of the tramps under Waterloo Roundabout if they could sell you a shot. I'm sure you could trade it in for a … rat, or a damp newspaper, something.'

I think of all the other drinks I've ever heard of. I can't think of many. I keep thinking of Cary Grant in an airport lounge, asking for something – but I can't remember if it's a 'High Ball', or a 'Screw Ball', and I don't want to get it wrong. What drinks *are* there?

'A cider and soda, please,' I say, eventually. Kenny stares at me.

'A cider … and soda?' he repeats.

'Yes!' I say, brightly. 'It's a Midlands thing. Sir.'

ZZ looks up at me, momentarily. He's from the Midlands. He knows it's not a Midlands thing.

'Well, I'm living and learning,' Kenny says, going over to the bar and putting the order in. I can see the bar man's reaction to 'Cider and soda'. Kenny shrugs at him. 'It's apparently big in the Midlands,' he tells him. 'You may wish to make note of the recipe – lest Slade come to town.'

When Kenny brings it over, saying 'Your cider and soda, Wilde' – clearly still amused by the whole thing – I reply, 'Thank you very much, sir.'

'Are you, in fact, being Elvis Presley there?' Kenny asks.

'Yes, sir,' I reply. 'Thank you very much, sir.'

'Okay,' he replies.

The editor raises his glass. 'Cheers, everyone!'

'Cheers!'

We all clink glasses. It feels like the Three Musketeers, clinking swords. I'm in a gang I'm in a gang I'm in a gang.

'Is there a reason you're all in black?' Kenny asks, sitting next to me.

'It's for all the future lovers I'll kill,' I say, cheerfully. I feel *very* cheerful. Invincibly cheerful. Like Debbie Reynolds in *The Unsinkable Molly Brown*. I could so easily do a musical number *right now*. Instead, after ten minutes of discussing REM ('I've known them for five years. Wankers,' Kenny says) I feel brave enough to finally ask Kenny why I've had so little work recently.

'Kenny – why aren't I getting any more big features?'

'Well,' Kenny says, awkwardly, shifting in his seat. 'Ah. Wilde. The thing is. Your John Kite interview …'

'What?' I say, with all the braveness of King Arthur.

'We were kind of … disappointed, to be honest,' he said, not unkindly. 'You want the truth?'

No! Of course I don't!

'Yes.'

'It read a bit … fannish,' Kenny says, almost apologetically. 'You sounded like some hysterical teenage girl at Heathrow Airport, banging on the doors and shouting "WE WANT THE ROLLERS!"'

He looks at me, and then remembers I *am* a hysterical teenage girl, and that I also probably don't know who the Bay City Rollers are.

'No offence,' he adds. Then, gentler: 'Hey – do you have a bit of a crush on John Kite?'

'No,' I say, miserably. It's an obvious 'No' of 'Yes'.

'Because it felt like the last paragraph was basically a marriage proposal. You know? I mean, we've all been there. But Dolly – we're music *critics*, not … *fans*. I'm thinking of you. How you come across to the *reader*.'

I can't really hear him, because, in my head, I am very busily writing a massive note to myself, that reads: 'CRUCIAL INFORMATION FOR THE REST OF YOUR LIFE: DO NOT WRITE LIKE A FAN, OR BE IN LOVE.'

Kenny can see that I'm on the verge of crying, and so he steers the conversation into less fraught territory.

'And your musical reference points were a bit … off. You compare Kite's album to Deacon Blue and one track off *The Best of Simon & Garfunkel*. No mention of American Music Club, or Nick Drake, or Tim Buckley?'

I shrug, in further misery. Nick Drake is next on my list of albums to get out of the library, when I get some money. And I've never even heard of Tim Buckley. How many fucking bands do you have to listen to, to be a proper music journalist?

If it's more than 200, this is going to take *ages*. I can only get five albums out at a time on my teenage ticket.

'Can I claim getting CDs out of the library on expenses?' I ask, suddenly. 'They're 20p each. Can I claim it like travel, and "refreshments"? It would be useful.'

For a minute, Kenny seems so astonished that, for the first time I've ever witnessed, he is silent. He finally says:

'Wilde – you can get any album you want. Ring up the PRs and they'll send you a Jiffy bag full of every Godforsaken hairy attention-seeking bunch of onanists, bed-wetters and arse-holes in the canon of Western rock. You can fill your boots with as much Superchunk, Ned's Atomic Dustbin and Bum Gravy as you can handle. And then, if you decide you don't like a particular platter of substandard grebo hackery, you can sell it, for a tidy sum. Bryce Cannon of this parish has been subsidising a healthy, by which I mean fatal, cocaine addiction on the proceeds of this system for nearly four years, now. This is Club Tropicana. Linx are free.'

He looks at me.

'Linx are a band, Wilde.'

Four hours later: we're at a party, somewhere in Soho.

We'd left the pub at 5pm, in a gang. It is a majestic thing to walk out of a building, in a rangy booze-squad, and out into the very beginning of a long spring evening. The buildings on the South Bank are pale grey, like dirty bridesmaids; women in bright dresses, promenading to their next destination. London feels like an infinite toy. Evenings never end – they just, without you noticing, turn into tomorrow.

I was booked on the 7pm train back to Wolverhampton – but on the pavement, as I start to say goodbye, talk turned to the party they're all going to tonight.

'Come along,' Kenny said. 'Come out in the wrecking crew. *Disc & Music Echo* men are here – we drink your men and fuck your beer!'

'I should really go home,' I say. I do not want to go home.

'Your man John Kite's coming,' Kenny says, slyly.

'The last train to Wolverhampton is the 22:35,' Zee offers.

'And John Kite's coming,' Kenny says again, looking me right in the eye.

So here I am, at my first ever music industry party. First ever party, really – if you don't count wedding receptions for cousins. At the last one of those we went to, we sat underneath the buffet table and sucked the cream out of a whole plate of eclairs – then played a game where we went on the dance floor and high-kicked our shoes off to *Star Trekkin'* by The Firm. It was unfortunate that Lupin was wearing wellington boots, and that cousin Ali was sitting where she was sitting, but generally, it was an amazing night out.

This party is very different to a cousin's wedding. The main problem is that I don't know anyone. Obviously I've come with all the *D&ME* people, but I still don't really know what to do with them. They walk in and stand by the bar – which, despite being free, has been abandoned by the staff – and wait, tetchily, to be served. I feel, in some odd way, that this is something I should be doing something about – not least because I can't join in on their conversation, about the band Faust, because I've never heard of Faust.

After two further minutes of waiting, I take matters into my own hands.

'What do you want, boys?' I ask – climbing over the bar, and starting to serve them. I am *bold* with MD 20/20 and cider.

'I'll have a Jack and Coke, Wilde – but, erm, should you do this?' Kenny asks.

'We call this "Wolverhampton self-service",' I say, enjoying being legendary. 'I once ran the bar at the Posada pub for twenty minutes on Christmas Eve. Given how much I was helping out, I thought it was churlish when they later banned me.'

All of this is a total lie – I've never drunk alcohol in a pub before today – but everyone seems excited by my legendariness, and what is the point of being seventeen years old if you can't totally make up your back-story? I'm just doing what Bob Dylan did – but in a dress, with some free drinks.

Rob Grant's giggling delightedly, like a girl – 'I'll have a beer, Wilde' – so I double-up on my legendariness, and throw some nuts onto the bar.

'Snacks, anyone?' I ask. But then the bar man comes and does a very bad face at me, so I have to jump back over, saying, 'Just trying to help a brother out!' in a cheerful way, and knock back the gin I served myself in one throw – basking in the *D&ME* boys' camply scandalised air.

'We've got a live one here,' Rob says, approvingly.

I love being 'a live one'. It is an admirable substitute/ upgrade for 'being able to fit in'.

Still, once the 'freelance barmaid' excitement is over, I continue not being able to join in with the resumed conversation about Faust.

John Kite isn't here yet – 'He's shooting a video in East London. He'll be here by nine' – and so I wander away from the *D&ME* crew, with a good two hours to kill before I have someone I can party *with*.

A party is definitely a collaborative effort, I observe, looking at all the other people having conversations, and dancing together, and, in the corner, kissing. Oh, kissing. I watch the kissing until it's obvious I'm watching the kissing, and then I walk away, quickly. It's bad to be seen watching kissing.

By now, my un-kissed kiss feels like gunpowder on my lips – if anyone comes near me with even the vague heat of attraction, I will go up in a sheet of flame – mouth first. I feel a sexual fury, for a moment. Oh, God – why won't you let me fuck you! *All* of you! *Everyone in this room.* I have a feeling I'll only ever properly make sense in bed, on my back. You would understand what I mean if we were there.

Anyway. Over the next ninety minutes, I try a variety of different tactics to make it look like I'm not lonely at this party. My findings on how to 'party on your own' are as follows:

1) The buffet. There is a fabulous spread here, and no girl can truly say she is alone if she is standing next to a plate of honey-glazed miniature chipolatas! I eat six, thoughtfully – then worry that I simply look like an abandoned girl eating a lot of small sausages. Under the common teenage misapprehension that anyone is a) observing and b) gives any kind of a fuck what I'm doing, I then take two paper plates, and load them up – as if getting food for a friend, who is over the other side of the room. I give this scenario all I've got – deliberating over slices of miniature quiche, and then rejecting them, because my friend – 'Claire' – does not like quiche, 'remembering' that, unlike me, what 'Claire' really likes are Scotch eggs – then walk across the dance floor, 'looking' for my 'friend' 'Claire', until me and my two loaded plates reach …

2) … the toilet, where I bolt the door, and eat both platefuls. When I finish them, I can't fit the two paper plates into the Bin of Shame with all the sanitary towels in it, because of the uneaten Scotch eggs, so I leave them neatly stacked on the floor, instead. By the time I leave the toilet, a small queue has built up outside. The woman at the front of the

queue looks in, and sees the plates with their Scotch eggs, on the floor. 'They will hatch soon!' I tell her, cheerfully. 'They are dragon-eggs! Good luck!'

3) Being a very busy journalist. If you're a writer, are you ever *really* off-duty? The human condition never has the evening off – it must be reported upon, 24/7. I sit up the corner with my notebook, and write down all the astonishing observations that are occurring to me. When I find the notebooks, years later, I see that this consists of a drawing of a cat wearing a top hat; my bank account number – which I am trying to learn by heart; and, on a page all on its own, 'I wish Krissi was here.'

4) A conversation with a stranger! 'Do you know where the toilet is?' 'Yes – over there.' 'Ha – thank you.' I'm glad I look like the kind of person you can trust to tell you where the toilet is. Whenever Krissi gets asked, at a party, he always points people towards a cupboard, and then watches, laughing. God I miss Krissi.

5) And, finally, smoking. There's no two ways about it – this shit is useful. I have long observed its application in society, and concluded it to be needful. Everyone smokes – it just has to be done. Having finally acknowledged this, last night, I had bought a packet of ten Silk Cut from the newsagents up town. This shop is legendary for its relaxed attitude to selling cigarettes to children. Until recently, they used to vend a single cigarette, threaded through a Polo Mint, for 15p – in order to capture lunch-time smokers who needed to freshen their breath before going back in for PE. Sitting on the grass outside St Peter's Cathedral, I doggedly taught myself to smoke. I'm impressed by how determined I am, because it is – and there's no two ways about this – filthy. It tastes of the worst *brown* ever. It's like

sucking in everything you'd ever put in a bin – ashtrays, burnt pub carpet, yellow snow, death. Dadda at 2am. As my lovely clean throat and pink lungs sucked in the smoke, I felt very, very sorry for me: this is not what a child should be doing. In a right world, I should have needed to do nothing more than spend that money on eight Curly Wurlys and a couple of Refreshers.

But here, now, at the party, I am glad I have the cigarettes in my rucksack – because I now have a little task to attend to, and keep me busy. I go over to the window, take the packet out, light a cigarette, and smoke it, while looking thoughtfully out on the street below. I try to remember how I've seen Elizabeth Taylor holding cigarettes, and hold it up by my face. In my reflection in the window, I see that it looks less *Cat on a Hot Tin Roof*, and more like I'm doing shadow-puppets of a swan. I put my arm back down, and cough a bit. Jesus, it is *disgusting*.

'Aaaaaaaah,' says a man standing next to me, lighting his fag. 'You've gotta love a fag.'

'Yes indeed,' I say, in a slightly strangled voice. 'I've been dying for this all day. And then of course,' I continue, with the dark humour I presume all smokers will have, 'I'll be dying for it *literally* when I get to fifty!'

It seems this is the wrong thing to say.

'Yeah,' he says, before wandering away.

That's okay. I've got other things I can concentrate on. In the street below, a posh-looking drunk man is reading the card of a prostitute, Blue-Tacked up by a doorbell. He's examining it with all the forensic care I presume he puts into reading a wine list.

'What are you looking for?' I ask him, in my head. 'What woman will go best with your main course of terrible, horny loneliness?'

I speculate, briefly, on how different the world would be if it were run by women. In that world, if you were a lonely, horny woman – as I am. As I always am – you'd see Blu-tacked post-cards by Soho doorways that read, 'Nice man in cardigan, 24, will talk to you about The Smiths whilst making you cheese-on-toast + come to parties with you. Apply within.'

But this is not that world.

I watch the posh, drunk man – obviously not captivated by what he has read – stagger off down the street, into the dark-ness, still alone. I lean my head on the glass. I am still smoking.

At 9.59pm, John Kite finally turns up – a flurry by the door heralds his arrival, and the sound of a pissed Welsh man going, 'I've got to get this bloody coat off – the rain has made it smell like a zoo. An *animalarium*.'

I go over and there he is – taking off his huge, soaking fur coat, and hanging it on the coat-rack, wet hair plastered over his eye, fag in mouth.

'Duchess!' he says, seeing me. His hug – huge – is the fourth-best thing to ever have happened to me, after birthdays, Christmas, and the Easter when it snowed on the first roses. I feel the battered gold rings on his hands press into my back.

'You're like a bad drink in a good world. I didn't know you'd be here! That's fucking – *Gold Run*, man. Where's the gin?' he asks.

I hand him a gin and tonic. I bought it at exactly 9.29pm – anticipating his arrival. Most of the ice has melted now. The drink is quite watery.

'Do you want me to get you one with ice?' Ed Edwards asks. Kite has a small entourage with him.

'No, no – this counts as the glass of water between drinks,' Kite says, knocking half of it back in one. 'It's healthy.' He coughs. Kite's entourage are still hanging around him.

'Shall we go for a fag?' I ask Kite. I am holding the packet in my hand – the box that acts as a shield against loneliness, each cigarette a tiny wand that I can wave, to re-order a room however I wish. With this cigarette, I can spirit Kite away from people.

'Yes!' Kite says.

We're over by the window – entourage left way behind – before he realises what's happening.

'You smoking now, Duchess?' he asks.

'I thought it was time for me to get another hobby,' I say, with a daring air, trying to light it.

Kite leans forward. 'It's just, most people smoke them the other way round.'

He gently takes the cigarette out of my mouth, and puts it back in the right way. My mouth fills with the taste of burnt filter.

'But never be afraid to experiment, sweetness,' he says, lighting the proper end with a flourish. 'If anyone could invent Backwards Cigarettes, it's absolutely *you*, my love.'

For ten minutes, I'm about as happy as I've ever been. Standing in this big window with John, smoking our fags – clever decision, me – and gabbling about what we've been up to. He tells me an anecdote about touring in Canada that creases me, and I tell him about Lupin's teeth and play it for laughs, very successfully, I think. At one point, he takes my hands in his and says, 'And thank you for that *lovely* interview you wrote with me. You made me sound like Owain Glyndwr with a twelve-string, bombing his own castle. It was a beautiful thing to read on the tour bus. I read it out loud to Ed Edwards until he told me I was acting like a monkey in a zoo, touching its own cock and laughing.'

But then John grinds out his fag, knocks his drink back in one, and does the equivalent of pressing a massive cannon-snout right against my heart.

'Right – I gotta go now, Duchess. It's bed-time for John-John.' I laugh.

'You're leaving early? Kite, the only way you'll ever leave anywhere early is on a gurney – paramedic pumping your heart and shouting, "WHAT DID YOU TAKE, JOHN? JOHN, TELL ME WHAT YOU TOOK."'

There is no way this joker is leaving early.

This joker is leaving early.

'Seriously, Dutch. We're doing MTV in Holland at 8am tomorrow. I have to go,' he says. 'I've been read a riot warning. Apparently I am never again allowed to stay up all night with you, then die by a swimming pool.'

I look up and I can see Ed Edwards holding the door open for him – waiting for him to go through it, into the car, and away, to Holland.

'Fucking hell – you really are.'

I am silent for nearly ten seconds – the longest, I think, I have ever been silent in my life. I climb into a coffin. I nail down the lid. I basically die during this silence.

'Well,' I say, finally. 'Well. Good luck. Remember – always ride out as if meeting your nemesis.'

He leans in, and kisses me on the mouth. I don't know what it means. I just stand there, and get kissed. One kiss. As gentle as snow.

My heart explodes like a swarm of bees.

'Goodbye, Duchess,' he says.

And then he is gone – my entire point of being in the room; in London; alive. My £18.90 train-fare and my whole life getting into a taxi, leaving me this room full of people – a party – as a parting gift.

I have never wanted anything less.

*

I stand there, alone, for a few minutes, his kiss still shouting in my bones. While I try and work out what I think, I smoke another cigarette. God, they are *useful*. I should have started this *much* younger! Perhaps if I'd been smoking while I was still at school, I wouldn't have felt so lonely!

This is the first time a man has ever touched my mouth. Ever. It was just a goodbye kiss – dry, quiet – but it was the first time anyone had ever not kissed to the left or to the right of me – but gone right into the centre, as men and women do.

'The mouth is the heart of the face,' I think, taking a glass of free wine off the table and knocking it back; hands vibrating; bee-headed. I don't really know what to do with myself. I want to do more of the kiss. I want to finish the kiss – go on and on and get to the bit where someone just eats the clothes off my body, and just fucking *does* me. *Why* do I keep not having sex? What is going on? This is a massive operational error.

I look around the party. I should go and be in this party. Zee is over by the bar, holding a pint and talking to someone. Zee is nice, my five gins tell me. I go and join him.

'Hiyarrrr!' I say. 'Hiyarrrrrr!'

'Dolly – this is Tony Rich,' Zee says, introducing me. 'Anthony, this is Dolly.'

'Hello,' Rich says.

I know who Rich is, of course – he's *D&ME's* star writer. Exotic courtesy of doing his degree at Harvard – he's been to *America*! Where *Marilyn* is from! – Rich is both incredibly clever, and incredibly vicious. His vibe is a general dissatisfaction with the majority of music that's in the charts. Last week, he described jolly indie Midlands' heroes The Wonder Stuff as 'The sound of five idiots laughing with their mouths open. They are the point where music finishes its amazing, expansive outward journey into space, docks at a desolate space-station, and then starts proudly colonising the rubbish-chutes, holding up turds as treasure.'

Anyway, none of that is important right now. What *is* important is that I've just realised that Tony Rich is incredibly hot. A tall boy with a big mouth and very pale skin, whose eyes are as clever as rockets – guns – the sun – and the *exact* colour of Coca-Cola.

I am astonished that they don't have reports on how scorching he is on the News pages, every week. Why would they not headline this news? The paper has really dropped the ball here. This is what comes of having an all-male environ-ment: not only do they not advise you to wear a sports bra in the mosh-pit, but Grade A perving opportunities for the ladies are being missed left, right and centre.

I can't believe how kind the timing is on this issue: thirty seconds after John Kite, my future husband, has left – leaving me hot, and useless, with kiss – the world has served me up my second future husband. Or maybe I'll have an affair with Rich, while I'm married to John. Or maybe I'll just have sex with both of them – proper, total sex – and then marry Gonzo from *The Muppet Show*, as I'd planned since I was nine. It's all still definitely to play for. I am *full* of potential right now.

'You're Jewish, aren't you?' I ask Rich, in my best 'chat' manner. 'I found out I'm half-Jewish last week, too! On my mother's side!'

'Mazeltov,' Rich says, laconically. I didn't find out I was half-Jewish last week at *all*, of course – Mum is from Peterborough, and her parents are from the Hebrides – but I *have* read all of Harpo Marx's autobiography (*Harpo Speaks!*, Limelight, 1985), so I know what a 'shiksa' is, also 'pinochle', and I sometimes *wish* I was Jewish – and that's got to be basically the same thing. Besides, lying has worked very well for me tonight. I'm just making me up as I go along! I'm jazz! I drink another gin.

'There aren't many of us in Wolverhampton,' I sigh, in the most Jewish way I can.

I consider running down Wolverhampton as a town full of gentiles, but I'm still not sure how you pronounce it – I've only ever read the word – and I figure it would be pretty gentile to pronounce 'gentile' wrong, so I abandon my burgeoning ethnicity to ask: 'So – who are we slagging off? I hate them too. Deal me in.'

'Just discussing your man John Kite,' Zee says, mild-eyed and blinking. 'Trying to work out how much he does for effect.'

'*Effect*?' I say. I am so astonished I momentarily stop perving Rich – which is a *lot* of astonishment. I feel as offended as a Christian who's just walked into a conversation on whether the cross that Jesus carries at Calvary secretly had retractable wheels – like carry-on luggage – and that Jesus has, in effect, cheated.

'*Effect*? I don't think John Kite's *pretending* to be John Kite,' I say. 'I've hung out with him. In Dublin, he pissed next to me while I was in a bath, wearing his fur coat and smoking a fag. John Kite is 100 per cent John Kite, 100 per cent of the time. I believe in him like I believe in Elvis singing psalms on Sunday.'

'Is that a Eurythmics album-track you've just misquoted, in a defence of John Kite?' Zee asks.

'Yes. I panicked.'

'Well done,' Zee nods.

Rich has winced at the mention of the Eurythmics – a band, I now recall, that he once described as, 'The sound of approximately nothing, masturbating while watching itself in the mirror.'

Not only do I love the Eurythmics – me and Krissi do a great version of 'Sex Crime'; he's always Annie Lennox – but I've also masturbated whilst watching myself in a mirror, as well. Well, the back of a CD. The CD's hole kept lining up with my hole. It was very annoying. Maybe me and Rich will not marry, after all.

'People become aware of their own legends pretty quickly,' Rich says. 'After you've read half a dozen reviews of yourself, every artist loses the innocence that fuelled their original persona. Every act is condemned to eventually turn into their own tribute act. ABBA had turned into Bjorn Again *years b*efore Bjorn Again came along.'

'What's *my* legend?' I ask Rich.

Rich looks me up and down – taking in the eyeliner, the top hat, the laddered hold-ups, the short dress, the cigarette. I like him looking at me.

'Well, you're still making it,' he says, looking me right in the eye. 'But I suspect it includes trouble.'

His mouth is outrageous. I don't care what it's saying. I just want it on me. Christ, imagine it on your belly. Imagine him dipping down, and making the fur wet. Like in the pictures in *The Whole Earth Catalog* – but happening to me. To my actual me, everywhere.

Dear God! GOD! GOD IN HEAVEN! Attend my words, now! Because I warn you – there's going to have to be some kissing, soon. Some kissing – if I'm not going to die. Kissing will have to happen to wet my lips, and cool the heat out of me – I have something in my mouth that needs to be taken. Like how baby birds take seed, from the mouths of their mothers. I wonder if I could fit Rich's whole mouth in mine – if I held his head perfectly still, and pressed up against him. If I *made* him.

If I just went round and made people kiss me. Maybe that's what I should do.

I am mad with kissing.

I have to catch my train.

On the last train home, an hour later – still half-drunk on wine, and gin, and kiss, and Rich's mouth – I think about this. I think about the whole day – smoking, and drinking, and the important information that interviews are not love-letters; and that I am a journalist now – not a fan. And that I am trouble. I must be – Rich has reviewed me, and he is the cleverest critic I know.

In my bag, I have my notebook, in which I'd started making notes for the next album I am supposed to be reviewing, by a failing band called The Rational.

The album is resolutely average throughout – just an indie potboiler – and I have started to sketch out whimsical descriptions of the guitars, and made a couple of jokes about the band coming from Dunedin – 'They Dunedin some tunes, to be honest.'

It's all very jolly stuff – just a gentle piss-take of their essential hopelessness. Right at the end, I have started to describe the lead singer, Alec Sanclear – a rather dim, vain man with a blond mullet, spiked up on top: 'It makes him look a bit like someone stuck a picture of a confused man's face on a cockatoo,' I have written.

I scribble everything out except this last line, and start again.

'Oh, God – why has this cockatoo-haired cunt been allowed out of his cage to make a *second* album?' I write. 'Can we not ring some kind of helpline, and send in the RSPB with big nets – to re-capture him? Or perhaps we could drug some raisins, and leave them scattered around his squat – like they do in

Danny – Champion of the World. Actually, yeah – that would work. That plan's a goer. So we spike The Rational's rider with Seconal, yeah, go into the audience, and watch, as flocks of hapless Sanclears fall from the sky. Wheee! Thud. Wheeee! Thud! There they go. Crashing from the ceiling.

'That last bit, by the way, is also the perfect onomatopoeic description of pretty much every track on here: it's all wee and thud.'

I am on the last train home, being trouble.

SIXTEEN

The next two months I feel drunk, permanently. Half of this is because of the instant success of my new role: that of a hell-raising gunslinger. Trouble.

I rock up at gigs, with my notebook, and watch a succession of middling indie-bands with a sarcastic look on my face, who I then go home and eviscerate. It's so much easier than what I was doing before – being nice about bands – and, if I'm honest, it's more fun. Why stand there trying to politely join in on a conversation about Faust, when you can just jump over the bar and give everyone STRONG DRINKS? Everyone loves a bad kid on a roll.

The subsequent reviews are a hit – my profile at the paper rockets. I'm working six days a week – sitting in my bedroom, with my latest financial acquisition – a brand new computer – turning out hatchet jobs at 7p per word. Trouble is profitable. Trouble is a good, steady job. Trouble is the future.

'If you want to get ahead, get a hate,' Kenny says, gleefully, as he gives me lead review after lead review.

The thrill is giddying – letters start appearing about me on the Letters Page, bands talk about me in interviews. For someone who lives in a house without mirrors, seeing yourself talked about by others is exhilarating. I'd always had a slight worry that I might not exist – that I was a very long dream I was having. Or maybe that Krissi was having, and that he was desperately trying to wake up from.

But I am incontrovertibly real now – now that other people are discussing me. Now that my byline is on page 7, and page 9, and three from pages 17 to 20, and the Gossip Page has a picture of me, drunk, at a party, standing on a table in my top hat, captioned, 'Slash has let himself go.'

Because the other reason I feel drunk, permanently, is because I am drunk, permanently. Well, not permanently. But every night, at every gig I go to, I drink – who would let a penny of their £20 'refreshment budget' go undrunk, save the mad? In the long days, the unnerving, violin-like screeching of worry can be firmly sat-up with the thought, 'By 9pm, I shall be *partying*.' And besides, I'm drinking for practical reasons. Having spent all my money on my computer, I walk home from gigs, down the A449 to our estate, and the alcohol keeps me warm, and means I do not stint on the top-notes when I sing. *High Land, Hard Rain* by Aztec Camera gets me as far as the Springhill turn off, and then up the black, empty streets to our house – past Violet's house.

'What did you say to them?' I wonder, as I walk past – the net curtains like stiff white cataracts on the windows, making the house look myopic, and stubborn. 'What will happen next?'

At one gig in Wolverhampton – drunk, of course – I bump into my goth cousin Ali.

'Alright,' she nods, over her pint. I note that she is not a goth any more – she's now dressed like a classic shoe-gazing indie-kid: black ankle-boots, jeans, stripey Breton top, huge fringe.

'Ali!' I say. 'Oh my God! Hello! I love John Kite too, now! I slept in his bathtub! I heard him piss!'

'I've gone off him,' Ali says, flatly. 'I'm into The Nova. They're brill.'

I have no idea who The Nova are.

'They're over there,' Ali says, nodding towards a corner of the club where five skinny boys in black jeans with black hair, also in Breton tops, are hanging, sullenly.

'They're *nova* there, you mean,' I say. '*Nova* there. They're *nova* there.'

'I'm shagging the bass-player,' Ali says, adding: 'I've heard him piss, and all. And do the other.'

'I've never heard a popstar do the other,' I admit. Ali *always* has one up on me.

'I wonder who does the loudest poos in pop?' I muse. 'I bet Celine Dion has one of those fancy porcelain Victorian toilets, with all flowers on the inside of the bowl, which she fills with millions of tiny dry pellets – like a rabbit. Pting ting ting ting ting!'

'Ar,' Ali says. Her expression doesn't change – it's the same, cold, blank face she's had since birth – but she's clearly intrigued; as she then says, 'Prince does it secretly behind the sofa – like a cat. And then scratches at the carpet a bit, before going off to shag Sheena Easton.'

'I reckon Nick Cave emits a pellet from his mouth, like an owl. He opens his mouth and it comes out – with all little bones in it.'

We carry on like this for a while, until we've described the toilet-habits of pretty much everyone in the Top 40. Then:

'So – did you shag him, then?' Ali asks, after a contemplative, fag-smoking silence. 'Did you shag John Kite?'

'Maybe,' I say.

'No, then,' Ali says. 'You still look like a virgin, anyway.'

'I am not a virgin!'

'You am.'

'I'm not! I know … what spunk tastes of!'

Ali looks at me.

'It tastes of bleach.'

I once read this in an interview with Sally from the band Bleach, who was explaining why the band was called 'Bleach'. Apparently, Sally's information was good, as Ali looks satisfied.

But her inquiry has stirred something in me. My un-kissed kiss is now a palpable weight – like a goitre; or an unlucky horse-shoe, on a chain, that I must drag round with me. Sometimes, it feels like it stops me talking. Sometimes, it feels like it stops me breathing.

'I haven't got off with anyone for ages, though,' I confess, which is true: my seventeenth birthday has now passed, and, in every year, I haven't got off with anyone. An entire life *is* ages. John Kite doesn't count – there were no tongues.

'I'm gagging for it.'

Ali looks at me for a second, and then nods towards The Nova.

'See the lad with the band?' she asks. There is a gangly youth of indiscriminate hair and face standing with them.

'He'll get off with you. He's "The Kisser".'

I look at him again. The Kisser. I don't know how to describe him. He's just … normal. All the parts in the right place, and facing the right way. He's got, like … a head, and stuff. Legs. Doc Martens. The Kisser.

'He will get off with you, if you want,' Ali says. 'That's what he does. He's got off with all my mates. You know those things they have outside shops that's like a giraffe, and you put 10p in and have a ride? He's like one of those. You just … get on him, then get off with him. He's a man-slag.'

I look at The Kisser again. I then, because I've had a couple of drinks, look at my watch. I think subconsciously I'm seeing if it's time for me to have my first proper kiss. My watch tells me that it's 9.47pm on Wednesday, 17th May, 1993 – but then, it is a little fast. Like me! I'm about to be fast! Because I'm going to get my first kiss!

'How does it … work, then?' I ask.

Ali starts walking across the dance floor, and I follow her.

'Alright, lads,' Ali says, to The Nova, and The Kisser.

'Alright, Al,' they reply.

'This is Jo – Dolly Wilde. My cousin.'

'You're Dolly Wilde from *Disc & Music Echo*?' one of The Nova asks, looking impressed.

'Yes,' I reply. 'Almost all the time.'

'Whoa – nice one!' He then frowns. 'Hang on, though – you slagged off Uncle Tupelo last week. They're alright, Uncle Tupelo.'

Oh, for fuck's sake – I've come over here to procure a kiss – not get drawn into an argument about Americana.

'I'm off duty at the moment!' I say, with an expansive hand-gesture.

'Was yours the review with all that stuff about how Neil Young owns, like, 70 per cent of all the buffaloes in America?' another member of The Nova asks.

'Yeah,' I say.

'Is that true?'

'I believe so,' I reply.

'Is it just me, or is that weird?' he asks. 'Neil Young owning all the buffalo. That's just weird.'

'Yes,' I say. 'It's like finding out that Mike Nesmith from The Monkees' mum invented Tippex.'

The Nova are astounded.

'She never!'

'She most surely did,' I reply. 'Presumably after she saw how badly her son had typed the phrase "The Monkees", and needed to correct it with some kind of … liquid paper.'

Ali's boyfriend reveals how the first time he ever got high, it was from sniffing Tippex – 'Well, it was own-brand corrector fluid' – and the conversation veers off into a knowledgeable, five-minute discussion of what, exactly, can be bought at a stationer's shop that gets you high. Glue, marker-pens, butane gas re-fills for lighters – I had no idea. Basically, the WH Smith in the Mander Centre is Wolverhampton's version of Studio 54. It's a narcotic goldmine. I had no idea. I've only ever used it to buy staples.

But none of this is getting me kissed, so I stare at Ali – who then tactfully takes The Nova away 'to do … stuff', and leaves me with The Kisser.

As I've not been kissed before, I'm not really sure how you activate this function on a man. I think of all the kissing I've seen. I know that saying, 'You may now kiss the bride!' has a 100 per cent success-rate – but that seems inappropriate here. Leia got Han to kiss her before they swung across a chasm in a spaceship on a rope together – but that's going to take a lot more infrastructure than I have available.

I'm just trying to remember how the kissing starts in *The Sound of Music* – usually, when it gets to the soppy bits, we fast-forward them, because Lupin starts screaming 'YUCK!', and all I can recall is images of Christopher Plummer and Julie Andrews pursuing each other around a pergola at high speed – when The Kisser lives up to his name, and just … kisses me.

It appears to be some kind of 'Factory Pre-Set' kiss – one, two, three kisses on the lips, and then in with the tongue – but it's happening! I'm in a kiss! The captains of this nightclub are picking their teams of Sexually Active Teenagers – and my name, finally, has been called!

I carry on being in the kiss for a couple more minutes – it's a bit difficult, because my hair keeps getting in the way, and we have to keep removing it from our mouths. In the end, I get practical, say, 'Hang on a minute,' and put it into an easy, convenient ponytail – and then I get straight back into the kissing again. Kissing, as I always thought it would be, is brilliant: I would put it just below telly – but definitely above drinking, squeezing blackheads or fairgrounds. Or squeezing Krissi's blackheads, on his back – which he let me do one Christmas, if I promised never to tell anyone.

At one point, I open my eyes, and see Ali on the other side of the room, watching me – arms crossed, smoking a fag.

'*Get in there*,' she mouths.

Me and The Kisser kiss for nine minutes – I check on my watch, later – and then the band comes onstage, and The Kisser says, 'Oh, I like this song,' and goes off down the front, to mosh – but there are no hard feelings. The Kisser has done his job. I am grateful for his services. If I had needed sheep moving from one field to another, I would have called a shepherd. If I'd lost my wedding ring down the U-bend, I would have called a plumber. And as I needed my first kiss before I got another day older, I have used The Kisser. I feel better now.

'What's his name?' I ask Ali, later. 'The Kisser, I mean.'

'Gareth,' she says. We looked at each other.

'Let's just keep calling him The Kisser,' I say.

When I get back home, Krissi is in the front room, watching *Eurotrash*, with Lupin asleep on him.

'I thought it would be educational for him,' he says, looking down at Lupin. 'But he fell asleep before the naked male gimp cleaners came on.'

'I got my first kiss!' I tell him, triumphally. On the walk home, all I've been able to think about is telling Krissi. It seems very important to tell him what I did.

'Oh,' he says, still staring at the TV.

'First kiss! I did my first kiss!' I say, again.

'Right,' Krissi says.

'I didn't want you to be … worrying about it,' I say. 'I thought you might think there was something wrong with me. But nuh-uh! I'm someone people will kiss!'

Krissi looks at me.

'Was it Gareth, by any chance?' he asks. 'Looks like … an average boy?'

'Yes! Yes – it was Gareth!' I gasp. 'It was Gareth!'

'He got off with Fat Tommy last year,' Krissi says, factually.

I'm still working out what to do with my face when he adds, 'Dad wants to talk to you. He's in the garden. He's pissed.'

I'm pissed too, so that's okay – we can be pissed together! That's the point of being drunk!

At the bottom of the garden, Dadda's sitting on the bench that he made – of course – with a plank and some bricks. His cigarette hovers in the dark, above his hand, like a tiny orange marsh-light.

'Heya, Johan!' he says, making room for me. 'Good night?'

'Yeah,' I say, sitting next to him.

I like us sitting together like this. When I was younger, I was Dadda's Shopping Companion. He liked to be in the supermarket early, before anyone else was around, so we'd sit on the wall outside, waiting for it to open, and he'd tell me stories about what his life was like when he was a little boy, in a Shropshire village, with seven brothers and sisters.

'There was no benefits then,' he'd say, as we sat and waited – a teenage boy in a tabard rounding up last night's abandoned trolleys from the car park, with a thunderous rattle. 'The parish would come round and assess your needs, and if you had any furniture that could be sold – bang! Your parish money was gone. So when you got the knock on the door, your nanna would stall them at the door, and all the kids would grab the chairs and the tables, and go down the bottom of the garden and hand them over the wall, to the neighbours. And they'd do the same when the parish knocked on *their* doors. The whole street lumping mattresses over fences when the knock came. It would have looked fucking funny from an airplane. All this furniture, constantly emigrating, ahead of trouble.'

'There must have been a great sense of community,' I said, earnestly, swinging my legs in the early sun.

'Oh no – it was fucking horrible,' Dadda said, cheerfully. 'The war had just finished, and half the men in the village were shell-shocked and on the beers. Men used to knock their missuses around, and no one would say anything. "I've walked into a door," they'd say, with a black eye, at the butchers. It was grim, Johan. Everyone was a lot harder, back then. At school, the nuns would hit you with a ruler if you were left-handed.'

'Did they hit *you?*'

'Yeah! I was an angelic little thing. I was fucking gorgeous, love. And they'd have you up in front of the whole school – five whacks on the left palm – so you couldn't hold your pencil in it any more. Fucking cows.'

I think about Dadda's handwriting. He writes with his right hand now, and we've always made fun of the spidery, slopey script, with the occasional backwards letter. One of his favourite things about being diagnosed disabled is that he doesn't have to sign his full signature – 'Just an X! Like a fucking *spy*!'

'That's why I ran away and joined the band,' he said. 'Get out of that poxy little place. I came back six months later in flares out to *here*, and my hair down to my arse, with the rest of the band. We came back with hashish pipes from Turkey, and incense from London. Blew everyone's minds. They made the bass-player eat his tea sitting on the porch roof.'

'Why?'

'He was black. They'd never seen a spade in Shropshire before.'

'Where was he from?' I asked.

'Bilston,' Dadda replied.

I loved these conversations with Dadda. These stories of this utterly foreign place – here, right here, but twenty-five years before. So recent, but feeling as if it were nearer to medieval times than 1993, with its violent nuns, priests giving out money, hunger, rats, war and fear of dark-skinned men. It gave me the powerful sense that everything that made *my* world – benefits, multi-culturalism, rock 'n' roll, even writing with your left hand – were quite recent inventions – a world so new, we'd only just torn the wrapping-paper off. I saw what an achievement it was – the will of a small, countable number of men and women, who wrote, and thought, and marched, and sang. If you'd killed the right 200 people, this future would never have come at all. Perhaps this future had come so late because, previously, they *had* killed the right 200 people – over and over, through history.

Whenever Dadda tells me the stories of what it was like when he was young, I shiver again in relief and glee that I am here, now. I do not think I would have been me at any other time. I would not have been allowed. I know what happens to girls like me, in history. They are hard-handed, oily and unper-fumed in manual labour. They drudge so hard they look fifty at thirty. I would have been in a factory, or a field, with no books, or music, or trains down to London. I would have been one of a million sad cattle, standing in the rain, wholly unrecorded. I would not have been trouble, in my top hat, in London.

I let out a small, sympathetic 'Mooooo' to the Johanna of the sixteenth century.

'You what, kid?' Dadda says. I remember where I am: drunk, in the garden.

'Oh, nothing. Just glad I'm here,' I say, putting my head on his shoulder.

'Kidder, we got to make a plan, yeah?' Dadda says, kissing the top of my head, and rolling another ciggie. 'Your mum's on the warpath. We got a letter from the DHSS today. They've finished their in-vest-i-gation, and they are keeping the bene-fits as they are.'

'Brilliant!' I say. 'Oh, thank God!'

'No,' Dadda says. 'Keeping them as they are *now*. Cut.'

'Why? Did they say why?' Oh, please let it not be my fault.

'Nah,' he says, shiftily. 'Just … one of them, innit. They found out they were over-paying us. So we are brassic.'

'I can give you more money!' I say. 'If I don't do the savings. Savings are stupid. We need the money now.'

'Your mum's not having that,' Dadda says. 'So we've got to box clever. We're a family – we can't depend on you. It's not fair on you for a start, babba. Nah – we got to *utilise* our *assets*. Which is – me and you. You write about music. I make it.'

He pauses, and lights his fag.

'You've got to get me in there, kid. Get me a break. Get me in that paper. And we'll be millionaires by Christmas.'

Because I'm pissed, and I love him, and I'm excited about living in the twentieth century, I hug him.

'It's a deal,' I say. And we shake on it.

SEVENTEEN

As I'm now a regular on the *D&ME*, Jiffy bags start arriving at the house – ten, fifteen, twenty a day. Every record released in Britain is being delivered to my house – the postman sweating, his bag newly pregnant with parcels. Where once the rattle of the post box meant only red bills and the threat of brown envelopes from the council, these tiny posts are now drowned out by CDs, seven-inches, twelve-inches and white, pre-release cassettes. It feels like Christmas, every day. It's raining music.

I gather them all in the washing-basket and take them to my room and listen to them, splitting them into two piles: ones I love, and therefore will not allow myself to write about (DON'T BE A FAN), and ones I can tear to bits in amusingly vituperative broadsides, against whichever bunch of foolhardy chancers are trying to waste the time and money of Britain's youth.

Three weeks into this new bounty, I go to the toilet halfway through an album, and come back to find an unexpected visitor in my room: Krissi. He's sitting on floor, looking through the washing-basket.

'Helloa,' I say.

This is a surprising development – Krissi has not set foot in my bedroom since SatanWankGate. Indeed, he hasn't really talked to me since SatanWankGate – not even when I tried to jolly the situation along by referring to it as 'SatanWankGate'. When I did that, he just put his Ready Brek down, sighed, and left the room.

Another sad corollary of 'SatanWankGate' is that I've stopped being able to think of Satan while I wank. I now irrevocably associate The Great Lucifer with Krissi being tetchy – and that's scary.

'Hello, repulsive,' Krissi replies, still looking through the washing basket.

'What are you–'

'Have you got any Bee Gees?' Krissi asks.

'I think there's a Best Of over there …' I say, pointing to my shelves: plank and bricks, like in Krissi's room; but where he has seedlings, I have hundreds and hundreds of CDs. I stare at him as he wanders over.

'I was watching *Grease* again yesterday, and remembered what a tune it is,' Krissi says, examining the shelves. 'I need some *Grease*.'

I get the album out, and hold it near the stereo – shall I? Krissi nods, and I put it on while he carries on rifling through the shelves.

'And have you got any Velvet Underground?' he says, as the ultra-slick, ultra-tight swoon of *Grease* fills the room, and I start hitch-hiking in the corner.

'Well, they haven't released anything recently, since they broke up in 1973 – so I'd have to ask for it,' I say.

'I'm aware they're no longer touring,' Krissi says, witheringly. 'I had noted them not appearing on *Going Live!* recently, being back-announced by Gordon the Gopher.'

'Gordon the Gopher couldn't back-announce them – he's mute.'

'He could *gesture*,' Krissi says, making a pile of CDs on my desk. 'He could … point at Lou Reed.'

'So – you're into music, then?' I say, lying casually on the bed.

'I've always been into music, you div,' Krissi says. I have a sudden flashback again to us doing 'Sex Crime' by the Eurythmics. On Boxing Day. For Fat Nanna. Before she died. He's got a point. 'Just different stuff from you. I've been going to the library too.'

'OoooooOOoooooh, whatcha get?' I ask. 'Hey – you're not the one who pre-ordered the Smashing Pumpkins album before me, are you? I'm still waiting for it.'

'I eschew the Smashing Pumpkins,' Krissi said. 'You can't *do* anything with it.'

'What do you do with music?'

'Dance,' Krissi says. 'The KLF, and Pet Shop Boys, and Public Enemy, and Ice T, and NWA.'

'The hip-hop? You like the hip-hop? How do you know about the hip-hop?'

'I read.'

'You read the *D&ME*? Do you read my stuff?'

This is an insanely exciting development. Krissi has never, once, referred to my job. The idea that he's been secretly reading me for months fills me with joy – I feel like Bruce Wayne when Vicki Vale casually mentions she fancies Batman.

'No, I don't read the *Dame*,' Krissi says, dismissively. 'No offence, but it's massively wanky – like sitting in a sixth-form common room with a dozen wannabe Fonzes, arguing over the stereo. I like *music*, Johanna. I read fanzines. I like *Thank You*.'

Thank You is the Midlands' premiere fanzine, written by ZZ Top – the one he runs on the side, that got him his job with the *Dame* in the first place. It's 50p, and the latest edition has a thrilled, speeding, 2,000-word analysis of Ice T's *O.G. Original Gangster*, which concludes that this is 'Sour, furious, militarised funk – as if Bootsy Collins had been in a high-speed police-chase pile up, and emerged from the wreckage with his flares and fro burnt from his body, holding a machine gun, ready for warfare.'

ZZ only writes about people he likes. Apart from Sting, with whom he has a long-running imaginary feud. ZZ writes like a fan. This is why he is still the lowliest writer on the *Dame*. I once heard Kenny refer to him, dismissively, as 'the groupie'.

'*Thank You*? No, thank you,' he'd said, before laughing hysterically, and giving ZZ another tuppeny ha'penny shit-hole indie gig in Derby to review.

'Oh,' I say, now, to Krissi. I don't really know how to respond. It had never occurred to me that I might not be my brother's favourite writer. It's a bit of an awkward moment. I consider apologising for SatanWankGate again, just for something to say – but Krissi, sensing it's all become a bit sensitive, fixes me with a stare, and points at me, dramatically: 'Staying Alive' has come on.

Krissi starts dancing towards me in a showy disco-jog. Still a bit hurt, I do vague, place-holding 'Disco Fingers' at him.

Krissi reaches past me, and turns the light off. This is what we used to do when we were younger – have Dark Discos. Turn off all the lights and dance to Stevie Wonder's *Hotter Than July* in the black-out, so that we could dance as dramatically as we wanted, without the embarrassment of seeing each other's flailing limbs, and hopelessly unfunky bum-shakes.

I will always dance in the dark with Krissi. He always has my dance-card filled. In less than thirty seconds, he funks me into a corner. By the green glow of the stereo light I find my bottle of MD 20/20, take a swig and offer it to Krissi – he pauses for a minute, and then takes a shot.

'GARRRRRGH!' he falsettos.

'YAHHHH!' I falsetto back.

We dance and drink all the way through 'Night Fever', 'Jive Talkin'' and 'Tragedy', and then collapse onto the bed for 'I've Got To Get A Message To You', sweaty, and a bit pissed.

'God, the Bee Gees are *so gay*,' I say, in between singing the words. I'm lolling against Krissi the way we used to when we were very little – like puppies on a blanket. 'I'd love to have a gay friend. I wonder if there's *anyone* gay in Wolverhampton. I guess they'd probably be shot.'

Krissi stiffens a bit, on the bed, then gives a huge sigh.

'Isn't Kenny gay? At the magazine?' he says. 'Isn't he your friend?'

I consider Kenny for a minute. Kenny, in his cut-off jogging-bottoms, doing his horrible sulphate, and secretly listening to Yes.

'He's the wrong *kind* of gay for me,' I say.

At that point, the lights suddenly come on, and Dadda comes into the room, furious.

'What are you, thumping around like fucking heffalumps? The twins are trying to get to sleep,' he says, staring at us on the bed.

He takes in the stereo, and me lying on Krissi, and the bottle of MD 20/20 in my hand.

'Oh, I see,' he says – anger immediately dissipating. He puts out his hand towards me.

'Corkage.'

I pathetically try to hide the bottle of MD 20/20 under my jacket, but his hand remains out. I give him the bottle, and he knocks it back like a pro.

'That looks like about 15 per cent,' he says, holding up the bottle to the light and evaluating the new, low level. Then he takes another swig.

'Plus tip, of course,' he says, handing the bottle back.

He comes and sits on the bed, making us shuffle up, and then takes the bottle back off me.

'And VAT,' he says, having another sip. There's hardly any left.

'So, what you doing?' he says, looking at the CDs and Jiffy bags all over the floor.

'Sorting out the post-bag,' I say. 'Being a rock critic. Those are the winners,' I point to one pile, 'and those are the losers, whom I smite.'

Dadda looks at the pile of Jiffy bags, rather oddly. I can't work out what his expression means, for a moment, and then I think: these are exactly like the ones he's been sending off to London – only for them to be returned, with polite rejection notes: 'Dear PAT MORRIGAN, Thank you for submitting to us for deliberation, but unfortunately …'

There's a long pause.

'I'm going to review you soon, Dadda,' I say. 'Just got to choose my moment.'

'Yeah,' Dadda says, nodding. 'You've got to choose your moment. It's all about timing. The rhythms of the universe. Wheels within wheels.'

I look at him. His eyes are pinned. He's clearly had quite a lot of his medicine today.

EIGHTEEN

It's just … I'm kind of busy doing other things. With my mouth.
Two months later, and I've got off with Tony Rich six times.
The last is back at his flat, where I 'crash' for the night: three
long, slow, wet hours kissing by the light of his computer which
glows, green, in the corner – showing a half-written essay on
My Bloody Valentine, until I climb on top of him, and put his
face into shadow.

He won't fuck me that night, as he's 'kind of seeing
someone', but the 'someone' has gone by the next time I come
down to London:

'I'm single, now,' he says, in the pub, after the editorial
meeting, before pulling me outside and kissing me in the hot
summer doorway. When I look up, half the editorial staff are
looking out of the window, and cheering sarcastically. I wave
like the Queen, and Rich gives them a V sign, before we start
kissing again, and they eventually lose interest and melt away.

We go back inside, and try to re-join the conversation –
but we're both so fuck-drunk it gradually becomes untenable:
his hands are on my thigh, under my skirt, and sitting next to
him, leaning against him, I can feel his heart booming under
his shirt.

'Don't you think we should leave the pandas to breed in
private?' Kenny asks the table, eventually, when my dilated
pupils and Rich's increasingly distracted answers make it clear
we're not really capable of socialising right now.

I take Rich by the hand and take him outside again, and this, now, is amazing kissing. This is not like The Kisser. This is … thrilling. Rich's mouth is so huge and billowy – it's like an endless feast, a banquet of man that I have finally been invited to. He's kissing me in a way that could save the lives of the dying. He has my face in his hands, and there's a lazy, urgent joy in the way he moves – I'm pretty sure there can't ever have been any kissing better than this. There can't ever have been *any* kissing before. We are inventing it, in these last ten minutes. If you follow all the kissing in the world upstream, you will, eventually, end up here – in the doorway of a pizza place opposite Waterloo Station, with the taxis and the people passing, feet away, oblivious, and Tony Rich kissing the corners of my mouth – slowly, thoughtfully – before falling back into me again. The first two people to ever think of doing this. Ever.

And when you are being kissed like this, you are Christmas Day; you are the Moon Shot; you are field larks. My shoes were suddenly worth a million pounds, and my breath was the ethyl in champagne. When someone kisses you like this, you are the point of everything.

I was the one who suggested the cab – I was the one who undid the first button, as we went over Waterloo Bridge. In books, a gallant man always says, 'Are you sure?' before they open their front door, but Tony didn't ask that, because it would have been a sad waste of time. I was exhaling so much desire that we were both dizzy – and when you've had a man's hard-on pressed against you for nearly an hour, it's not a question you need to ask in return.

And we got into his bed, and we fucked.

Losing your virginity is an odd thing, when you've thought about it for years. Nothing about the sex was surprising – other than that supernova kissing, which not even the Nostradamus of masturbation could have foretold, until it had happened, to his mouth. The basic mechanics of it were all that I'd thought – wet fingers, mouths; suddenly – finally! – having someone inside me.

I didn't come – but that, also, didn't surprise me. Because all I had wanted was to have sex. I had never known what *kind* of sex. I just wanted – some sex. It was all enormous, tumbling, urgent fun, and when we were exhausted, we lay next to each other, laughing. And that was losing my virginity, to Tony Rich, who had once been just words in a magazine, but had now left bruise-marks on my thighs, where his fingers had gripped, when he called out my name. I made him call my name – 'Dolly!' – loud, like the first word ever. And when he said it, I was momentarily and unexpectedly sad he wasn't saying 'Johanna!' – but I ignored that feeling, for now.

I could finally see myself appearing in the world. Having sex, and printing words. I was slowly assembling, into vision, at the end of a telescope.

So no – the sex wasn't the surprising thing, the unknown thing, I needed to actually fuck to know.

It was all the other stuff that was the surprise. Here's the amazing thing about sex: you get a whole person to yourself, for the first time since you were a baby. Someone who is looking at you – just you – and thinking about you, and wanting you, and you haven't even had to lie at the bottom of the stairs and pretend you're dead to get them to do it.

I enjoyed taking Rich's shirt off so much I thought I would die – to take the shirt off a man is to finally feel like a grown woman. That's no fourteen-years-old shit. Only women do this.

And you are in a room with a closed door, and no one else can come through it. No one can come and interrupt – no one will come and sit next to you, and spoil the conversation. There is no kicking-out time. There is no sad moment where the phone call will end – or the lights will suddenly come up, and the music ends, and you have to go home, alone, at the end of the gig, or a party.

It seemed to me that this was the real reason people wanted to fuck so much. To get here. To get to this tiny, quiet place where there was nothing else to do but be with each other. Just to be two humans who had – for a short while – stopped wanting. This is the beautiful, final destination. The end of things.

It's so friendly, lying here. In the lamp-light, he holds my hand, and turns my arm, to see the inside. There are bite marks all up inside it, from when I was unhappy.

'Have you been giving yourself love bites?' he jokes. 'Have you been getting off with yourself?'

'Yes – but it's a pretty open arrangement. We're seeing other people, too.'

He makes cheese on toast that has mushrooms on it, too – 'The main thing I learned at Harvard' – which feels exotic, and he finds red wine – 'From the corner shop, sorry' – and we drink it out of green glass tumblers, and oh! It's so *lovely*. I didn't think picking up and casually fucking someone was supposed to be lovely.

Books had always led me to believe that the second fuck was supposed to be slow, and dreamlike, and more satisfying, but when we had finished eating, the second fuck was even more urgent than the first one, and I still didn't come, but when *he* came, I felt enormously … useful. Men need to come – and I had made it happen. I had a simple purpose.

And in the morning, I said, 'We should do this again,' and he said, 'Come back soon,' and kissed me at the bus stop until my bus came, and took me away – my mouth pressed up against the glass to cool it, now, from all the kissing. Kissing hadn't cooled me at all, in the end. It had made me hotter.

Walking back into the house, in Wolverhampton, was bizarre. I felt fresh from battlefield victory. Within the weekly achievements of our family, I had, surely, pulled off the greatest deed. In any just world, I should have been able to kick the front room door open, like Lord Flashheart in *Blackadder*, and shout, 'OH YEAH. THAT HYMEN'S GONE. DON'T YOU WORRY ABOUT THAT,' and then run round the room, getting high-fives from my parents, and siblings. I had taken one, literally, for the team.

In reality, of course, I knew that was not the correct thing to do. However unfair it was – and it was massively unfair – I had to pretend that this was just another normal week, where I'd gone around making no erections, had not been half of an Olympic-standard kissing double, and had failed to make a man who went to university IN AMERICA ejaculate into my comprehensive-educated genitals.

Trying to find a way to mediate this clash of my instincts *vs* societal boundaries, I settled on walking around being very smug, instead.

'What are you doing with your face?' Krissi asked, as I made myself a cheese sandwich in the kitchen. Having been away for two nights, I had a sudden, giddying perspective on just how much margarine seemed permanently smeared on our work-tops. This whole room was a health risk.

'What do you mean?' I asked – increasing the smugness as I sliced the cheese.

'Your face – it's clearly telling me to slap it,' Krissi said, staring at me. 'It's communicating with me on a frequency you can't hear. It's begging me to slap both cheeks at the same time – like Cannon & Ball.'

'Nothing's up,' I said, continuing to grate cheese onto the sandwich. 'Just … feeling kind of hot right now. You know. Kinda … foxy.'

'You *are* quite foxy,' Krissi said. 'Really quite foxy.'

'Thank you!' I said.

'… foxy, like Basil Brush,' Krissi continued. 'You have the same ability as Basil to laugh, piercingly and lengthily, at your own jokes. And,' he added, leaving the room, slyly, 'you've had a man's hand up your bum.'

Later that evening, I say the word 'Ptarmigan' to Krissi, which is our old code word, meaning 'Meet me in the wardrobe, for secrets'. We tell all our secrets in here. This was where I admitted I fancied Jason from *Battle of the Planets*, and Krissi told me he did, too, and we agreed that, when we grew up, we would marry someone from G-Force, or no one at all. That was a long time ago.

We sit in the wardrobe, crushed against each other – so much bigger than we used to be, when we started doing this.

'Yeah?' he says, cagily. 'What?'

'What did you mean – when you said I'd had a man's hand up my bum?' I ask.

'*You* know,' Krissi says.

'What?' I say.

'*You know.*'

'I don't!' I do.

'It's obvious,' Krissi says. 'Well done.'

Silence.

'Do you want to ask me any questions about it?'

Krissi, immediately: 'NO!'

Silence. Krissi was obviously wrestling with his curiosity vs his horror. Finally:

'Did it hurt?'

'N–'

'Actually I don't want to hear this.'

Krissi starts climbing out of the wardrobe. I pull him back in, and we sit in silence, until his obvious nausea subsides.

'Did you,' he asks, eventually, 'take *all* your clothes off?'

'Yeah,' I say.

'Oh my God.'

'Sorry,' I add.

'It's okay.'

Krissi sighs, repeatedly. He huffs and puffs. Eventually: 'Thing is, I want to ask you questions – but the answers are literally intolerable, because then I imagine you having sex and that, inevitably, makes me want to kill myself, and everyone in this family. And everyone I've ever met. And God. I don't want to think about you having sex.'

'You have to think about me, having sex.'

'No! It's *disgusting*.'

'Think about it … me having sex.'

'NO!'

'Me having sex me having sex me having sex.'

Kriss gives me a sibling-punch. Anyone who has a sibling will know what that is – a punch which really hurts quite a lot, and which is meant to, but which you cannot take offence at, or retaliate against, because you went out of your way to get it – because, sometimes, you *want* your sibling to punch you. No one knows why this is. We sit in silence again.

Eventually: 'Why don't we give the protagonists different names?' I suggest. 'Not me and Tony Rich. Say, Peter Venkmann and Dana Barrett?'

Krissi agrees.

And so I tell him all about Dana Barrett from *Ghostbusters* losing her virginity to Peter Venkmann in *Ghostbusters*, and he asks a couple more questions, and only says 'UGH!' or 'I WANT TO DIE' three times.

At one point, he puts a pillowcase over his head, and says, in a very quiet voice, 'And what did his cock look like?' and I tell him:

'The skin was dead soft, like baby cardigans, and it curved a little, to the left – I think because he's left-handed, and bent it that way from wanking. I was dead proud of working that out. I felt like … David Attenborough, working out what some ants were doing.'

And when I finish, I have told Krissi all about what it is like to have sex for the first time, and we both agree, without saying a word, that we will never, ever discuss this again.

When we get out of the wardrobe, we leave the loss of my virginity in there, among the black bin liners full of old coats. And Krissi goes downstairs and puts 'Gotta Get a Message to You' on at full blast until the twins wake up, and cry, together – the only sound on Earth higher and more persistent than the Gibb brothers' harmonies.

NINETEEN

All this time, I have been writing to John Kite – two, three, four letters a week, and the same back from him. Mine from my desk, looking up at pictures of him, flicking ash into his ashtray; his from the studio in Wales, where he's recording his new album.

He is the first person I tell about losing my virginity – long before I pulled Krissi into the airing cupboard and traumatised him, I'd been on the train on the way home – still sore – writing to John about what had happened that night.

Even though I had, at that point, been a non-virgin for nearly fourteen hours, it was still essentially the letter of someone very inexperienced – I would blush to write something so oddly, innocently pornographic now. I did not know that you don't usually write letters to 'friends' that have graphic descriptions of being turned over and fucked until you wail – that talking about being slicked with sweat, and riding someone, naked but for the necklace banging on your collarbone, was ... *too much*. I thought that once you entered the land of fucking, this is how all the fuckees and fuckers talked to each other – regardless of the social situation.

'People of Fucking probably talk like this in the supermarket,' I thought, 'or whilst waiting, at Kwik-Fit.'

And, to be honest, even if I *had* been aware, I still would probably have written that letter, anyway. And all the filthy ones that came after it. It was no coincidence that I'd gone after the first man I set eyes on after John had kissed me – John had started something that he couldn't finish and, sparking, I had gone to find someone who could. I basically lost my virginity *at* John. When I wrote to him about it, I wanted him to imagine himself in the fuck. I wanted these letters to *disturb* him – to make him come and get me.

But his reply was peerlessly even-handed: 'Christ, Dutch, you're wasted on music criticism. This is top-quality grumble-mag stuff – you could send this stuff off to *Razzle* and never have to review Bum Gravy at the George Robey again. It's definitely five wanks out of five. Although you will forgive me if I pretend it was someone other than Rich you were boffing? It's just that I find his support of Lou Reed intolerable. I hate Lou Reed. He looks like fucking Erik Estrada from *C.H.i.Ps*, with a cob-on.'

But then, if I'm being honest, I want *everyone* to imagine they're fucking me. Because, now I've lost my virginity, I use it as the springboard to go on what is basically a massive Shag Quest. I wish to be like James Bond, who never leaves a party without either shagging someone, or blowing something up. That is my role model here.

And it is one initially chosen more in hope than expecta-tion. For, up until I got off with Tony Rich, my understanding of the world had been that, as a fat girl, I might only get laid three or four times in my life – half of those fucks instigated out of pity; all of them drunken, and careless – before I settled down with a fat husband and left casual sex, once again, to the beautiful thin girls, for whom this pastime was constructed. If I *were* to be a Lady Sex Bond, then the film I would be in would be *You Only Shag Twice – If You're Lucky*.

But now I've discovered the truth of the matter: that any woman can get laid, any time that she wants. *Any woman. Any time*. It is the greatest and most amazing secret on Earth. It really doesn't matter if you're some fat chick wearing a top hat and speaking with a Wolverhampton accent. It's ridiculously easy. You go to a party, or a gig, start talking to someone, introduce the topic of sex – it doesn't matter how; and everything's kind of about sex *anyway* – and, twenty minutes later, you'll be frantically getting off with someone in a dark corner, trying, in between kisses, to find out where they live.

For, in the summer of 1993, I have a carefully calibrated map of which areas of London I will fuck in – all triangulated out from Euston Station, where I will inevitably have to return to in the morning, to get back to Wolverhampton. No further east than Clerkenwell, no further west than Kensal Green, no further north than Crouch End, no further south than Stockwell. If it's more than twenty-five minutes in a cab from whatever inevitable Soho venue we're in, I will, ultimately, decline sexual intercourse – having learned the hard way how unpleasant it can be, at 9am the next morning, to get from Putney into the centre of town with a love-bite on your face.

I also have an irrational hatred of the District Line, and will use it as the final decider in borderline cases:

'Why don't you come back to mine, and let's [putting hand down bra] talk about this further?'

'Where do you live?'

'Earl's Court.'

'Sorry. I'm working a shift in a homeless hostel tonight, and I'd rather get laid there. Bye.'

I learn a lot along the way. If you talk about sex to every drunken man you meet, you access generations of sexual attitudes in a matter of minutes – a stockpile of received wisdoms and beliefs. One rock star tells me that he 'can always tell how intelligent a girl is by the way she walks'.

This confuses me. I have very weak ankles that mean I basically walk like a penguin. I'd always thought I was fairly bright – but perhaps my ankles know better? Or maybe it's just my ankles that are stupid?

I spend weeks trying to alter my gait – trying to guess how a clever girl walks. The most likely answer seems to be 'Quickly and determinedly' and so I start moving very much like the T-1000 in *Terminator 2: Judgment Day*, when it starts running after the car. It's absolutely exhausting, and also, I can't help but think, quite menacing. I'm not sure it says 'clever'. I wish I'd asked for more details.

A bass-player tells me, during a drunken interview, that the key to a woman being good in bed is to 'Never leave one hand idle – always be doing something with both hands'.

Again, this leads to worry. The next time I'm having sex, I remember it, and end up absently patting the back of the man on top of me – as if trying to wind a baby. Is this what he meant? It doesn't seem very sensual. All these men are being too vague.

Other men are not vague enough. A Cockney A&R man – who isn't the person I want to have sex with, but is standing next to the person I want to have sex with, and so gets caught up in the flirty cross-fire – tells me, confidently, that he knows 'all about' fat girls: 'They're great at two things: swimming and blow jobs.'

He explains that this is because, at school, fat girls don't like sports that involve running, 'Because their tits all jiggle about, innit?', and so enjoy being in the water, 'Because they don't feel heavy. They like floating.'

As for blow jobs: 'You don't have to take your clothes off. Fat girls don't want to take their clothes off.'

Needless to say, I don't have sex with him – even as I'm thinking, 'My God! I *am* very good at swimming!' and grudgingly wonder if he might actually be right about blow jobs. I haven't tried one yet – but it's definitely something I want to be good at. Getting good at blow jobs is totally something I intend to do, in this year that most of my peers are concentrating on their A levels, instead.

I want to be knowledgeable about sex – most of my jokes are heavily based on innuendo, and I need to know what it is that I'm actually making all these jokes *about*. So far, I'm just doing a lot of guesswork, based on books, and things I've read people saying in interviews, and in films.

I feel, urgently, that I want to be knowledgeable about fucking. It's an attribute I wish to have. I want to be respected and admired for what a legendary piece of ass I am – I would actually like to be introduced as 'This is Dolly Wilde – she's a *legendary piece of ass*' – but the only way of doing that is by going out and having a lot of sex. And that has repercussions.

For in a way that feels quite unfair, the only way I can gain any qualifications at this thing – sex – that is seen as so societally important and desirable, is by being a massive slag – which is *not* seen as societally important and desirable. This often makes me furious.

'You wouldn't denigrate a plumber with a lot of experience in fitting bathrooms!' I rage to myself, whenever I see the phrase 'massive slag', and remember it applies to me. 'You wouldn't hiss about a vet who'd saved the lives of over 300 guinea pigs! Well it's the same here! I'm learning on the job! I'm expanding my CV! I'm becoming a safe pair of hands – around a cock!'

By way of a shame-busting exercise, 'massive slag' is a phrase I often repeat to myself, in order that it not seem as hurtful as I find it. 'I am a massive slag!' I think to myself, in a motivational way. 'I'm a Lady Sex Adventuress! I'm a Pirate of Privates! I'm a swashfuckler! I'm a friendly, noble, massive slag – and now I'm going to have my slag breakfast.' I think of 'Teenage Whore' by Courtney Love as by way of my personal anthem.

I have several areas of sex that I wish to be 'specialist' at. The first is S&M – pervy sex. I've listened to enough of Krissi's Velvet Underground records to be aware of the whip, and the mistress; and in the yearnings of a masochist, I hear a furious sexual hunger like my own. A man who wants to be dominated has the same, desperate, almost incoherent need to be subsumed that *I* feel. I want to *help* these fellows. I want, again, to be *useful*. If a man ever wanted to be my gimp, I would be *delighted* to help him out. Like a small start-up business, I would delight in fulfilling an untended niche market. I would whip those craving boys with all the kindness I have.

The second is blow jobs. Blow jobs are, mythically, what all boys want the most – and so, again, as a good student of market forces, I am very interested in them. Margaret Thatcher has basically made me pro-blow job. Having read all I can about them, I'm given to understand that the key thing is that you *must* swallow. Girls who don't swallow are fussy, and must be coerced into swallowing – which is annoying for all parties. To gain dominance in the market, I fully intend to swallow. So all my blow jobs will be utterly *stress-free* in that respect, and no one will feel awkward, or ashamed.

I also have one non-sexual skill I want to master: typing whilst smoking, like in *His Girl Friday,* and all pictures of Hunter S. Thompson. I've attempted it before, but the smoke always goes right into my eyes – leaving me smoking, weeping and typing, all at the same time.

Last time I did it, Krissi saw me, left the room, and came back with a pair of swimming goggles.

'To help you look cool,' he said, putting them next to my laptop, and patting me on the head, pityingly.

Three weeks after having sex with Tony Rich, I've made a start on this list – I've tried some S&M, using Madonna's 'Justify My Love' video as my primary source of practical information.

One hapless man who takes me back to his house seems very excited when I say to him, 'Have you seen the "Justify My Love" video?', and then very alarmed when I purr 'Can you handle it?' while dripping molten candle-wax onto his balls.

'JESUS CHRIST!' he roars, leaping out of bed and pawing at his genitals, spreading red candle-wax everywhere.

Next time I see him, at a gig, he's still standing slightly awkwardly, and will not make eye contact with me. He looks a bit scared. I hear later that there was so much dried wax on his balls that he eventually had to shave the entire right side, to get rid of it, and that his mates are calling him 'Phil Oakey' as a result.

Obviously, I injured *that* penis too badly to fellate it – but, a week later, I'm in a flat in Ladbroke Grove – right on the borders of my Sex Map; four more streets to the West and I would have bailed – doing my first ever blow job.

I've absorbed a couple of principles from Jilly Cooper: primarily that it's all about enthusiasm, and that the top of the penis – the bit I keep thinking of as 'Captain Jean-Luc Picard's head' – is where all the action should be centred.

Also, logically – learning from my own masturbatory habits – I figure it needs to be rhythmic, and to speed up a bit at the end, like 'Release' by Aztec Camera.

The penis turns out to be a pretty straightforward, easy-to-understand mechanism. At first, anyway.

At the beginning, I find it unexpectedly enjoyable to have it in my mouth – it's quite comforting, really. Like sucking your thumb, but whilst making someone else very, very happy. I like how *friendly* it is – I feel oddly honoured that he trusts me enough not to bite it, which perhaps proves how young I still am. Forty-three-year-old women probably don't think, 'Look! I'm not biting it.'

'Here I am,' I think to myself, 'being totally capable with a penis – and no one ever taught me how! I'm an auto-didact! Well done me!'

Things, however, become more complicated on the approach of orgasm – at which point he starts thrashing around a bit, making confusing noises, and then pushes my head down onto his cock.

Now, not only is this last action impolite – I am, at the end of the day, doing him a big favour. Suddenly putting an extra, unannounced amount of cock in my mouth is basically like cadging a lift, then trying to blag six mates and a Welsh dresser into a Mini, too – but it's also thunderously impractical. Because when you push a cock too far down someone's mouth, they are, almost inevitably, going to be a bit sick. That's just reflexes.

Startled, I do a small, discreet lady mouth-sick – at which point, he comes.

In many ways – although initially unwelcome – the sick makes the subsequent sex-admin easy: at least I don't have a last-minute dilemma over whether I am actually the kind of person who spits or swallows – because, for the sake of politeness, I just have to swallow the sick anyway. That's the common-sense thing to do. There's nowhere to spit a medium-sized amount of vomit out, unless – I scan the immediate vicinity – I use *either* an empty wine glass *or* his pants, neither of which seem in keeping with the mood we've established: one of heavy sensuality.

I wonder – as I so often do in sexual moments – if this has ever happened to Madonna: if she's ever given someone a blow job in a shabby bedsit, mouth full of sick.

Eager to seem still 'welcoming' re: the blow job, I keep on sucking long after he's come – until he jack-knifes over in bed with a hand on my head, going, 'Careful, sweetheart – it's very sensitive.'

We try to do some sex again, later – but my over-enthusiastic sucking has led to him getting a tiny tear in his foreskin, and so the penis is out of bounds: we both look at it, sadly, for a while, and then I look out of the window, and say, 'Oh well, I suppose I'd better get the bus,' and leave.

I can't even kiss him goodbye, because my mouth still tastes of sick and come, and I don't want to put him off – even though it's all his fault anyway.

'Farewell, then,' I say, formally, as he moves in for a kiss, on the doorway – only for me to take his hand, and shake it, instead. He looks very confused. Also, still, residually, in groin-pain. But none of it was my fault! Oh, it's all so complicated.

'I keep breaking penises,' I think to myself, dolorously, on the 37, heading towards Euston Station. 'And, also, no one, yet, has made me come. I am still the greatest lover of me. I'm still the best I've ever had.'

Some of these men have tried, of course – starting the kissing on the belly that is the prelude to oral sex: looking up through their fringes, eyes asking 'Shall I?' – but I have always stopped them.

Why? I'm trying to work it out. I can't decide if it's because I feel I don't deserve it – that they wouldn't *enjoy* doing it, they're just being polite, and so the correct thing to do is demur – or whether it's because I don't feel *they* deserve it, instead: that I don't want these men to see me lose control, and come by their hand, as I do when I'm on my own.

I have, after all, never seen a woman come, except in *When Harry Met Sally*, which to me is still more a scene about an amazing sandwich than some sex. These are the days before internet pornography. In all the dirty films I've seen, only the men ever come. In a way, I would have to invent the female orgasm from scratch before I could do it with someone else in the room. I have no template for where you would fit it into sex – or how. Should I come before we fuck – or after? When *is* the usual schedule for these things? How long should you take to come? Do I take too long? Should you not even ask it of a man if you take more than, say, four minutes? Is that simply unreasonable? I don't want to be a difficult case, and give someone RSI. I don't want to get a reputation as a 'hand-wearier'.

Also, I have to admit that a large factor in my not-coming is because some of them have been absolutely hopeless. One man's hand in my knickers is so achingly adrift from where it might be useful that, in the end, as he tries to manipulate my thigh to orgasm, I looked up at him and say, 'You know what? If it's there, I'll give you the money myself.'

But he doesn't get the reference, and the joke falls flat. Later, as I make myself come next to his sleeping body, I whisper, resentfully, 'Bette Midler wouldn't put up with this shit. Everyone gets Bette Midler's jokes,' come, and fall asleep.

TWENTY

This intense training season of casual sex reaches its peak with Big Cock Al.

Big Cock Al is in a band from Brighton called Sooner, and I keep bumping into him at gigs and getting off with him – but then having to stop, because he needs to get the last train home.

The next time Sooner have a gig in Brighton, he invites me to stay the night in a phone call that might as well be called the 'Shall we have sex next Thursday?' phone call.

So here I am in his flat in Brighton – four storeys up, looking out over the rooftops from a room filled with batik throws, joss sticks, Buddhas and guitars.

I'm wearing only a dark-blue nylon petticoat, and Al's down to his trousers. I've just unzipped the fly – and released the biggest penis I have ever seen. It takes two hands to get it out of his pants. I feel like a snake-handler on *Blue Peter*. It's alarmingly huge. In my startlement, I believe I hear it go 'thump' as it comes out. The last time I saw something like this, it was at dead Fat Nanna's house, across the bottom of the front door, as a draught excluder, with two buttons for eyes. There were boys I went to school with who had legs shorter than this.

'Blimey!' I say – agitated into speaking like a Cockney chimney-sweep on spotting a silver sixpence.

'I *know*,' Al says, with the lazy, triumphant grin of the gigantically endowed.

Now, everything I have ever read, up until this point, has led me to unquestioningly believe that the more penis, the better. Jilly Cooper has been very, literally, firm on this: that men's cocks are basically like buffets, at parties – there is simply no such thing as too much. Whatever you can't handle that night, in the heat of the party, can simply be cling-filmed and had for breakfast, the next day – as a treat.

This, however, clearly is not the case here. This penis is so large, it's basically a medical emergency. If I'm going to risk getting even half of that in me, we're going to need some paramedic units hanging around, just in case of a terrible accident – like they do on the difficult bends, on F1 race courses.

With something of this size, Al's not really asking me for sex. That's not what's going on here.

'You don't need a vagina,' I think. 'You're simply trying to avoid rental charges on an appropriate storage facility, instead. My friend, you will need *council permits* to park something like this.'

Al's lying on his back, eyes closed, so I get a chance to look down at it again. Oh, it does make me smile. It is an *insane* body part – it looks like child's arm, or the snout of Alf from *ALF*.

It has the air that I'm starting to realise all erect penises have – one of hopefulness, coupled with something that almost borders on pleading: 'Please stroke me! I am nice!' – but, given its sheer size, it can't help but look slightly, inevitably menacing. The scale is all out of whack. You know – like the giant fluffy white kitten in *The Goodies*. It's a lovely, fluffy white kitten! But it is undeniably stepping on your house, and crushing you to death!

This penis will undeniably step on my house, and crush me to death.

'That,' I say, in a very friendly voice, 'is a very large penis.'

'Yes,' Al says, quite urgently. 'Suck it, and make it bigger.'

Haha, I will do no such thing, you joker. I'm not a lunatic.

But what *am* I going to do? This is quite the dilemma. If I continue touching this cock, it will – as I have just been fairly warned, although it seems, frankly, impossible – get even bigger. If I try and fuck it, it's just going to go straight through me and come out of the top of my head, like the stake on a scarecrow. And if I just back off completely, that's the end of sex – which would be a massive and frankly *intolerable* waste, given that I've spent £25.90 getting down here, I'm wearing a hot new petticoat, I want to have sex, and there is a whole, naked man here in a locked flat – which is the thing I always want, but almost never have.

I spend one second thinking about the 'not sex' plan, and have a quick flashback to my parents' house. Thursday night. If I go home, tonight's tea is potato soup, and then we'll be playing charades. Oh fuck that, no.

What I really need is for Al to offer to go down on me – because that is the sex we can have without it killing me – but it appears not to have occurred to him, and my understanding about men eating women out is that the rules are a bit like the Prime Directive in *Star Trek*. You know – where the crew of the *Enterprise* are forbidden from telling other, more primitive cultures about astonishing and enjoyable technological advances on other planets.

I, Tiberius Kirk, cannot tell this non-oral man about the glorious eating-out revolution. This is news from the future he will not be able to handle yet.

I look at his cock, and sigh. He looks up.

'You alright, love?' he asks.

We end up having sex, of course. Never look a gift hose in the mouth. In the end, I find what works is to stop thinking about what *I* am thinking about this particular sexual intercoursing – mainly 'I am alarmed! This is the biggest penis of all time, surely! Quick! Call Norris McWhirter!' – and start thinking about what *he's* thinking, instead. How clearly excited he is by my mouth, and the 'grab a handful' aspects of my arse.

'He's having such a great time with me!' I think, cheerfully, as he climbs on top, and diligently starts trying to feed into me nineteen miles of extraneous cock. 'I am being a generous lover!'

In later years, I find this is called 'physical disconnect', and is all part and parcel of women having their sexuality mediated through men's gaze. There is very little female narrative of what it's like to fuck, and be fucked. I will realise that, as a seventeen-year-old girl, I couldn't really hear my own voice during this sex. I had no idea what my voice was at all.

But right here, in this room in Brighton, with the batik bedspread knotting underneath us, and a pile of *D&ME*s stacked up in the corner, all I know is that his desire is making me desirous, and I am pretty pleased with me for getting at least half of this cock inside me without shouting 'Blimey! No pushing at the back! Settle down there!' Really, my sex-behaviour is borderline … noble.

And in between enjoying the sex – which I do, at several moments – I find time to compile, in my head, a little list of hints and tips for a future putative help-sheet, entitled 'Ladies: How YOU Can Deal With An Unfeasibly Large Penis, Too! By A. Friend'.

1) When in the missionary position, place your palms flat on his chest and brace brace brace with your arms. This limits thrust-depth. It also, pleasingly, pushes your tits together, so it's kind of like a good tip for looking hot, posing for future photographs, etc., too.

2) In doggy, you can subtly but essentially keep *crawling away* from the penis – making it impossible to get more than the first five inches inside. During our ten-minute session, I manage to make a whole circuit of the bed, on all fours, as Al ardently pursues me, kneeling. A speeded-up film of this would make Al look like Bernie Clifton, very slowly riding his ostrich (me) around a putative Bedsit Fuck Arena.

3) Over the course of an hour or so, you will find that, helpfully, eventually, everything within a woman stretches, to accommodate. Although there's probably some technical term for this, at the time I think of it as 'Using the penis like a small trowel, to dig a bigger hole'.

4) Think of Han Solo.

5) Keep on pretending you're Al. Think about how amazing it is for him to be able to have sex with you! He must be looking down at your arse – shuddering with each rush – and thinking it's Christmas. Yes – this is a good day for Al. Lucky, happy Al.

6) Think about how little you would like to eat potato soup and play charades. Everything is relative. Particularly your relatives.

7) Use blow-job breaks in the same way American football uses ad-breaks. Everyone has a chance to get their breath back, and attend to running abrasions and injuries, etc.

8) Think of Han Solo and Chewbacca doing it together – all tenderly after some huge intergalactic laser-fight. Mmmmm, so hot.

9) This is quite fun.

10) Never, ever, ever going to come from it, though.

Al finally comes, with a rather plaintive roar – such as Aslan would make, having a thorn removed from his paw. I make a supportive sound – kind of an 'Mmmmmroooo!' – and he falls off me, and lies, breathless, next to me, as if he's completed the last foot of a parachute jump, and the tangle of my petticoat is the silk.

I still don't really know what to do in post-coital situations. I presume the basic rules must be like chatting in the pub. After a minute of silence, I decide to get the convo-ball rolling:

'Did you read Tony Rich's piece on the Cocteau Twins?' I say, gesturing to the pile of *D&ME*s. 'In it, he uses the word "basorexia" – the overwhelming need to be kissed. Isn't that an amazing word? "Basorexia". I keep thinking I might get a tin, and keep amazing words in it. "Basorexia".'

When this is greeted with silence, I turn on my side, to look at him. While I'm bright as a button, Al's demeanour is very strange – as if he's just been hit on the side of the head with a massive Acme frying pan, by the Road Runner. I later learn this is called 'being post-coital'.

'Mrrrrwww, nah?' he says – eyes oddly loose in his head. 'Din read. Sorry, babe.'

'I had *sex* with Tony Rich!' I add – half proudly, half to keep the conversation going. People love talking about sex! It is the best topic of all!

But Al is asleep.

'Well done on fitting all of my penis in you, Dolly!' I say, brightly. 'Thank you for making that effort! It wasn't bad at all, given that this was your third-ever shag! Given that you're essentially still a child, and I'm a grown-up, you managed that with aplomb!'

Al doesn't move. He's gone.

I don't feel sleepy at all. What I feel like, is having some more sex. Better sex. Sex with more of me in it. Indeed, with a smaller

penis – one that doesn't live in two separate postcodes at once
– I can see how I would like to have sex pretty much all day,
to be honest. The idea of sex only taking, like, forty minutes
seems odd – like those people who only watch television for an
hour each day. You just keep the telly on in the background, all
the time, surely? IT'S TELLY.

'Women,' I think, 'can keep the sex-telly on all day.'

But Al's asleep, and so the only sex I'm going to have is
with me. I chat myself up for ten minutes, and then come –
hard, like a car-crash, trying to be silent – next to him.

I wonder how many dead men I'm going to come next to, in
the next ten years, I think. How many times I will come alone,
next to a still not-friend, whilst the pale ghost moon watches,
through the window, and sighs.

By the time Al wakes up, I've been an utter dick and tidied
up his whole flat. I've put throws over his grimy sofa, emptied
his ashtrays, and dusted his mantelpiece. I've also made a
bread and butter pudding, out of all his stale bread – in three
half-empty bags – and fashioned rudimentary air-freshener by
boiling up a couple of half-lemons in a pan (as recommended
in *Mrs Beeton's Book of Household Management*), to boot. What
am I trying to do? Prove I'm useful, I guess, and friendly, and
practical. That I know how to do things other than gracefully
and consistently edge away from a massive penis.

'Alright, love?' Al says, wandering into the room – face and
pyjama bottoms rumpled from sleep, and lighting a fag.

'Fairies came!' I say, gesturing around the flat with an
expansive hand. I am sitting at the table, eating the bread-and-
butter pudding. I hand him a spoon.

'Fucking hell – amazing! Gonna finish this fag first,' he says.

'Oh, give us one – I'm dying,' I say.

I don't want a fag at all – but you always smoke a fag when someone else is smoking a fag, even if you find the idea a bit repulsive. That's how cigarettes work. The smokers all have to clock in together. There is an agreement.

He gives me a fag. I light it, inhale, and go a bit light-headed.

'That was … amazing,' Al says, gesturing towards the bedroom with his head.

'Thank you,' I say. 'I never had any formal sex education. I'm entirely self-taught. From the … School of Hard Cocks.'

I put my head on the table.

'You alright?' he asks, sitting at the table. 'You've gone a bit … pale.'

'Yeah,' I say, woozily. 'Just – having a little table-nap. It's okay. Carry on.'

Al goes over to the stereo, and fiddles around.

'Here,' he says, eagerly. 'Do you want to hear our new stuff? I've got some demos.'

Normally, the idea of hearing music that is still-forming – new music, music still hot from being inside someone's head – would thrill me. I make that part of me say, 'Fuck yes!', whilst the rest of me goes, 'No. I would actually not like to hear your new music. I feel very odd, and have one ear resting on your table. I am transmitting Signs of Unwellness. You might as well ask me if I want to have a go in your new rowing boat, and sail away across the Sea of Ink.'

Al puts a cassette in the player, and I get to listen to my first ever rough demo of a band.

I quickly realise why rough demos are never released. If I were reviewing this, my review would consist of the phrase 'Bitty, muffled, half-formed bollocks'. This is a magic-ruiner – like being shown the tubes magicians' rabbits escape down.

'Wow, it's so … thrillingly nascent,' I say, which is a phrase Krissi once used when I asked his opinion of my dance style.

The demo keeps on playing. Al stares at me, straight on, throughout – pausing only to close his eyes in dreamy appreciation during various, particularly awful bits.

'Gonna have some backwards clarinets there!' Al shouts out, at one point. Or: 'Gotta fix that balance in the mix – Steve's keyboard sounds a bit prickish.'

With my head on the table, I feel increasingly odd.

Up inside me, there is a bad feeling.

At first it just feels a bit 'tetchy' – understandable, given the definitive, pounding workout it's just been given. It's been a hard day's night, up my wedge. I have managed at least half a mile of cock in the last three hours. I've basically fucked all the way to the train station and back. Half a bus route.

But, after half an hour, this tetchiness is definitely morphing into a palpable anger – it's starting to feel like there's a war going on up my fnuh.

I think of pictures I have seen, in history books, of castles, at siege. That's how it feels up there, now. Like something is attacking me from within, and the defences are failing, fast. Scared peasants tipping boiling oil over the ramparts. Livestock panicking. Horses rearing up, and neighing. Princesses hastily trying to leave, via a secret back-way – their tall, pointy hats jamming in my urethra. Lots of screaming.

Al notices that I'm phasing in and out of the conversation – increasingly distracted by the urgent telegrams from my toilet-parts.

'You okay?' he asks, finally – turning the demo down.

'Ah. Hmmmm,' I reply, dashingly. 'Just going to the loo.'

I sit on the loo. There's a mirror opposite – making this the first time I've ever seen what I look like on the toilet. Although

I'm glad of the fresh and novel information, I have to admit, it's not very sensual. I get the chance to observe my natural 'hunching' posture, and send a note to myself: 'Note for future: unlikely to pull whilst on toilet. Would have fared badly in the days of communal toilets, in Rome.'

I begin my tinkle, and have the exciting chance to watch my face contort in sudden and total agony. HELLO. This piss is apparently made of boiling poison. Boiling poison, a billion Lilliputian arrows, and a wildly rotating whirligig, made of Satan's pin-like teeth. What's going on? What is this malfunction?

I haven't had enough sex to know. Perhaps this is what 'post-coital' actually means. I'd always thought it meant 'being a bit sleepy' – but perhaps it *actually* means 'feeling like someone has lit a bonfire made of swords in your vagina' instead. Perhaps that.

I come back into the kitchen, and sit down on the chair, carefully. I have been thinking hard.

'I believe,' I say, slowly, but in what I hope is also a statesmanlike manner, 'that I have cystitis.'

'Christ!' Al says, alarmed. 'Shit! Fuck!'

Pause.

'What is that, then?'

'My mum gets it,' I sigh. 'She told me all about it.'

I feel as teenage werewolves must, the first time they explain the hereditary nature of lycanthropy to their adolescent peers, the night after something awful happened with the full moon, and a friend's cat.

'It's passed down from my *mother*'s side,' they would say, apologetically – collar still hanging from their mouth, displaying a small bell, and a disc bearing the legend, 'Tibbles'.

But now: 'It means it really hurts when you go to the toilet.'

Al's expression is that of a man trying to get a handle on wild, unfamiliar, oddly alarming information.

'Well, that's not *too* bad?' he tries – clearly adding up how many times a day he urinates, and coming up with 'less than ten minutes of commitment'.

'Except, you need to go to the toilet *all the time*,' I clarify. 'Indeed – excuse me,' and I go back into that cold, cold room, and sit back down again.

Despite the desperate, bearing-down pressure in my bladder, I manage to squeeze out less than a teaspoon of what appears to be mulberry jam, heated to 1,000 degrees Celsius. The mirror allows me, once again, to see what I look like pissing out jam heated to 1,000 degrees Celsius. The answer is 'red-faced and unhappy'.

I hear Al's voice, outside the door.

'Can I get you anything?' he asks.

'You can come in,' I say. 'Three hours ago, you were bumming me sideways off a futon. The time for coyness is at an end.'

He opens the door, and hovers, uncertainly, on the threshold. As the mirror swings away, I see my teary eyes above the hand-towel I am biting on, as if in the early stages of labour.

'Shit,' he says, helplessly.

'No – piss,' I say, like Oscar fucking Wilde.

'Er, this sounds bad,' Al said, fiddling with the door-handle, 'but, erm ... have I got it, too, now? Can you ... catch cystitis? Is it like crabs or something? I don't mind, like – I've had them before.'

Oh God. Tiny crabs in this toilet. This is a bad day.

'No, Al,' I say. 'You can't catch cystitis. It's an infection triggered by tissue trauma.' I feel like Dr Chris on *This Morning*. So wise.

Although he tries not to make it obvious, Al breathes a sigh of relief. 'Can I get you anything?' he asks – looking much happier.

I try to remember what my mother does.

'I need codeine, and cranberry juice, please,' I say. 'These are the medicines of cystitis. Codeine, and cranberry juice.'

He immediately takes his keys and wallet off the chest of drawers.

'Righty tighty hold on to your nightie – back in ten minutes,' he says, slamming the door behind him.

I pass another seven drops – each feeling like a burning coal slag – and allow myself, now alone in the house, to go, 'AHHHHHHHH,' in pain.

There is a very particular noise women make when they have a pain in their reproductive chutes, caused by something unhappily trying to negotiate its way out. Years later, during childbirth, I recognise the self-same noises. I'm sure a musicologist could pin-point the exact pitching of 'vaginal immolation'. Perhaps they could play it on a church organ, whilst a room full of women wince.

Piqued by the noise, Al's cat comes into the room, and sits – a few feet away – staring at me. Its eyes are like plates of pale jade. Its fur is a very beautiful tortoise-shell. I both appreciate it as an animal, and would also dearly like to wear it as mittens, tippet or hat. I would use the eyes as buttons. I want to wear this cat. This cat could be my best thing ever.

'Male cats have spikes on their penises – so, beware,' I tell the cat, leaning my head against the wall. 'I read it in *Your Guide to Cats and Kittens*. One night on a hot tin roof, and you'll be like this, too.'

I stare at the cat. The cat stares back at me.

'Or maybe you *are* a man-cat,' I continue. 'In which case – fuck you. Fuck you, you vagina-ruiner.'

Al's bathroom is in old, green-and-white tiles – probably Victorian, or Edwardian. The floor is cold, black lino. The air is 'crisp' – the radiator is stone cold. It has the feeling of a well-run butcher's shop, or a larder. I feel like a truckle of cheese, on a shelf. I will not mould here.

The bath tub is similarly old fashioned – a huge, cast-iron ship, with rust marks where the taps have dripped, for, perhaps, centuries. I start running the bath – water coughing out of cranky pipes. I feel warm water will make this all so much better.

As soon as there's one inch in the bottom of the tub, I take everything off, and sit next to the taps, swooshing the water over my poor, unhappy cunt, shivering. The relief is immediate. It doesn't *cure* me – but the pain-relief is significant enough for me to stop fearing that I might actually start screaming. I know, instantly, that I must stay in this bath for many hours. This is the sole and only place for me now. There is no way I will be able to leave this bath, ever. How will I get back to Wolverhampton? Eventually, they'll have to put me in one of those transportation tanks they use to relocate dolphins, from SeaWorld, and take me on a massive flatbed truck, up the M1.

'A massive flatbed truck up the M1,' I think. 'That is a good euphemism for what has caused this pain. I've had a massive flatbed truck up the M1.'

When Al comes back, half an hour later, with codeine and Ocean Spray cranberry juice, I'm up to my neck in water, listening to *Screamdelica* by Primal Scream, reading an old jumble-sale copy of *Adrian Mole* that I've found in his bedroom, and crying.

These are not tears of sadness at all – just sheer agony.

'Here!' he says, handing me pills and juice, still looking quite awkward. I don't know why. Yes, he's broken a woman with his penis who's now weeping in agony in his bathroom, but, you know. Surely this is what sexy grown-ups who have sex do? I presume this kind of thing happens all the time.

I take the pills, and drink the juice straight from the carton, and continue to cry.

'This is what the Manic Street Preachers' song "Slash 'N' Burn" is about,' I say. 'Also, possibly what Dire Straits were trying to warn us about in "Tunnel Of Love".'

'Do you want anything to eat?' Al asks, still looking mortified.

'Nah. I've drunk nine pints of water,' I say. 'I'm good. Full.'

'Thing is,' Al says, looking even more awkward. 'Thing is, I've got that gig tonight.'

'I know!' I say. 'IT'S WHY I'M HERE.'

'And, erm, well. I said the support band could sleep here tonight. They've come down from Ayrshire, and I don't think they've got anywhere else to go, and …'

'Al,' I say, putting an imperious hand up. 'Don't worry. I'm sure that this will all be over in an hour and, when you return, triumphant, from your gig, I shall be sitting in the front room, wholly cured, bright as a button, mixing cocktails, for the aftershow.'

11.48pm.

I hear voices in the corridor, and then Al's key in the lock. They are back, finally.

I have had an interesting afternoon, and evening. By which I mean fucking terrible.

When the codeine kicked in, I felt well enough to finally get out of the bath – as pale and wrinkled as ET, when Eliot and Drew Barrymore find him dead, in the stream.

I lie around weakly for half an hour – pain is enormously draining – and then slowly get dressed, and prepare to leave the house. I should go home, really – although Al invited me to stay the night, things still feel pretty weird down below, and, besides, it's fairly basic common sense to quarantine myself from his penis for the foreseeable future. It would be an insanity to live through the pain I've just lived through – and then fuck him again. Like Luke effortfully blowing up the Death Star – then rebuilding the Death Star, then stuffing it back up his vagina.

No – I'm going back to my parents' house, and my bed, and I'm not going to put anything up inside me again until at least after Christmas. This whole area – and I pass my hand over my pants – is closed for maintenance.

I make it out of Al's flat and as far as the shop on the corner before the pain kicks back in. Whatever the small, brave codeine pills have managed to do, they have now, clearly, been overwhelmed. I go very, very hot and then very, very cold, and go into the shop for a minute, to buy crisps, because I am somehow convinced they will make it better.

Three minutes later I am hobbling back to Al's house again with three bags of Ready Salted McCoy's – thankful that I know he keeps the key under the mat. I, clearly, will not be going anywhere for a while. As I put the key in the door I do a bit of agonised wee in my pants, much like mice do. Would do. If they wore pants. Apparently mice constantly piss themselves. I'm scoping out a bit. I must stop thinking about mice.

By the time Al comes home, at 11.48pm, I have been able to make some preparations for his arrival. Between 3pm–6pm, I simply wept, exhaustedly, in the bath, feeling very, very scopey. Then at 6pm, I sat in the bath and ate the crisps, as my tea – a useful tea, as it turned out, as, by then, I'd drunk so much water my salt levels were dangerously low, hence my confusion.

After the bath crisp-picnic, I felt a bit more together, and finished *The Secret Diary of Adrian Mole* and then *The Growing Pains of Adrian Mole*. Bored, I then found an extension cable, and dragged Al's TV and video out onto the landing, and angled them so that I could watch his video of *Withnail & I* from the bath. I'd always wanted to see it, and, in the circumstances, found it inspiring – they were both taking so many drugs that I felt confident in my decision to take twice the recommended amount of codeine. I hauled the huge sash window open, and looked out over the rainy rooftops of Brighton, as I sat in the boiling bath, hair piled on top of my head and held with a knitting needle I'd found in the kitchen.

Withnail and his I were fantastic company for the afternoon. Indeed, if it weren't for the racking agony, I'd put that afternoon up there as one of the best of my life so far. By the time Withnail was reciting *Hamlet* in the rain to the uncomprehending wolves in Regent's Park Zoo – broken, under his umbrella, with love – I was crying my eyes out, off my chanks on codeine, and smoking a fag.

Hence, by the time Al returned, my fantastic plan. I was still definitely in too much pain to leave the analgesic effects of the hot bath – but, on the other hand, I acknowledged that Al's guests – and, indeed, Al himself – would need to use the toilet, and would find a naked woman in the tub somewhat disconcerting.

'Al!' I cried – cheerfully, and woozily, from the tub. 'Al's friends! Come and say hello!'

I heard them coming down the corridor – uncertainly – and Al saying '… not very well …'

Al appeared at the door with the entire line-up of a band I later found out were called Plume – all in black, all looking quite worried.

'Hello!' I said, expansively – cigarette in hand. I felt so very warm and fuzzy.

'I am very sorry,' I said, 'but I am temporarily confined to this bath, due to a woman's agony. However, as this is, clearly, massively inconvenient to anyone who wishes to use the toilet, I am attired in my petticoat –' I gestured to myself, sitting, in the hot bath, in my soaking wet petticoat '– and will temporarily vacate the bathroom, to stand on the landing, whenever anyone needs to use these facilities.'

And that is what happened, until 2am. I leave the bathroom door open, and am a fairly lively member of the party, even though I say so myself. Like that film where Glynis Johns is a mermaid that someone keeps in their bath, I, too, am an enticing siren, who must be kept wet at all times – but who, nonetheless, charms all who meet her.

At first, the men stay in the front room, and I shout witticisms as and when I see gaps in the conversation – pausing only to occasionally get out of the bath, and stand on the landing, in Al's towelling robe, while they use the toilet – door coyly locked.

By the end of the evening, however, everyone's so drunk that all the boundaries have dissolved: those social ones between men and mermaids; those physical ones between someone using the toilet, and the people standing outside. The party moves first to the landing, and then into the bathroom – I partake of Plume's bottle of Polish vodka ('It's a clear liquid – it'll clean yer insides out, love') whilst they sit on the radiator, or on the windowsill – window open onto the rooftops, and the stars. Everyone pisses in front of each other, and I make one of Plume and Al kiss each other, because these are the days of Suede, and everyone's pretending to be a little bit bisexual between 11pm and 4am.

Finally, at 4am, the pain passed enough for me to crawl out of the bath, drape my wet petticoat over the radiator, wrap a towel around myself, and fall asleep at the bottom of Al's bed, like a dog.

The next morning, I feel amazing – that clean, light rebirth feeling you have when pain finally lifts, and you have slept. I have clearly pissed out my infection. I'm up first, and tip-toe past the living room – where all of Plume sleep on the floor, covered in old blankets – and into the kitchen.

The room is a pig-sty – empty cans and vodka-bottles, ashtrays humped, Pompeii-like, with ash and dead stubs, and a broken wine bottle in the sink: the wine splashed over the stacked plates, like blood.

Pain has made me older and wiser. Yesterday, when I found this house messy, I cleaned it from top to bottom, like a good girl.

Today, they can all go fuck themselves. Housework is endless. I am never opting in again.

I make myself a cup of tea, roll a fag, open the window, and sit on the windowsill – looking at Brighton across, and below. The way I sit, in my petticoat, anyone in the street can see my cunt – but I don't care. After the day it's had, it's a miracle it's still there. I'm proud of it. Passers-by *should* acknowledge its survival. And besides, the breeze on it feels soothing.

I'm gently squawking back at the seagulls – kwaa, kwaa – when I hear a rattling behind me. It's one of the Plume boys, looking very dishevelled, searching for fags.

'Do you want a rollie?' I say, offering him Al's tobacco pouch.

He blearily accepts it, and sits at the table by the window, going about the process of assembling a cigarette, and himself, for the morning.

'Good night,' he offers, eventually, after the first dry drag, and cough.

'Yes!' I say, brightly. 'It's the best bath party I've ever been to.'

'You feeling okay?' he asks, looking up from under his hair. 'You looked really rough.'

'I thought I looked lusciously opiated – like Stevie Nicks,' I say.

'Nah. Rough,' he says, taking another drag. The CD player is on, in the corner – still playing, quietly, from last night, on endless repeat. It's Serge Gainsbourg's *Melody Nelson*. I had insisted they put it on – 'This album is *amazing*! It's like – *eating a sexy kaleidoscope*!' – while I told them all about John Kite – 'I ended up in *his* bath, too! This is not my first time at a rock star bath-party!'

'It's amazing that this album's about a ginger girl from Newcastle,' I say.

'Is it?' the boy asks.

'Yes. If you listen, in a minute, he goes "blah blah blah French French *Newcastle*",' I say.

We listen, in silence, as the strings become tidal, and wash the song along.

'See!' I say, when Serge sings it. 'See! Newcastle!'

The boy makes tea, and we spend the next hour talking about what we know about Serge Gainsbourg. In the days before the internet, this is how you found out things about music – there was nowhere all the facts were kept. You learned things piecemeal, in conversations, instead – sometimes having to go all the way to a bar in New York, at 3am, to find out something that twenty years later, you could have just discovered using an iPhone, on a bus. We share all our knowledge about Serge like it's thrilling village gossip – 'Well, *I* heard …'

At one point as the boy – his name is Rob – rolls another fag, he looks up and says, 'You know, you're not a thing like I thought you'd be.'

'You thought I'd be like a thing?' I ask, pleased. I have a reputation! 'What thing did you think I'd be like?'

'You know. The way you write. I thought you'd be …' he struggles to choose the right words. 'Scary. But you're alright'

'Scary?'

'Yeah. You know.'

I think, for a moment, about the things I've written recently. The review of C+C Music Factory's 'Gonna Make You Sweat', with a joke about how one of the band – '+C' – had recently had meningitis: 'And that *will* make you sweat when your temperature hits 102. Unlike this hateful piece of house music, designed solely and only to make secretaries get dry-humped by their bosses at Christmas parties.'

The review of the Inspiral Carpets, where I spend the whole thing repeatedly going on about how they're all too ugly to be popstars – 'Popstars should look like David Bowie: all ice and bone and imperiously-shouldered furs. To buy one of Bowie's singles is like walking into Tiffany's, and treating yourself to a tiara whenever you get the Mean Blues. By way of contrast, whenever the Inspiral Carpets release a single, it's like that awkward day a week before Christmas when the bin men ring on your doorbell and say "Happy Christmas, missus", waiting for a tip. They're too ugly to be a band. They are, instead, a *bad*.'

Or, indeed, the review of U2, where I refer to The Edge throughout, simply, as 'The Cunt' – even though, as I've said before, I secretly love U2.

'All the bands I know are scared of you. Here – don't come and review us,' Rob says – with the half-joking, half-serious look of a man who worries he might have said too much.

'Oh, I wouldn't review you! I like you!' I say. 'These days, I only review bands I don't like.'

'Bands you *don't* like?' Rob asks. 'Why?'

Why?

Because I believe pop music is too important to be left to the leaden, dullardly and unambitious. Because rich people, powerful people, cool people or the kind of swaggering men that form these bands, are the kind of people who would usually look down on a fat teenage girl from a council estate, and in the one place I am more powerful than them – the pages of *D&ME* – I want my revenge – revenge on behalf of all the millions of girls like me. Because when I sit at my half-a-table in my house, at my laptop, with the smell of the chip-fryer still lingering on the curtains and the twins wailing downstairs, I want to pretend I'm those other lady-journalists – Dorothy Parker and Julie Burchill – and they would have wielded their stiletto daggers in the same way I wield mine, before draining their martinis, and hailing a cab. Because I get paid by the word, and it's a thrill when that word is 'cunt'. Because I don't run or swim or cycle, and I only dance in the dark, and so the adrenalin I get from hating these bands is the nearest I get to physical exercise. Because I wrote John Kite a proposal in a feature and he notably never married me. Because Kenny told me to.

Because I'm the weakest, youngest one in the gang at the *D&ME*, and need to kill to prove my loyalty. Because I am still learning to walk and talk, and it is a million times easier to be cynical, and wield a sword, than it is to be open-hearted, and stand there, holding a balloon and a birthday cake, with the infinite potential to look foolish. Because I still don't know what I really think or feel, and I'm throwing grenades and filling the air with smoke while I desperately, desperately try to get off the ground: to get elevation. Because I haven't yet learned the simplest and most important thing of all: the world is difficult, and we are all breakable. So just be kind.

At the time, I think of my own, new pugilistic air as utterly righteous. I am a lone gunslinger, come to town. I am Travis Bickle, taking the scum off the streets. If someone has the right to do something, then I have the right to try and *undo* it. Every time I shoot down some no-hoper band, I leave a little more room for the new David Bowie to appear.

Of course, the thing about Travis Bickle, and lone gunslingers, is that they're not really the kind of people you want to invite to parties. For if your self-appointed role is coming into the party, late, dressed in black, and shooting over everyone's head towards the stage, the party will begin to … sour. People who have quieter voices, or who aren't so sure of themselves, do not want to speak up any more. They will not take to the stage. Only the more confident, and boisterous, will want to address the crowd.

The atmosphere changes – for now, it's just the extroverts left, shouting each other down. The introverts have gone back underground – taking with them the quieter notes, the minor chords. The playlist constricts, stultifies: people only play old favourites. Everyone is too scared to stand up and risk something new, that might sound odd to impatient ears.

For when cynicism becomes the default language, playfulness and invention become impossible. Cynicism scours through a culture like a bleach, wiping out millions of small, seedling ideas. Cynicism means your automatic answer becomes 'No'. Cynicism means you presume everything will end in disappointment. And this is, ultimately, why anyone becomes cynical. Because they are scared of disappointment. Because they are scared someone will take advantage of them. Because they are fearful their innocence will be used against them – that when they run around gleefully trying to cram the whole world in their mouth, someone will try to poison them.

Cynicism is, ultimately, fear. Cynicism makes contact with your skin, and a thick black carapace begins to grow – like insect armour. This armour will protect your heart, from disappointment – but it leaves you almost unable to walk. You cannot dance, in this armour. Cynicism keeps you pinned to the spot, in the same posture, forever.

And, of course, the deepest irony about the young being cynical is that they are the ones that need to move, and dance, and trust the most. They need to cartwheel through a freshly burst galaxy of still-forming but glowing ideas, never scared to say 'Yes! Why not!' – or their generation's culture will be nothing but the blandest, and most aggressive, or most-defended of old tropes. When young people are cynical, and snarky, they shoot down their own future. When you keep saying 'No' all that's left is what other people said 'Yes' to, before you were born. Really, 'No' is no choice at all.

When other people begin to bring their guns to the party, it's not a party any more. It's a battle. Without realising it, I have become a self-defeating mercenary in a pointless war. I'm shooting my own future.

But it's okay – I've got plenty of time to be nice … later on. Plenty of time. When you're seventeen, the days are like years.

You've got a billion lifetimes to live and die and live again before you're twenty. That's the one positive thing about being so young. You've got plenty of time left to make things right.

Except, as it turns out, I haven't got plenty of time.

RIP
IT UP
AND
START
AGAIN

TWENTY-ONE

So, a couple of months ago, it really *was* fun being me. I would turn up at the *D&ME* and 'Morning Cruella de Ville!' the men would cry, fondly. I would sit on their desks, smoking fags, and telling stories about all the rock stars I'd got off with.

My colleagues love these stories – my recounting of my night with Big Cock Al brings the office to a halt. Sometimes, I get off with rock stars just so I can come back and tell the stories – I think of myself as a little drone robot, going off and accumulating samples of sexual behaviour, then bringing them back here, to the lab, for everyone to analyse. This is my unique contribution to the gang: if this were *Dungeon Master*, and we were assembling a crew, then Rob's talent would be 'Drunken havoc-making, 7', Kenny's would be 'Drunken bitchery, 8' and mine would be 'Sexual Raconteuring, 10'.

In interviews, I get songwriters hopelessly drunk and make them tell me what their sexual fantasies are – 'Off the record! I just want to know! It … informs your beautiful songs!'

When the lead singer of one band tells me that his fantasy is getting a nun wearing lipstick to give him a blow job – 'So there's lipstick all over … it' – I go straight from the interview, in a taxi, to the office, to tell everyone.

'A *nun*,' Rob boggles. 'That's these Catholics for you.'

'Jews aren't perverted like that,' Rich says, in one of his rare, light-hearted moods. 'We never imagine getting blow jobs from rabbis.'

Eventually, after a couple of stories, Kenny will shout, 'Chop chop. The freak-parade is over. Everyone start writing,' and I'll go over to a spare computer and start writing up that day's work – taking all the things I've test-run in front of my try-out audience, and putting them into copy, for the paper. Carefully crafted bitchiness.

Today, I'm 600 words into a feature when I suddenly remember something: my dad's demo, in my bag. He'd put it in there this morning, as I left the house: 'Get your dadda a million quid. Just one million. It's all I want,' he'd said, standing on the front doorstep holding a pint of milk. 'Just play it to someone. Get my foot in the door.'

I looked down at his feet. He was wearing my mother's slippers, which are novelty bee ones.

'Rightio!' I said, waving goodbye.

'Kenny,' I say, going over to his desk. His computer has a sticker on it which reads 'Just FUCK OFF (who are you?)' on it, which he points to, whilst still typing. I ignore it. 'I've got a demo of a band. Can I play it to you?'

He doesn't look up from his computer screen, and holds his hand out: 'Fifty quid.'

'What?'

'To listen to a new band. Fifty quid.'

He looks up at me.

'I'm too old for all that "new band" shit, darling,' he sighs. 'I'm still reeling over Genesis P. Orridge leaving Throbbing Gristle. I still think they could have been the biggest band in the world. Play it to one of the younger boys. One who still has hope.'

I go into the Meeting Room, where Rob and Zee are doing the crossword in the *NME*.

'Five down *has* to be Iggy Pop,' Rob is saying, sitting on the windowsill and smoking a fag.

'I've already got Status Quo on 17 across,' Zee says, doubtfully. 'It would make him Iggy Poo.'

'That could still work,' Rob says, musingly.

'Hey you blokes,' I say, knocking on the door, coming in and going over to the stereo in one move. 'I've got a demo.'

'Hit it with the Bible. In the morning, if it hasn't gone down, see a doctor,' Rob says.

'What is it?' Zee asks. Zee has started up his own, tiny record label – also called 'Thank You' – on which he presses flexi-discs, and sells them with his fanzine. In honour of the big independent labels – Factory and Creation – Zee's record label is referred to in the office as, variously, 'Zeeation' or 'Cacktory', depending on how much the speaker likes Zee.

'It's a mystery,' I say, mysteriously, putting the cassette in the stereo. 'A new band. From the Midlands. See what you think.'

There's a hiss and clunk, as the cassette spools on. Then the unmistakable sounds of James's *Sit Down* blares out.

'There could be some copyright issues,' Rob says. 'It's quite derivative. Of "Sit Down" by James.'

'He – *they* – have obviously recorded it on an old tape,' I say, stopping it and fast-forwarding it. 'The stupid bastard.'

'Is this some horrible goth band?' Rob asks. Rob is convinced I'm a goth.

'I'm not a goth,' I say, pressing the button on the stereo, to make it re-wind faster. 'I just like wearing black. Like the Beatles in Hamburg. You wouldn't say they were goths.'

'Do you write poetry?'

'Yes.'

'Have you danced to "Temple of Love" by Sisters of Mercy?'

'Well, who hasn't?'

'Have you imagined Robert Smith from The Cure is your big brother?'

'That's a very common–'

'Would you leave the house without eyeliner?'

'I made a decision–'

'When you doodle, do you draw a picture of a sad willow tree, with all the leaves falling off?'

'You saw my pad!'

'You know what I've noticed?' Rob says, thinking. 'You actually can't *help* it if you're a goth. It's in your genes. You're born that way – it's like being black. I reckon you could identify goths if they were naked, in a line, God forbid. 'Cos your goth birds – they all have a bit of chubble, don't they? They're all a bit fat – no offence, Dolly. They gone goth because black's slimming, innit? And the make-up's because they're insecure, so they try and look scary, to frighten off the … predators. And your goth boys, meanwhile, without exception, are fucking short-arses – because they can wear those brothel-creeper shoes if they're goth. Get a bit of elevation. When two goths mate, it's fucking hilarious. A goth couple coming down the street looks like a number "10", perambulating. It's in their *genes*.'

Briskly thanking ex-punk Rob for his thoughts on goth body-dysmorphia – and pointing out all ex-punks I've ever met only appear to have nine teeth left, 'From a combination of bad sulphate and getting punched in the mouth for being *incredibly fucking offensive*' – something which clearly wounds Rob, who has teeth like fragments of cheese – I fast-forward the cassette to the bit where my dad's songs are. I press 'play', and 'Dropping Bombs' plays, tinnily, in the room.

This is the first time I've ever heard his songs, outside our house. In our house, they sound huge – mainly because Dadda plays them very loudly, on his massive speakers. And his audience is us, and we pat them as they go past, like a farmer would a cow as it passed through a gate. These songs are our livestock. Our family's pets.

Here, however, on the tinny office stereo, with two grown men sitting and listening quizzically, the songs sound very different. I'm quite startled by how *small* Dadda sounds. Small, and oddly lonely. Like a busker who's been chucked out of a pub, for annoying the other customers, and is now standing outside. I suddenly have a terrible pang of sympathy for him. He was so happy making these songs – but they come across so *sad*.

Dadda is singing '*And the bombs you make/And the lies you fake*' (Rob: 'Here. How can you fake a lie?' Zee, reasonably: 'Well, a lie *is* a fake. That's what it is.' Rob: 'It's a fucking *tautology*, is what it is.') when Tony Rich comes in – taking off his coat and putting it on the back of a chair, and putting his bag on the floor.

I have a momentary flashback to the last time I saw his coat come off – me taking it off him by candlelight before he fucked me on the floor, while I patted his back with my hands – as instructed to by that man, at that party.

'This sounds fucking awful,' he says, blankly, nodding at the stereo.

'I've already filed that review,' Rob says, cheerfully.

Everyone listens for a little while longer.

'Oh, you could have a *lot* of fun with this,' Rich says. 'Who's reviewing it? This bloke's so Brummie. And God, it's so *mawkish*. It sounds like a poster of Noddy Holder holding a dying unicorn, and crying "But WHY? WHY?"'

So far, I haven't said anything. I'm standing in a room with my colleagues and my kind-of boyfriend, listening to my dad singing while they all slag him off like any other wannabe chancer who sends a demo into the *D&ME*, and I haven't said a word. I wonder what I'm going to say?

'I'll review it,' I say, eventually pressing 'Stop' and taking the cassette out. 'I can just cut out and print everything you boys have said. Easiest job of the week.'

Later, I go to the Ladies, take the demo tape out of my bag, wrap it up in toilet paper, and put it in the bin. I push it right down to the bottom. Then I put more eyeliner on, and get into the lift with Tony Rich, and press against him until he gets hard, because it still thrills me that I can do that. That I can make a man hard. This is my main job, right now. Making Tony Rich hard. That's all I'm thinking about.

That night, the whole *D&ME* crew is off to see Teenage Fanclub at the Brixton Academy. We all walk in, like a gang, with a vaguely menacing air: aftershow passes inside our leather jackets, smoking fags and talking at the back. I have learned quickly that 'talking at the back' is the right thing to do – after going down the front at a Primal Scream gig, moshing against the barrier, coming back sweaty and having Kenny ask, in a pained manner, 'Are you covered in *peasant sweat*? Did any of them touch you? Show Kenny on the doll where they touched you, darling. We can get you whatever inoculatory jabs you might need.'

And so I moved, permanently, to the back of the room, by the bar, where my kind should live – doing a running commentary of the gig, with the other writers, instead.

Recently, however, it's become quite difficult to go out – even if I stand at the back, with my gang. The indie-rock world is a small world, and I soon realise I have insulted around a third of it.

Standing with the other *D&ME* writers, instantly recognisable in my top hat, I am pretty visible to the enemies I have made – something I first realised when a small goth girl came up to me last month, and berated me at length for slagging off the Sisters of Mercy.

'Where do you get off calling Andrew Eldritch "a weasel in painted-on trousers", when you're just a … fat cow, in the Child Catcher's hat?' she asked – a fair point well made, really.

A couple of press officers have refused to send me CDs any more – Kenny has to blag them and forward them to me when I need to review them, saying, 'They fear your hatchet, Wilde – I had to tell them it was for ZZ Top, instead.'

And then, tonight, at the Brixton Academy, halfway through Teenage Fanclub, I am enjoying several whiskies when the bass-player from Via Manchester comes up to me at the bar, says, 'You are Dolly Wilde, aren't you?', and waits for me to give my now-traditional reply – 'Almost all the time' – before throwing his drink over me.

'And *that's* a waste of a good drink,' he says, standing over me as I blink, vodka running down my face. 'I was going to make it piss – but my manager said to save it for next time.'

I try and remember what I said about Via Manchester as I cry in the toilets, where Kenny is giving me my first line of his legendarily terrible sulphate, 'To cheer you up.'

Previously, when he's offered it me, I've turned it down, as I'm scared of putting anything up my nose. But now, I feel like I *should* have something, to make me better. I need something new inside me, to counteract this equally new and bad feeling. It's like medicine, really.

'I can't remember if I said they were the ones who proved the threat of Mad Cow Disease was real – or if they were the ones I said should be buried up to their necks in all their unsold records, then stoned to death by angry peasants,' I say, crying, as Kenny chops out my line.

I do it – chopped out on the top of the cistern – in a devil-may-care way, and notice that it tastes like money. I don't know what I'd previously thought drugs might taste like – dry ice, maybe, or some kind of metallic snow – but this tastes exactly like a £5 smells.

I wonder, with a sudden clarity, if this is because *every* £5 I've ever smelled has traces of sulphate on it. If *all* money is dusted with drugs. God, *everyone* is on drugs. I can't believe I've left it so long. Thank *God* I'm doing some now. Otherwise, I'd never catch up.

'Kenny, I don't want to go around *upsetting* people,' I say, as the sulphate makes me start crying again. 'I didn't think they'd actually *read* it. I just thought, like, their press officers put it in a box, and it just kind of stayed there, and they just carried on doing what they're doing, and we carry on doing what we're doing, and we all know it's just some *fun*, I was just *riffing*, I mean why do they *care* what I think? This is a band who said they wanted to put an E up John Major's bum.'

They had indeed – live, on *The Word*. It had caused quite the controversy.

The speed has kicked in so rapidly that I have said all of this on one furious exhale, whilst crying. I look up – Kenny is staring at me.

'Fuck them,' he says, briskly. 'They're all big boys. This is the game. This is what we all do. They make records, we write about them. They make the records they like – we write the reviews *we* like. Everyone gets their go. If you don't want to be written about – don't put records out, or prance around on stage like a tit.'

I think about this for a minute. I feel comforted.

'This is the game,' I repeat. I take a tissue, and blow my nose.

'Oh my God – your drugs, Wilde!' Kenny says, in horror – staring at my tissue. 'Don't blow out your drugs!'

I look into the tissue, where I've just deposited the half of the line my nose didn't have time to absorb. I look at Kenny. It seems I have made a drug faux-pas. He stares at me.

'Should I … eat it?' I ask him, trying to work out what the done thing is.

'Not now,' Kenny says, bending over to do his line, screwing up the empty wrap, and flushing it down the toilet. 'But maybe keep it in your pocket, for later. For who knows where the evening might lead?'

In the short-term, the evening leads to coming back to this toilet three more times, and doing some more of Kenny's speed. I am finding it a surprising experience. It isn't like I thought it would be at all. Even though the truism about Kenny's speed is that it's awful – 'Rat poison and aspirin,' someone at *D&ME* had explained, briskly. 'Even Shane McGowan from the Pogues won't take it' – it doesn't really have much effect, other than making me want to talk a great deal more, ie: to unbearable volumes.

But – like smoking and drinking – I find it pleasingly communal, and bonding. I guess if we still lived in an agrarian society, we would feel the same bonding experience when bringing in a harvest, or pulling together, as a village, to raise a clapboard house in a day, like in *Little House on the Prairie*. Robbed of this opportunity, we all pulled together, as one, to smuggle me past Security's eye into the men's toilets, to culmi-natively pile through two wraps, instead. It gave the evening a pleasant sense of *questiness*.

But the evening leads, eventually, as so many evenings do, to having sex again in Tony Rich's flat. We fall through the door all over each other – in the white-hot state where you're just pawing at each other – kissing in that way that is a series of questions. If I do … *this*, then you will do … *that*, and then I will *do all these other amazing things*.

By the time we fall onto the bed, shoes, coats and half our clothes are off, I'm so high on lust that I feel like some kind of kiss-drunk werewolf. I feel happily, dumbly animal. This is the best remedy to a bad night – to fuck. I am at my best when I am taking my clothes off with a boy. I can make no mistakes, or offend anyone, here. Here, I am a force for the good – making boys who need to come, come. This is the purest humanity. In a way, it's very noble.

My thoughts of intense nobility are interrupted by Tony.

'So – lipstick nun blow jobs,' he says, amusedly, pausing in our fumbling on the bed. We've taken a break to get our breath back. I've been on top of him, grinding him, hard.

'You've been getting around a bit.'

'Yes!' I say, proudly. 'I've been having Lady Sex Adventures!'

I start unbuttoning his shirt – grinding down into him again. No talking! Let's get back to being animal!

'So you're quite *adventurous*,' he says, hands in my hair. His voice is heavy, and slow.

'Yes,' I say, kissing the chest revealed from the unbuttoning. 'I'm like Christopher Columbus – voyaging around the world, always looking for Newfoundland in someone's trousers. Oh look! I've just found New York!'

I unbutton his flies.

'You're so *dirty*,' he says, delightedly. Then he says it again, but more seriously. 'You're so … *bad*.'

It's an oddly simple and reductionist word for Tony to be using – usually he would qualify any moral judgement with a paragraph of social context, like the time in the office that Rob Grant said that Sinead O'Connor was 'a bald goon-eyed mentalist', and Tony lectured him for half an hour about the Catholic Church in Ireland, and the need for feminism to have feral out-runners, in order to 'grenade impacted assumptions'. All the way through that speech, Rob had stood behind Tony, making 'blah blah blah' faces, and doing an impression of Sinead O'Connor being bonkers. Anyway.

'Super-bad,' I agree with Tony.

'You know that story you told everyone about the guy with the candle …' he says. 'And all the hot wax. That was an … interesting story. You know, you have to pick the right kind of person for that kind of thing. The *right* kind of person.'

He looks at me in a significant way.

Oh, okay. Right. I *get* you, my handsome, posh pervert. There's a candle by the bed. I give Tony my very best 'dominatrix look' – seeing my reflection in his eyes, I see it looks less 'Venus in Furs', and more 'Mrs McCluskey from *Grange Hill* when Gonch has set off the fire-alarms again', but still – and reach over to get it. I will drip hot wax onto this man's genitals! I take requests! But Tony suddenly rolls over on top of me.

'The thing I like about you, is that you like doing all the *wrong things*,' he says, pinning my hands above my head.

The next half-hour is odd. I had always thought if I did have some kind of S&M sex, *I* would be the S, not the M. I feel like a natural S. The S has to make all the effort – the S is put to work, soothing, controlling and relieving the gratitude-drunk M.

As someone not afraid of a hard day's work, I've always presumed I would be the sadist, in any sexy games. I am a sexual grafter! A lovely, beneficent, hard-working mistress, in a great leather outfit – like out of Madonna.

But it appears I have got me all wrong – as Tony has seen the secret masochist in me. He must have – or why else is he doing what he's doing now?

For the first few minutes, I feel quiet … huffy. To be honest, I feel I would be a better sadist than Tony. I've read about it, in dirty books, in the library – I've read de Sade, and Anaïs Nin, and *Gravity's Rainbow*, and *Story of O*. First you have to have pleasure – *then* pain. I know how you should never strike the same place twice in a row; how you should choose the softer, fleshier areas, rather than the bone. How you coax, and cajole, in between the crueller moments. How you *tell the story* of your fuck.

What Tony's doing, by way of contrast, is essentially like the 'wrestling' matches I have with Lupin. Except Tony's actually hurting me. At one point, I say 'OW!' in a very broad and indignant Wolvo accent, but I can see this is ruining the mood – so I make the next one more of a 'MmmmmOW!' instead. I am nothing if not helpful.

Really, *I* should be in charge of all this. I feel a bit like I am the Bob Dylan of sadistic fucking, and have turned up at a party, and offered my sexual genius to the room – only for the host to say, 'Oh, it's okay – my brother has a Bontempi organ, and is going to do us a couple of Hue & Cry numbers, instead.'

The thought I can't have is 'I don't want to do this' – because how do I *know* if I don't want to do this? I'm still terra-forming me. I'm learning so many new things about me, every day. Perhaps this is the day I find I *am* secretly a masochist – even though each blow does just feel like someone thumping me, rather than some high-octane sexual release.

In the end – not really getting the point of being, essentially, told off by a man with a hard cock – I do what I have always done during sex: concentrate on how much *he* is enjoying it, instead. I imagine what it's like to be sexy posh Tony Rich, with a dirty seventeen-year-old girl in his bed. I think how much it must delight him. I think how incredible it must be to put your cock into someone – how magical to have something so hard and full, and to push it, over and over, in this hot, friendly place. To be able to move a girl around a bed, and put her in the positions you want. To have someone want you.

He must want to do these things very badly. I'm making his dreams come true. That's a pretty cool thing to be doing, I think, on all fours, as he slaps my arse in the same place, over and over, like an amateur who's never read any pervy books, until my bones hurt. I am making dreams come true.

'You're amazing,' he says, afterwards, as we lie on the bed, breathless. He strokes my hair, and looks at me quite tenderly – admiringly.

Am I? Was I amazing? Is what I just did amazing? If I think about it, what happened here tonight was Tony Rich had sex with someone who was *pretending* they were Tony Rich. I don't think *I* was here at all.

'You are so adorably filthy,' he says, kissing me. So I smile, because I am so adorably filthy. This is, after all, the best thing anyone has said to me for months.

'You are so adorably filthy,' I think to myself, the next day, back in Wolverhampton.

I'm lying on my bed, thinking about Tony Rich. I'm doing my usual thing, of trying to look at things positively. I can't help but think what we did yesterday means, ultimately, we are at a new stage in our relationship.

I have a sneaking suspicion that Tony Rich is falling in love with me. Last night was as some kind of bonding ceremony. He *trusts* me. The girl he was going out with before – maybe she *wouldn't* let him do those things, and that's why they split up. That's why he's with me, now. Because he's falling in love with me. A girl he can do bad things with.

As the weeks go on, my only problem is, I'm pretty certain it's against all the rules of being a foxy chick to ask outright. Popping your head around the door on the way to the toilet and saying, 'I'm going to make a brew – anyone want one? And, hey! By the way! Are you completely demented with love for me? Those things you write – are they about me? Do you dream of me? Am I the thing? Are you in this with me – or am I here alone?'

But then, on the other hand, the opportunities to casually, accidentally find out if we're in a relationship seem few and far between. All the conversations we have are either about music, or fucking. I can't see any way I can trigger in Rich the sentence '… and, of course, obviously, I am your boyfriend' in *either* a nerdy deconstruction of Nile Rodgers' guitar-playing, or the instruction 'More. *More*,' as he slaps me. I just don't have those chat-chops.

All that summer, as I end up in his flat over and over, drinking his wine, having his bad pervy sex, and then lying on the bed, talking about Auden's influence on Morrissey, I feel like we're in a huge, ongoing, surreal session of the Rizla game, in which Rich has stuck a Rizla on my head on which is written either 'My girlfriend' or 'Not my girlfriend', and I am having to guess which it is with a series of questions which he can only answer 'yes' or 'no'. This whole situation seems like a massive societal problem. Why have we not yet discovered a way to find out if someone's in love with you? Why can't I press a litmus paper to Tony's sweaty brow, when we're fucking, and see if it turns 'pink' for love – or 'blue' for casual fuck? Why is there no information on this? *Why has science not attended to this matter?*

Whether I'm in love with *him* seems far less important than whether he's in love with *me*. I never take me to one side and ask myself, 'Do you actually *want* him?', because I feel like I never really see me around, any more. This is another drawback of living in a house with no mirrors.

As if trying to confuse me more, in the middle of July, while I'm back in Wolverhampton, Rich calls me, and invites me down to his parents' for the weekend – LIKE YOU DO WITH A GIRLFRIEND – then adds, 'But don't worry – lots of friends are going.' Like you exactly don't with a girlfriend.

'Are you having hot filthy perverted casual sex with lots of your friends, as well?' I ask, like a cheerful yet cunning love detective.

'My parents have an amazing cellar!' he replies. 'Who knows?!'

At my parents' house, which does not have an amazing cellar – just a shed, full of old cans of petrol – I eventually put the phone down on this peerlessly gnomic phone call, and go and seek out Krissi.

He's in his room, tending his seed propagator, which he bought at a jumble sale for 50p, and which is mint apart from a massive crack across the lid, which he's Sellotaped up.

'Whatcha growing?' I ask, throwing myself on his bed, and taking a swig from my bottle of Jack Daniels. I've upgraded to Jack Daniels now. It's what Primal Scream drink, and Slash, and Ernest Hemingway. I have graduated on from the nursery slopes of MD 20/20 in impressive time.

'Get off my bed – I don't want you perioding on it again,' he replies. 'You're too free and easy with your bodily fluids. I found evidences of your viscera on my pillowcase last week. Marrows.'

I look at the rows of tiny marrow seedlings – each so small, they look like a tiny green needle, with a single pair of leaves at the top. They are the most fragile thing I have ever seen. I do not know how they stay upright. This is a box of impossible.

'I don't know if I'm Tony Rich's girlfriend or not,' I say, sitting obediently on the floor, and fiddling with his mist diffuser.

'Well, you're not,' Krissi says, briskly. 'Or he would have told you.'

'It's not that simple!'

'Well, it is,' Krissi says, crumbling compost into the tray.

'Not it's not.'

'It is. He's your smashing posh paedo not-boyfriend.'

I stare at him, open-mouthed.

'He's not a paedo!'

'Johanna, he's twenty-three and you're seventeen.'

'So?'

'Bit paedo, innit? I mean, it's not *not* paedo.'

'Age is nothing but a number,' I say, loftily. 'Tony and I don't think of those things. We're just two hot equal hacks, having sex with each other.'

'Yeah, you're right,' Krissi says. 'Age *is* just a number to Tony Rich. It's a number he keeps saying over and over to himself – 'I'm fucking a seventeen-year-old! I'm fucking a seventeen-year-old! Gonna get some high-fives for this back at the office!'

I decide, angrily, that this is not the moment where I will tell Krissi about the slapping. Sex is complicated, and he doesn't understand it. He's just a commentator, on the sidelines. I'm the one on the frontlines of sex, actually *dealing* with it.

I sit sullenly on the bed, and take another swig of Jack Daniels. The problem is, Krissi is still treating me like I'm an unfucked fourteen-year-old trying to talk to him about *Annie* – despite my top hat, and my byline, and my shagging.

'You know, in a couple of years, you'll understand,' I say to Krissi, crushingly. 'And I will look forward to being more understanding than you have been today, when *you* finally start having sex.'

As soon as I say it, I know I shouldn't have. It's unfair to mention that Krissi is still a virgin. It's not his fault – it's an unfair point to score – I shouldn't have said it, and I was wrong.

'Kriss, I shouldn't–'

He stands up, face white. I've never seen him so angry – actually *furious*, and not just annoyed.

'Fuck off out of my room, you shit,' he says. His face is cold. Colder than I've ever seen it. He looks like he's going to say something else – say a billion things – but then he just says again, even more icily, 'Fuck off, you shit.'

I immediately leave the room, and lean against the door that divides Krissi's room from the kitchen. I say, through the wood, 'Kriss, I'm sorry. I'm really sorry. I shouldn't have said that.'

From the other side of the door, in a cold, cold voice: 'You're an utter turd.'

'I am a turd.'

Dadda comes into the kitchen, carrying a plate with toast crusts, and smears of fried egg on it, which he wedges into the sink.

'You're a turd, hey?' he asks.

'Not now, Dadda,' I say, still leaning against the door.

'In a way, we're all turds,' Dadda says, expansively. I can hear Krissi say, in a low monotone, 'Well, *you'd* know,' in his room.

'It's just a sibling conversation,' I say, to Dadda.

'I will kill you,' Krissi says, in the same monotone.

'Just a sibling conversation.'

'You played anyone at the mag that tape yet?' Dadda asks.

'Still waiting for the right time,' I say, as positively as possible. 'You gotta know when to hold 'em, know when to fold 'em.'

'Ah, Kenny Rogers,' Dadda says, nodding, and leaving the room. 'Yeah. Do it like Kenny.'

I keep leaning against Krissi's door for some time, saying 'Sorry' over and over. But all I can hear is Krissi spraying the tiny seedlings with his diffuser.

I sit on the floor, leaning against the door, just listening to Krissi moving around. I know I can't go back in for a long, long time.

TWENTY-TWO

So it's good to get away for the night – to Rich's parents' house. It is beautiful – you could kiss the front of it, like a girl's face.

'It's the old vicarage,' Rich had explained, on the train, as we sped into the bosky Cotswold August. We had met at Paddington Station, and kissed so hard, and for so long, some children came and stared at us. When I finally broke off from the kiss, I gave them a 'thumbs up'. I want adult sexuality to have good nascent connotations for them.

But when we get to Rich's parents' vicarage, I see it isn't like the vicarage on the Vinery estate, which is from the 1970s, and has an odd, yellow concrete wall on which some local wag has sprayed 'OH GOD!'

This is a Victorian vicarage with table-like lawns, and willows, and a doorstep wide enough to sit my whole family on. There are roses swagged around the windows, and an arthritic Labrador comes out to investigate our cab when we pull up outside.

Rich's parents are standing on the doorstep to greet us, like parents out of a sitcom where the casting-call went out for 'Lovely, posh, slightly ditzy mum' and 'Ostensibly gruff, pillar-of-society dad with a penchant for whisky'.

Everything about them makes me instantly feel scruffy – when they show us to Rich's room, with its double-bed, I feel ashamed of my worn Doc Martens on the white carpet, and the ex-army canvas rucksack I have, still splattered with dried mud from an all-day festival at Finsbury Park.

I immediately vow not to put it on the floor, bed or dressing table, with its beautiful crocheted cloth. I don't want to despoil this place with my inappropriate things.

'This is a lovely room, Mr and Mrs Rich,' I say.

'Isn't it?' Mrs Rich says. 'It was Tony's when he was a boy. Look!' she says, pointing to a clay dish on the dressing table, gaudily splashed with purple paint. 'That was his Mother's Day present to me, when he was seven.'

I look at it. Tony has painted a picture of his mother on it that makes her look like a half-melted Data from *Star Trek*.

'How lovely!' I say, staring at it. The plate-mother has only one eye.

'When you've settled, come and join us for drinks on the terrace,' Mrs Rich says, withdrawing.

We 'settle' by me giving Rich a blow job as he sits on a beautiful oak rocking-chair – his hand on my head, repeatedly saying 'Shhhh!' every time I move too fast, and make the rocking-chair creak – because I am a great, as-yet-unannounced, girlfriend.

And then we get on the bed and kiss for a while: those long, slow-motion kisses he does so well; all his cleverness in his mouth, as I make myself come, because it's now traditional that he doesn't even try, and he whispers 'Shhhh' again, lest I make a noise. All my sex is done by me, and is silent.

And then I put my rucksack in the en-suite bath, where it won't dirty anything, and put on a dress, and clean my boots with wet tissue until they shine, and join his parents on the terrace, as they call out: 'Hello! You're just in time for champagne!', and the cork pops, and the glasses clink, and the butterflies fly up, beautiful and dim, and get trapped in the canopy of the giant parasol.

I have never been anywhere like this before – somewhere so devoted to calm, orderly, lavish pleasure. The stone terrace looking down over the lawns, to the slow-moving river at the bottom, draped with willows. The borders lush with lavender, euphorbia and rose.

I give his parents the gift I have brought – a Wolverhampton mug, from the Wolverhampton Tourist Information office in Queen's Square. They boggle at its existence, and I tell them they're quite right to: 'While I was in there, two people came in and asked "Do yow do chips?".'

Everyone laughs.

We drink champagne, and I spread my dress out nicely on the chair, and they tell me what Tony was like when he was younger, as Tony squeezes my hand under the table in a 'don't mind my parents' way: 'Spending all his allowance on these *awful* sounding records–'

'–*experimental* records.'

'–and bunking off important exams at Harvard to go see the Pixies.'

'He was very much the black sheep of the family,' his mother says, looking at him indulgently.

Apparently all their lawyer-friends had been disappointed in his lack of interest in following in the family firm – 'They'd been eyeing him up for their practices for years!' – until they remembered their friend Martin who works for the *Observer*, and had passed Rich's writing on to him: 'And he said the boy could write! Next thing we know, he's got a piece in there explaining about how these *raves* are the future of music.'

Rich is very silly and self-deprecating about the whole thing – 'It's just a passing fad, Dad,' he says, lighting a cigarette while his mother tsks, but brings him an ashtray.

'Isn't that what they said about the Beatles?' his dad says, re-filling the glasses. 'Just a passing fad?'

It's all very pleasant for an hour. Then Rich's parents leave – 'We'll leave you all to your … *wild bacchanaling*! See you later,' Rich's mother says, kissing Rich's upturned face – just as Rich's friends start to arrive. Will! Emilia! Christian! Frances! Confident boys and girls with glossy hair, calling out as they come across the lawn.

I am excited by all the young posh people turning up. One of the things I can never confess to my father, in the middle of his Class War rants, is that I quite like posh people. Well, to be specific, confident, slightly foppish Oxbridge graduates: boys in tweed jackets; girls with glasses in flowery dresses, studying physics.

In another world – where I had not run away from school to earn money – I would have gone there, I think. My mock-exam results were high enough, and I would have left Wolverhampton and entered that intellectual Gormenghast, where there are no boys standing on street corners, shouting at you; no men threatening to put an axe in your dog's head.

I would have taken the dog, of course – if Byron could take a bear, I could easily have hidden an Alsatian in my 'digs'. Perhaps in a cupboard.

I would have read English, and written for *Varsity*, and gone out with the younger siblings of Hugh Laurie, and taken a punt to the corner shop, for fags. It would have been like a three-year-long holiday, spreckled with banquets. I would have *luxuriated*.

But instead, I ran away, and joined the rock 'n' roll circus, for cash.

And so it is as a member of the rock 'n' roll circus I greet them. Now Rich's parents have gone, I can revert to type. Tilting my top hat at its most rakish angle, and putting a lit cigarette in my mouth, I stand to greet them.

'Hello!' I say, putting my hand out. 'I'm Dolly Wilde! So lovely to meet you! Come and get some booze up you! I brought you a memento, from Wolverhampton.'

I hold up the bottle of MD 20/20 that I bought from the off-licence near the station.

Will says, 'I might have a beer, thanks' – I mark him out as a troublemaker, and immediately put his name in my Feud Jotter, under 'drink refuser' – but the others all gamely sit down, and have a shot.

'Just like being back at uni!' Emilia says, cheerfully, as they knock back the gleaming green medicine.

'So you are the *enfant terrible* of *D&ME*,' Christian says, cheerfully, sitting down. 'I read your stuff.'

'Rob Grant calls me the *elephant terrible*,' I say, gesturing to my body, 'which is rich, coming from an ex-punk with no teeth. Rob holds the record for being the journalist most frequently physically assaulted by musicians he's slagged off – although I am coming a close second. The bass-player from Via Manchester threw a glass of piss over me, at a Teenage Fanclub gig last month.'

'It was vodka, Dolly,' Tony says, as the others laugh, in sympathetic horror. 'And it was in June.'

'He said it would be piss *next time*. And besides, the vodka in the Academy tastes like piss. And besides – *nuh*.'

Quietly, in the back of my head, I am scared that these golden children might turn the conversation to the clever things I have not yet read in the library – Kant, Greek philosophers, Schopenhauer. I've read Rimbaud, yes – but I'm still not sure how you pronounce his name – *surely* it can't be Rambo? But if it *is*, I've got fifty Sylvester Stallone jokes ready to go – and I still feel the burn of shame from when I interviewed a band and pronounced 'paradigm' as spelt, and they mockingly corrected me.

This is the terrible thing about learning everything from books – sometimes, you do not know how to say the words. You know the ideas, but you cannot discuss them with people with any confidence. And so you stay silent. It is the curse of the autodidact. Or 'autodidiact', as I said, on the same, shameful day. Oh, that was a conversation that went so wrong.

And so I do what all insecure people do – I pull the conversation onto territory I feel safe on. Me. I talk about me, all afternoon. I tell all my battle-stories – the lipstick nun blow job, Big Cock Al, 'fat girls are good at swimming'. I even tell the story about going on *Midlands Weekend*, because I feel I can laugh at that girl, now. Dolly Wilde can laugh at Johanna Morrigan, with her unpainted face, and bad clothes.

'I am the life and soul of this party!' I think, as I pour myself another drink, and watch them all laughing, happily scandalised, at my stories. Christian is particularly taken with my story of how, when I interviewed Mark E. Smith from The Fall, I'd asked him if he got much groupie action, and Smith replied – gimlet-eyed – 'I've had more birds than you've had hot dinners, love,' to which I replied, patting my ample belly, 'I very much doubt *that*.'

'Hahaha, fucking *brilliant*,' Christian says.

I don't tell him that, in reality, I only thought of saying 'I very much doubt *that*' four days *after* the interview, while I was in the bath. At the time, I just nervously said, 'How lovely for you! And them!', and moved onto the next question.

But tiny lies do not matter. I *feel* as if I could have said it – and that's basically the same thing as actually having said it. Little lies do not matter when you are being legendary. And when you are being legendary, it doesn't matter that you keep talking over people.

6pm, and the alcohol has had the unforeseen consequence of making many people feel sporting.

'No more talking!' Rich says, firmly – herding his slightly restless guests onto the lawn for a game involving shuttlecocks and badminton rackets.

'I don't really have the right *bra* for it,' I say, when they ask me to play. I note, with a tiny pain, that Rich seems relieved I am to be left here. I decide to be noble about it – waving them onto the lawn, in the manner of an imperious Maggie Smith.

There is no way I am going to engage in a physical activity in front of these lithe people – I am *not* top-dog in a scenario that involves running around, and hand-eye co-ordination.

Instead – nodding to them beatifically – I sit and watch them play, in the late evening sunlight. They look – languid, now. It's like the video to Roxy Music's 'Avalon' – all misty focus, and gilded youth.

'Come and play, Dolly!' Will calls out – breathless, holding out a racket.

I shake my head, with cheerful regret.

Because they come and ask you to play, in paradise, but you do not know how to board their caravel, and you do not know how to ride their swans. They call out their names – 'Emilia! Will! Frances! Christian!' Names that do not have to bear heavy weights, or be written on benefit application forms – pleading. Names that will always be just a joyous signature on a birthday card, or cheque – and never called out, in a room full of anxious people.

Oh, your names – your names! Will you ever understand how anxious they secretly make me? That I worry I cannot say them unsarcastically. Your names are jokes, where I come from.

I sigh, and light another fag.

Two hours later, and dusk has fallen. I am sitting with Emilia, who has invalided herself out of the game after Tony accidentally smashed into her hand with his racket.

Her hand is resting on a bag of frozen peas, and we are medicating her pain with gin – the MD 20/20 having all gone, now. We are quite, quite drunk – that warm stage where you are just two floating faces, talking to each other.

We've had an interesting and wide-ranging conversation – Marxism, Suede, Chanel No. 5, fear of insanity, Guns N' Roses, how her parents like her best and how awkward that is, what the best animal is – consensus reached on 'centaurs' – and whether all velvet jackets make you look fat (yes).

She spends a long time discussing my writing on *D&ME*, which she's 'a fan' of – particularly my review of The Breeders, where I said Kim Deal's calves were so bulgingly, disproportionately muscular that I presumed she 'spent all day riding a very, very tiny bicycle up hills'. 'It was abso-fucking-lutely *hilarious.*'

And then, around 9pm, she says a very big thing. She leans forward confidingly, and tells me that she knows all about me – because she and Rich used to go out with each other, until recently. She dumped him, and he was 'very cut up about it', but, 'We still fuck occasionally, now. It's not a big thing. You know what I mean?'

So here comes something I'm not prepared for, on this delightful evening, when I am very drunk: a sudden, emergency delivery of pain and embarrassment. I feel like I'm signing for a parcel that now takes up the entire lawn.

When she first tells me, I want to burst into tears. I want to run away. I want to run away – maybe whilst setting fire to my hair – and never come back.

He's still in love with this girl, who he's fucking – and he brought me here, to meet her? What a *horrible* thing to do. Amusingly, for someone whose heart should be breaking, the thing I'm initially most angry about is that he didn't even offer to pay my train-fare down.

'I've spunked nearly fifty quid getting here, to meet the girl he likes better. *And* I bought his parents a mug,' I think. 'For that kind of money, I expect some kind of exclusivity – not some "Oh Dolly, here's the person I usually think of when I'm coming in you" surprise party.' This is total bullshit.

'But we're cool, yeah?' Emilia says – rattled by the look on my face. 'I mean, he said you sleep around a lot – that it's just a sex-thing. That you … do things … I mean … that you're …'

'A Lady Sex Adventurer? Yes. Yes I am,' I say, to relieve her awkwardness. 'I'm a Swashfuck-ler. I'm Indiana Bones!'

'That's so cool. I'd like to be that, too,' Emilia says. 'A Lady Sex Adventurer!'

And we clink glasses, in a toast, to Lady Sex Adventurers.

And in my tiny, weaselly drunk mind – desperate not to go anywhere near the shame that sits, on the lawn, looming over me – I make a decision, to save my pride.

I decide I will show that I'm okay with this humiliating situation I knew nothing about – and that the best way to do that is to get off with Emilia. This is how I will remain top dog, in this situation: I will get off with the girl he likes best. After all, everyone is bisexual after 11pm.

Thirty seconds later, I'm finding that kissing a girl is weird. Well, this girl, anyway. She's so soft, and her face is so small, that it's almost like nothing's happening at all. It's a tiny, gentle, lapping thing – like kittens nuzzling their mother. But that's cool. Who doesn't like kittens? I like kittens. I kiss on.

On the lawn, I can see the others have stopped playing their game, and are watching us.

From the lawn, I can hear Tony say, appreciatively, 'She's so *filthy*.'

I thrill to hear him say it again.

'That's *right*!' I think to myself. 'I *am* absolutely filthy! Listen to Tony, telling everyone of my legend!'

I redouble my kissing-Emilia efforts – stroking her face; putting my hands in her hair. I'm putting on a show.

After a few minutes of this hushed watching from the lawn, Tony leaves the others, and comes to sit at the table, next to us. He smokes a cigarette, silently – occasionally reaching across to stroke Emilia's hair, or mine – but otherwise, nothing is said.

In the end, I break off the kissing, and look across at Tony, and say, 'Hello,' in a sexy way.

'Oh – don't stop on my account,' Tony says, in his slow, low way that means he's very turned on. 'I'm glad you girls are getting on so well.'

But I notice he's stroking her hair more than mine.

And so it is my little weasel-mind – hammered on MD 20/20 and gin – that decides to get back in control of this situation by taking it up a gear: suggesting a threesome. I cannot argue with my logic – mainly because I am pissed. But my deduction is that if I am the less-fancied girl who, nonetheless, then suggests the most-wanted thing, I will become the most-fancied girl again.

And when Tony gently takes Emilia by a tendril of her hair, and pulls her away from me so he can kiss me, I think, 'Yes! I have done the right thing!'

And when he then kisses her, I think, 'Well, he's just being polite. And besides, it was all my idea. I'm still in charge here.'

I stroke Emilia's hair while he kisses her – just so I'm joining in.

'*So* outrageously filthy,' he says, pulling back – staring at me, and then her, pupils blasted.

'Well, this is all going splendidly!' I think. 'I am about to go up a Sex Level!'

'Excuse me for a moment,' I murmur, standing up – and then almost falling over again. I have had a lot of gin since I last stood up. 'I'll be back in a … Sex-mo.'

Waving ostentatiously over my shoulder, in the manner of Carmen Miranda, I walk very carefully back into the house, and go up to our bedroom. I have to be ready for my first three-some! Gotta look good for this!

I take my eyeliner out of my bag, and apply it until my eyes are circled with black. I apply underarm deodorant – gotta smell nice for the girl! Girls are picky! – and then perfume: Body Shop Vanilla Musk, the nineties' most sophisticated way to cover up fag-smoke. I then go to the toilet, and clean my teeth while sitting there. I am like a dirty goth bride, preparing for her bisexual wedding night.

The bathroom window is open, and I can hear the conversation, slightly muffled, outside. Tony is talking to Christian, Will and Frances – they are clearly being encouraged to leave. I stop cleaning my teeth for a minute.

'We should go for a walk,' Will is saying. 'To the pub.'

Christian seems reluctant.

'I'm tired,' he says, petulantly.

There's a scuffle, and some laughter – Tony appears to be mock-fighting with Christian.

'Ow!' Christian says – still laughing. 'Alright! Alright!'

Then he says something in a murmur I cannot hear, but which ends with, '… your bit of rough.'

And then the sound of them leaving – bottles clinking, Christian moaning, 'Well, I just hope it's not too full. I don't want to *stand* at a *bar*.'

I sit there for a moment, trying to absorb what I've just heard.

A bit of rough. I'm his … bit of rough.

And for the second time this evening, I tell myself how to deal with this situation. I *order* myself to be okay with this. I will be whoever the situation demands. Fake it 'til yow make it, kidder. I *will* be his piece of rough – like when Rochester is won over by the impoverished Jane Eyre. Or … like Julia Roberts and Richard Gere in *Pretty Woman*. There is nobility in this! I have triumphed against the odds of society, sexually – simply by being me! I'm two-for-one here! I'm the working-class S&M threesome girl! My sexual CV has *all* the kinks in it! *Man*, I am well-qualified. Hot tramp, I love me so.

But when I get back onto the terrace and greet my two future fuckees with a cheerful, 'So – let's get this threesome *started*!', I see Tony grinding Emilia up against the wall, with his hand in her bra.

'Oh,' I say. 'I see you … already have.'

I stand there for a minute.

For the first thirty seconds, I have absolutely no thoughts at all – I feel like Wile E. Coyote when he goes over the side of a cliff, and his legs are just bicycling in the air. Is this bad? Is it bad I feel bad? Should I tell me not to feel bad?

'Er … hello?' I say.

Tony and Emilia turn to face me. Emilia is totally pissed, but still has her hands on Tony's chest. Tony holds a hand out to me.

'Come and join us!' he says, cheerfully.

I don't move.

'Come – join us!' he says again – arm still outstretched.

I actually can't think of anything to say.

'You look … *unhappy*,' he says – as if geeing up a sulky child.

'Well,' I say. I reach around for the locus of my discontent. All I can do is state fact: 'You had your hand in Emilia's bra.'

'You agreed to a threesome!' Tony says.

'Well, yes – but then *you* started having a twosome,' I say, slowly.

'A twosome is contained *within* the threesome. It's inherent,' Tony says, laughing. He comes over to me – leaving Emilia against the wall, looking confused – and kisses me. 'Come on, darling,' he says. 'Let me show you something *really* dirty.'

And suddenly – for the first time in years – I get angry. I have always, previously, shied away from anger – I do not like the way it speeds your thoughts and emotions up; it feels too like anxiety to be welcomed. Anger is like putting acid into already boiling water – it makes things effervesce uncontrollably. It makes you act and speak with dangerous rapidity, and I already feel too rapid.

But now – now, it feels like an unexpected rain-burst of power. It feels like – if I can get a handle on it – the solution to this troublesome day. For I am *indignant*. I am *affronted* by this. My carriage has arrived, it's a high dudgeon, and I am getting into it.

'Let's get one thing straight,' I say, pushing my top hat back into place, and trying to keep on top of this galloping rage.

'Let's get one thing *very* straight. *I* – am the dirty one here. *I* – am the sex-expert. *I* have had more fucks than you've had hot dinners. *I* was coming, thinking about talking lions in Narnia while you were doing your fucking *A levels*. I've actually *read* de Sade – rather than just listening to the Velvet Underground whilst wearing stupid pointy boots. *I've* had sex with a penis so big it nearly killed me. *I've* seen attack ships on fire off the shoulder of Orion, and c-beams glitter in the dark near the Tannhauser Gate – *in my pants*. It's pervy for me to be fucking *you*. Not the other way round. I pulled *you*.'

I've started crying whilst saying this. Not from sadness, but from … sorrow that, I've *had* to say it. That I stupidly came here, with this stupid boy.

'I was objectifying *you*,' I continue, trying to suppress any sobs that will ruin this soliloquy. 'I have a *scorecard* for shagging nobs. I'm on a fucking *Gold Run* for banging you. I'm getting *high-fives* down the Working Men's Club. We make our *own amusements* on the council estates. I'm not … your *bit of rough*. You're … *my bit of posh*.'

He's my drummer. He's my drummer. All these men I've fucked are my drummers.

I look at him – just staring at me. And behind him – Emilia. Also staring. I see what I have done: I have launched into a drunken rant about the class system. I know what this means. I've finally turned into my dad. There is only one way I know to end a speech like this.

'I am the bastard gypsy Jewish son of Brendan Behan,' I say, 'and one day, YOU FUCKERS WILL BOW DOWN TO ME.'

I pause. Rich and Emilia are still just looking at me.

'I'm going away now – to smoke an angry Marxist cigarette,' I conclude.

I smoke it all the way up the stairs, and into our bedroom, even though you're not allowed to smoke in the house. I then put the cigarette out in the small clay bowl that Tony made when he was seven – grinding it out on his mum's melted *Star Trek* face – and pass out in the bed.

TWENTY-THREE

I wake amidst the opulence of the dawn chorus – the yolk and phoenix feather, and the particular pearly grey leather of a cockatoo's feet, which would make a beautiful Chesterfield sofa, at the price of 50,000 dead cockatoos. Birds are outrageous. Listen to them singing up the sun! Their voices fill its limp golden skin until it floats up over the horizon, like a glowing zeppelin of noise; oh God, I'm still drunk.

I fall back asleep, and wake again at eight. It is bright.

I get out of bed – Rich is still sleeping, sprawled where he must have thrown himself, hours after I left him, love-bites on his neck. *What* a cunt – dress, pack, find the *Yellow Pages*, and order a cab.

Sitting on the front doorstep, smoking a fag as I wait for it to arrive, I feel a sudden, unexpected moment of calm – as if I've pressed 'pause' for a second, on a life that seems to have been on 'fast-forward' for some time.

Watching the smoke coil upwards, like an Indian Rope Trick, I look at my hands, and think, 'Those look like the hands of a grown-up. You have grown-up hands, now, Johanna. Grown-up hands smoking a grown-up fag, the night after preventing a sex debacle.'

I feel excitingly … free. Things were going to happen to me last night that I did not like – and I *stopped* them. I have never prevented my own doom before. I have never stood in the path of certain unhappiness, and told myself – lovingly, like a mother to myself – 'No! This unhappiness will not suit you! Turn around, and go another way!'

I have previously been resigned to any and all fates ahead – mute and compliant; worried about seeming weird, or unfuckable, or about making a fuss.

But now, things have changed: it seems I am now the kind of girl who can instigate a threesome – then *cancel* a threesome, *then* order a cab. I am in charge of me. I can change fates! I can re-order evenings! I can say 'Yes' – and *then* 'No'! This is new information to me. I like this information. I like all information about me. I am compiling a dossier. I am my own specialist subject.

When the cab arrives, it's trailing behind Tony's parents' BMW. They both crunch up the gravel driveway, amusingly disparate – the gleaming BMW, for them, and the battered Ford Fiesta with the huge aerial, for me.

His parents get out of the car carrying their overnight bags, and walk to greet me. Putting my rucksack on my back, I go over to shake their hands.

'Mr and Mrs Rich, thank you for having me over,' I say, in my poshest voice. 'You have a very beautiful house. A very, very beautiful house. But a very bad son.'

And I get into the cab, and drive away.

On the train back to London – dizzy with hangover – I realise that I am not going out with Tony Rich any more. Partly because I've drunkenly shouted at him, but mainly because I never was in the first place. And that, actually, I had never really *wanted* to. I had just acted like a peasant girl, desperate to be wed, who offered herself to the first dashing pedlar who visited the village, selling hair-ribbons, and tonics.

Pressing my head against the window, I have a little chat with me.

'So, what *do* you want?' I ask me, in a friendly manner. 'Where do you *want* to be? What is good for you? Who do you actually *like*?'

And that is obvious: John Kite. I would like to sit and talk with John Kite. I would like to go and have a conversation with John Kite where we do all the things we do together: agree on things, and end each other's sentences, and feel like we are the best two people in the world. And I know where I will find him: The Good Mixer, in Camden. This is where he will wash up, if I wait long enough. I am getting off this train, and I am going to find John Kite.

I go in there, at midday. An otherwise unremarkable old man's pub, in Camden, 1993, the Mixer is essentially the *Cheers* of the indie-music world: if you sit at the bar long enough, all the regular cast-members will turn up. James from the Manic Street Preachers, Norman from Teenage Fanclub. Miki from Lush. Blur seem to have the pool table permanently reserved – pints on the table beside them. As I am but a very minor cast member of this indie sitcom – basically Cliff's mum – I nod at the ones who I vaguely know, then put my head back down, head for an empty corner-table, light a fag and wait for John Kite.

At 1.30pm I feel restless with waiting and go outside, where the rickety market-stalls are, and buy a battered copy of *Ulysses* and a bag of tangerines. Sitting on the kerb I peel the tangerines, reading Joyce in the weak-tea sun. I've never tried to read Joyce before. For twenty minutes, I enjoy how he appears to be writing across all space and time – his past, present and future; as himself, and a dog, and the sea itself – and then I realise I've read the same page twice, go, 'Oh God, I can't handle this right now,' and buy *Viz* instead from the mini-mart opposite.

Finally, at 2.59pm, when I'm back in the pub, John advents – shabby linen suit, brogues, gold rings. He's with a group of people – but walks away when he sees me, and looms over my table, beaming, face like a lighthouse; already a little drunk.

'Duchess!' he roars. 'Christmas in August – delivered to my pub, to my very *table*, for my delight! What a salve to incipient cantankerousness you are!'

'How you doing?' I say, pretending everything is normal.

'Oh, you know,' Kite says, lighting a cigarette and sitting down beside me, forcing me to budge up. 'Westward-leading, still proceeding. What' – he looks at me – 'is happening with you?'

I burst into tears.

Kite spends three minutes trying to calm me down – 'Dutch! Dutch!' – and then just hugs me with his huge arms, so I am completely wrapped up, and inside him, like an owl inside a hollow tree. This is my most enjoyable crying ever – if all crying were this pleasant, I would do it more often.

I slow down the crying – partly because I'm feeling better, and partly so I can illicitly inhale Kite's cologne – and then shudder to a halt, like a car that has slalomed down a hill, and finally come to rest in a hedge.

When I emerge from his arms, I see that the bar man has brought a bottle of gin to the table, and Kite has poured us both a measure.

'Go and wash your face,' Kite says, gently, 'and then we will sit here and set the world to rights. And if you're unhappy for one second more – some cunt will RUE me!'

I go to the toilet, and wash all my streaky make-up off. I start to apply Dolly Wilde's face to my own again – then decide

I can't be bothered. Kite's seen my old face, without make-up, before. There's no need to make this effort.

When I return, his entourage have gone – 'I set them free, to wander' – and he is holding up a glass of gin to me. I take a sip, and immediately feel calmer.

'I got into a huge argument with Tony Rich in front of his *real* girlfriend, and dumped him. I don't think I can go to nice places, or talk to nice people,' I say, eventually. 'I don't think I can do that. I belong in the ghetto, with my people.'

'Bollocks – you would adorn the Palace of the Doge,' Kite says, firmly.

'No, really – I'm too … *early* to be let out yet,' I say. 'I keep breaking social situations. And penises.'

And so I tell him about Rich's house, and his friends, and what I said, and how it ended. He yelps with laughter frequently through the story – 'Attack ships off the shoulder of Orion, *in your pants*! Hahaha!' – but winces more frequently towards the end, as I tell him about the awful sex. Finally:

'So – what's up with you and this Rich, then? Is it not true love's first kiss, after all?'

I look down into my gin-glass.

'You know when Princess Diana said there were three people in her relationship? I think there was only one in ours: me,' I say. 'I was not the thing, for him.'

'No – I think he is not the thing for *you*,' Kite says. 'I would say you're only interested in him because he's a writer, and you're a writer, and you basically want to fuck a writer, because that's the nearest thing to fucking yourself. You just fancy yourself, darling. As of course, you should. Would you have gone out with him if he were a … cowboy, or a … spy?'

'Haha, no,' I say.

'Well, then,' Kite says.

I think about this for a minute. I think about what I like best about Rich: the dirty phone-calls; the way he describes sex as we're having it. I realise something:

'I think … that I might have only fucked him for the review,' I say, finally. 'I think I just wanted to be reviewed by Tony Rich. To see what I was like.'

'HAHAHA! And I'm sure it would have been five stars,' Kite says. 'I'm sure you were Album of the Year. Bumming of the Year. But, you know? You can't go out with the writing. People aren't their *work*. We are not our art.'

'*I* am,' I say – then notice Kite is looking at me, eyebrows raised. 'I mean, not *now*. Not all the … bitchy stuff. But I *will* be. I want to do something great. Something great, like men do.'

'I'm sure you will, honey,' he says, kissing the top of my head. 'I'm sure you will be great art, one day.'

And so then we drink more gin, and then more gin, and have one of the loveliest afternoons of my life – the same kind of dreamy, unreal wandering as we'd done in Dublin. We took the gin bottle with us out of the Mixer – 'We shall return!' Kite told the landlord, with a flourish of his hand – and walked up Oval Road, towards Regent's Park, in the late-summer after-noon sun, swigging and smoking as we went.

'That's Alan Bennett's house,' Kite said, pointing with a be-ringed finger to a Georgian house with a tatty van parked outside it. 'And over there – Morrissey's.'

The magic of London is obvious, that afternoon – that every street has a pet-genius; that this is the place everyone runs to.

We reached Regent's Park, and walked through the rose garden, and I kept running off to particularly skittish roses who called out, like sexy girls, to me, burying my face in their myrrh-ish whirls, and calling out to John, 'This is the best one – no, this! No – this!'

I was mad with roses – I wanted to be filled with the scent of roses. I saw myself as a glass bottle that swirled with them. I am decanter; I am atomiser. I am in love with the opulence of rose.

I don't need to critique things, or have an opinion, or pose, with John – we just go around, being alive, and pointing at things. We're just, simply, in the world. It had never occurred to me what a wonderful thing this was. Or perhaps it had, a long time ago – but I had forgotten. I am full of how great life is. I am so happy to be alive. That point of life is joy – to make it, to receive it. That the Earth is a treasure-box of people and places and song, and that every day you can plunge your arms in and find a new, ridiculous, perfect delight.

We found one tumble of yellow roses, and looked for its name on the plaque below – 'Golden Showers' – and became hysterical. After three minutes I was fearful a park-keeper would chase us away, as John boomed, 'GOLDEN SHOWERS! You spend thirty years grafting cutting onto root-stock onto cutting, and then you call the fucker GOLDEN SHOWERS! Why not call it CASCADING BUMHOLES, you mad cunts? Or FLORAL SPUNKINGS?'

I paddled in the fountain while John sat on the edge, smoking, telling me about his latest visit to his mother – 'She won't even look me in the eye, now, Dutch – she just sits by the window, looking out, describing things, until visiting time is over' – and I bang his thigh with my fist, in sympathy, as he says, wonderingly, 'I never talk about these things with anyone apart from you, my sister.'

*

We wander on to the Zoo – Kite paying for the tickets – and sit, smoking, and listening to the gibbons making their high, looping, electric cries to each other, from the tree-tops.

By this time, we're very drunk – draining the very last drops of the gin – and we quietly sing along with the gibbons; Kite dueting with one lonely male; singing snatches of his own songs inside the wails. There's something very beautiful about watching a man you love dueting with a monkey – the gibbonous melancholy suits the moon, rising pale in the blue sky, over the cages.

In order to maximise this experience – to be having the most of the most – I have been chain-smoking all afternoon. As I open my second packet of Silk Cut, John looks at me, for a moment.

'I have never seen anyone smoke with the rapacity and dedication to the cause you show,' he says, mildly.

'*You* can't say that,' I say – pausing with my lighter. 'I only *started* because of you.'

'Ah, well – I only started because of John Lennon,' he sighs, taking one from my packet. 'Rock 'n' roll is a terrible babysitter, baby.'

Watching him, I have a thought I am so excited about that I know I cannot keep it in much longer. I have something to tell him.

I drag Kite to the wolf enclosure – bubbling, bursting, stumbling – because that is where Withnail made his great speech, and I am about to make mine. John adjusts his cuff-links, and says, 'Well?'

'I've run all the science and maths on it, and the conclusions are: we should *kiss*,' I say, decisively. 'We must kiss, and it must be now. I cannot leave you unkissed any longer. We need to kiss, so that we know. Let's not shilly-shally any more. Let's start our kissing. LET'S GET ON WITH IT!'

When I wake up the next morning, that's the last thing I properly remember – talking about kissing with John Kite, in front of the wolf enclosure at Regent's Park.

What then? What then? I don't know. Everything after that is gin-blasted darkness – the brain cells that would hold the troubling memory have been destroyed by the alcohol. It is a workable system, of sorts.

I open my eyes.

I'm in Kite's hotel room – lying in his bed, fully dressed. He's still asleep, in the bath-tub, fully dressed. A memory of him saying, 'My turn to sleep in the bath, Duchess,' and climbing in, to sleep. So we were still talking then? I can't have done anything *too* bad – except I know I did. I talked about kissing. Oh, Johanna – *never* talk about kissing. Stop. Stop doing things, and *think* for a while.

Right. I am going home – to think.

I bundle everything into my rucksack – taking the ashtrays from the table, as Kite has taught me – and write him a note: 'Got to get home. THANK YOU. Sorry. Have ashtrays, of course. xxxx.'

I leave the hotel – where are we? Soho, I think. Am I still drunk? Yes. I start walking to the train station, trying to sober up. I talk to myself, as I would a troubled child, or Lupin, in the middle of a terror. Johanna – what are you doing?

I remember again my vision of what I thought my adult life would be like: attending a party in London full of my peers, applauding me when I entered the room in honour of the new thing I have written, or have done. People calling 'Bravo!' and sending over champagne, as they would when Wilde opened a new, daring play.

I think of what I'm actually getting: a new issue of *D&ME* coming out, and me getting lager thrown over me by my peers because I've called one of them 'A bucket-faced time-wasting fuck-Womble'.

But surely they will know *underneath* it all I'm a good and noble person, in love with the world? Surely you get a *sense* of that, underneath what I'm actually saying? People must be able to smell that, underneath all the harsh words, I'm someone who still wants to own a sausage dog, and cries about Nelson Mandela.

When I get to Euston station, I go to the newsagent and buy a copy of the *D&ME*. I'm going to do an experiment. I'm going to pretend I'm John Kite – waking up, and confused about why one of his friends tried to proposition him last night, and wondering if she might be a bit mad – and I'm going to read everything I've written in this week's paper, and see if he would conclude I'm a good person or not. I'm going to put my written self on trial, to see if it's actually *me* or not. If I *am* art, as I wish.

On the train, I get a seat – a whole table to myself! Bullseye! – and start drinking my emergency hangover McDonald's chocolate milkshake, flicking through the new issue with shaking hands. There's a momentary panic when I see a lead review by Tony Rich – don't think about Rich! Don't think about Rich! – but then I go back and read it anyway, doing what I always do: seeing if there's anything, even obliquely, about *me* in there.

But there's nothing – nothing about love, or fucking, or any kind of woman at all: it's clear that however many times I suck this man's cock, he will *not* immortalise me. John's right. The only place I will ever see myself in this paper is in what I have written – and here, on the next page, is *my* lead review: bigger than Rich's, I note, gleefully.

It's my 'analysis' of the new Soup Dragons album – a Scottish band who'd jumped onto the Madchester bandwagon, to much derision all round. Kenny had mentioned something on the phone about it, after I'd filed, but at the time, I dismissed it. I note now, with alarm, that he has given it the headline 'Finally – Wilde Goes Too Far'.

The review centres around the conceit that the band are in the dock, charged with crimes against humanity for their career.

'If we are to take the Geneva Convention seriously…'
– I began –

> … *if we are to hold to account those who commit atrocities that lead to the destruction of humanity, then surely the knock must come, soon, for the Soup Dragons. They will be taken from their jangly Scottish hovel squat – do not drink of the milk in the Soup Dragon's house! For, surely, it will be suppurating whey and dreck! – by stern-faced security-forces with guns, and put up in the dock. Observe them, in their shackles.*
>
> *'What is your defence?' asks the judge – a kind-eyed man, wearied by all the evidence he has heard; a man still having screaming, traumatic flash-backs to all four minutes of 'Dream-On (Solid Gold)'.*
>
> *'We were just trying to entertain The Kids!' the Dragons will bleat. 'We were just trying to be free, to do what we want, any old time!'*
>
> *'But did you wilfully, and with fore-knowledge, take your previous, shambling, jangling indie-rock, and cravenly nail onto it a Funky Drummer back-beat – much like a previous inhabitant of that dock, Dr Mengele, coldly sewed together the*

bodies of Romanian orphaned twins – but not even in the name of medical science, but simply for the procurement of cash, and a startlingly ineffective placing at Number 72 in the Independent Charts?'

'I want my mother!' lead-singer Sean Dickson cries, as the Visitors' Gallery starts calling out, as one, for the ultimate penalty – for the Soup Dragons to be placed onstage at the Reading Festival at 11am on Sunday, and pelted to death with bottles filled with urine, by their peers.

I can't read any more of me. I close the magazine. Oh God. I've compared a drummer, a bass-player, a guitarist and a man with some maracas and a bowl-cut to the Nazis, and their music to the medical experiments of Mengele. I've trashed a load of working-class kids from the provinces, who just love music – kids like me – and tried to make them feel *ashamed* of wanting to do that glorious thing: write a song. Write a song that someone, somewhere, might need. Of all the jobs in the world that need doing, *this* inglorious task is the one I've given myself.

Even though I have written every word, this – just like Rich's review – has none of me in it, either. I'm not here – in this bile-filled persona I have gone to all the time and trouble of making.

I started writing about music because I loved it. I started off wanting to be part of something – to be joyous. To make friends.

Instead, I've just, bafflingly, pretended to be a massive arsehole, instead. Why would I do that? Why would I put all this effort into pretending to be … less than I am? After nearly two years on the *D&ME*, I have to conclude: this experiment has been a massive failure.

As if the *D&ME* were contaminated, I get up, and put it into the bin in the toilet. I come back to my seat, but am finding it increasing difficult to handle sitting in a chair. I feel bad. I feel bad in every place and part of me. I have no comforting thoughts to fall back on.

My ultimate bad thought is this: that I have offended John Kite. He will wake up this morning – confused about what I have done – and read this, and decide he never wants to see me again. There's nothing here that would make someone love me, or wish to be on my side. Even *I'm* not on my side, here. I have lost my one friend. My good mirror.

This thought is the thought to end all thoughts. I find it makes me quite breathless. My breath gets shallower and shallower, until I have to lean against the train window and suck my thumb, and breathe, raggedly, around the knuckle. I despair at myself. I wonder how many times in my life I'm going to burst in on me being a dick, and have to shout 'What are you *doing*, Johanna? What have you *done*?' at me, like I've just found Lupin scribbling on the wall.

I spend the next hour of the train-journey thinking about how – and if – I can make this all better. I must first write a letter of apology to the Soup Dragons, of course. And C+C Music Factory, and the Inspiral Carpets, and U2, and roughly one-third of all bands in existence, to be honest. Christ – being a reformed bitch is going to cost a fortune in stamps.

Then, I must exile myself away from John Kite, for a while – so I don't have the unbearable moment of seeing him looking at me in sorrow.

And after that, I need to go back to how I *used* to write – before I turned into some weird, angry old man, puncturing the ball of every band who kicked their ball over my fence. I must go out there and prove that I am a halfway decent human being. That will be my next, new career.

But all of these things will, of course, take time. They don't answer my most urgent question: What do I do *now* with this bad feeling? Today? This afternoon? This second?

The only thing I can think of is a sudden, longing regression to childhood – to be found lying at the bottom of the stairs again – but, this time, really broken. Because to break yourself means that you are sorry, and I am so sorry. I have the wild, wild comfortless remorsefulness that makes you want to run into walls.

Back at home, in my room, having drunk the best part of half a bottle of Jack Daniels, I am doing the nearest thing I can think of to throwing myself down the stairs, or running into a wall: I am very quietly cutting my thigh with a razor. I have chosen my leg because a thigh looks like a piece of pork, and I have scored pig fat before, in the kitchen, on a Sunday. If you're going to start self-harming in a fury of self-flagellation, you might as well fall back on skills learned in the 'Meat' section of Dorothy Hartley's *Food in England*:

'*Pig Pye* (Fourteenth century)*:* Flea Pyg and cut him in pieces. Practically nothing is wasted in a good pig. A pig killed in November would still provide fresh meat, brawn and pie until Christmas.'

The first cut hurt so much that I made the second one just to distract myself – this time on my arm. And then another eight – quickly. With careless anger.

It really hurts. I am surprised.

It had never occurred to me that self-harm would be … harmful. For the rest of my life, it's a truth I just can't believe – in the same way that I never really believe the only way to stop smoking is not to have another cigarette, the only way not to get drunk is not to drink, and the only way to keep a secret is to never, ever tell anyone.

But then – the payback. For as I sit there, in pain, I suddenly notice I have changed. I am not self-loathing anymore. These billion cheap blackbirds inside me – beaking the wires of the cage, frantic – are now on the ground, sleeping. This billion-eyed mess, which I cannot comprehend, contain or name, has now disappeared – replaced by these hot, red lines on my leg and arm.

'So this is the point of self-harm!' I marvel. 'It is translation of emotion into action! It is simpler! It's admin! It's just *paperwork*!'

The essential boringness of it almost puts me off. I thought I'd become high and Byronic on endorphins. Instead, I'm just being kind of … stupid and angry at my limbs. I am just being angry at my skin.

For a minute, I feel quite clever and calm. Then I notice that I'm bleeding quite a lot.

From upstairs, I can hear the Velvet Underground's 'The Black Angel's Death Song' on top volume, coming from Krissi's bedroom. I go down, and knock on Krissi's door, saying, as cheerfully as I can, '*C'est moi*! *C'est le* party!'

Usually this is met with 'Fuck off!' – but this time, there is silence. I open the door, and see Krissi lying, fully dressed, on his bed, surrounded by shelves and shelves of seedlings. The volume is deafening – John Cale's awful, slate-scratching violin, the occasional, ferocious piston-hissing of feedback, and Lou Reed singing like a chained Gollum. The room has all the cheerfulness of the catacombs in Paris. This room is like some terrible Midlands ossuary.

'You'll kill your veg like that,' I say, eventually.

'This town is killing me,' Krissi says. His voice is utterly flat. I continue standing in the doorway, until he looks up at me. When he sees me, his face changes immediately.

'Jesus Johanna – what have you *done*?'

'I tried to make things better,' I say. 'But I got it wrong.'

He springs off the bed, and rolls up my shirt-sleeve.

'Fucking hell. Bleeding. Right,' he says, business-like. 'We need a tourniquet.'

He goes to his drawer, and takes his school tie out, and ties it around my upper-arm.

'Put your arm up in the air,' he says. 'It will stop the bleeding. Christ, you *reek* of whisky.'

Absolutely mute, I do as he says. The blood drips on the floor, but slower – until it stops.

'Sit on the bed,' Krissi orders. 'I'm going to clean you up. And then I'm going to ask you what the absolute fuck you're doing.'

He gets his plant-mister, and a clean towel, and starts cleaning my arm, carefully, as I wince.

'This is like that bit in *Indiana Jones and the Temple of Doom*, where Marion cleans Indie up, after the fight,' I say, trying to make conversation.

'Put your arm down now. And I'm not going to get off with you,' Krissi says, still wiping, very gently. 'You are *not* a hot archaeologist.'

After a minute of cleaning, he suddenly stops.

'Johanna, you've … what the fuck?'

He looks at my arm.

In my panic and blindness, I did not look at how I was cutting myself, and the incisions have landed so that it appears, surreally, to spell something out, on my arm.

'*NWA*?' he says, staring, incredulous. I look at the arm again. Yes. The cuts appear to form the letters 'NWA'. I look like the world's maddest Niggas With Attitude fan.

'I had a self-harming accident!' I say. 'It's not a *statement* – it's a typo! Razors are very hard to spell with! I wasn't really looking! The sub-editors will change it, later.'

He continues looking at the arm.

'You look mental.'

'I am! I am mental!' I say, starting to cry, very hard.

Krissi wipes the last of the blood from my arm, and says, very gently, 'Johanna. Would you like to tell me what the sheer cunt is going on?'

And so I start to tell him everything – about Rich, and Kite, and the panic, and the review, and being horrible. Halfway through, I start crying because my arm hurts, and he goes over to his drawer again, and comes back with two pills – taking one himself.

'It's Dadda's medicine. Just have one. They're very strong. And you can't have any more than one,' he says, warningly. 'You can get addicted to them.'

I take one, and look at him. I think about how quiet he has become recently.

'Are *you* addicted to them?'

'I don't know,' he says, breezily. 'I haven't tried stopping yet.'

As the pill kicks in, I curl up next to Krissi, on the bed, and he puts his arm around me, and strokes my hair. I carry on telling him about John Kite – but the whole thing doesn't feel so bad now, because I'm safe in Krissi's bed, and I could probably just stay here forever. Everything is very warm. I'm very tired.

'We've always got the Bee Gees, Kriss,' I say, sleepily. 'We've *always* got Robin, Maurice and Barry.'

'Johanna,' he says, staring up at the ceiling. 'Sometimes, I think it won't be enough.'

But I've already fallen asleep.

In my dream, I'm back with John Kite, at Regent's Park Zoo, in the late evening. I am remembering what happened. We're close close close – we are the same thing, woozed together with gin. We're like the voices of the Bee Gees. I've known him forever and there's nothing I can't say to him, and I know what I *do* want to say: it's a speech I've made a thousand times, in my head.

It's written in my diary over two pages – I quote it by heart while I wait for trains, or walk in the rain, or need a mantra to get me through. And it is this:

'Since I met you, I feel like I can see the operating system of the world – and it is unrequited love. That is why everyone's doing everything. Every book, opera house, moon shot and manifesto is here because someone, somewhere, lit up silent when someone else came into the room, and then quietly burned when they didn't notice them.

'On the foundation of the billion kisses we never had, I built you this opera house, baby. I shot the president because I didn't know what to say to you. I hoped you'd notice. I hoped you'd notice me. We turn our unsaid things into our life's work.

'Loving you is the dirty fuel that powered me, during my industrial era. You've got to have a hobby – and mine is you. Mine is being in love with you. It was never the sun coming up in the morning that lit up the room. It was me, quietly flaring, when you said, "One more?"'

That's the speech I've had in my heart for a year. That's what I want to say to him. But I know I can't. You can't make book-speeches to someone's face.

So this is what I said, drunk, at Regent's Park Zoo, instead. I explain that I am Chrissie Hynde, and that I have brass in pocket, and that I'm going to make him notice by 'gonna using' my 1) arms 2) legs 3) staah 4) stansta 5) fingers 6) mah mah mah magernation. Result = giffertoome.

'We'll be like Burton and Taylor,' I conclude, brightly. 'Amanda Burton, and Dennis Taylor.'

I say this to John Kite, and he looks up at me, and opens his mouth, and the wolves howl, and the gibbons spool, and I wake up, in Krissi's bed, with my face pressed into his chest. And that's all I remember.

Something's wrong. Fugged with Dadda's medicine, it takes me a while to work out what that is: it is agonising pain in my arm. It feels like it's going to burst.

'Krissi!' I shout.

He wakes up with a start.

'I'm bursting!'

Krissi puts the light on, and looks at my arm. It's gigantic – swollen, purple and with the fingernails an alarmingly dark blue.

'Jesus! The tourniquet! You're only supposed to leave them on for twenty minutes!' Krissi says – undoing the tie as I hold my arm out, like Frankenstein's monster.

'Fuck! Fuck!' he says.

'Am I going to lose my arm?' I weep.

'Don't be silly, Johanna,' Krissi says. 'Open and close your hand. Get the blood moving again.'

'I can't! I can't feel it!'

Krissi puts his finger in the middle of my palm.

'Squeeze this,' he says.

I pathetically curl the fingers a bit.

'More than that,' Krissi says, firmly.

I try again – a little harder now. I can feel his finger on mine.

'See,' Krissi says, relieved. I squeeze his finger, hard.

'I love you, Krissi,' I say.

'I love you too, you unbearable item,' he says back, staring at my hand. Then he looks me in the eyes. 'That's actually true.'

For the next few weeks, I cover the cuts on my arm with long-sleeved shirts – the scabs catching, slightly, on the fabric, when I move, to remind me of what I did.

The scars feel like I have a message on my arm. Something that needs to be read, urgently, by someone. It was only years later that I realise the person I had written that message to – the person who wasn't listening – was *me*. I was the one who should have been staring at that arm, and working out what the red hieroglyphics meant.

Had I translated them, I would have realised those lines read: '*Never* feel this bad again. Never come back to this place, where only a knife will do. Live a gentle and kind life. Don't do things that make you want to hurt yourself. Whatever you do, every day, remember this – then steer away from here.'

But I don't have a thought as clear as that then. Instead, I attend to what I think is the most pressing lesson to be learned from all this: I borrow Krissi's NWA albums, and learn the whole rap from 'Fuck Tha Police' – just in case someone should ever see the scar on my arm, and quiz me, on my devotion.

TWENTY-FOUR

So what do you do when you build yourself – only to realise you built yourself with the wrong things?

You rip it up and start again. That is the work of your teenage years – to build up and tear down and build up again, over and over, endlessly, like speeded-up film of cities during boom times, and wars. To be fearless, and endless, in your reinventions – to keep twisting on nineteen, going bust and dealing in again, and again. Invent, invent, invent.

They do not tell you this when you are fourteen, because the people who would tell you – your parents – are the very ones who built the thing you're so dissatisfied with. They made you how they want you. They made you how they *need* you. They built you with all they know, and love – and so they can't see what you're *not*: all the gaps you feel leave you vulnerable. All the new possibilities only imagined by your generation, and non-existent to theirs. They have done their best, with the technology they had to hand, at the time – but now it's up to you, small, brave future, to do your best, with what *you* have. As Rabindranath Tagore advised parents, 'Don't limit a child to your own learning, for he was born in another time.'

And so you go out into your world, and try and find the things that will be useful to you. Your weapons. Your tools. Your charms. You find a record, or a poem, or a picture of a girl that you pin to the wall, and go, 'Her. I'll try and be her. I'll try and be her – but *here*.' You observe the way others walk, and talk, and you steal little bits of them – you collage yourself out of whatever you can get your hands on. You are like the robot Johnny 5 in *Short Circuit*, crying, 'More input! More input for Johnny 5!' as you rifle through books, and watch films, and sit in front of the television, trying to guess which of these things you are watching – Alexis Carrington Colby walking down a marble staircase; Anne of Green Gables holding her shoddy suitcase; Cathy wailing on the moors; Courtney Love wailing in her petticoat; Julie Burchill gunning people down; Grace Jones singing 'Slave To The Rhythm' – that you will need, when you get out there. What will be useful? What will be, eventually, *you*?

And you will be quite on your own when you do all this. There is no academy where you can learn to be yourself; there is no line manager, slowly urging you towards the correct answer. You are midwife to yourself, and will give birth to yourself, over and over, in dark rooms, alone.

And some versions of you will end in dismal failure – many prototypes won't even get out of the front door, as you suddenly realise that, no, you *can't* style-out an all-in-one gold bodysuit and a massive attitude-problem in Wolverhampton. Others will achieve temporary success – hitting new land-speed records, and amazing all around you, and then suddenly, unexpectedly exploding, like the *Bluebird* on Coniston Water.

But one day, you'll find a version of you that will get you kissed, or befriended, or inspired, and you will make your notes accordingly: staying up all night to hone, and improvise upon a tiny snatch of melody that worked.

Until – slowly, slowly – you make a viable version of you, one you can hum, every day. You'll find the tiny, right piece of grit you can pearl around, until nature kicks in, and your shell will just quietly fill with magic, even while you're busy doing other things. What your nurture began, nature will take over, and start completing, until you stop having to think about who you'll *be* entirely – as you're too busy *doing*, now. And ten years will pass, without you even noticing.

And later, over a glass of wine – because you drink wine, now, because you are grown – you will marvel over what you did. Marvel that, at the time, you kept so many secrets. Tried to keep the secret of yourself. Tried to metamorphose in the dark. The loud, drunken, fucking, eyeliner-smeared, laughing, cutting, panicking, unbearably *present* secret of yourself. When really, you were about as secret as the moon. And as luminous, under all those clothes.

TWENTY-FIVE

It is October, 1993 – two months since I fucked up so badly that I nearly exploded my arm.

I'm at a Take That gig, at the NEC in Birmingham. I'm with ZZ Top. I know. I know! My social circle has changed quite a bit, in the last few months. I don't go out with the *D&ME* crew any more – no more bitchy Kenny, at the back of the venue; no more of the Tweedledum and Tweedledee of insanity: gin and sulphate.

I've learned what my contemporaries will have learned in their first terms at college, or university – that the first friends you make in a new place are the ones you usually spend the next three terms trying to lose: and that it's the people who are quietly holding back, and standing in the corner, that you will want to be with when your second year comes around. The quiet mammals, working in the shadow of the fabulous, fatal T-Rexes you are so flattered not to have been eaten by, when you first walked through the door.

Zee is one of those quiet mammals. 'We're going to Take That,' he said, on the phone, to me. 'You need to see loads of girls, screaming, because that's what you are. A big screaming girl from the Midlands. You're an *enthusiast*, Dolly. Come and enthuse. Come and be a teenage girl again. Come and be a *fan*.'

I think about him saying that, now, as I scream – like all the other girls – at Robbie Williams. His words are like Glinda's kiss on my forehead. I'm an *enthusiast*, who's been pretending to be a cynic. But I have been correctly labelled, now. I am *for* things – not against them. I must remember this. Mainly because this is more fun. It's *exhausting* being cynical. You are trying to be an immovable, angry rock in the middle of a stream. But the stream will not move. It is you that will be worn down to dull silt.

I scream, but the person standing next to me is screaming louder.

'Krissi!' I say.

'I LOVE YOU, ROBBIE!' Krissi screams. He's wearing glitter across his face, like the girls standing next to him, and is vibrating with joy. 'Johanna – which order would you do them in? Which order? Go on.'

I look at the stage.

'Robbie, Jason, Mark,' I say. 'Howard, the roadies, the roadies' friends, a man in the street, Robbie again – but wearing a mask so he doesn't realise, and say, "I've already done you." Everyone else in the world. Then I'd sleep. Then sort my sock drawer out. Maybe put the tea on. Then Gary. How about you?'

'ROBBIE!' Krissi screams. 'Robbie, until security pulled me off him. Then I'd wank at him, from behind a door. OH, ROBBIE!'

I'm so touched Krissi's entering into the spirit of things. He really is a good big brother.

It's going to be so easy to write this review. First of all, no one else at *D&ME* wanted to review Take That – 'Darling, they're just … wank-fodder for teenage girls,' Kenny said, in horror, as I nodded my head, and replied: 'Yes! And you can *never* have too much of that!'

And, secondly – just like I did, in the beginning – I can go back to explaining … *why I love a thing*. Explaining why you love something is one of the most important jobs on Earth.

*

The day after I nearly exploded my arm, I lay under my bed, with my arm still bandaged, and thought: 'I have to die – *again*.' And again, this thought makes me very cheerful.

I sorted through the inventory of what I had become, so far, and divided it into two piles – like I do with the records I get sent. What to keep, and what to throw away.

TO KEEP:
The top hat
Fags
T. S. Eliot
Dolly Wilde
Writing. Obviously
Eyeliner
Booze
Sturdy boots
Larkin
Listening to the Pixies and pretending to be Kim Deal
Having sex with as many people as possible
Staying up until dawn
Adventure (see also: having sex with as many people as possible)
London

TO REJECT:
Cynicism
Shit sulphate
Standing at the back
Hanging out with people who make me feel uncomfortable
Self-harm – the world will come at you with knives anyway.
    You do not need to beat them to it
MD 20/20

> *Going out with people without checking – with me – if I actually*
> *want to*
> *Any penises over eight inches long*
> *Taking sexual advice from strange men at parties*
> *Saying 'No'. I will always say 'Yes'. With God as my witness,*
> *I will never 'go angry' again*

After being reborn again under the bed, I have three interesting conversations. The first is with my mother.

It felt like I hadn't seen her for ages, and we sat in the garden – me with the twins on my lap – as she sat ten feet away, assiduously blowing her cigarette smoke away from the twins. David and Daniel. 'Daniel – short for "denial",' as my mother said, when she returned with the birth certificates.

'Anti-depressants are a great thing, Johanna,' she says, now, watching David wriggle off my lap, to go play with the Snail Farm in the roasting tray.

We've resurrected the Snail Farm – we did a Snail Race at the weekend that took nearly three hours. Lupin had to keep picking up Carol Decker from T'Pau and make her face the right way again – she kept crawling up the sides of the tin, and away from the others. She clearly wants to go solo.

'If you ever accidentally have twins and feel like throwing yourself under a bus whilst screaming, I recommend them highly,' she continues.

'I'll remember this,' I say, solemnly. Putting Daniel down, to play with David, I go over and join my mother.

'Twos?' I say, holding my hand out for the fag.

'No,' she says. 'I'm your mother. I'm responsible for you. I gave birth to you. I'm not going to give you something that kills you.'

I take a fag out of her handbag and light it. She nods. Fair enough.

'I've found a flat, in London,' I say, finally, exhaling. 'I can move in at the end of the month. I'm going to use my savings as a deposit.'

I put my hand on her arm.

'It is good to have savings as a deposit. Thank you.'

My mother looks at the end of her cigarette.

'You really want to?'

'Yeah. I'm spending so much money on trains down to London that it's actually cheaper, and I'm excited about living on my own, and having my own toilet.'

'It's not all it's cracked up to be, you know.'

'What – having your own toilet?'

'Yeah. You'll soon learn to hate limescale. You can get these tablets for the cistern – but it turns the water blue, and poisons the dog when it drinks from the bowl. Are you taking the dog?'

'Of course!'

'Oh good. We can start using the tablets again. More Blu Loo for me. Hurrah.'

I see Mum is crying. I hug her.

'I'll be back *all* the time.'

'Make sure you tell me in advance. I'll put a chicken in the oven. Just a small one.'

I put my arm around her.

'You'll always be my baby,' she says, in a small voice.

'Your big, black, depressed baby?'

'My big, black, depressed baby.'

'Now I'm going, you can finally say how proud you are of me, and that I'm the best one,' I say, giving her a shove.

'I'm proud of you *all*,' she says, fiercely.

'Well, yeah, obviously. I've always admired how you've treated us all equally, whatever our abilities.' Pause. 'But I *am* the best one, aren't I?'

'I was just as proud of David, when he started using his potty,' she says.

'Well, yeah – *theoretically*. But working for a national magazine at the age of seventeen is *quantifiably* better. That's a proper, notable achievement.'

'You've never potty-trained a toddler, have you, Johanna? It's like working as a ball boy at Wimbledon, but with shit. And it goes on for months. With people *crying* at you.'

We carry on smoking.

'So I've got spare pots and pans in the loft, and cutlery, and you can take one of the Buddhas,' she says, starting to fuss. 'Just pick whichever one you like, apart from the big one. They'll bring you luck. And I've got a spare dream-catcher.'

'Awww, thank you, Mum. I wouldn't want my dreams … *roaming* around the flat. It's good to trap them, in a window.'

She smokes more.

'Mum. Will you be able to do without the money? Do you need the money I give you? Are you going to be okay?'

My mother is silent for a minute.

'You're sure you want to move out?' she says.

'Yeah,' I say. 'London's the place for me.'

'Then we'll be fine, love,' she says, putting out the cigarette. She smiles in an odd way. 'We'll be fine.'

The second conversation is with Krissi. There is a leaving party for me, at Uncle Jim's house – 'Because we're not having a party here,' my mother says, firmly, dishing out shepherd's pie in the front room. 'Last time we had all your dad's family over, I found your Uncle Aled trying to climb into the cot with the dog.'

It's not just my leaving party – as my father romantically puts it, 'Your Aunty Soo's kid's got some boiler in Halesowen knocked up – so this is their engagement party, too.'

When I get to the party, I locate the 'boiler from Halesowen' and try to congratulate her – but she's playing football in the garden with some of the kids, and tells me to get the fuck out of the way when I impede her impressive on-target shot at the goal (two swing-bins, by the fence).

'I hope you have a very happy future together,' I say, clutching my breast where the ball hit, and making a dignified retreat to the front room. She plays an unexpectedly competitive game for someone five months pregnant. She is a true Black Country woman.

In the front room, Krissi is sitting on the windowsill with cousin Ali, who looks very different to last time I saw her. She's smoking out of the window. My tits still hurt. I tell them this.

'She's gone rave,' Krissi says, gesturing to Ali, as soon as I approach them. I see this.

'I'm on a Ragga tip,' Ali says, doing some vaguely E'd-up hand gestures. She's wearing tie-dyed dungarees and a day-glo beanie hat.

'What happened to the bloke from The Nova?' I ask. 'What happened to the shoe-gazing dream?'

'I found a raver with a big cock,' Ali says, smugly. Krissi visibly blenches.

'So what's big in the … rave?' I ask.

Ali tells me about some records she's been 'banging' recently, and drones on about the mythical rave bass-note that makes some people poo their pants.

'And is that an … *advantage*?' Krissi asks, drily. Ali ignores him.

'What I want to know, Ali, is how you reconcile your love of so many different musical genres?' I say.

'Oh, I'm a goth in the kitchen, a shoe-gazer in the parlour and a raver in the bedroom,' Ali says, flicking her ash out of the window.

When Ali goes to get a drink, Krissi leans in and goes, 'I cannot *stand* her. Stupid bloody female. Come on. Let's go.'

He jumps out of the window. I look around to see what the kids are doing – David is carefully trying to push his finger into the VHS player. His concentration is total – and, reassured that he's occupied, I follow Krissi out of the window.

We walk over the road, to the swings and slides at the playground. Krissi takes two cans of cider out of his pockets.

'So, you're off, then,' he says, as we swing on the swings – legs too long for the ropes.

'Yeah,' I say. 'You going to be okay without me?'

'I managed for the first year of my life perfectly fine.'

'Yeah – but you spent those mainly crying and wetting yourself,' I point out.

'I guess I can re-discover those early pleasures, then,' Krissi says, swinging – knees almost touching the ground.

'Kriss – I've got to ask you: do you think you really will be able to manage without me? I mean, I can't not go – if I don't leave home now, I'll die. A lot. But is everyone going to … manage?'

Krissi sighs: 'Yes, Johan, we'll be able to manage. You're one less mouth to feed, after all.'

My indignation is instant, and considerable. 'Hey, *man*,' I say. 'I'm not the one who can *drink* an entire can of rice pudding. And, anyway, half the time, it's my work that puts food *on* the table. I eviscerate the Soup Dragons – and then *you* get soup. That's the food-maths.'

'Well, to be fair,' Krissi says, slowly, 'if you look at it another way, you could just as well say it's you working that's taken food *off* the table.'

I stare at Krissi. I can sense my face is dim-looking, and uncomprehending.

'What … do you mean, I took food *off* the table?' I ask. 'Also, can we stop saying "table" – we haven't got one. The table's in my room. It's a desk with a load of Primal Scream CDs on it.'

After graciously conceding the table point – 'Okay. Your work took food off our *laps*, where we had plates, balanced on cushions' – Krissi sighs, rubs his forehead, and then explains what's been going on, all this time.

When I left school to work for the *D&ME*, that was why they'd cut our benefits. Because I'd left full-time education. That was the 11 per cent cut.

Our impoverishment *was* all my fault, after all. Not because of anything I'd said to Violet – but because I'd left school. I *had* been the ruin of my family – but by trying to save it.

Oh, the tangled web of panic and causality. I suddenly feel a massive affinity with Marty McFly in *Back to the Future*, who goes back in time, and then almost causes his own non-existence by heroically stopping his father from being run over by his mother. Poor Marty McFly. Poor me.

'Bloody hell,' I say, absolutely still on the swing. 'I'm Marty McFly. I'm Marty McFly, Krissi.'

Krissi hands me a can of cider.

'Yes. Yes you are,' he says, soothingly. 'You're Marty McFly. Drink your cider up, little lady. You're obviously in shock, because you've started talking bollocks. You probably need a tin-foil blanket or something.'

'Not with these shoes,' I say, automatically, opening the can. 'They would clash.'

'So, who knew then?' I ask Krissi. 'You, obviously – and Mum, and Dad?'

'Yeah – that's what all those arguments were about,' Krissi says, looking into his can. 'And then Mum told me and Dadda not to mention it to you, in case you freaked out, under the pressure. So, now you know. Now you know the big secret! Just in time for you to solve the problem – by fucking off.'

'Yeah – thanks for the summary, Ceefax,' I say, drinking some cider. 'Fucking hell.'

'We were very *noble*,' Krissi says, reflectively. 'We were all very noble about you.'

'But ... you called me your saviour when I bought the new telly!' I said.

'Yeah – we were aware of the irony.'

'Fucking hell.'

I hang on the swing utterly limp, like a potato. I don't really know what to say. I'm learning a whole new thing: that sometimes, love isn't observable or noisy or tangible. That, sometimes, love is anonymous. Sometimes, love is silent. Sometimes, love just stands there when you're calling it a cunt, biting its tongue, and waiting.

'As soon as you leave, we should be alright. We'll lose your Child Benefit, obviously – but to be honest, it's costing us more than £7.50 a week in loo roll. You use an *extraordinary* amount of it.'

'All girls do,' I say. 'Being a girl involves a lot of wiping. You have no idea. And it's usually better than tampons. They are tricksy. I once had an incident in a toilet in Vauxhall where I was trying to put a new one in, and found an old one up there. It's like some kind of ... mad cupboard in there.'

'Your vagina never ceases to amaze me,' Krissi says. 'It's just a massive repository for trouble.'

'Oh, I know,' I say.

We stay a bit longer, on the swings, as it gets colder, until Aunty Lauren calls us in, from the house across the road.

'ARE YOU DANCING?' she roars. I can hear Dee-Lite's 'Groove Is in the Heart' being bumped up on the stereo, loud.

'COME AND GET YOUR LEGS AROUND THIS!' she shouts. 'I'VE GOT THAT SALT-N-PEPA ON NEXT, AND YOUR DAD SAYS HE'S GOING TO DO THE DANCE!'

We run across the road.

The final conversation I have is a late-night phone call with John Kite. I haven't heard from him since the bad kissing thing in Regent's Park – I cannot bring myself to write a letter, even though it's my turn. I've banned myself from even thinking about him, lest I become panicky again. I have clanged shut the door in my head that leads to the thoughts of John Kite.

This is hard – as, over the last year, I've taken to saying his name, over and over in my head, like a rosary, in moments where my brain idles, or is stressed: 'JohnKite JohnKite JohnKite.' I say it at bus stops, and when I'm walking, and when I hurt myself, and when I'm lonely. 'JohnKite JohnKite JohnKite.' In the way some people count, or recite psalms.

Sometimes I say it like it's the name of a new mineral, or rock: 'Jonkite. Jonkite. Jonkite.' Something ribboned with colours, but made hard by the moving of tectonic plates, and the compression of the Earth. I would like to go to the Natural History Museum and find a piece of Jonkite, lying on a velvet cushion. I imagine it would warm to my touch. I would wear a necklace of it, casually, until he noticed. I would wear it with a red dress, and it would go with my eyes. I could have *won* John Kite if I'd had a red dress. I frequently berate myself for not having one. I was one right dress away from having him.

However, since that day in the park, every time I do that, I have to imagine a bunch of policemen busting into my head shouting, 'NO NO DO NOT THINK OF THIS MAN ANY MORE. YOU MAY NEVER THINK OF JOHN KITE AGAIN.'

But now, at 2am, the phone goes in my room, and I pick it up before the first ring has finished. I know who it will be, and it is – it's John, drunk, somewhere in Spain:

'I'm in bed with a straw donkey, Dutch,' he says, slurring slightly.

'Still a hit with the ladies, I see,' I whisper. I can see Lupin shifting a little, in his bunk bed, and I climb into the wardrobe with the phone, and shut the door, for privacy.

'So, how you doing?' I ask, voice slightly wobbly.

'Oh, you know life on the road,' Kite says. I can hear him light a fag. I wish I could light a fag, but even I know that's a bad idea in a wardrobe.

'I've bought a new fur coat,' he says. 'I found it in a flea market. It's magnificent. I think it's made of dog. It doesn't have arms – just holes.'

'That's a cape, then,' I say.

'SO IT IS!' he roars. 'SO IT FUCKING IS! I thought they were just ripping me off!'

'Well, now we've established that, I want to state that it's lovely to hear from you,' I say. 'I've missed you.'

'I've missed you *too*, Dutch. I've had to drink too many bottles of gin on my own in the last month.'

'I thought I might not hear from you again, after … last time,' I say.

'WHY ON EARTH WOULD YOU THINK THAT YOU MENTAL?' he roars.

'Well, you know,' I say. 'I was a massive twat.'

'*Were* you?' he says. 'I was too busy being a massive twat myself to notice.'

'I think I was the most massive twat,' I say. 'You know.'

'I really don't,' he says, sounding confused. 'What happened? I was totally gattered. I'd been on the piss since eleven. I didn't do anything ... *inappropriate*, did I?'

'No, no – God, *you* didn't,' I say. 'Do you really not remember anything?'

'Er ... I seem to remember there being wolves, and penguins. We had a great day, yes? What happened?'

He seems genuinely not to know – and now I've put myself in the position where I have to tell him. For the first time in a month, I find myself picking at the scars on my left arm. Oh, Johanna – why do you keep *talking*? Why do you say the things you do? I try and tell him in the breeziest way possible.

'Well, we got very drunk, and we sang with some gibbons, and then I ... appeared to be overcome with bestiality, and said that I was both Chrissie Hynde and Elizabeth Taylor, and that it was fated that we have sex,' I say.

I had planned to do a laugh at the end of this sentence, but find I can't. There's a pause.

'Oh well, you know – we probably *will*,' he says, gently. 'That's just statistics, baby. How will we *not* have sex at some point? You're a you, and I'm a me. It's just the age thing right now, babe. Too young.'

'Too young? I'm *seventeen*,' I say, with all the huffy world-weariness I can.

'Not you, Dutch – *me*. I'm far too young for you. I'm hopeless.' He sighs. 'Christ, you terrified me there – for a minute, I thought something *bad* had happened. I once pissed myself on stage, you know. *That* was bad.'

He goes on to tell me about how this had happened – 'It was for some talk; I'd been on stage for *hours* ...' – but I'm not really listening, as I'm so happy I could cry.

Oh look, I *am* crying.

It's like being born again – like surfacing after long months of drowning. I have made my confession in this wardrobe, and been absolved by my drunken priest – and now I may go back out into the world, and do it all again. My future has come back online again, with a brrr and a thump, and all the barnacle-like cancers of my heart have died. I did *not* misjudge the world when I was drunk! I did *not* do the wrong thing! I acted as pissed people should! I can simply carry on, as I am! And I will! I will carry on with these adventures!

'Dutch?' Kite says, finally. I haven't replied to the last thing he said. 'Dutch? Are you still there? Have you nodded off?'

And I sigh, and I sigh again – from pure happiness – and I say, 'No – I am still here,' and then I get to say the most beautiful thing in the world. I say: 'John – we must go for a drink.'

When we finally finish talking, an hour later – after I tell him about moving to London, and going mad, and then getting better again – light is shining through the crack of the wardrobe door. I presume it's the dawn – but when I emerge, I see that it is, in fact, the night-light: Lupin's turned it on, and is sitting on my bed.

'Can I snuggle?' he asks.

'Oh, always, baby,' I say, pulling him into bed with me. 'You can always snuggle with Johanna.'

We curl up, in the hollow left by Nanna. This is the last time I will sleep here.

EPILOGUE

MOTORWAY SERVICES, M1. THURSDAY

Dadda comes out of Burger King, eating a Whopper.

'Life on the road, eh?' he says – sauce all over his face. 'Keep your motor running.'

We're at Watford Gap Services – the border between the south and the north. It's cold and windy – my top hat keeps blowing off. Really, there are so few circumstances in which it's possible to wear a top hat consistently ... I don't know how Slash does it. He *must* use Velcro somehow. Maybe using his hair as the other bonding agent.

The caravanette is parked in the Disabled bay – Disabled sticker carefully displayed on the dashboard. The windows show how full the caravanette is – duvets and bin bags full of clothes pressed up against the glass, like some kind of jumble-sale terrine, all resting on top of my chest of drawers and my third-choice Buddha ('Oh you can't take that one either, Johanna – I like his face').

All my worldly possessions are in this van.

I've paid for Dadda's Whopper – 'Corkage, Johanna.'

I've also paid for the baccy-money – 'To keep me alert, during the migration' – and the large chocolate milkshake in his hand – 'An old man's gotta have his treats.'

On top of this, I've also paid the petrol-money, which Dadda assured me, with his most serious face, came to £90. It was only years later that I found out what petrol actually cost in

1993, and frankly admired the old bastard: rinsing me, right to the end, even as he says goodbye.

We get into the van, and the old man slurps more of his milkshake, as we watch everyone outside, scurrying in the rain.

'If we had to, we could camp here,' he says, comfortingly, patting the dashboard of the car. 'We've got a cooker, and a sink, and the bunk beds – we could *live* here, if we needed to. Fly-camp. Make this our new home.'

'What a fucking terrible idea.' Krissi's voice comes, from the back.

I can see Krissi, in the rear-view mirror. He's squashed in between the duvet and my curtains, with the dog on his knee. The dog, like me, suffers from travel sickness, and can't travel on the floor or it pukes.

'Can we just get the fuck out of here? This van now stinks of meat, and I can't wind the window down, because there's a *whole dog's face* in my way.'

Last night, Krissi came into my bedroom – 'Knock knock. Promise me you're not fapping yourself off with a bottle of Elnett, Johanna, or I swear to God, I'll end you' – and told me that he was coming down to London with me, for my first few weeks, 'To make sure you're okay, and you don't accidentally write your shopping-list on your arm with an axe.'

This is what he says – but I'd seen him surreptitiously looking at the club listings in *The Pink Paper* in a newsagents, and I know what he's *really* coming down for: to take me to my first-ever gay club, so I can finally make a gay best friend!

'Please, gun the hog,' Krissi says. 'This car park is starting to oppress me.'

Dadda turns the engine on, eases out of the parking bay, and fiddles with the stereo: 'Any requests?'

This is a question that I have been ready for for some time. I have Blur's new single, 'For Tomorrow', on cassette. I've been obsessed with it for the last month. Still with a weather-eye on legendariness, I have long-planned that this is the song I will listen to as I emigrate to the south – Damon singing all about London, and getting lost on the Westway, during which I intend to look as noble and full of destiny as possible. I have even imagined my dad turning to me and saying, 'Aye – that's you, kid. *You're* a twentieth-century girl,' and me lighting a cigarette and saying, 'You bet your *ass*, Da.' It will be like casting a fortunate spell on my future life. It will charm my way. It will be a key moment in my life.

Everyone listens to it in silence for a minute, as we pull onto the motorway.

'This is Cockney shit,' Krissi says, eventually. 'Put the Bee Gees on.'

I put the Bee Gees on – 'Tragedy' – as Dadda overtakes three cars.

'So,' Dadda says, conversationally, as he swerves in front of a Vauxhall Astra, 'So. I see that Bjork is playing tomorrow night. You can get us on the guestie, can't you, Johanna? Old Pat Morrigan plus one? Because I've got a plan. We're gonna hit the aftershow party, yeah, and start talking to the wankers.'

He looks excited.

'The big wankers. The *powerful* wankers. The *worst* wankers. To be honest, I feel like a right prat with all this "sending off demos" and "poxy journalists" bullshit – no offence, love. All this time, I should have just been getting *in* there, instead. Be in the room when all the blow and hookers come out – *that's* when the business gets done. I bet it's still the same fuckers it was back then. I'll put *money* on knowing someone there. I used to know them *all*. There was this one A&R guy, right ...'

I look at the road ahead – where all the signs say, with impossible thrillingness, 'LONDON and THE SOUTH'. I'm seventeen. I've got my brother, my dog and a laptop with 'John Kite' Tippexed on it. I believe in music and gin and joy and talking too much, and human kindness. I have warning scars on my arms, a new blank wall to fill with faces and words. I still want to change the world in some way, and I still have to get my dad famous. I've eaten drugs off a hanky, had sex with a medically inadvisable penis, confused The Smashing Pumpkins, binned off a threesome with a quote from *Blade Runner*, and tried to kiss my hero whilst being serenaded by singing gibbons. And, like all the best quests, in the end, I did it all for a girl: me.

'... and he *definitely* owes me one,' Dadda continues, starting to roll a ciggie with his left hand, trucker-style. 'I can't remember his name. I can't remember anyone's name, to be honest. But when you've carried someone else's unconscious wife down the fire escape of a hotel in Berlin as a favour to a dude, you tend to remember that dude's face. If I see him, babba. If he's there tomorrow, love, then –'

Dadda lights his fag.

'Ker-ching. We'll be shitting fucking *diamonds* by Christmas.'

ACKNOWLEDGEMENTS

Writing a book is literally worse than giving birth to a baby – in hell – then dying, then being brought back and having to have *another* baby that, this time, is coming out of your eyes – even though your eyes aren't holes, and there's no way a baby can come out of them. But worse than that. Did I say it's difficult? It's really difficult. When you sit on a chair all day, your arse *really* hurts. I mean, really. And then, there's that baby coming out of your eyes. Oh, it's a palaver. And so these 'acknowledgements' aren't really acknowledgements – more abject, weeping gratitude to the people who dragged me over the finish-line. My British editor – Jake Lingwood – and my US editor – Jennifer Barth – both of whom put so much time, love, attention and stone-dead skillz into *How To Build A Girl*. I really can't imagine having better people on both sides of the Atlantic. It's like being edited by Godzilla *and* Mothra. You are extraordinary. Double-bubble.

And Louise Jones and Claire Scott at Ebury UK, and Gregory Henry at HarperCollins US – there is nothing more sexy than cheerful eminence and the cry of 'Cocktails?', and you all do both *constantly*.

John Niven, who was so nice about the draft I showed him that I cried. See you in hell, Shitbix.

My brothers and sisters – bad-asses to a man/woman. I'm really sorry – I've written *another* book full of wanking and shagging. Don't worry – I won't ever ask you if you've read it.

We can all pretend this whole 'book thing' never happened. You are the greatest people I have ever met, without a doubt – and I've met *all* of the Inspiral Carpets, *and* the man who wrote *Bagpuss*, so that's a pretty big statement. To be fair.

Simon Osborne and Imran Hussain at the Child Poverty Action Group, who worked out what benefits the Morrigan family would have been on in 1990. THANK YOU. The maths was making me want to jump out of a window.

Most importantly, THANK YOU to Georgia Garrett – an agent so extraordinary that I can't actually believe other agents actually exist. Georgia answered an emergency call in July, came to my house, and found me sitting in the garden, face down on a picnic table, next to my laptop, and crying whilst listening to Daft Punk's *Get Lucky* over and over again. 'I can't write this book,' I said. 'I've made a terrible error. Also, I am the worst person who has ever lived, I don't even know words, and I'm going to change my name and go and live in another country. Perhaps as a cabbage-farmer. Or a night-soil porter. I'm getting the fear. I'M GETTING THE FEAR. Oh God, I've lost all the sensation in my head. I'M GOING NUMB.'

And she got me a cup of tea, and sat there and just kept… asking questions, and suggesting things, until, suddenly, I saw that I might actually be able to finish the book, after all.

And then she did that another nine times. NINE TIMES. It was actually quite funny by the end. For me. Maybe not for her. George – this book really wouldn't have happened without you. That's not an exaggeration. I keep saying this, but if you ever stop being my agent and friend, I will simply throw myself down a well.

The band Elbow, whose entire back-catalogue I caned mercilessly during the writing of *How To Build A Girl*, as the best example of how the working classes do it differently –

with hard work, 'universal emotions rendered in potent details' (copyright Dorian Lynskey), and love.

Lauren Laverne, who handed me my sanity back on a plate, literally, in Giraffe.

And, finally, to my husband, Pete, who has helped build three girls, now. And is also the only person who would have noticed that when I mentioned Grant Lee Buffalo in the first draft, they had, at that point in the timeline, 'only released one limited-edition EP, and would not, in all likelihood, be known of in Wolverhampton', and that I really should change it to Uncle Tupelo, instead. And then he went off to build his own gramophone. I love you.

If you enjoyed How *To Build a* Girl, keep reading for the first chapter of the hilarious, bestselling sequel, *How To Be Famous*

I'm **Johanna Morrigan**, and I live in London in 1995, at the epicentre of Britpop. I might only be nineteen, but I'm wise enough to know that everyone around me is handling fame very, very badly.

My unrequited love, **John Kite**, has scored an unexpected Number One album, then exploded into a Booze And Drugs HellTM – as rockstars do. And my new best friend – the maverick feminist **Suzanne Banks, of The Branks** – has amazing hair, but writer's block and a rampant pill problem. So I've decided I should become a *Fame Doctor*. I'm going to use my new monthly column for *The Face* to write about every ridiculous, surreal, amazing aspect of a million people knowing your name.

But when my two-night-stand with edgy comedian **Jerry Sharp** goes wrong, people start to know *my* name for all the wrong reasons. 'He's a vampire. He destroys bright young girls. Also, he's a total dick' Suzanne warned me. But by that point, I'd already had sex with him. Bad sex.

Now I'm one of the girls he's trying to destroy.

He needs to be stopped.

But how can one woman stop a bad, famous, powerful man?

ONE

When I was eleven, I formally resigned from the family dream.

From the earliest moment I can recall, the family dream was simple: that, one day, we would get money from somewhere – win the pools, discover a medieval chalice at a jumble sale, or, least likely of all, *earn* the money – and leave Wolverhampton.

'When the bomb drops, we want to be on the other side of *those*,' Dadda would say, at the end of our street – pointing across the flat fields of Shropshire, to the distant Black Mountains. We practically lived in the country.

'If they nuke Birmingham, the fallout won't reach Wales – those mountains are like a wall,' he would add, nodding. 'We'll be safe there. If we get in the van and drive like fuckers, we'd be over the border in two hours.'

It was the mid-eighties, when we knew, for a fact, that the Russians would launch a nuclear war against the West Midlands at some point – the threat was so visceral that Sting even had written a song about it, warning that it would, by and large, be bad – so we were absolutely braced for it.

And so we made our plans for escape. Our dream house was a survivalist bolthole, with its own water supply – a spring, or a well. We'd need enough land to be self-sufficient – 'Get some polytunnels up, get your fruit in,' Dadda would say – and we'd have a cellar full of dried grains, and guns – 'To shoot the looters, when they come. Or commit suicide,' he added, still cheerfully, 'if it gets too much.'

The dream house was talked about so much that we all presumed it was real. We would have passionate hour-long arguments about whether to keep goats or cows – 'Goats. Cows are fussy fuckers' – and possible names for the property. My mother, who had been made simple by many pregnancies, favoured a ghastly option: 'The Happy House'. My father didn't want to give it a name – 'I don't want any bastard to be able to find us in the phone book. Come the Apocalypse, I'm not going to be feeling *sociable*.'

We were poor – which was a normal thing; everyone we knew was poor – so we all made each other Christmas presents, and that Christmas – Christmas 1986 – I had drawn a picture of The Dream Survivalist House, as a present to my parents.

Because it was just a drawing, I had spared no expense on this house: there was a swimming pool in the garden and an orchard at the back. The front room was painted the colour of a peacock's wing, all the children had their own bedroom, and Krissi's had a slide in it that went out of the window, and straight into his own fairground. The house was *magnificent*.

My mother and father looked at it with tears in their eyes.

'This is beautiful, Johanna!' my mother said.

'This must have taken you ages!' Dadda marvelled. And it had. The roof was covered in fairies. Their wings had taken hours. I'd drawn veins on them. Wings, I reasoned, must have veins. There must be a vascular system.

Then my mother looked at it again.

'But where's *your* bedroom, Johanna?' she asked. 'Have you forgotten to draw it?'

'Oh, no,' I said, eating my breakfast mince pie. The pastry was very tough; my mother was not a gifted chef. I was glad I had topped it with a slice of Cheddar cheese, by way of precaution. '*I'm* not going to live there. *I'm* going to live in *London*.'

My mother cried. Krissi shrugged: 'More room for me.' My father lectured me. 'It's absolute certain death to live in a city!' he said, at one point. 'If the Russians don't get you, the IRA will. Civilisation is a trap that will blow your knickers off!'

But I didn't care if the Russians, or the IRA, did drop a bomb. They could drop a million billion, and I still wouldn't want to live on the side of a mountain, with goats, and rain. Even if it was radioactive, and full of mutants, and lead to my certain death, London was still the place for me. London was where things happened, and I wanted – with utmost urgency – to happen.

And so at nineteen, here I am in London – and London, it turns out, *is* the place for me. I was right. I was right that this was the place to go.

I moved down here a year ago, to a flat in Camden, to pursue my career as a music journalist. I brought three bin bags full of clothes, a TV, a laptop, a dog, an ashtray, a lighter in the shape of a gun, and a top hat. That was the sum total of my possessions. I didn't need anything else.

London provides everything else – even things you'd never dreamed of. For instance, I'm so near Regent's Park Zoo that I can hear the lions at night, fucking. They roar like they are trying to let the whole city know how sexual they are. I know that feeling. I want to let this whole city know how sexual *I* am. I see them as another one of those unexpected London bonuses – en-suite sexy lions. This is something Wolverhampton would never give you. Although the downside is that the sexy lions drive the dog crazy. She barks until I order a Meat Feast pizza, and I give her the meatballs whilst I eat the crusts, and cheese. We are a good team. She is my pal.

If I imagine the dog is a horse – which is easy, as she's very large – I live a life that could largely be described as 'that of Pippi Longstocking, but with whisky, and rock music'. To live in a city at nineteen, alone but for a pet, is to engage in adult pursuits, but with the vision of a child.

I spent three days painting my flat electric blue, because, in 'Sound and Vision', that is what David Bowie did, and there is no better person to take interior decorating tips from than David Bowie.

I then tried to paint white clouds on the wall – to make it *celestial* – but it's surprisingly hard to paint clouds with a big paintbrush and some white emulsion. The clouds look like empty speech bubbles; the walls look full of spaces where things should be said, but I don't know what those things are yet. That's part of being nineteen. You don't yet know what your memorable speeches are. You haven't said them yet.

When I have money, I have takeaway spaghetti bolognese for breakfast, every day, because that is the most treat-y meal, and children buy themselves meals that are treats. When I don't have money, I live on baked potatoes – because they are treat-y, too.

I wake at noon, and stay out until 3 a.m., and then I have a bath, when I come home, because I can. It doesn't wake anyone up. Every single one of those baths makes me happy. You leave home to have baths in the middle of the night. That is true independence.

My phone is regularly cut off, because I forget to pay the bills – they come so often! Who opens their post in the month it arrives? Only the dull – and, when the phone is cut off, people ring my local pub, the Good Mixer, and leave messages there for me. The landlord complains about this often.

'I'm not your fucking secretary,' he will say, handing over a pile of multi-coloured Post-it notes when I come in, with the dog, for a pint.

'I know, Keith. I know. Can I borrow your phone?' I will reply. 'I just need to get back to the most urgent ones. They want me to interview the Beastie Boys in Madrid!'

And Keith will hand over the phone, from behind the bar, with a sigh, because it is the responsible thing to do, when a lone teenager needs to make a call. It takes an inner-city village to raise a child!

I keep all my dirty clothes on the floor – because who would waste their money on a washing basket, when you could spend it on roast chicken and cigarettes?

Once a month, when all the clothes have made it to the floor, I put them in my rucksack, and take them to the laundrette. One of Blur uses the same laundrette. It's nice to use the same laundrette as a pop star. We nod at each other, silently, and then read the music press, whilst popping out every so often for a cigarette. I once watched him read a bad review of Blur, as he was doing a whites wash. I have never seen anyone transfer their underwear from a washer into a dryer so sadly. It's hard to combine being a public icon with your day-to-day domestica. The disjuncture is jarring. Grace Kelly never had to unclog lint from tumble-dryer filter while Pauline Kael shouted abuse at her.

And what this makes me aware of is that London isn't just a place you live: London is a game; a machine; a magnifying glass; an alchemist's crucible. Britain is a table, tilted so all its loose change rolls towards London, and *we* are the loose change. *I* am the loose change. London is a fruit machine, and *you* are the coin you put in – with the prospect of it coming up all cherries, and bells.

You don't *live* in London. You *play* London – to win. That's why we're all here. It is a city full of contestants, each chasing one of a million possible prizes: wealth, love, fame. Inspiration.

I have the pages of the A-Z stuck to my wall – so I can stare at the entirety of London, trying to learn every mews, alley and byway. And when you take four paces back from the wall – so you're pressed up against your chest of drawers, staring at it – what those network of streets most closely resembles is a computer circuit board. The people are the electricity jumping through it – where we meet, and collide, is where ideas are hatched, problems solved, things created. Where things explode. Me, and the sad man from Blur, and six million others – we're trying to rewire things. We're trying, in whatever tiny way we can, to make new connections between things. That is the job of a capital city: to invent possible futures, and then offer them up to the rest of the world. 'We could be like *this?* Or *this?* We could say *these* words, or wear *these* clothes – we could have people like *this*, if we wanted?'

We are Henceforth-mongers, trying to make *our* Henceforth the most enticing. Because the secret of everyone who comes to London – who comes to any big city – is that they came here because they did not feel normal, back at home. The only way they will ever feel normal is if they hijack popular culture with their weirdness, inject themselves into the circuitry, and – using the euphoric stimulants of music, and pictures, and words, and fashion – make the rest of the world suddenly wish to become as weird as them. To find a way to be a better rock star, or writer. To make the rest of the world want to paint their walls electric blue, too ... because a beautiful song told them to. I want to make things *happen*.